The STORY *of* BLUE EYE

The STORY *of* BLUE EYE

TYLER TRAFFORD

thistledown press

National Library of Canada Cataloguing in Publication

Trafford, Tyler, 1949-
The story of blue eye / Tyler Trafford.

(Sun on the mountains ; bk. 1)
ISBN 1-894345-78-9

1. Quakers--Fiction. I. Title. II. Series: Trafford, Tyler, 1949- .
Sun on the mountains ; bk. 1.

PS8589.R335S86 2004 C813'.54 C2004-900864-1

Sun on the Mountains motif by Nicolas Trafford
Cover and book design by J. Forrie
Typeset by Thistledown Press

Thistledown Press Ltd.
633 Main Street
Saskatoon, Saskatchewan, S7H 0J8
www.thistledown.sk.ca

Thistledown Press gratefully acknowledges the financial assistance of the Canada Council for the Arts, the Saskatchewan Arts Board, and the Government of Canada through the Book Publishing Industry Development Program for its publishing program.

With special thanks to Rosaline Crowshoe of
the Piikani Nation, Alberta, for her translations.

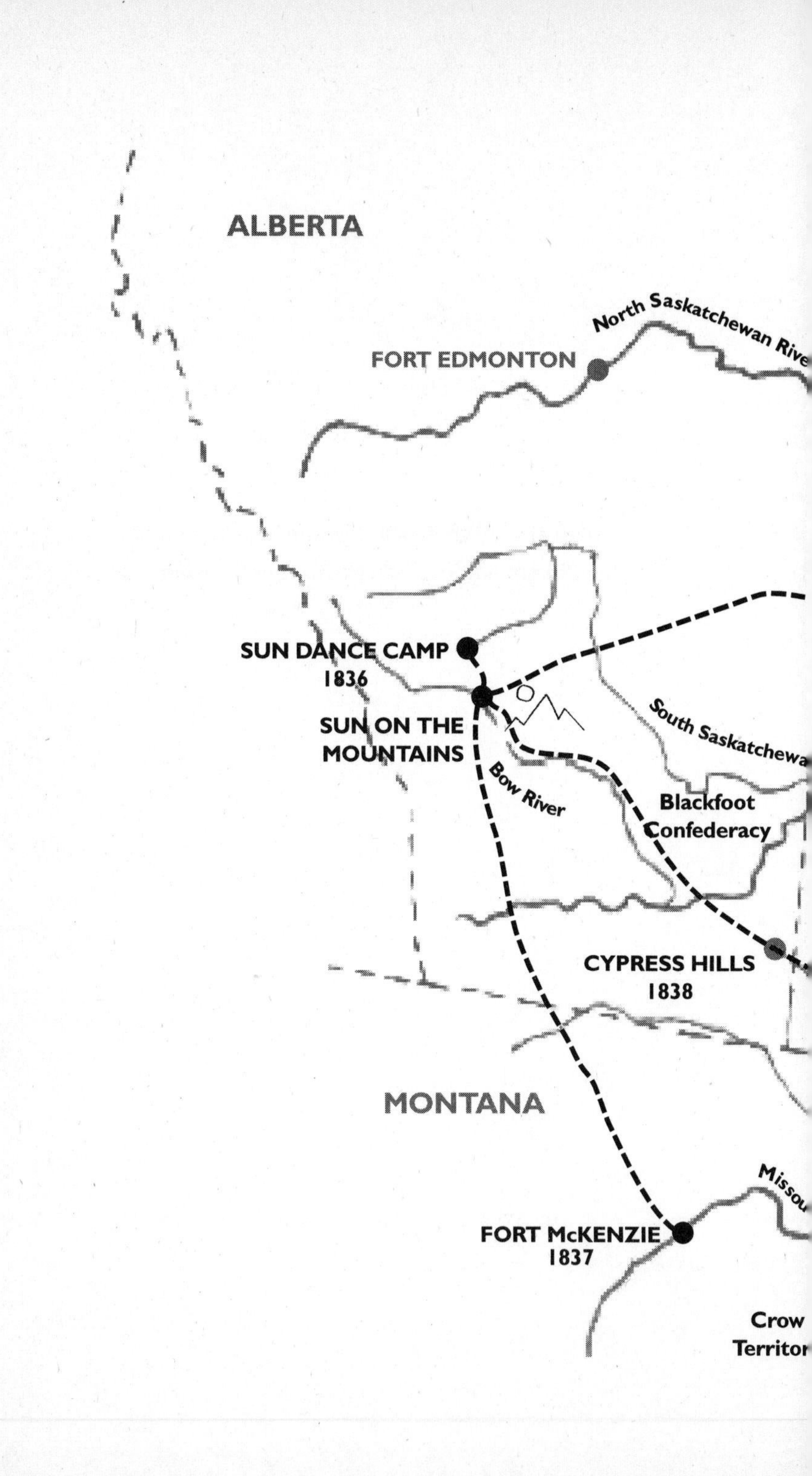
ALBERTA
North Saskatchewan
FORT EDMONTON
SUN DANCE CAMP
1836
SUN ON THE
MOUNTAINS
South
Bow River
Blackfoot
Confederacy
CYPRESS HILLS
1838
MONTANA
FORT McKENZIE
1837
Crow

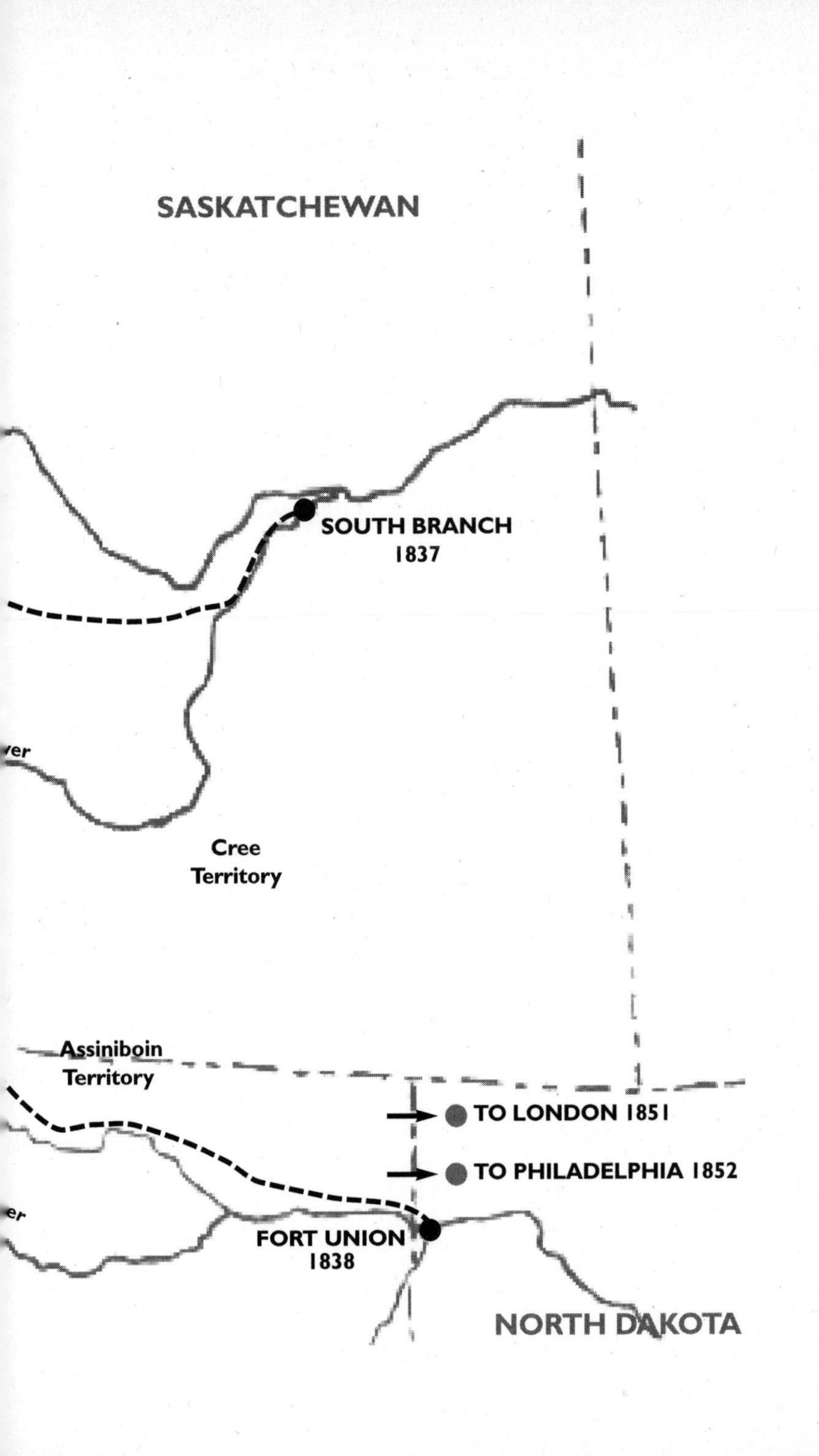
SASKATCHEWAN
SOUTH BRANCH
1837
Cree
Territory
Assiniboin
Territory
TO LONDON 1851
TO PHILADELPHIA 1852
FORT UNION
1838
NORTH DAKOTA

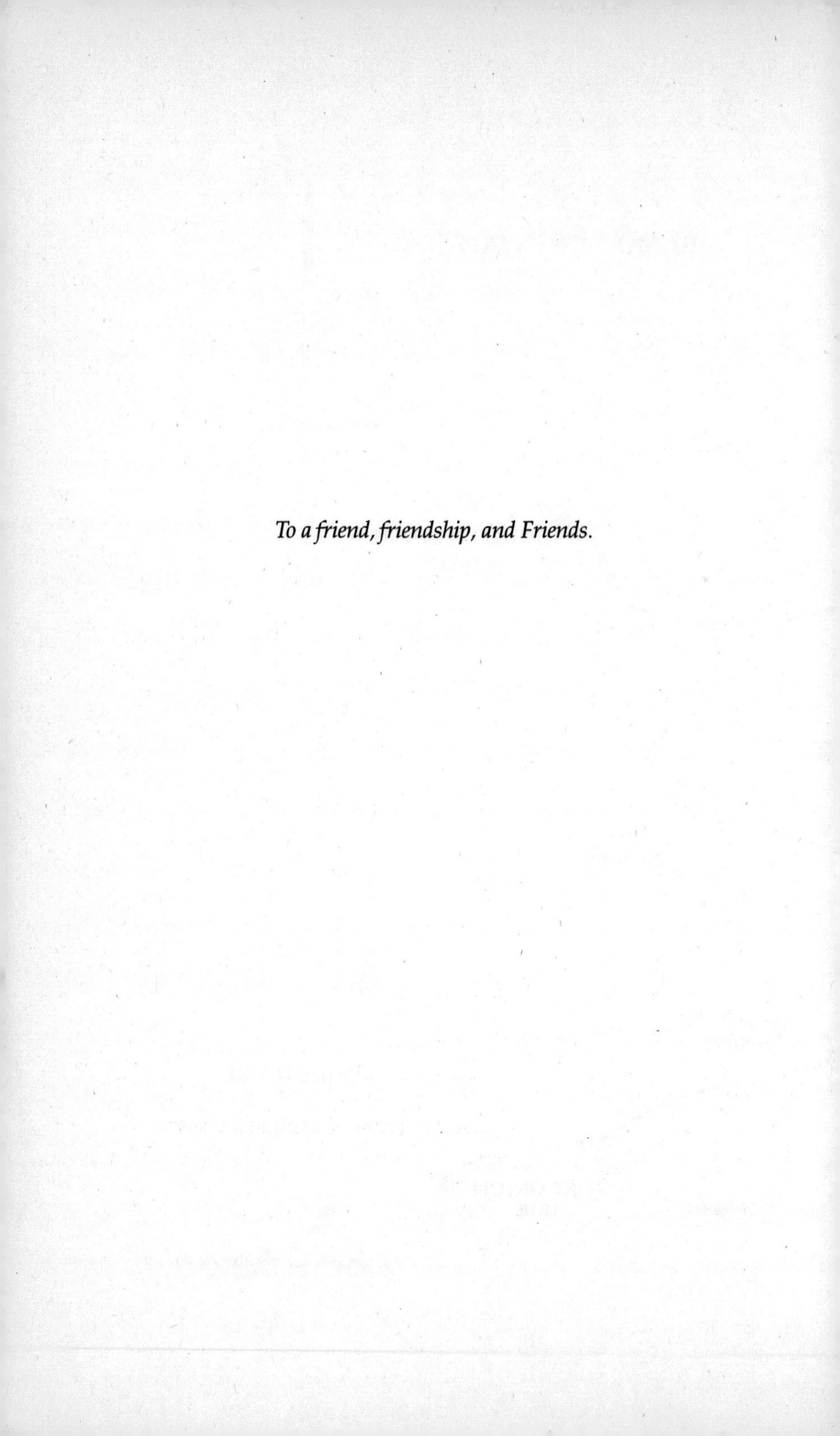

To a friend, friendship, and Friends.

1 THE TRADING HOUSE ON THE BOW RIVER

EARLY SUMMER, 1836. Alexander heard the horse coming. It was almost noon and the Piikani Sun had washed the prairie, slipping between the poplar trees by the river and carrying away the morning shadows. Reason told him there was only one sun, but living told him this was the Piikani Sun and its medicine could not be known in words.

The splash-necked pinto trotted into the clearing, head high and ears forward, its empty pad saddle twisted to one side and its long rein dragging in the dry grass.

It halted and began to graze quietly in front of the trading house.

"Hannah," Alexander called to the corrals where his daughter was supervising a Piikani boy riding a young bay gelding. "Blue Eye's pinto is back. He must have fallen off again."

The Sun On The Mountains trading house faced west to where the last snowfields of the Rocky Mountains spun the bright light back into the open sky. Behind the house, the long plains folded into soft-sloped hills and coulees, and the horizon eroded into a dusty haze that tracked the buffalo herds.

Alexander James and his wife, First Snow, had built the trading house on the bank of the Bow River more than fifty years ago. Since then, the James and their Piikani friends had often gathered on its front porch in Quaker Silence when the setting sun flowed crimson over the mountains.

Now in their seventies, Alexander and First Snow maintained a steady trade in furs and buffalo robes with the Piikani. Their daughter, Hannah, and an old Piikani, Grey Horse, raised and trained the Runners, the wide-eyed, fast buffalo horses that brought excitement and the best hunters to the house.

Blue Eye, Hannah's thin-faced, awkward sixteen-year-old son, had been spending his mornings with the Piikani teenagers and visiting their camps. More often than not, Blue Eye tumbled from his pinto along a trail and had to walk home, unless his mother sent one of the boys or girls from the corrals to find him.

Hannah had been thinking about her son that morning, and his curiosity regarding his grandfather. When she was Blue Eye's age, she had asked Alexander about his life before he came to the Bow River. He had shaken his head and turned away. This abrupt, negative response was so unusual she never questioned him again.

To Hannah, raising and training horses was straightforward, and talking about the past took up time she would rather spend with the horses. If her father didn't want to discuss it, why worry about it? How could something that happened years ago make any difference today? But her son saw complications. He wanted to know the why of everything.

Now, as Hannah watched Alexander, at least a head taller than any Piikani, lead Blue Eye's pinto toward the corrals, she frowned in discouragement. "Where do you think my son is this time?" she asked. "Did he say where he was going?"

"No," Alexander replied. "But he can't be far. The horse isn't sweating."

Hannah turned to the corral. She was dark-haired, muscular and had the same round, gentle face and oval eyes as her Nahathaway mother.

"Two Arrows," she called to the boy in the corral. "That's enough for now. Take my mare and find Blue Eye."

The boy slipped off the bay gelding and untied the bridle. The gelding followed him and, as he opened the gate, it stretched out its neck. He stroked its nose with a gentle touch. Two Arrows was very slender, and had a loose-limbed, effortless walk. He had handsome, dark Piikani features; a narrow nose, prominent cheekbones, and intense, restless eyes.

Alexander stopped by the gate. Two Arrows looked up, caught momentarily in the bright blue of Alexander's eyes, a blue that seemed to shine directly from the broad prairie sky.

"The pinto came back along the river," Alexander said. "Will you be able to follow its tracks?"

"*Aa*," Two Arrows answered. Simple Piikani words such as *aa* and *sa*, for yes and no, and *oki*, for hello, were frequently used around the trading house.

Blue Eye's pinto, a deep red chestnut with a distinctive splash of white across both sides of its neck and face, moved to Two Arrow's side as Alexander passed him the rein. "My grandson seems determined to ride this horse," Alexander said.

"Otssko Moapsspiksi should ride something quieter," Two Arrows replied, using Blue Eye's Piikani name. "This pinto is fast," he added. "It would be a good horse for a better rider."

Hannah nodded in agreement with Two Arrow's honest opinion. "You are right. But when my son makes up his mind to do something, he rarely quits. So far, he has worn out three pairs of moccasins following this horse home."

She rested her hand on Two Arrows' shoulder. "You know he admires the way you ride. He wants to keep up."

Two Arrows shrugged. "I don't mind riding slowly. I wait for everybody else, why not wait for my friend?"

Hannah looked toward the corral and clapped her hands sharply. "Come!" she called. Her mare, a fine-boned grey with alert eyes, lifted its head from the grass and trotted to Hannah's side. Hannah pulled a braided leather rope off the corral rail and knotted it around the mare's neck.

"Do you need the bridle?" she asked Two Arrows. The boy shook his head and swung easily onto the mare. Leading the pinto with his left hand, he nudged the mare with his heels and she trotted toward the river. Guided only by Two Arrows' legs and the rope around her neck, the mare turned up the trail and settled into a rolling canter she could hold for hours.

"I can't help but admire that boy," Hannah said as he left the clearing. "He already knows more about horses than I've learned in my entire life. He rides almost as well as Grey Horse."

"So do you," Alexander added. "The difference is Grey Horse taught you to ride. Two Arrows was born knowing how to ride. He has the Piikani gift. When your mother and I came to the Bow, the older Piikani told us they remembered the days before they owned horses. Now, the boys and girls ride as if the Piikani had been doing it forever. If the horses had come here two hundred years ago, there might not be an uninvited white person on the prairie today. The world has probably never seen better warriors on horseback."

Her father rarely talked about wars and conflict, and it was at moments like this she wished she could ask more about his life before Hudson Bay and the Bow River.

The hoofbeats of the mare faded into the steady washing of the Bow River along the bank. Hannah straightened the bridle Two Arrows had dropped, neatly coiling the rein.

"You know the Quaker saying that God exists in every person," she said to Alexander.

"Yes," he answered. "We are all born with the Light within us."

"I think God does more than exist in Two Arrows. He rides a horse."

He smiled. "You are probably right. God would enjoy riding with Two Arrows. And in Blue Eye?" he asked. "How does God exist?"

"I wish I knew," she answered. "The Light shines but my son still doesn't live his path."

"You are giving him choices," Alexander replied, his voice level and unemotional. "And God is giving him time. You can be patient."

"It would be easier to be patient if he would stay on his horse." Hannah frowned as she thought about her son's difficulties as he tried to keep up with his Piikani friends.

When Alexander saw her frown, he took her hand. "Your mother and I waited a long time for you to know your path," he said. "We always wondered if you would stay with us or disappear into the prairie with your horses and the Piikani."

"Well, I wasn't going to be a Fisheater!" she replied emphatically, releasing his hand.

Fisheaters! The expression almost made Alexander laugh. It was how Grey Horse scornfully described the whites and the Indians who paddled the rivers and camped in the damp forests. For Grey Horse, there was only one way to travel, by horseback, and only one place to live, the prairie. The Piikani way.

Hannah's heart had never needed encouragement to adopt any of Grey Horse's ways, or to learn his skill with the horses. She had ridden with Grey Horse before she could walk, held firmly in his arms as he cantered back and forth from the herd. By the age of ten, she was constantly riding at his side from camp to camp selling the Runners he trained. Women warriors and hunters were not common on the prairie, but accepted, and Hannah's almost constant presence at Grey Horse's side drew little more than an occasional comment. To prove the speed of a Runner and to obtain the best price, Grey Horse would accept any challenge to match the Runners against the best Piikani buffalo horses. He always chose Hannah to ride and she never let him down. After seeing the girl race to the lead in a buffalo run, a Piikani never haggled over the high price of a Runner. Grey Horse also taught Hannah about selecting mares to breed to the stallions, and buying new mares to bring new blood into the herd.

"If you see a mare that will improve our herd, buy it. Don't hesitate," he had told her. "A good broodmare will give us many colts, and some of them might turn out to be Runners."

While First Snow watched her husband and daughter as they talked by the corral, she continued to pack supplies for the Broken Ribs camped further up the river. The Broken Ribs were the most influential of the Piikani bands, and usually chose the locations for the annual gatherings. With strong, broad hands and unending energy, First Snow never tired and never complained about the days she spent hoisting the packs of supplies, bales of furs and buffalo robes onto the counter or onto the pack horses. First Snow rarely talked with the visiting Piikani, most of whom she found too excitable and aggressive compared to her Nahathaway family at Hudson Bay. Only a Piikani couple, One Person and Long Fingers, had become her close friends.

One Person, even-tempered and sociable, had been a wandering hunter when he had met Alexander. He and Long Fingers had travelled from band to band, hunting and selling the ropes and bridles Long Fingers braided. Now, they lived at Sun On The Mountains, delivering supplies to the Piikani and selling Long Finger's braiding. Blue Eye called them aunt and uncle, a familiarity he could rarely reach with Grey Horse. One Person was well-known in the bands for his sense of humour and easygoing manner. Long Fingers was more quiet and observant. She didn't mind being alone when she worked.

The couple always had the latest news about squabbles, celebrations, marriages, births, and deaths. It was Long Fingers who had explained to First Snow the reason for the Piikani's curiosity when Hannah was born. The women from the Badger band, a band with a reputation for gossiping and breaking promises, had ridden up the river to the trading house, almost overwhelming her as they examined Hannah. The Badger women weren't interested in trading, Long Fingers had told her. They had come to inspect Hannah and report to the other Piikani bands if she were dark like First Snow, or pale like Alexander.

"*Sa*," the women had announced after they had made their inspection. "The baby's eyes are not like her father's." The Piikani had hoped the girl would have Alexander's powerful medicine. All of creation, the Piikani believed, was controlled by unpredictable powers, powers they could sometimes direct to ensure good hunting, health, and victory over their enemies. Everything a person needed could be gained by learning the secret of those powers. But first, a person had to find the medicine that contained the power. A special eagle feather, for instance, might contain the power a hunter could use to enter an enemy's camp at night and capture horses.

Alexander's medicine, his white hair and blue eyes, had given him the power to become a respected trader and the owner of hundreds of Runners. His medicine, the Piikani believed, made him an entirely different type of person than the British and American traders on the North Saskatchewan and the Missouri rivers. Alexander understood and respected the Piikani traditions. For years, he had ridden with their hunters. To acknowledge Piikani ownership of the buffalo and their goodwill in allowing him to trade by the Bow, he had borrowed arrows from less affluent hunters and let their families claim the meat. Acknowledgement of a favour or a debt was as important to the Piikani as the repayment of the debt.

Today, as Blue Eye limped along the top of a treeless ridge toward the Bow River, he said to himself, "I should have held onto the rein when I fell. I don't know why Two Arrows never falls off." His hip and elbow were beginning to ache. He had been on his way home from the Broken Ribs' camp when a grouse flew up from the grass and his horse shied. Now he was on foot. Again.

"That's eleven times I've fallen off the pinto. And if the pinto steps on the long rein and breaks it, Grey Horse will make me repair it. That will be the fourth rein I've repaired.

"And if somebody comes to get me today, it will be the seventh time. But if nobody comes, then it will be only six times they have come for me. And, if I fall off once more and don't get a ride home, then I will have fallen off twelve times and will have walked home alone exactly six times and I will have ridden home with someone else exactly six times. That's progress, I suppose."

He had been relieved in the spring when his mother had suggested he spend less time with her in the corrals and more time in the trading house and delivering supplies to the band. Everybody had been waiting for her to make the suggestion and, once it had been made, Blue Eye's life had become simpler. Until then, he felt his family had been watching him, to see if he would grow to be like his Piikani father, Yellow Shield.

Although Blue Eye had inherited his father's black hair and red-brown skin, he was thin-shouldered and hollow-cheeked, and, as hard as he tried, never quite as quick or strong as his Piikani friends. Now, nobody wondered if Blue Eye would be like Yellow Shield.

"Why would I want to be like him?" Blue Eye said to himself as left the ridge and began to make his way down to the river. "He only spent one season with my mother and then rode off with the Elk Seekers as soon as he heard they were raiding the Crow by the Missouri. He has never visited me. I don't even know which band he's with now."

Alexander had recorded Blue Eye's birth in his trading ledgers of 1820 with the name David James but the boy's brilliantly blue, right eye would always be too startling for him to be called anything but Blue Eye. His left eye was as dark as his mother's.

Reports of the boy's different coloured eyes had spread quickly through the bands. Albino and pinto horses with a blue-tinged eye were rare and considered special by the Piikani. However, a person with two very different coloured eyes was extraordinary. Blue Eye would sit patiently on the trading counter while the Piikani men and women took turns examining his eyes. Nobody failed to notice his blue eye was almost identical in colour to Alexander's eyes, with the same fine black flashes radiating through a bright blue iris. Seeing this, they concluded he carried the great medicine of Alexander. Many Piikani still called him The White-Haired Piikani, the name given him when he had shared the glories of their buffalo hunts.

As a child, Blue Eye absorbed all he heard at the counter where his grandparents and his aunt and uncle traded, discussing hunting, weather, trading values, guns, horses, illnesses, and the endless raiding between the Piikani, the Assiniboin and the Crow.

One Person, always looking for tricks to play on visitors to the trading house, showed Blue Eye the startling effect his different coloured eyes had on first-time visitors. They would always look once, for just a moment, directly at Blue Eye, and then quickly shift their attention away, as if they had glimpsed something ghostly. Invariably, they couldn't resist sneaking a second, sideways glance, all the while wondering if they had simply caught an odd reflection in the light, or if they had been mistaken. One Person showed Blue Eye how to anticipate this second glance, and to tease the visitors by lowering his eyelid to cover the blue iris. They would then watch as the visitors continued their trading, all the while trying to catch an unobserved glimpse of his right eye.

Blue Eye played number games with his grandfather. Alexander would pile furs onto the counter and ask him how they could be divided equally into smaller piles. Blue Eye would count the furs and unerringly tell his grandfather the right answer. In his tidy memory, Blue Eye kept inventory for his grandfather, priding himself on always keeping track of how many guns, kettles, blankets and other goods were on hand and where they were stored on the shelves. He remembered who had paid Sun On The Mountains and who had promised to pay but hadn't.

Alexander taught Blue Eye to be resolute in making a trade and to never offer less than a fur or robe's full value. If two well-tanned robes traded for one gun, then that is what he should offer. To offer less, Alexander told him, was to lie. To offer more, was also to lie. It was that simple.

Always be truthful. Only ask for what you wanted, never more, never less. That was what the Piikani called The Sun On The Mountains Way. To follow The Way, Alexander said, was to trade fairly and, when in doubt, err on the side of generosity.

The sun was nearing the horizon when Blue Eye found the tracks of his splash-necked pinto on a trail by the river, worn into a deep rut by Piikani riding to trade at Sun On The Mountains. Seeing how far he was from the trading house, he doubted if he would be able to walk home in time for the evening meal. And, he was sure, he would be too late to help his grandmother pack the supplies for the Broken Ribs. He should be there to help her; otherwise she would not know to put in the extra knives and kettles the band had ordered from him today.

He climbed down to drink at the river and rest. "Maybe Two Arrows will bring the pinto," he thought hopefully. "He won't have any trouble following its tracks on this trail."

Blue Eye leaned back against an old poplar tree. Sitting quietly by the river reminded him of the summer he had spent a year ago with Firekeeper, his grandfather's partner at the South Branch. There the South Saskatchewan swirled and foamed beside the trading house, and he and Firekeeper had spent many evenings sitting on the bank, talking about trading. He liked the good-natured Nahathaway and listened carefully as Firekeeper had told him how he and Alexander and First Snow had left Hudson Bay and built this trading house. The Hudson's Bay Company traders Blue Eye had met along the river talked impressively about their firm's headquarters in London and Blue Eye had stored this information on the shelves of his mind, not sure when it would be useful, but sure it had a value.

Firekeeper had shown him the loans and gifts he always made to the trappers in the spring that the trappers almost always repaid in furs or favours.

"What if they don't repay you?" Blue Eye had asked.

"If their trapping goes poorly, I give them time. We all need help sometimes," Firekeeper had replied without concern. "Helping is my way."

Firekeeper had let Blue Eye look over his year-end tally of the Sun On The Mountains' profits in his ledger. "See," he pointed out proudly, "we lost nothing on the loans and gifts. Those who repaid us more than made up in trading for those who didn't repay us."

Blue Eye had returned to the Bow River that fall, his frame tall and spare, his voice deep.

As Blue Eye rested, his mind began creating a plan. Bit by bit, he assembled the details of how he would proceed, how he would explain it to his mother and grandparents, who he would ask to help, and all the supplies he would need.

"You're lucky I'm not a Crow," Two Arrows said from the top of the bank, startling Blue Eye. "Why did you fall off this time?"

"*Oki*," Blue Eye said as he saw his friend. "Never mind the Crow and never mind why I fell off. Tie the horses to a tree and talk with me. I have an idea."

"You always have an idea. And it is always complicated."

"This is different. I want you to come to Fort McKenzie with me and trade next spring," Blue Eye replied. Not concerned when Two Arrows started shaking his head, he continued, "I've heard the Americans are bringing boats up the Missouri to buy robes and furs. We should see those boats for ourselves. Of course, we'll probably have to take somebody older with us. Maybe Grey Horse. If he comes, I think my mother will let us go."

"Fort McKenzie?" Two Arrows said incredulously. "There's always trouble at that fort. They trade a lot of whiskey there."

"We'll be careful," Blue Eye said. "My grandfather wants me to take the winter furs and robes to Fort Edmonton next spring and I've already been there twice. Nobody from our trading house has been to Fort McKenzie. We'd be the first!"

Two Arrows took a deep breath. "I'd like to go. Especially if Grey Horse would ride with us." He paused, thought for a moment, then said, "But there's something I need to tell you about before I agree."

"Are you in trouble with your parents again?" Blue Eye asked. "What is it this time?"

Two Arrows wasn't surprised his friend had guessed so quickly. Everybody knew his parents weren't easy to get along with. They weren't like Hannah. "They don't want me to spend so much time at Sun On The Mountains," he began. "I was at the trading house all of the bull hunting this summer, and now it is fall and my family are preparing for the Great Circle and the Sun Dance. They expect me to go with them."

Traditionally, the Sun Dance was held during the last days of the Great Circle, the largest social gathering and most important communal hunt of the Piikani. In the fall, after the buffalo calves were weaned and the cows began to gain weight, the Piikani began building up a winter supply of dried meat and robes.

"But you like hunting," Blue Eye said.

"I do. But Hannah promised me a Runner if I stay and help her finish the two-year-olds. You know how much I want a Runner. I can't make up my mind."

"It's easy," Blue Eye offered. "Here's all you have to do. Tell your parents you will hunt with them . . . if they let you come with me to Fort McKenzie next spring."

"What about the Runner that Hannah said I could have?"

"She'll understand. Just tell her your family wants you with them at the Great Circle. She knows how important it is. You wait, she'll figure out a way for you to get a Runner. You're her favourite. She even let you bring her grey mare to find me. She won't let anybody else ride that horse."

Two Arrows grinned at the compliment. "*Aa*. You're right. As usual. Too bad you don't ride a horse as well as you make plans."

Blue Eye rubbed his hip. "I don't understand horses."

"That's because you think too much," Two Arrows said with a quick laugh. "Just ride, don't think, and you won't fall off."

Blue Eye and Two Arrows cantered back to the trading house. Two Arrows rode in front, keeping an easy pace for his friend. They turned their horses out with the riding horses by the river, and slipped into the house just in time to help with the evening meal.

Blue Eye kept his proposal to himself as he and Two Arrows set the places at the table for The Family, as the James referred to everybody who lived at Sun On The Mountains. This evening, they were all home: Alexander, First Snow, Hannah, One Person, Long Fingers, Blue Eye and Grey Horse.

At least once every day, usually before the evening meal, the James participated in a Quaker Silence, inviting any guests to join them. A Silence might last a minute or fifteen minutes, and was a time when they were fully open to the presence of God. They believed all men and women possessed the Light equally and had no need for the help of churches, clergy, ceremonies or sacraments in finding the presence of God. Everybody was welcome to interrupt a Silence with a short comment about a spiritual experience. First Snow would occasionally speak, but mostly to encourage Hannah. Blue Eye often had his mind on other experiences. Only Alexander spoke regularly, but lately he had been in a thoughtful mood and was unusually quiet.

The Family followed the Quaker traditions of simplicity and truthfulness. Only when asked directly by their Piikani friends would they do more than briefly explain the Light of Christ Within, that sense of God they believed every person contained which made clear the difference between right and wrong, and the importance of working for the good of others. They accepted the equality of the Piikani Sun and the Light Within, and never considered converting any Piikani to Quakerism.

As the Silence began, the trading house became still. An evening breeze blew through the open door, but before Blue Eye could rise to shut it, the door swung closed and the Silence ended. That was quick, Blue Eye said to himself.

He waited for everyone to start eating and then bluntly asked Alexander and Hannah to send him with Two Arrows and Grey Horse to trade on the Missouri River. That was the best way with his mother and grandfather. Go straight to the point. They always saw through his preparations, no matter how carefully he made them.

"I've heard the Americans are buying robes and furs. It could be an opportunity for us," Blue Eye explained. Alexander looked into his grandson's serious face, saw something that reminded him of his own father, and immediately agreed.

"You may go next spring as soon as there is green grass. You may take pack horses with furs and robes, and a small herd of riding horses," Alexander said. Robes, furs and horses! Blue Eye nodded solemnly. His grandfather didn't like a show of emotions, even for good news like this.

When Hannah said her son was too young to trade that far from Sun On The Mountains, Grey Horse reminded her he was younger than Blue Eye when he raided the Assiniboin and Crow horses. "You should be pleased," he added with a confident smile. "Your son wants to do something peaceful like his grandfather. Besides, when you were younger you wouldn't stay in the trading house every day. You lived on the prairie as much as you lived in the house."

Hannah knew she couldn't argue with Grey Horse and win. "You're right," she said as she relented and gave her permission.

"But he will probably fall off his horse or something!" One Person said, making everybody laugh, even Blue Eye.

"Maybe you should quit riding the splash-necked pinto," Two Arrows suggested. "Sun On The Mountains has the best horses in the Piikani territory. You can take your pick."

Blue Eye shook his head. "That's my horse and I'm riding it to Fort McKenzie."

Two Arrows left the house that evening with a thoughtful look and didn't return until morning. Hannah made him ride two-year-olds all day and by evening he was so tired he could barely stay awake for the Silence.

Afterwards, he asked Blue Eye to talk with him outside.

"I need your help," he said, his voice unusually serious.

"*Aa*," Blue Eye responded. "I'll help you with anything. We are friends. Tell me what you want."

"You are my good friend," Two Arrows said. "I know your family doesn't get involved in the Piikani dances and celebrations, but I want you to come with me to the Little Red Deer River when I make my sacrifice at the Sun Dance. I'm asking you to be my guide."

Surprised, Blue Eye considered his friend's request. Two Arrows must be very determined to find his path if he was willing to endure a Sun Dance, the most dangerous ceremony of the Piikani.

"Shouldn't you pay a warrior to be your guide? Isn't that the tradition?" Blue Eye asked.

Two Arrows shook his head. "Not always. I'll be looking for my future at the Sun Dance. Should I be a Piikani hunter, or should I be Sun On The Mountains and train horses with Hannah? If you're with me at the Sun Dance, I think it will help me make my choice."

"I'll go with you," Blue Eye replied. "I wish my family had a Sun Dance to show us our paths. But we don't dance or sing. All we do is discuss things."

"*Aa*," Two Arrows agreed. "You discuss things a lot."

Two Arrows did not want to go into the house to talk with The Family about his request. "My parents talked with me almost all night. I'm tired of talking. You have said yes. I know you will come." Two Arrows slipped onto his horse and trotted into the twilight.

Inside the house, Blue Eye told The Family he had agreed to be Two Arrows guide at the Sun Dance. "He is my friend and he asked me to help."

"You did the right thing," Alexander assured him. "But maybe you should have talked to us before committing yourself. Don't be surprised if this doesn't turn out according to your plans. Nothing will be the same for Two Arrows after the Sun Dance.

"There is as much to learn in the Sun Dance as there is in our Silence. Our hearts can be changed. One Person and Grey Horse made sacrifices at the Sun Dance and they are no longer seekers. They live their paths."

Seeing his grandson's look of concern, Alexander reached over and rumpled his black hair. "You are a good boy, Blue Eye," he said. "And you will be a good man. No more can be asked of anyone. I'm just being cautious. When a friend asks for help, you must give it without question." Blue Eye felt the familiar, steady strength flowing from his grandfather's hands and it settled him.

"I want to help Two Arrows, but I don't know if I can," he admitted. "I've never seen a Sun Dance."

"When the time comes, you will know what to do," Alexander said. "Perhaps all he will need is someone to stand by him and be a witness to his sacrifice. Just remember to be a good Quaker: Be cheerful and speak to the Light in every one."

"I don't understand," Blue Eye said.

"You will," his grandfather replied. "Be prepared to accept whatever you see."

Blue Eye looked over at One Person who was grinning at Blue Eye's still serious expression. One Person's hair was almost silver, and he had a deeply lined, dark face. When he smiled, everybody felt his warmth.

"Yes," One Person said. "Be cheerful. That's the best thing to do."

"Now," Alexander suggested, "this might be a good opportunity to take your busy thoughts outside and let the less important people of this house remember what it was like to be young and invincible."

Blue Eye, wishing his grandfather had given him more practical advice, went to sit on the porch. "Some days I wish I were Piikani," he said to himself. "Speak to the Light in every one? What does that mean?"

He had been sitting on the porch in the twilight, thinking about the Sun Dance and Two Arrows, when First Snow sat by his side.

"Hannah says you've been asking her about your grandfather," she said.

Blue Eye turned to face her. "Yes, I have. He never talks about what he did as a boy. It's as if his life started when he came to the Bow with you. Last summer Firekeeper told me how the three of you started the trading house on the South Branch. He said he didn't know anything about where grandfather came from before he met him at Hudson Bay."

"I can tell you a little," First Snow offered. "Your grandfather talks about a lot of things, but not much about when he was young." She had a low, steady voice. She spoke slowly and always told her stories step-by-step.

Alexander, she said, was born in Philadelphia. He had an older brother and sister. "I don't know where Philadelphia is and I don't know if any of his family are still alive. He told me his family were Quakers and they owned a bank.

"He said he was a boy when he started working in the bank with his father and mother. Then the Independence War started between the British and the Americans. The Quakers wouldn't fight. They believed war was wrong. They wouldn't pay money to the American army. Alexander said the leader of the American army — a man named Washington —persuaded his brother to join. That started the family's troubles. Other Quakers refused to talk to them. They lost everything. Nobody would pay what they owed the bank.

"I met Alexander at Hudson Bay. He said he was starting his life over. He traded with my people, the Nahathaway. The other traders called us Cree, but your grandfather always called us Nahathaway."

First Snow fingered her long braids while she recalled Alexander as a young man. "He had respect for everybody. He was big and tall. He had white hair, just like it is today. Everybody knew him, even though he tried to keep to himself. One day American soldiers came to Hudson Bay looking for him. I never found out why. There was a fight and he had to leave quickly."

Blue Eye found his grandmother's description of the events in Philadelphia and Hudson Bay puzzling. It didn't sound like his grandfather to have this kind of trouble. He was always calm. He didn't get angry. He was polite to everybody.

First Snow continued, "He asked if I would go away with him and Firekeeper, and I said I would.

"That's when we built the trading house on the South Branch. That's where I found an envelope in your grandfather's jacket.

"He said it was a letter from his mother, one he would never open. When I asked him why he didn't read it, he said he had left that life behind. He still has that letter and he hasn't opened it.

"We stayed one winter at the South Branch. We knew a boy named David Thompson at Hudson Bay and we met him again on the river. The next summer we rode to the Bow with David and some other traders. I had never ridden a horse before. We've been here ever since." She stopped, and then said, "I can't tell you anything else. Maybe one day your grandfather will tell you more. It's up to him."

"Should I ask him?"

First Snow shook her head. "No. Let it come from him. He knows you are interested."

Alexander's letter intrigued Blue Eye. He could not think why his grandfather had not read it. "Aren't you curious about the letter?" he asked his grandmother.

"A little," she replied. "But I'm not in a hurry. The Nahathaway believe life explains itself slowly. Usually the answers we receive are simpler than we expect. And some questions don't have answers. It is what we learn along the way that is important."

Work resumed around the trading house the next day, and Blue Eye's decision to go with Two Arrows to the Sun Dance was not discussed by The Family again. Blue Eye continued to ride to the bands where the news spread quickly that he would be at the Sun Dance. He would be the first from Sun On The Mountains to attend a Sun Dance.

Blue Eye's young friends joked with him, asking him if he would be riding the splash-necked pinto to the Great Circle — or walking. He assured them he would be riding the pinto.

In the joking, Blue Eye heard the beginning of the Piikani's acceptance of him, not as Alexander's grandson, or as Hannah's son, but as Blue Eye.

Blue Eye and Two Arrows left for the Little Red Deer River ten days later, promising to return in two weeks.

2 The Sun Dance

THE LITTLE RED DEER RIVER, FALL, 1836. Two Arrows' band, The Round Robes, was camped on the poorest side of the Great Circle, the side farthest from the river and the shade of the cottonwoods. They had to walk across the Circle every day for water while the larger bands had just a short walk. Each summer for the last five years, the Round Robes had been losing families to more prosperous Piikani bands, and now they had only six families. They hoped Two Arrows would lead their hunts soon. Then the Round Robes would be camped beside the river and be turning aside gifts of horses from families hoping to join the band.

For two days, the band had been watching the horizon to the west, impatiently waiting for Two Arrows to arrive and begin his preparations for the Dance. "If he's riding with Blue Eye, he will be riding slowly," they said as they waited. The families talked about the many days Two Arrows' spent at Sun On The Mountains, and how he had become one of Hannah's favourites. She had kept him all summer at the trading house with the promise of a Runner. To make up for the hunting he would miss, she had sent two riding horses to his family, and Two Arrows had agreed to meet his family at the Great Circle in time for the Sun Dance. After the Dance, he had told them, he would decide if he would stay with the band.

Two Arrows and Blue Eye had been cantering their horses most of the morning, travelling steadily northwest. Blue Eye's pinto cantered calmly, content to follow Two Arrows' horse. The boys had just watered their horses at a stream in a small coulee and were letting them walk up the long bank when Little Ears, a Badger about five years older than they were, splashed across the stream.

"This is how warriors ride," Little Ears shouted as he galloped up the bank. Blue Eye's pinto pulled hard on its rein as the Badger approached. Two Arrows stopped and waited for Blue Eye. "Let him run by," he said. "Your horse will settle down after he is gone."

As the Badger galloped past, he swung his bow and smacked the pinto on the rump. The pinto bucked and Blue Eye rolled off. The pinto raced after the Badger's black.

Two Arrows glanced back once to make sure Blue Eye was all right, and then pressed his horse into a gallop. He caught the pinto's rein at the top of the bank and slowly brought the nervous horse under control.

Little Ears circled back, laughing as he followed Two Arrows to where Blue Eye was waiting.

"What happened to you?" Little Ears called to Blue Eye. "Didn't you want to race me?"

Blue Eye ignored Little Ears and took the pinto's rein from Two Arrows. As soon as Blue Eye had mounted, Two

Arrows turned to Little Ears. "You go ahead. We don't want to ride with you."

Little Ears ignored Two Arrows and lifted his bow to strike Blue Eye's pinto again. Two Arrows reached over and jerked the bow from Little Ear's hand.

"Don't you want your bow?" Two Arrows said with a laugh, holding the bow just out of Little Ear's reach.

Little Ears kicked his black forward. Two Arrows backed his horse a few steps. Little Ears kicked his black forward again and Two Arrows trotted to the side, staying out of his reach.

"Still want to race?" Two Arrows asked, enjoying the game he was playing with Little Ears. "Think you can keep up?"

Little Ears jerked hard on the black's rein, and the horse tossed its head in pain. "Give me my bow."

"Don't you want to race?" Two Arrows asked, holding the bow above his head.

Little Ears looked across at Blue Eye on the pinto. "I'll race, my horse against that pinto — if Blue Eye rides it."

"It's a race," Two Arrows answered, not giving Blue Eye an opportunity to respond. "The first rider to the camp wins." He tossed the bow to Little Ears.

"Hang on, Blue Eye," he called back as he turned his horse and started at a gallop. "Don't stop until you are at the camp."

Blue Eye twisted both his hands into the pinto's mane and gave the horse a quick kick. Moments later, he caught up to Two Arrows.

"I can't stop him," Blue Eye shouted as he passed Two Arrows.

"Don't try," Two Arrows laughed. "Just ride." He kept his horse about four lengths behind the pinto. Blue Eye held on, just directing the horse slightly to keep it running along the faint trail to the camp.

When they could see the tops of the poplars along the river, Two Arrows slowed his horse to a canter and leaned forward, as if he had a pain in his side. Looking back, he watched as Little Ears galloped closer.

Little Ears pulled alongside and swung his bow at Two Arrows. He hit him twice on the back and each time Two Arrows winced. When Little Ears edged closer, Two Arrows stretched down and twisted Little Ears' foot, tossing him off the black.

Without stopping, Two Arrows grabbed the black's rein and galloped after Blue Eye.

Blue Eye raced through the camp, the pinto running wildly until he could bring it under control. He had just dismounted and was leaning against the lathered horse when Two Arrows trotted into the Great Circle leading the black.

Two Arrows slid his horse to a stop in front of the Round Robes' camp and swung off with a wide smile.

"Blue Eye just won Little Ears' black," Two Arrows said to his family as they crowded around. "Little Ears fell off this time — not Blue Eye!" His family followed him to where Blue Eye, still breathing hard, was now sitting on the grass.

"You probably didn't know how fast you could ride," Two Arrows said to Blue Eye. "You've probably only seen your pinto run like that after you've fallen off!"

Two Arrows told his family how Blue Eye had wrapped his hands into the pinto's mane and let the horse run. "You couldn't have pulled him off!' he said.

As Two Arrows described the race to his family, Blue Eye saw concern develop in their faces. The Badgers were always involved in disputes with other bands over hunting and horses. A dispute with them over a horse race on the first evening of the Sun Dance preparations would spoil the good atmosphere in their camp.

"You talk with your family," he said to Two Arrows. "They want to hear your news. I'll cool the horses." But before he could lead the horses behind the tipis, he heard shouting in the Badger camp and turned back.

Little Ears, riding behind another Badger, had trotted into the Badger camp and was surrounded by five men.

"Poor Little Ears," Two Arrows said in a mocking tone, "having to tell his friends that Blue Eye won his horse in a race."

"You made the bet, not me, "Blue Eye pointed out. "It was a bad idea."

"I knew you'd win. I've seen his horse run before. Your pinto is faster."

"It was still a bad idea," Blue Eye said, smiling slightly. "But I should thank you. I always wondered if I could ride that fast. Now I know."

Two Arrows laughed. "Yes. Now you know . . . a little."

As the Round Robes watched the Badgers, Little Ears and his friends crossed the Circle to the tipi of Heavy Shield, the tribal chief and leader of the Broken Ribs band. He had been sitting by its entrance, talking with three or four band chiefs, but rose when while Little Ears and his friends began arguing with him. With a wave of his arm, he sent one of the band chiefs across the Circle to the Round Robes. Blue Eye saw the disappointment in the faces of the Round Robes families as the band chief walked towards them.

"Wait here," Blue Eye said to Two Arrows. "I am your guide for the Sun Dance and I'll handle this. Stay with your family. Tell them I'll settle it."

He walked straight to the band chief. "Is this about the race?" Blue Eye asked.

The chief shook his head. "I don't know anything about a race. Little Ears claims you and Two Arrows stole his black horse this afternoon. Heavy Shield sent me to get you and Two Arrows.

"I will speak for both of us," Blue Eye replied. "The sun is beginning to set, and Two Arrows must begin his preparations for the Sun Dance. He has chosen me as his guide. I will speak for him."

The chief smiled. "Always thinking, aren't you? If it was my decision, I'd say there was lots of daylight left, and Two Arrows should speak for himself. But it's Heavy Shield who will decide if you can speak for Two Arrows." He turned and led Blue Eye to the tribal chief's tipi.

Heavy Shield, wearing his ceremonial clothing, welcomed Blue Eye to the Great Circle. His lined face was framed by his shoulder length hair, parted in the middle with a handful of locks knotted on his forehead. Five long, pale white shells hung from each of his ears. The hundreds of red and yellow quills and beads sewn into his entire leather outfit of leggings, shirt, jacket, and moccasins had required months of work.

"The sun is setting and the Dance preparations are beginning," the tribal chief agreed after hearing Blue Eye explain why Two Arrows was not with him. "The Sun On The Mountains boy may speak for his Round Robes friend. This dispute will be settled now."

"Sun On The Mountains!" Little Ears said, shaking his head in disgust. "Why is Blue Eye here? He is not Piikani. He should not be at our Sun Dance."

Blue Eye kept his face impassive, not wanting his face to reflect the insult to himself and his family.

"Two Arrows has asked Blue Eye to be his guide in the Dance," the chief said. "He has the right to be here." He continued on, telling Little Ears and Blue Eye the chiefs would listen to their accounts and then consider their judgement privately. "Little Ears will speak first."

Little Ears told the chiefs he had been riding toward the Circle when Two Arrows and Blue Eye had galloped alongside, laughing at him for not riding faster. He had tried to ignore them until they challenged him to a race.

"I told them I would not race," Little Ears told Heavy Shield. "I am not wealthy like Sun On The Mountains, and have only one buffalo horse, the black. I could not bet my only horse in a race. We argued and they pushed me off my horse so they could steal it. They left me on foot. I was lucky someone gave me a ride to the camp."

Heavy Shield turned to Blue Eye. "Is this what happened?" he asked. Blue Eye looked back to the Round Robes' camp where the families had surrounded Two Arrows and the horses.

"I will not dispute what Little Ears says," he said.

Heavy Shield considered Blue Eye's response. "Are you admitting you and Two Arrows stole Little Ears' horse?"

Blue Eye knew the chiefs expected him to say Little Ears was lying. They had punished Little Ears twice at other camps for stealing horses, and each time he had given them a plausible explanation that turned out to be a lie.

Blue Eye's face did not change as he repeated his answer. "I will not dispute what Little Ears says."

Heavy Shield talked with the band chiefs, turning his back on Little Ears and Blue Eye.

It took only a few moments for them to reach a decision. The chiefs stepped back, and Heavy Shield announced, "The black horse belongs to Little Ears. Blue Eye will return it to him."

Little Ears grinned, and his Badger friends slapped him on the back in congratulations.

"Come to the Round Robes' camp now and get the horse," Blue Eye said to Little Ears.

Little Ears refused to let the dispute end. "Two Arrows should have a Piikani as a guide. The Sun Dance is for warriors. Sun On The Mountains are afraid to be warriors."

The crowd of Badgers waited for Blue Eye to reply to this insult.

"You are right," Blue Eye agreed. "My friend should have a Piikani warrior as a guide. You will be his guide — and mine. I will make a sacrifice at the Sun Dance as well. We will pay you one horse for this. My pinto."

Heavy Shield stepped between Little Ears and Blue Eye. "Wait," he said, his hand on Blue Eye's shoulder. "Think carefully. A guide must be someone you trust."

"I know what to expect," Blue Eye replied.

Heavy Shield turned to Little Ears who, glancing across the Circle at the splash-necked pinto, said, "*Aa*. I will be their guide."

At the Round Robes' camp, Two Arrows reluctantly handed the reins of the pinto and the black to Little Ears. As soon as they were alone, he said to Blue Eye, "I thought you knew how to plan things. You won the race. Now you have given the black away — and your pinto."

"It doesn't matter about the horses," Blue Eye said. "Look at your family. They are pleased that the Sun Dance will go ahead without an argument over the race. This is an important time for you and for your family."

"Yes. But you didn't have to give your pinto to Little Ears."

"You're right," Blue Eye said. "I didn't have to. But I have a reason. I've been thinking about the Sun Dance."

"No!" Two Arrows interrupted. "Please don't tell me you've been thinking again."

"I have," Blue Eye admitted. "If I make a sacrifice at the Dance, everybody will know I am Piikani, not just Sun On The Mountains. That's important to me. You and I will find our paths together."

"You could have chosen somebody better than Little Ears to be our guide," Two Arrows said. "Somebody we trust."

"I'm not afraid of another race with Little Ears," Blue Eye said with a smile Two Arrows hadn't seen for a few days. "We'll beat him again, and this time everybody will see for themselves how our horses run."

Two Arrows shook his head in amazement as he understood what his friend had done. "When did you think this plan up? When you were talking to Heavy Shield?"

"No. I had most of it figured out before I left the Bow. I was waiting to see how things would develop before I told you about it."

Blue Eye and Two Arrows began fasting at sunset. The Piikani women would begin praying the next morning, after the men erected the centre pole by the river.

The Dance would begin in four days with all the dancers standing beneath the pole. The guides would cut two slits in the skin on each side of the dancers' chests and push saskatoon skewers underneath the skin. Then they would tie the ends of the skewers to ropes fastened on the top of the centre pole. Blood would cover the dancers' chests and the guides' hands.

The Sun, pulling on the ropes, would lead the dancers from the paths of their past and onto the paths of their tomorrows. As the dancers fell from exhaustion and pain, the skewers would tear their skin apart, completing their sacrifices. Their scars would signify the bravery of their dancing.

To prepare Two Arrows, the Round Robes took turns telling him stories of how the Creator had given the prairie to the Piikani, and had provided buffalo to feed and clothe them, and had sent them the first horses. They told Two Arrows how the Piikani fought with their enemies to protect the Creator's gifts. They described how Two Arrows' ancestors had been hunters and had provided meat for the band and had led the hunters, always caring for the Round Robes.

Heavy Shield visited Blue Eye on the afternoon before the Dance, dressed in a plain leather jacket and leggings, his hair tied in a single braid. He sat by Blue Eye's side, smoking a stone pipe. He puffed a few times and then set the pipe on the grass to cool. The tobacco went out quickly. He continued to sit until the mood struck him to light the pipe again.

Just before sunset, he offered the pipe to Blue Eye. "Smoke," he said. "I have often smoked with Sun On The Mountains." Blue Eye accepted the pipe and puffed it lightly while Heavy Shield continued to speak.

"Your people are not warriors or hunters," he said, "and stories of war and hunting will not help you find your path.

"You must take into your Dance a story about Sun On The Mountains and Alexander. I was the first to paint the Sun On The Mountains symbol on your trading house and the first to paint the symbol on a Runner, so that is the story I will tell.

"The story begins when I was young, like you. Alexander and First Snow came to our camp from the North Saskatchewan.

"Many Piikani did not like Alexander and First Snow wintering on the Bow and would not trade with them. We did not like First Snow because she was Nahathaway. Alexander's white hair and blue eyes puzzled us. We learned later his hair and eyes are a powerful medicine that can change the paths of men. But in those days we didn't know about his medicine. Alexander and First Snow surprised us. They did not hunt the Piikani buffalo. They traded for meat. They built their house on the Bow and invited us to visit, even if we did not trade. The British on the North Saskatchewan built forts, hunted our buffalo and only invited us inside to trade. They had no respect for the Creator's gifts to the Piikani.

"We saw Alexander's medicine revealed after he met Grey Horse. The Sun had shown Grey Horse the path where the horses ran, but Grey Horse did not fully understand it. At first, we envied him. Nobody could ride as far or as fast as Grey Horse. Then we saw he was dangerous to others. Many warriors who rode with him died. Soon, he rode alone. We did not see Grey Horse for a long time and thought he was dead. Alexander found him in the prairie, a Crow arrow in his leg.

"Grey Horse learned from Alexander. They made a bargain. If Grey Horse would raise and train buffalo horses with Alexander, then Alexander would trade for enough good horses to start a herd.

"Along the Missouri River, they met a Mandan trading party returning to the Dakotas. They had better horses than Grey Horse had ever seen. Alexander and Grey Horse did not have enough supplies to trade for the horses. Grey Horse could think of nothing but these horses. For the first time, he could see all of his path and he was afraid he would lose it. He knew the only way he would own the Mandan horses would be with Alexander's help.

"Alexander and Grey Horse returned to the Bow where they loaded all their spare supplies and guns on pack horses, and Grey Horse rode to the Missouri to find the Mandan and trade for the best horses. Two full moons later, he had not returned. We told Alexander he had made a mistake trusting that Badger with his supplies.

"But the next full moon, he returned with twenty mares and two stallions. He had galloped them west from the territory of the Mandan in the Dakotas and through Assiniboin and Crow territories.

"We had never thought horses like these existed. They weren't like our horses. They had fine legs, arched necks, and narrow, elegant heads. We called them Runners and we all wanted to own one.

"That winter I went to the Bow with my father and the band chiefs and invited Alexander and First Snow to stay on the river for as long as they wanted. We named their trading house Naato'si Otatsmiistakists, Sun On The Mountains, and I drew the symbol on their door. When I owned a Runner, I painted the symbol on it, too."

Heavy Shield paused in his story. With his fingers, he traced the air above Blue Eye.

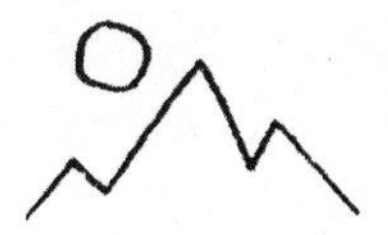

"Alexander says the buffalo run is the greatest story of the Piikani. We know how to kill a buffalo with one arrow. We know who dares to lean from his horse to pull an arrow out, so it will not be said his first shot failed. We are horsemen, and the Runners acknowledge our ways.

"The Runners have the speed to bring a Piikani hunter beside the buffalo cows that lead the herd, and glory if he kills several in one run. The Runners can gallop inside the herd, blinded by the dust. The Runners have the courage and intelligence to crowd close to the buffalo. They know the pattern of the run and are not afraid of the final twist when a dying buffalo turns its horns against the horse.

"That is the story you must carry into the Dance, of how the Runners have brought the Piikani and Sun On The Mountains together. You and the Sun must finish this story and that will be your path."

Blue Eye felt clear-headed and sure of himself the next morning. He sat by Two Arrows and waited for the ceremony to begin.

Little Ears made the cuts first on Two Arrows. He pinched the skin a hand's width below Two Arrows' collar bone, drawing the skin forward as he pushed the knife point through the fold. Blood poured over his hands as he withdrew the knife and slid a skewer through the slit. Two Arrows forehead beaded with sweat as he stared into the sky.

When it was his turn, Blue Eye pressed his fingertips against his thighs so he would not clench his fists or flinch as Little Ears pulled on his skin. He felt Little Ears' fingers digging deep into the muscle of his chest. He refused to look down. The knife slid through skin and muscle and Blue Eye felt a sickness roll in his stomach. He ground his teeth to hold the sickness down. The second cut went deeper than the first.

"You'll die here," Little Ears whispered as he knotted the thongs on the skewers. Blue Eye leaned back and the skewers twisted inside the muscles of his chest. His arms writhed uncontrollably as the pain burned through his shoulders and into his fingertips. The medicine of the Piikani Sun danced him into the sky.

THE TRADING HOUSE, FALL, 1836. Hannah waited five days for Blue Eye and Two Arrows to return from the Sun Dance before she asked Grey Horse to ride to the Great Circle and find them.

"I hope the pinto hasn't hurt Blue Eye," she said to her mother when Grey Horse left the trading house. "I wish he would change his mind and let me give him another horse."

"He has to prove himself," First Snow replied. "He has your reputation to live up to."

"My reputation?" she replied.

"Yes. He understands he'll never ride like you, but how else can he show everybody he is a man now? No matter what, he's always going to be compared to you." Hannah looked puzzled as she asked her mother, "What about the trading house? He's smarter than all the rest of us in there. Isn't that enough for him?"

"No. The Piikani accept the trading house, but they respect the horses. The horses are everything to them and, for now, they are everything to Blue Eye."

THE LITTLE RED DEER, FALL, 1836. Grey Horse had barely ridden into sight of the Great Circle when the Piikani children ran out and swarmed around his dappled grey Runner. There was not a boy or girl who had not heard the story of Grey Horse's gallop with the Runners through the Crow and Assiniboin territories.

And who had not heard how, at the Great Circle in the summer of his ride, Grey Horse had turned aside the honour of a warrior's name, declaring he was now a horse trader and would always ride with Alexander? When he chose the name Sikssikapii, Grey Horse, the Piikani assumed the horse herd had captured his loyalty. However, after Hannah began to ride with him, nobody doubted Grey Horse's loyalties. "The Runners," he would say when anyone asked why he had chosen to ride as Sun On The Mountains, "tell you everything you need to know about me."

Although Sun On The Mountains had turned Grey Horse's reckless energy from horse raiding toward raising and defending a horse herd, Alexander was sure Grey Horse's love of danger would never leave him. Alexander and First Snow had never traded alcohol when they travelled west from Hudson Bay, and would not on the Bow. Grey Horse liked to drink, and he and Alexander almost parted over this several times. Finally, Alexander divided the horse herd and told Grey Horse to take his share and leave; Grey Horse chose to stay and never drank again near Sun On The Mountains.

"Grey Horse is here!" the children shouted as he trotted his Runner into the Great Circle. Grey Horse, more than sixty years old, was considered an old man but his presence still attracted attention. As he rode through the camps of the Piikani bands, the men and women stood in acknowledgment, smiling as he guided his horse without reins toward the tipis of the Round Robes. The grey's long black mane and tail swung like flags celebrating the horseman's arrival, its ears flickered as it watched every movement. Responding to a shift in Grey Horse's balance, the horse slowed to a walk. Grey Horse's plain Sun On The Mountains clothing, never adorned with feathers or paint, made a stronger impression than if he had worn the brightest colours and feathers. He was Grey Horse, the Piikani who rides as Sun On The Mountains.

His hair hung to his shoulders in two braids. Beneath a wide forehead, his deep-set eyes moved with such self assurance that many Piikani could not return his steady stare.

He wore only one ornament, the string of blue beads around his neck that First Snow had given him when he had announced his intention to ride as Sun On The Mountains.

His horse turned nimbly to the right or left as Grey Horse greeted his friends. Seeing two small boys standing shyly to one side, Grey Horse urged the horse into a jog and, leaning over, swung the boys up, one in each arm, and lifted them onto the horse. The astonished boys waved as they rode through the camps with the marvellous Grey Horse. This Great Circle would never be forgotten. He had chosen them!

Grey Horse found Blue Eye in a small tipi on the edge of the Round Robes' camp, delirious, his chest swollen. Blood and pus oozed from the two skewer wounds. Two Arrows had been rubbing herbs onto his friend's chest.

Grey Horse knelt by Blue Eye and brushed the sweat-soaked hair from the boy's temples. "Listen to me," he whispered. "I am here now. I will take you back to Sun On The Mountains." Blue Eye showed no sign of understanding. He twisted feverishly on the buffalo robes, and Grey Horse stroked the young man's forehead again.

Turning to Two Arrows, Grey Horse asked, "Why did Blue Eye make a sacrifice to the Sun?"

Two Arrows described the race and the decision of the chiefs to return the black to Little Ears. "Blue Eye refused to defend his claim to the horse. It was wrong, but Blue Eye wanted the Sun Dance to go peacefully. Then Little Ears insulted Blue Eye, saying Sun On The Mountains were afraid to fight. That's when he decided to make the sacrifice with me. He offered Little Ears his pinto as payment for being the warrior guide for both of us."

Grey Horse looked at Blue Eye and said, "It must have been important to him, or he wouldn't have offered his pinto."

Two Arrows continued, "Little Ears cut Blue Eye so deeply that the skewers couldn't be torn out. After I fell, he hung from the centre pole for another day and night. He would have died if I hadn't cut him down."

Grey Horse's concern for Blue Eye turned into a hot anger. He went to his horse and brought back a small lump of vermilion. Carefully, he drew a Sun On The Mountains symbol on Blue Eye's chest.

"There. Now Little Ears' failings cannot kill Blue Eye. The power of Sun On The Mountains will restore him. Stay here. I'm going to get Blue Eye's pinto."

Grey Horse hurried across the Great Circle to the Badgers' tipis where he found Little Ears, sitting in front of a tipi and painting blue bands across his face and shoulders. Blue Eye's pinto grazed on a picket a few paces away.

Grey Horse cut the picket line and began leading the horse away. Little Ears jumped up. "That's my horse!" he shouted.

"*Sa,*" Grey Horse replied, his voice not revealing his anger. "This horse belongs to Sun On The Mountains. If you say it is your horse, then the only explanation can be that you stole it."

"*Sa,*" Little Ears countered with malice in his voice. "That horse isn't stolen. It is mine. The horse is Blue Eye's payment to me for the Sun Dance."

"There is no payment." Grey Horse responded. "A warrior is paid for providing guidance and advice during the ceremony. You did neither for Blue Eye. You cut too deeply. He is almost dead. You did not earn anything."

The Badgers crowded around the two men, trying to start a fight. Urged on by his friends, Little Ears pulled a knife from his belt and waved it towards Grey Horse.

Grey Horse showed no sign of being intimidated by the knife or by the crowd of Badgers. He turned and continued leading the horse to the Broken Ribs' camp. The shouting and the crowd attracted the attention of two men from the Weasel Society, the men selected by the band chiefs to police the camp. Fights over horses, gambling, and women were common during the Great Circle and the Weasel Society patrolled the camp, breaking up quarrels before anybody was seriously hurt.

Suddenly, Little Ears swung his knife high, striking downward onto Grey Horse's back. Grey Horse stepped sideways, turning to bring his left elbow around hard, smashing Little Ears in the mouth. Little Ears fell backward. Grey Horse stood over him.

"Stop!" a Weasel ordered, moving quickly to Grey Horse's side. A thin line of blood trickled from Grey Horse's forearm where Little Ears' knife had nicked him.

"I should kill him," Grey Horse said.

The Weasels pulled Little Ears from the ground and pushed him toward the centre of the Great Circle. Grey Horse followed, leading the pinto. The Badgers, still shouting abuse at Grey Horse, called him a traitor to the Piikani. Grey Horse, his face impassive, did not respond. One of the Weasels walked across the camp and returned to the centre with Heavy Shield.

Little Ears, his mouth bleeding, spoke first, relying largely upon his role in the Dance to substantiate his ownership of the pinto. Grey Horse argued that Little Ears had not earned any payment for his role in the ceremony; the cuts he made were too deep. The Weasels then described Little Ears' knife attack on Grey Horse.

Heavy Shield ordered the Weasels to keep the two men separated while he and the band chiefs deliberated. Reluctantly, Grey Horse handed the pinto's lead to one of the Weasels to hold until the decision was announced. He returned to the Round Robes' camp.

When the chiefs summoned the Weasels to bring the two men to the centre of the Circle to hear their decision, Grey Horse walked with Two Arrows, his mind torn between his anger and his Sun On The Mountains' belief that conflicts should be settled without bloodshed.

The situation was complicated, Heavy Shield began. There were two matters to decide, the first concerning Little Ears' claim to the pinto; the second concerning the knife attack by Little Ears upon Grey Horse.

Concerning the ownership of the pinto, Heavy Shield said, Little Ears had no claim. Whether the incisions were made purposefully too deep, or were simply poor judgement, Little Ears had not followed the proper role of a warrior guide.

"Little Ears had the responsibility to cut Blue Eye loose. But he didn't. If Two Arrows had not intervened, Blue Eye would have died. The chiefs say Little Ears has not earned the horse."

The warrior scowled as Heavy Shield spoke, making it obvious he did not accept the decision.

Concerning the attack by Little Ears, Heavy Shield continued, Grey Horse had erred by trying to recover the pinto without consulting the chiefs. If he had, the entire incident might have been resolved without blood. "For that reason," Heavy Shield said, "Grey Horse must not seek revenge for his injury. The matter is closed."

Heavy Shield paused dramatically. When he spoke again, it was in an admiring tone. "The chiefs acknowledge Blue Eye for undergoing the Sun Dance with Piikani courage. He is a man who will always be welcome at the Great Circle."

Grey Horse and Two Arrows nodded, accepting the honour for Blue Eye.

"*Naato'si Otatsmiistakists*," Little Ears spat after Heavy Shield concluded. "Sun On The Mountains. Cowards and old men. They don't fight." He threw his knife at Grey Horse's feet, a challenge Grey Horse ignored.

Blue Eye woke in the evening, glanced back and forth between Two Arrows and Grey Horse and then fell asleep again. The swelling around his chest wounds began to subside in the night and by the next afternoon he was able to sit up briefly.

Two days later, they left the Great Circle. In the afternoon, Grey Horse caught a glimpse of Little Ears ducking behind a ridge to the south. Grey Horse turned south, telling Two Arrows to continue, but to watch Blue Eye who was riding hunched over in pain.

"Lead the pinto if you have to."

Grey Horse caught them just before they reached the Bow. Blue Eye looked up.

"You have returned," he said, his teeth clenched.

"I was not gone," Grey Horse replied.

Two Arrows looked across at Grey Horse with a smile. "You lost your knife while you were not gone," he said pointing to Grey Horse's waist.

"Thank you," Blue Eye said to Grey Horse.

Blue Eye mumbled a weak greeting at the trading house when they arrived the next day and fell unconscious to the floor. After Alexander laid him on the bed in the small room, Grey Horse opened his shirt. "This is what Little Ears did," he said with a hard edge in his voice.

Hannah stared at the raw wounds. After hearing Two Arrow's explanation, she said to him, "He wants to be like you, but he can't. You have found your path. He must accept his."

Two Arrows leaned over Blue Eye. The sleeping robes fell from the bed as Blue Eye rolled restlessly in his sleep.

For a moment, Two Arrows glimpsed the still bleeding cuts of the Sun Dance on Blue Eye's chest, and the faint vermilion symbol below. The Piikani way, and the Sun On The Mountains way.

"I am Piikani," he whispered. "Begin your own journey. Do not ride with me."

3

Riding to Fort McKenzie

THE BOW, SPRING, 1837. On a cloudy morning, Alexander and First Snow helped Blue Eye and Grey Horse prepare for their journey to Fort McKenzie. Two Arrows had chosen not to go.

"I have found my path," Two Arrows had told Blue Eye during the winter after the Sun Dance. "The Sun has shown me I am not a trader. I will hunt for my family, and protect them from the Crow and Assiniboin. I am Piikani."

Blue Eye protested, "What about Grey Horse? He is Piikani and he rides as Sun On The Mountains."

"I am not Grey Horse. I am Two Arrows."

While First Snow tied the pack horses to the rail in front of the house, Long Fingers and One Person began to load them with the heavy robes and hides. Nearby, two boys held a herd of twenty well-trained riding horses, chosen by Hannah to make the best possible impression on the Americans and set a precedent for future trading.

Blue Eye and Grey Horse wore plain, lightweight leather clothing. They tied their hair in single braids and wore no feathers or emblems. A vermilion Sun On The Mountains symbol on the flanks of the splash-necked pinto and Grey Horse's bay Runner provided the only identifying marks. Blue Eye wanted everyone they met to see they travelled as traders, not warriors.

Earlier that morning, Hannah had left the trading house to take a herd far up the Bow River. The trading house, with its constant noise and endless activity, often oppressed her. People were always coming and going, and she was determined not to place any unusual importance on this departure. Her son would return in a few months, she assured herself. Over the winter she had noticed he had begun to see himself as a man, and had taken charge of the preparations for this trip. Perhaps, she thought, the Sun Dance had done him more good than harm. Maybe he had begun to see a way that he could be Blue Eye; Piikani and Sun On The Mountains.

"When he returns from the Missouri, I'll spend time with him," she said, thinking of the pleasure she found on horseback and in the marvellous life of the prairie; the buffalo herds, the wolves, the coyotes, the hawks and eagles, and, most of all, the unending openness. As she had many times before, she felt thankful the Prairie People never allowed the whites to hunt in their territory.

The Piikani, the Blood, and the Blackfoot dominated their territory and way of life, controlling the best buffalo hunting grounds on the northwest plains fronting the Rocky Mountains. They called themselves the Prairie People, an alliance white traders would later call The Blackfoot Confederacy, and aggressively used their guns and horses to drive whites and neighbouring tribes to the perimeter. When the Prairie People travelled and hunted, others moved aside.

Just before Blue Eye mounted the pinto, Two Arrows cantered to him on a tall, sorrel Runner. Two Arrow's bare chest and face were streaked with grey, earthy chalk and his hair hung over his forehead in a loose forelock. He had twisted yellow, blue and red leather thongs into the back locks that hung onto his shoulders.

"*Oki,*" he said as he dismounted. Abruptly, he handed Blue Eye the rein of the sorrel. "I trained this horse as a gift for you. You will ride him to the Missouri and back."

Blue Eye did not know how to acknowledge the gift. Since the Sun Dance, he had wanted a quieter horse, but had been too proud to ask Hannah to choose another for him. Now, Two Arrows was making it easy for him to exchange the pinto for the sorrel. Blue Eye took the rein and handed Two Arrow the rein of the splash-necked pinto. "For you."

They mounted their new horses. Two Arrows reached over the pinto's neck and shook Blue Eye's left hand in the Piikani manner that recognized the left hand was the closest to one's heart.

"May the Light guide you," Two Arrows said.

"May the Sun guard you," Blue Eye replied.

Two Arrows spun the splash-necked pinto in a tight circle, raised his hands in acknowledgement of The Family, and galloped with a cheer up the river, his heels guiding the horse, and his arms spread apart as he flew along the bank.

"God should get ready for an exciting time," Alexander remarked as he and Grey Horse watched Two Arrows race away.

Blue Eye had prepared himself to handle every imaginable eventuality on the trip. Nevertheless his heart pounded with apprehension as he and Grey Horse rode from the trading house. His mind would not stop anticipating the dangers ahead. He had estimated the trip to the Missouri would take about twenty days, because of the heavy robes on the pack horses. Other than crossing the Oldman River, the riding would be relatively easy. The Oldman could be in spring flood and they might be delayed a few days until they found a safe ford. There was no way of telling what tribes they might meet along the way, and two men with ten cumbersome pack horses and a herd of twenty loose horses would be vulnerable.

As the herd left, Alexander put his arm over First Snow's shoulder, saying, "You know this trip is not without risk for us. Washington's men may be on the Missouri."

"This is Piikani territory," First Snow said as she moved to his side. "Washington's men cannot come here."

"They will try," Alexander said softly to himself. "They will not forget me and I will not forget them."

Blue Eye and Grey Horse saw a few Piikani camps in the distance near the Oldman River but nobody rode out to greet them, to Grey Horse's disappointment and Blue Eye's relief. Even inside Piikani territory, Blue Eye accepted that every encounter with strangers could be dangerous.

The grass grew shorter and dryer further south. The wind blew hard and the dust from the herd swirled across the flat ground. The mountains to the west gradually disappeared in the horizon. After they crossed the Oldman River and rode into the hills of the upper Missouri, they were able to find better shelter and the horses travelled more calmly.

THE MISSOURI, SPRING, 1837. Fort McKenzie, the westerly American trading house on the Missouri, was an untidy barricade against the wilderness and the Indians, built far below the standard of Fort Edmonton where Blue Eye and his grandfather had traded on the North Saskatchewan. At Fort Edmonton, the Hudson's Bay Company had built a solid, three storey log house, complete with a basement and, most impressively, a hall lit by panels of coloured glass. The factor there regularly greeted the Piikani chiefs with British ritual, sometimes firing a cannon before opening the gates in the fortification.

After setting up a camp overlooking the river, Blue Eye watched the men unloading crates of trade goods from a fleet of keelboats, and loading heavy bundles of buffalo hides and robes to be sold in St. Louis. As much as the narrow, flat-bottomed boats with their square sails attracted his curiosity, he made himself pay close attention to the disembarking passengers who were eager to buy horses. Many assumed the Piikani would find whiskey an overwhelming temptation. One trader grabbed Blue Eye and pulled him forward.

"That's a spooky lookin' eye," he jeered, his voice thick and slurred from drinking.

Instantly, Grey Horse's knife was at the trader's ribs. Slowly the trader released Blue Eye. "We are here to trade, not to fight," Blue Eye said.

"You're just a damn Indian," the trader spat. Grey Horse, seeing Blue Eye's lack of response to the trader's insult, backed away silently, his knife still balanced in his hand.

Fort McKenzie, pitifully small and the men poorly mannered, offered little of interest to Blue Eye. The fort had almost no trade goods on hand; everybody was waiting for trading to begin after the men unloaded and sorted the supplies brought on the keelboats.

Blue Eye kept to himself, responding to questions with hand signs and the few Piikani words the white men knew; *aa* and *sa*, yes and no. He overheard the fort's head trader, John Anderson, a stocky, lightly bearded man dressed in a thick brown wool jacket and black wool trousers, explain the fort was closed, and wouldn't reopen for trading for two days.

Most of the men around the fort showed no interest in Blue Eye; to them, a half-breed, no matter how unusual looking, was of little consequence. The Sun On The Mountains horses, however, attracted tremendous interest and Grey Horse moved the herd several miles from the fort for safety. Blue Eye wandered freely around the landing. The men ignored him and talked openly, their conversations mostly arguments about the number of kegs of whiskey they would sell to the Piikani and Crow. They bragged endlessly to each other about previous drunken exploits; exploits they planned to surpass as soon as the next supply boat landed.

Blue Eye noticed they usually talked in terms of money — dollars and cents — and almost never in trading values, such as beavers, horses or robes. Money, Blue Eye realized, was their most valued item. From a small pouch on his waist, he pulled out two silver and two gold coins he had taken in trade on the Bow, and systematically began testing what they would buy. The third offer he got was to trade a heavy steel knife for the smallest silver coin and he took it. By the end of the afternoon he had a reasonable idea of the value of each of the coins and his quick mind soon tallied the value of their hides and robes, and compared it to the value of the guns he planned to buy.

The value he calculated for the robes and hides surprised him. Unless he had made a big mistake, robes and hides on the Missouri were worth almost twice what Rowand paid at Fort Edmonton. He thought about it a long time, first thinking that Rowand had been cheating them. After more thought, he realized the robes and hides were simply less desirable on the North Saskatchewan than the smaller furs. Buffalo robes were too bulky to transport by canoe. But the American steamboats were loaded from the keelboats in the deeper waters of the Missouri and could carry thousands of robes.

Blue Eye recalled Firekeeper's fur auctions at the South Branch and decided that, if no Piikani competitors showed up to sell robes and horses at the fort, he would hold an auction. If other bands arrived to trade, he might have to change this plan.

Only one band of three Piikani rode to the fort on the day trading was to begin. Their horses were poor compared to the Sun On The Mountains horses, but their robes were good. Blue Eye let the Piikani trade first, rather than compete against them. The Piikani took their time and haggled over each item. While Blue Eye watched this trading, Grey Horse built a rope corral for the horses a hundred yards from the boat landing and stacked the robes and hides where they could be seen by everybody. Almost a hundred people of all ages disembarked from small boats in the morning, some of them families of trappers hoping to make a living on the upper Missouri, unaware they would be unwelcome in any Piikani territory. John Anderson and the men representing the smaller, independent firms were obviously disappointed by how few Piikani had come.

The Sun On The Mountains horses, more than the robes and hides, drew out a crowd. Grey Horse, amused by their insistence he negotiate with them, would not sell any horses. Blue Eye surprised the crowd on the third morning by announcing in English the start of the auction. John Anderson suddenly showed more interest in Blue Eye than he did in the horses, recognizing a shrewdness in the young half-breed.

Blue Eye announced the pack and riding horses would be sold by auction, as would the hides and robes. The terms would be cash. He would accept up to half the price in American paper money, the balance in silver or gold coins. After three days of listening to the conversations around the fort, he had learned paper money was as valuable as coins. The auction forced out many of the men who had been hoping to swindle Indians with whiskey and lies about the relative values of goods and robes. And, because of the crowd of eager buyers from the boats, the regular fort traders had no opportunity to control the bidding.

Grey Horse astonished the crowd with his horsemanship. Everything sold, even the rawhide ropes, packsaddles and rigging. The purchasers of the horses were pleased, having acquired well-trained, sound animals that were easy for even inexperienced riders to handle. Grey Horse kept aside their Runners and two pack horses.

After the auction, Blue Eye bought guns from John Anderson who congratulated him on his trading. He next spent almost all the paper money purchasing goods from the smaller traders. The few bills Blue Eye kept back would be taken later to Fort Edmonton to see what they would buy in British territory.

Grey Horse knew the journey had been a success, proving Blue Eye's ability to trade. All that remained now was for the old horseman and his nephew to return with the coins and supplies to the Bow River. But Grey Horse had one more thing he wanted to do before leaving Fort McKenzie — get drunk.

"Alexander is a great man," he told Blue Eye. "But he doesn't see that not all men have his medicine. He has a path and he never wanders from it. My path is not so easy. I drink once in a while. That's what I intend to do tonight. Everything is sold and we can relax.

"I promise we will leave early tomorrow. There is no need for you to tell Alexander about this. He and I are old men, and he has already guessed I'll be doing this. There is nothing to talk about."

Blue Eye, relieved the trading had gone well, agreed to join him. They tethered the horses on a hillside and buried the pouch of coins beneath a clump of brush. Grey Horse had often done this before and he told Blue Eye it was best not to trust themselves with anything of value once they began drinking. Uncle and nephew sat on the hillside above the fort, drinking into the evening until Blue Eye vomited and fell asleep. Grey Horse left and went to the fort to get another bottle. The men in the fort stayed well away from the drunken Grey Horse. He looked old but they had seen him ride and knew he was not frail.

Two trappers followed Grey Horse as he climbed the hillside to the camp. He could hear them rustling through the grass and brush as he knelt beside Blue Eye, trying to wake him. Blue Eye muttered incoherently. One trapper rushed forward. Grey Horse twisted around, jabbing his knife straight into the trapper's chest. The trapper died, falling forward onto Grey Horse and pushing him to the ground. As Grey Horse heaved the body aside, the other trapper came at him from behind, driving his knife hard into the side of Grey Horse's neck. Grey Horse roared, his elbow pounding against the trapper. The trapper spun backwards, falling into the brush. Grey Horse pulled the trapper's knife from his neck and blood began to run over his shoulder. He stood squarely, holding the knife, his eyes fixed on the trapper who turned and ran down the hill. For as long as his blood dripped onto the grass, Grey Horse stood beside Blue Eye.

Blue Eye woke the next morning as ten or twelve men from the fort climbed the hillside. The bodies of Grey Horse and the trapper were cold. Blue Eye had no idea what had happened. The men surrounded the camp and called out. Blue Eye answered. They took away the heavy knife he had exchanged for a coin the first day. Two men carried the trapper's body down to the fort, leaving Grey Horse's body on the hillside. Others led the horses and Blue Eye, his hands tied behind his back, to the fort.

John Anderson scowled as the trappers demanded he hold a trial and convict Blue Eye of murder. "I'll listen," the head trader agreed, "but I don't like the way you're accusing this boy of murdering a full-grown man."

The trapper who had stabbed Grey Horse claimed Blue Eye and Grey Horse had enticed them up the hillside to drink and had then tried to rob them. In the fight that followed, his partner had killed Grey Horse and Blue Eye had killed his partner in retaliation.

Blue Eye knew it was a lie. Grey Horse would never invite a Fisheater to share his camp. Something else had happened, although Blue Eye could not tell what it was. But he could see the men at the fort wanted revenge. They had liked him well enough when they wanted to buy his horses and robes; now they had no reason to take the word of a half-breed over a white trapper.

Blue Eye forced himself to think rationally. His head ached from the drinking. He had made a mistake drinking with his uncle and now his uncle was dead. He could do nothing about that. He must get out of this difficulty with the least cost to Sun On The Mountains. Within the Blackfoot tribes, a murder could often be settled by paying a price, usually horses. His calm thinking restored, Blue Eye studied the crowd of men. If he offered everything he had, the four remaining horses, the two packs of trade goods and guns, and the pouch of coins, most likely they would take it and then kill him. Even if he had been as good with a knife as Grey Horse, he could not hope to fight his way clear. He needed a better plan than that.

Blue Eye took advantage of something that the accusing trapper did not reckon upon; his accurate memory, trained by years of trading at Sun On The Mountains. He clearly remembered the two trappers from the auction, where they stood, and how they bid.

"My uncle and I were drunk last night," Blue Eye told the men. "We had sold everything we brought to the fort and we were celebrating. We had money, guns and trade goods. Why would we try to steal anything from two trappers?"

John Anderson listened thoughtfully but did not interrupt.

"I remember those two trappers from the auction," Blue Eye continued. "They stood by the rope corral on the side nearest the river. They tried to buy horses but always dropped out when the bidding went above sixty-five dollars."

Blue Eye pointed to John Anderson. "You paid ninety-five dollars for a gelding with a white blaze. This trapper only bid to sixty-two dollars on that horse. If he and his partner had any money, they would have bought at least one of our horses. Go, look for yourselves, and see the miserable horse they bought for twenty dollars from the Piikani before our sale. Why would we steal from men who didn't have enough money to buy one of our horses?"

Blue Eye scanned the crowd and he could see them being swayed. They had probably never heard a Piikani speak English so well, or so convincingly. "Empty their pockets and packs," John Anderson ordered. "See if they have any money."

Before he could be searched, the trapper glared at Blue Eye. "This here half-breed's lyin'. He and the Injun probably stole them horses they sold. They called me and my partner up to drink. They was plannin' to rob us."

Just then, a small voice behind the men spoke. "I saw two men following the older Indian last night. They waited until he was away from the fort before they began following him up the hill."

The crowd turned. A young girl, no more than seventeen, the daughter of one of the settlers, looked back at them with confident, hazel eyes. "I am sure of what I saw," she said.

She shook her thick, auburn hair emphatically, as if daring any of the men to doubt her word.

Her elderly father, standing by her side, spoke up in a formal, British accent. "I sent Frances and her brother to the fort just around dark to get some supplies. When she returned, she told me what she had seen. We did not think anything of it at the time." He paused, putting his arm protectively over the girl's shoulder.

"Frances is a good girl. She would not lie."

John Anderson turned to the trader. "If the girl is telling the truth, it looks pretty much like this is even. One Indian dead. One trapper dead. If nobody objects, I say we untie the half-breed and let him go."

The trapper stepped forward angrily. The head trader stopped him abruptly with a heavy hand on his chest. "You stay here with me for a while, until the half-breed is packed up and gone. This is over, and I don't want any more trouble at the fort."

The crowd murmured in agreement and John Anderson untied Blue Eye's hands. Blue Eye turned to Frances. "I am in your debt," he said with a firm shake of her right hand. She smiled, marvelling at the brightness of his blue eye.

John Anderson interrupted. "You'd better getting moving, young man. I've got this calmed down for the moment, but if they start drinking, they'll start thinking about all those coins in your bags. You're alone now, so you'd better find somewhere quiet to camp."

Blue Eye climbed the hill, dug up the money, packed everything on the horses, and tied his uncle's body onto the Runner. He rode further into the hills until he found a tall stand of poplars. There, he wrapped his uncle's body in a hide and hung the bundle as high as he could.

Unsure of what he should do next, he sat below the tree, holding the string of blue beads First Snow had given Grey

Horse. His head ached from the drinking and he knew if he tried to eat, he would be sick. For the first time in his life, he felt despair. He considered sleeping, but he was worried the trappers from the fort might have followed him to steal his coins and horses, and maybe kill him too. Thinking of this, he got up and checked the leads on the horses, and pulled a gun from the packs and loaded it.

He had just returned to the tree when a deep voice called out, "Hello!" He lifted the gun and waited.

"Hello," the call came again. The horses turned and, ears forward, stared into the trees to Blue Eye's right. John Anderson, the head trader, pushed through the branches and into the small clearing.

"I'm alone," he said, opening his hands to show he was not carrying a weapon. "I saw you ride off and thought somebody should be watching out for you. You were in bad shape when you left the fort."

Blue Eye stood. "I'm fine. I just hung my uncle's scaffold in this tree. I suppose I should keep heading back to the Bow before anything else goes wrong."

"Take your time. Get yourself thinking straight. I'll stay for a while and make sure nobody bothers you."

"Thank you," Blue Eye said as he sat down. "I am surprised you followed me here. I would have thought you had enough trouble at the fort.

"You aren't the usual sort of trouble."

Blue Eye smiled. "I don't know if I'm sick or if I'm dying. I've never drunk whiskey before." He held the gun across his lap.

John sat against a tree, facing Blue Eye. "Don't worry, you're not dying. You should sleep a while. You'd feel better afterward."

Blue Eye shook his head. "No."

"It's up to you. Do you have any water?"

"No."

John stood up. "I'll get some. Don't shoot me when I come back."

"I won't. I've never killed anyone and I probably never will."

John returned with a canteen and handed it to Blue Eye. "Don't drink it too fast or the cramps'll get worse."

"Thank you," Blue Eye said when he finished drinking. He stood and reached out his right hand. "My name is Blue Eye." As they shook hands, the trader said, "Call me John."

Blue Eye swayed slightly. John said, "You'd better sit down. More than just the whiskey is starting to catch up to you. You're going to feel poorly until you get some rest."

Blue Eye shrugged. "I'll sit down, but I don't want to sleep."

John waited for Blue Eye to sit. "What are those beads you're holding?" he asked.

"They belonged to my uncle. My grandmother gave them to him."

"I watched your uncle ride when you sold the horses. What was his name?"

"Grey Horse. *Sikssikapii*. He and my grandfather, Alexander, were friends."

"Your grandfather's name is Alexander?"

"Yes. We have a trading house on the Bow. Sun On The Mountains."

"Want to tell me about it."

"No. But I'll tell you about Grey Horse. I think he would like me to explain to you that he wasn't just another drunken Indian killed at the fort."

"I didn't think that. I may not run the cleanest fort, but that doesn't mean I don't recognize something good when I see it. Your uncle was something good. If you tell me about him, maybe I'll know better what I saw."

Blue Eye set the gun aside and began to tell the trader about Grey Horse, his famous ride, the herd, and even how Grey Horse had been disappointed with him when he fell from his pinto. He talked the rest of the afternoon and then slept. John covered him with a robe, made a small fire and brought more water.

"Feeling better?" John asked when Blue Eye awoke. "Have you eaten?" When Blue Eye said he hadn't eaten since the previous afternoon, John cut chunks from a loaf of bread. "It's plain enough for you to eat without getting sick," he said handing the chunks to Blue Eye. "You'll be fine in the morning. The whiskey we sell makes everybody sick."

Blue Eye sat against the tree while they ate. When they finished, John leaned back and said, "Would you mind if I gave you some advice?"

"I wouldn't mind. I think I need some."

"I see lots of people at the fort, whites and Indians. They come and go, and I don't care much either way. My job is to size people up, to know how to make a profit from them. But every now and then somebody comes along who's a little different and I know I'm not going to be able to make much from them. Your uncle was one of those different ones. I could tell from the way he rode the horses and the way he handled himself. He didn't care about the money. He was there because he wanted to be with you. From what you told me, I'd say your uncle wasn't just a great rider. He knew things.

"He knew what he was doing when he got drunk. He knew you thought you were pretty clever trading those horses and robes. But he wanted you to see that clever isn't enough. He wanted you to see things differently. To see both sides at once, the good and the bad. Those coins you have can bring trouble into your life, or . . . who knows what? He wanted you to never forget that if you're not careful you can end up as another drunken Indian killed in a fight at a white man's fort and nobody will care what a great rider or how clever you were at trading.

"So you should pay attention to what your uncle was telling you. You don't need to run home scared. You can spend some time here, look around, and meet some of the other people. See for yourself what's here. Just be careful. See both sides.

"If you don't take advantage of your uncle dying here, then he might as well have stuck his knife in both trappers and you could have ridden home together. But that wasn't what he wanted for you."

Blue Eye thanked him for the advice, adding, "I'm still having trouble thinking clearly. If I'm not sick in the morning, I'll look around like you suggested."

After John left, Blue Eye slept again. In the morning, his thoughts clear, he rode to the Missouri to thank Frances and her family. They were camped outside the fort, waiting for another family to join them. Her slightly-stooped father, George Watson, a Methodist minister, was almost as old as Alexander. Her mother, Anne, was much younger, possibly the same age as Hannah. They were English and had brought their three children, Frances and two younger brothers, to America to establish a Methodist mission on the Missouri.

"What is a minister?" Blue Eye asked George after being introduced to the rest of the family. "What do you do?"

"I show people the way to God and Christ," George answered.

"Are you a guide?" Blue Eye asked, thinking of the Sun Dance.

George raised his eyebrows at this possible interpretation. "Yes, I suppose I am a guide."

Blue Eye nodded. "I understand that." He opened his shirt to show the Watsons his thick Sun Dance scars. "I had a guide in the Sun Dance," he explained, "but he almost killed me. I expect you are more careful with your people."

The next boat up the Missouri with settlers was not expected for at least two weeks. Until they arrived, George and his family planned to stay near Fort McKenzie rather than risk travelling into the mountains on their own. After repeating his thanks to Frances for speaking up at the fort on his behalf, Blue Eye considered returning to the Bow but changed his mind, deciding to stay longer with the Watsons and learn more from George. He could see no urgency in telling The Family about Grey Horse, and they were in no hurry to receive the goods he had bought at the fort. He camped near the Watsons, hunting for them during the day and talking in the evening with George.

George explained to Blue Eye how he had served for many years in the British army, starting as a Redcoat drummer-boy fighting Washington's army in the colonies and then as a sergeant fighting Napoleon in Europe. After the wars he had turned to the church, spending twenty years in the Methodist ministry. The decision to bring his wife, Anne, and their young children to America and start a mission on the Missouri had not been made hastily. George had first looked carefully into the possibilities of remaining within the British colonies. They had met a group of American Methodists from Boston who had convinced them to follow another group of Methodist missionaries who had gone up the river earlier and were heading west to Oregon.

Blue Eye heard more about London and the cities in the east — Boston, New York, Philadelphia — where thousands of people worked in factories, producing the tools, guns and cloth traded to the Piikani. As a soldier, George had seen these cities and he explained in detail to Blue Eye their locations and how the ships transported people and goods across the oceans.

Blue Eye described Sun On The Mountains and the trading. George's eyes flickered momentarily when Blue Eye mentioned Alexander James' remarkable white hair and bright blue eyes, but he did not comment.

The next day Blue Eye saddled horses for Frances and her two brothers and rode with them to see the hills above the Missouri. Frances and the boys found Blue Eye's confidence with the horses exciting and reassuring. The boys felt secure in his company, no longer afraid of the unseen dangers. He pointed out animal tracks and showed them how to follow their own trail back to camp. Frances, less sure on her horse, stayed close by his side.

Frances was bewildered by Blue Eye's open ways, and by his generosity in providing meat for her family. It was odd, she thought, to see an Indian with a braid and wearing deerskin leggings and jacket, conversing seriously with her father. To Frances, Blue Eye hardly seemed to be an Indian; at least not one of the wild type she had been told lived on the frontier. Blue Eye spoke English more correctly than many of the passengers on the boats, and had much better manners. Although she was sure that much of what George told him about life in cities and towns was hard for him to imagine, she knew he absorbed the information. She was not sure if she had ever met a person who appeared to think as much as Blue Eye, or in such an odd manner. For instance, he appeared unconcerned now by the killing of his uncle only a few days earlier, and yet he spoke very lovingly of his family at their trading house.

His frankness and naivety sometimes took her aback. The first time Frances brought out her brushes and combs after bathing in the river, he watched intently as she untangled her wet hair and then asked if he could try brushing her hair.

"We have never seen these at the trading houses," he explained as he ran a brush through her hair. "I may go back to Fort McKenzie and see if I can find one as a special surprise for Long Fingers. She can braid hair and ropes in more ways than anyone else. She would make good use of a brush like this."

As he spoke, his hands absently stroked Frances' shoulders. "Your hair is almost brown but look at all the bright golden strands." He lifted a few locks and held them up against the sky. "They are like the light that creeps into my thoughts when I sleep in the sun." Frances turned to face Blue Eye, her face flushed. "I'll give you one or two of my brushes to take to your family," she said hurriedly. "Mother may have one to spare as well."

The families from the fort disapproved of the Watson's familiarity with the blue-eyed Indian rumoured to have killed a trader, but were unable to dissuade them from enjoying the young man's company.

In the evening George apologized to Blue Eye, saying he should have spoken sooner; he had often heard soldiers talking about an Alexander James during the War of Independence. "Your grandfather sounds like a remarkable man," George continued. "He knows what is in the hearts of soldiers. I'm certain he is the Alexander James that the Americans were so anxious to capture. I wish I could tell you why they wanted him. Perhaps if you ask he will tell you."

George only asked once about Blue Eye's religious beliefs. "Alexander says we are Quakers," Blue Eye replied. He described The Family, the Silence, and The Light Within. George said Quakers also called themselves The Religious Society of Friends. When Blue Eye heard this other name, he could imagine The Family sitting at an evening meal with their Piikani 'friends', enjoying their conversation and sharing their ideas.

"Friends," he said to George. "Yes, that's what we are."

George glanced over Blue Eye's unadorned clothing, and said, "Yes. Christianity written plain."

Another boat arrived. Instead of eagerly hurrying down the gangplank, the passengers crept dispiritedly from the boat, their faces downcast and troubled. A baby boy on board had broken out in a smallpox rash three days earlier, and five more cases had been found before the boat arrived at Fort McKenzie. Nobody knew who else was infected. The smallpox had spread all along the river, they said, and the settlers who had intended to go further up the Missouri had left the boat before it had arrived at Fort McKenzie.

George explained the disease to Blue Eye. Unless vaccinated, he said, most people died. Only a fortunate few had a natural immunity. George immediately moved the Watsons upstream to isolate them from the passengers. There they camped, anxiously watching each other for signs of the disease. Blue Eye camped a short ride away, leaving the family fresh meat on the riverbank in the evenings. The two boys broke out in rashes that turned to blisters five days after the boat arrived. Then Frances and her mother, Anne, developed rashes. Only George showed immunity. They buried the boys on the fourteenth day and Anne on the sixteenth day. Frances recovered with only faint scars on her face and shoulders. George, although never ill, became haunted by the deaths. He stared for hours at the campfire, unable to eat or sleep. Desperate, Frances called to Blue Eye when he left them meat, asking him to help. Believing he must have the immunity George had described, Blue Eye joined her in the camp. George did not acknowledge Blue Eye's arrival, and continued to stare vacantly at the fire.

The next morning Blue Eye woke when Frances screamed. George was swaying waist deep in the Missouri, his arms spread wide as he prayed loudly to be forgiven for bringing his family into the wilderness. Frances screamed again, running to the bank as her father threw himself facedown in the swift current and floated without a struggle beyond their sight. Blue Eye held Frances' hand tightly to stop her from leaping off the bank in pursuit.

Blue Eye pulled her gently from the bank and sat with her as she cried beside the fire. At noon, he told her they should leave. "Show me what to load onto the horses." She wouldn't answer him and only pointed out her bags so he could load them on a pack horse. He lifted her onto Grey Horse's bay, and rode north into the prairie. He left all the other Watson's possessions in the camp. Maybe the disease would depart and somebody else could find a use for whatever was in the boxes.

The epidemic preceded them. Where there had been Piikani tipis along the river bottoms, there were only death scaffolds in the trees, a few with decaying bodies below. Horses grazed unattended, some trailing tether ropes or still wearing bridles. Blue Eye continued north to intercept the Oldman River. Frances, pale and silent, her hazel eyes outlined by black circles of sorrow, rode but refused to eat or speak. Blue Eye had to force himself to eat, wondering as he chewed if death waited for him inside the meat.

Frances spoke once, on the fourth evening. "Are you an Indian?" she asked Blue Eye. "Why am I here?" Her eyes, sleepless and dark-circled, flickered frantically as she searched for recognition in his face. "Who are you?" she asked. This time the anxiety broke her voice and Blue Eye knew she would not be able to ride much further.

"I am a friend. I am Sun On The Mountains," he said softly. From his pack he pulled out a lump of vermilion and drew Sun On The Mountains symbols on the back of her hands. "I am a friend," he repeated as he began to draw the same symbols on his own hands. She would not speak again until late in the summer.

THE BOW, EARLY SUMMER, 1837. They arrived at Sun On The Mountains in the afternoon and Blue Eye immediately noticed the stillness. There were no horses tethered near the trading house although a small herd, attended by a single rider, grazed on the flats to the north. From two hundred yards away, Blue Eye fired his gun, hoping to bring somebody out of the house. The rider tending the horses looked over, and then cautiously moved the herd further away. Blue Eye fired again. This time Alexander stepped out.

Blue Eye called to his grandfather, in English to reassure Frances. "It's Blue Eye. I have come from the Missouri river."

"Stay away," Alexander ordered, shouting across the flat. "We have the smallpox here."

Knowing it would now make no difference, Blue Eye led the horses closer. "Don't worry, grandfather," he said. "We were in a camp with the smallpox but survived. We will not get ill now."

"Grey Horse?" Alexander asked, looking at the four horses and Frances.

"He is dead. Trappers killed him at Fort McKenzie."

"I wonder what they were afraid of."

Blue Eye said nothing, then handed Alexander the string of blue beads. "I kept these for you. There was a man named John there who talked to me about Grey Horse. He said Grey Horse died so I would not end up a drunken Indian killed in a fight."

"He was right," Alexander replied. Blue Eye would only hear his grandfather mention Grey Horse again on important occasions. "When trappers killed Grey Horse on the Missouri," Alexander would say, "I felt the greatest sorrow I have known; not for Grey Horse, but for those who killed him."

Inside, Hannah sat beside First Snow, wiping the sweat from her mother's forehead with a damp piece of deerskin. Blue Eye put his arm over Hannah's shoulders. "Grey Horse is dead, killed by two trappers on the Missouri. I know you cared for him and he was proud of you. He always told me you were the best rider on the prairie . . . next to him."

Hannah smiled briefly at her son and continued cooling her mother's forehead. A tear dropped from Hannah onto First Snow's face. Then one more. Two tears for Sikssikapii who lived his path so well.

Blue Eye returned to unpack the horses and led Frances to Alexander. "This is my grandfather, the man your father talked about. He will look after you."

Blue Eye shuddered as Alexander's black pupils opened, drawing in light. His blue irises almost disappeared into the darkness of his expanding pupils. Blue Eye had seen this happen only a few times before, and it always caught him unawares and pinned him into stillness. Apparently seeing what he had looked for in his grandson, Alexander turned his attention to Frances. Taking her hand, he led her to the steps of the trading house. "Sit here with me." That is where they stayed, the grandfather with the always-white hair, and the scared, auburn-haired girl with black smudges around her hazel eyes. There they sat and waited for the smallpox to take whomever it chose.

When First Snow died, Hannah dried her forehead, bound her in a buffalo hide and, alone, hung her scaffold in the poplars near the Bow. Death had come to the Piikani lands. Alexander and Frances sat on the porch of Sun On The Mountains and waited for death to leave.

4 The Bow River

SUMMER, 1837. The Piikani recognized and accepted many of death's faces; the white face of a blizzard, the painted face of an enemy, the cruel face of treachery. But the Piikani had never before seen the pocked face of death that indiscriminately stole one in three, stole children but left mothers, stole parents but left grandparents. The Piikani had never seen the full face of smallpox. Within three or four days, a band of twenty or thirty people, with five or six healthy hunters, might be reduced to a band of ten or twelve, with no hunters. Children without parents fought the camp dogs for scraps. Across the southern Piikani territory, survivors wandered, lost in their once-familiar prairie.

The Family acknowledged the deaths of First Snow and Grey Horse with a morning Silence and then turned their attention to the living. Hannah hired boys and girls to herd the Runners. Blue Eye led a band of teenagers to gather and redistribute the broodmares lent on shares to the Piikani bands. Each year, The Family loaned mares to several bands who earned a share of the colts in return for looking after the mares. During the epidemic many of these mares and colts had been neglected or had wandered away from camps. Blue Eye inquired about Two Arrows, but nobody knew if the smallpox had killed his friend.

One Person and Long Fingers rode ceaselessly, delivering meat to the prairie camps and returning to the Bow with Piikani orphans, widows, grandparents, mothers, and fathers. Sun On The Mountains supplied these survivors with tipis, robes, guns and ammunition, and helped them form new families and bands. An orphaned Round Robes girl, Stands Early, about ten, adopted One Person and Long Fingers, and determinedly resisted any efforts to be reunited with her band.

Blue Eye told Alexander about Frances' father, George, and his plans for a Methodist mission. "I told him we were Quakers."

"Quakers," Alexander exclaimed. "I wonder if we are still Quakers. I know I once closely followed the path of the Quakers but it was like walking in moccasins that did not fit. I could not change my feet, so I became Sun On The Mountains."

"But George was sure we are Quakers," Blue Eye insisted.

"In some ways, he was right," Alexander agreed. "We still follow many of the Quaker customs. But those customs don't make us who we are. The Light Within makes us who we are. What we wear and the languages we speak are not important.

"During your life, you will be many things and see many changes. Everything we see today could be gone tomorrow. Sun On The Mountains, the Piikani — everything we rely upon could be gone. That is the nature of the world. But the Light Within will never change. You will always have that."

Each morning, Alexander led Frances to the bank of the Bow where he wrote in his ledgers. In the afternoons, he and Frances rode to the horse herds or tidied the trading room. In the evenings, Frances sat by his side while The Family discussed the day's events. Frances, still not having spoken since leaving the Missouri, began to listen more carefully and to notice The Family welcomed the Piikani who arrived at Sun On The Mountains. She noticed that, when the visitors left, they always were given more supplies than they had requested, and Sun On The Mountains asked for nothing in return.

THE TRADING HOUSE, SUMMER, 1837. As the summer passed, Frances began to assist Alexander. She began to hand him things she guessed he needed; a blanket, a saddle, his ledger. "You are strong," Alexander said to her as she held a pack in place while he tightened the lashings, "and work will make you stronger." Afterwards, she began to pack the horses and sort supplies on her own. About a week after she had begun to help around the house, one of the evening Silences seemed to last a long time. Frances, who often sat with downcast eyes, glanced up and then quickly averted her eyes when she caught the attention of the others. Finally, just as the late sun began to shine through the top corner of the doorframe and onto the golden strands in her auburn hair, she returned Alexander's calm gaze. For the first time since her arrival at the Bow, she saw the deep water of his tranquillity. He held her eyes for only a moment.

"The Light is found," he said.

Hannah took Frances' hand and led her onto the porch of the trading house. Alexander and Blue Eye followed. Frances felt the warmth of The Family around her, much stronger than the warmth of the sun over the Bow. The Family, she thought. Grandfather, daughter, grandson, uncle, aunt... and where does Frances fit in? The tears came without warning and she involuntarily squeezed Hannah's hand. Hannah, not normally inclined to intimacy, drew Frances close and Frances rested her head on her shoulder. The unfamiliar smell of Hannah's deerskin shirt reminded Frances that her mother lay buried in the bank of the

Missouri — that her mother's cotton dresses with their familiar scents would never be pressed against her face again. Frances clung to Hannah and wept, not in sorrow as she had when her father drifted in the Missouri current, but in acceptance. The path ahead glistened through her tears. It was a path she had known of all her life.

For the rest of the day, Alexander and Blue Eye wrapped loads of dried meat to be delivered to Fort Edmonton. Hannah and Frances rode up the Bow to the summer camp of Long Fingers and One Person. One Person, upon the arrival of the two women, made a quick excuse about tending the horses and left with Stands Early. After Long Fingers had made tea, the women leaned on the willow backrests to talk. Long Fingers spoke Piikani for a short time with Hannah. Frances simply nodded in reply to any questions. From her tipi, Long Fingers brought out a plain deerskin dress she had been making for First Snow. "For you," she said in English, handing it to Frances. Hannah urged Frances to stand up to measure the dress against her frame.

"It will fit you well," Hannah said to Frances. "First Snow was just about your size. Maybe a little bit bigger here, in the shoulders and the waist, but not much. Try it on."

Inside Long Fingers' tipi, Frances shyly slipped out of her cotton dress and pulled on the deerskin dress.

"Do you like it?" Hannah asked as Frances stepped out of the tipi. Frances responded with a small smile. Long Fingers reached forward and knotted the belt around the waist of the dress. Frances stood in front of the tipi for a few moments, stretching her arms and getting accustomed to the freedom the soft leather gave her upper arms and shoulders. She slowly shook her head from side to side. "What is wrong, don't you like it?" Hannah asked, puzzled. Frances nodded her head to show that, yes, she liked the dress.

"Don't you want it?" Hannah patiently asked. "Is there something wrong with it?"

Long Fingers interrupted in Piikani, with a question for Hannah.

Hannah translated, "Long Fingers thinks you don't want the dress as a gift because it was intended for First Snow. Is that why you don't want it? Do you think Alexander will be hurt when he learns it was intended for First Snow?"

Frances nodded her head in agreement. Long Fingers grasped Frances' young hand and, stroking it with her callused palm, spoke in a reassuring tone. "Alexander is a good friend of Long Fingers," Hannah translated. "She is sure he will be pleased to see you wearing the dress."

Frances slowly pulled away from Long Fingers and entered the tipi, returning a few moments later with her old cotton clothes neatly bundled. "I will trade," she said softly as she handed the clothes to Long Fingers. "The old for the new." Hannah held her breath while Frances spoke, as if releasing her breath would blow away Frances' words. The three women spent the rest of the afternoon talking about the upcoming Great Circle that Long Fingers believed would be a sombre event after so many smallpox deaths in the recent months.

When Hannah and Frances returned to the trading house, Hannah was unsure whether or not Frances would continue to talk. Frances remained quiet throughout the preparations for evening meal. She and Hannah exchanged hidden smiles. Blue Eye's curiosity about Frances' new deerskin dress was obvious.

Frances spoke after the evening Silence, surprising everyone as the meal began. "Pass the meat, please," she said with a characteristic shake of her head that tossed the golden strands into the light. "You folks certainly take a long time to start eating."

Blue Eye's head snapped around to look at Frances. "You are talking again!" he said with surprise.

"Of course she is," Hannah responded with a light laugh in her voice. "Pass her some food — she's hungry!"

Alexander began his first conversation with Frances by commenting on the dress. "The deerskin dress fits you well. But if you want we could order some cotton to make a dress like your old one."

"I like this one. It is a gift from Long Fingers. She made it for First Snow." Frances waited to see how Alexander would respond.

"You do not have to be concerned," Alexander said pleasantly. "Our memories of First Snow are not adorned by dresses. We remember her spirit and that always brings us happiness."

"Yes," Frances agreed. "She must be in heaven now and looking down on us and seeing we are happy."

The Family suddenly focused its attention on Frances.

"Heaven," Hannah said. "What is that?"

Alexander shook his head, giving Frances a kind smile. "We have Quaker beliefs," he told her. "For us there is no heaven or hell. Our life is what it is, without punishment or reward."

Frances' puzzled look did not surprise Alexander, although it did surprise Blue Eye and Hannah.

"Come with me," Alexander said, taking her hand and leading her to the door. They walked to the edge of the river and Alexander led her into the water, to where the current flowed and tugged at their legs.

"This is your birth," he said as he cupped his hands and lifted them full of water from the river.

"This is your life," he said, holding the handful of water in the sunshine. "Be cheerful, enjoy the experience you are given. Enjoy the Light."

Then, letting his hands release the water back into the river's current, he said, "This is your death. There is no heaven or hell to enter; only the river we return to."

Until that moment, Frances had felt herself held back, unable to abandon her concern. Now she wanted a place in the trading house and began to look for opportunities to help the others.

THE TRADING HOUSE, FALL, 1837. "The smallpox is over," Blue Eye told The Family in late September. "But each trip to the bands I return with more of our mares because there aren't enough healthy men and women to look after them properly. We already have more horses in the Sun On the Mountains herds than Hannah can manage. Nobody can spare any horsemen to help. The situation will get worse, too, because scrub stallions from the Piikani bands are running loose on the prairie. Nobody wants to geld the scrubs and it is almost impossible to stop them breeding with our mares. Next year we will have poor quality colts mixed in with our herds. We have to find a way to sell horses outside the Piikani territory."

Hannah agreed. "Blue Eye is right. It is getting harder and harder for me to sell good horses because the poor ones are being sold so cheaply. The Company buys some for packing at Fort Edmonton, but they are not interested in buying Runners, unless the price is the same as for pack animals. The men at the fort are such bad riders that good horses are wasted on them."

"What we need is a way to sell several hundred," Blue Eye added. "If we could sell most of the pack and riding horses, all the scrubs, and a hundred Runners, we would be able to concentrate on improving the breeding herds."

Frances spoke up. "Why don't you take a larger herd to Fort McKenzie? Why not take two or three hundred, instead of twenty or thirty? Those American trappers and settlers buyers paid high prices in the spring."

Alexander thought for a moment. "That is a good suggestion, Frances. It's time to thin all the herds by making a big sale. We need to do it right. And we'll need the help of the Piikani. Tomorrow we will talk again. In the meantime I'll ask One Person for some suggestions."

Frances and Blue Eye left the house together, talking about trading on the Missouri.

One Person and Long Fingers joined The Family for supper the next evening. After the Silence, Alexander renewed the discussion by asking Blue Eye to describe again the situation of the Piikani herds.

"The problem is," Blue Eye began, "the Piikani like to accumulate horses and, although they want good horses, they place a higher importance on owning more horses than their friends, even if the horses are of poor quality."

"I agree," One Person interrupted. "There are too many horses around the Piikani camps. I have tried several times to tell the bands to only keep the good ones but they keep everything."

"Then we all agree our herds need to be thinned," Alexander said. "The question is how? Frances has suggested we drive a large herd to Fort McKenzie."

"I have thought more about it," Blue Eye interjected. "I agree we should try to sell more horses to the Americans but I don't think Fort McKenzie is the right place. Frances and I have another suggestion. It is Frances' idea and she should be the one to tell you."

At first, her words came cautiously. "When I came up the Missouri with my family, we travelled by steamboat from St. Louis. Along the way we stopped at an American Fur Company trading house called Fort Union. There we saw hundreds of Crow and Sioux and Assiniboin trading. Fort

McKenzie was very small in comparison. It would be a longer journey, but I think we could sell more horses at Fort Union where there will be more buyers."

"I think we should take three hundred," Blue Eye said.

Long Fingers shook her head. "*Sa*. I don't want to hear any more. You are planning to drive horses to an American fort through Assiniboin and Crow territory. This plan is too dangerous. *Sa*."

One Person reassuringly put his arm around Long Fingers' shoulders. "You're right," he said, "But there must be a way to do it safely."

"Yes. It can be done," Alexander agreed. "And there is another good reason for Blue Eye to drive a herd to Fort Union.

"We must learn how much time we have before the whites will take the Piikani land. We must go to the American forts and discover for ourselves what their plans are. In the east, they have already taken the Indian lands. We should help the Piikani prepare for when they come here."

He laid the steamboat map on the table and studied it, sometimes closing his eyes to visualize the course of the Missouri as it flowed north from St. Louis to Fort Union and then east to Fort McKenzie. On a page torn from a trading ledger, Alexander drew a rough map of the western prairies, placing the Blackfoot Confederacy in the centre, bordered on the north by the British trading houses along the North Saskatchewan, on the south by the Americans along the Missouri, on the eastern plains by the Crow and Assiniboin, and on the west by the Rocky Mountains.

"This is Piikani territory," Alexander said, indicating the land west of the mountains. He then marked the trading house's approximate position on the Bow River. "We live and trade here because of our friendship with the Piikani. It is their land, not ours." He pointed to the British and

American trading centres along the rivers to the east, north and south. "These are the threat, not the Crow and the Assiniboin. The British and Americans want everything, there is no end to what they want, and they will do anything to get what they want. The Crow and the Assiniboin only want the Piikani horses."

Seeing The Family's obvious concern, Alexander continued.

"The Piikani will not be able to defend this territory much longer," he said. "The Americans and the British will soon find reasons to cross the rivers. From the east and north, the British will force the Cree, Crow and Assiniboin toward the mountains, opening the way for their traders to follow." Blue eye noted that even his grandfather had begun to call the Nahathaway by the name given them by the white traders, Cree.

"From the south, the Americans will push north. They already have their keelboats at Fort McKenzie. It will not be long before they have more forts and steamboats on the Missouri, and many more settlers will arrive.

"If the Piikani had owned horses two hundred years ago and had learned to fight together, they might be able to keep them out. But individuals don't win wars, and the Piikani fight their enemies as individuals, not as armies."

"What will happen? Frances asked. "Will there be a war?"

"No. The British and Americans are too experienced at stealing land to take any chances by sending their soldiers in first. They realize the Piikani can give them a good fight, so they will wait until after the Piikani are defeated, and then they will send their soldiers to take the land without a fight."

As Alexander spoke, all Frances could think of the morning she met Blue Eye at Ft. McKenzie and how he described the death of his uncle Grey Horse. "You are talking about whiskey, aren't you?" she said.

"That is just one of their strategies." Alexander continued. "Think about the smallpox. They send a boatload of goods up the Missouri, goods to make life better for the Piikani. Kettles, blankets, needles, and the thousand little things they enjoy. And hidden away, unseen, is the smallpox. This is the white traders' way of fighting. They bring gifts that destroy. In one or two years, smallpox killed more Piikani than all their fights with the Crow and Assiniboin."

"But the Piikani live here. And we live with them," Frances said, shaking her head in disbelief. "The British and Americans will not take the Piikani land! It would be wrong."

Frances' straightforwardness and determination impressed Alexander, and like everybody else, he was pleased Frances had used "we".

"They will take it," Alexander confirmed, his voice remaining calm. "They will use their religion. Their laws. Their customs. They will use whatever they need to take all the Piikani territory."

Blue Eye sank back in his chair, thinking again about Grey Horse's death at Fort McKenzie. He knew about enemies, but he had never considered his grandfather's people to be enemies before, systematically destroying the Indians. Now, looking at the map and hearing his grandfather's warning, he felt himself strangled, choking as he imagined the white traders edging ominously closer from the north and the south. The Sun On The Mountains trading post lay in the centre of a trap, the British on one side, the Americans on the other.

"Haven't the traders at Fort Edmonton always treated Sun On The Mountains and the Piikani fairly?" Blue Eye said. "Perhaps the Americans have treachery in their hearts, but Grandfather's lack of trust may also have something to do with Philadelphia."

Hannah reached over and rested her hand on her son's back. "There are many things to understand," she said softly. "We must think carefully about this."

"Blue Eye is right," Alexander answered. "My judgement may be influenced by my experience in Philadelphia. Blue Eye must find out for himself if I am correct."

"The Light shines in everyone," Blue Eye said. "I will see the Light Within these people and understand the path they follow."

"You must do more than see the Light," Alexander replied, his tone soft. "When you speak with someone, you must speak to their Light and answer to their Light."

"Answer to it? How can I answer?"

"You will know," his grandfather replied. "When the question comes to you, you will have to answer."

The discussion ended, leaving Blue Eye puzzled by his grandfather's reply. Setting aside his thoughts about the Light, Blue Eye decided that, unless he travelled outside Piikani territory, he would never know for himself whether Alexander was right or wrong about the British and Americans. He might not be able to go to London, Boston, or Philadelphia, but he could go to Fort Union. Blue Eye picked up the map and began to plan how he would drive three hundred horses across five hundred miles of prairie to Fort Union. It would take a lot of preparation, and possibly all winter to find enough riders. Within minutes he had begun a list of what he would need. Then he stopped suddenly, his pencil above the ledger. "How," he asked himself, "am I going to drive the horses to Fort Union without risking the lives of the Piikani who help?"

The next day Alexander interrupted Blue Eye's planning by suggesting he make a journey that would keep him away from Sun On The Mountains for most of the summer.

"Old Firekeeper must be getting tired operating the South Branch," Alexander told The Family. "I think it is time we asked him if he would rather live on the Bow with us. He may want to go back to the Nahathaway by Hudson Bay. It is up to him. He may be like me and think it is time to let others handle the trading. South Branch will be between trading seasons. Now would be a good opportunity for Blue Eye to visit Firekeeper and suggest a change.

"And I am a little lonely without First Snow and Grey Horse," he admitted, surprising everybody. "I think Firekeeper and I would enjoy talking about the old days."

Alexander's concerns about the motives of the white traders had left The Family feeling threatened, and the prospect of bringing Firekeeper to the Bow gave them a reassuring sense of unity.

THE SOUTH SASKATCHEWAN, FALL, 1837. Blue Eye travelled alone, riding the sorrel Runner, and retracing the route Alexander and First Snow had taken almost fifty years earlier when they brought their trade goods from the South Branch. He could have crossed the five hundred miles faster if he had ridden to Fort Edmonton and paddled down the North Saskatchewan, but he wanted to ride through the Blackfoot tribes and see their condition after the smallpox. Like the Piikani, the other Blackfoot tribes were still struggling to reorganize. With leaders dead, with hunters dead, and with parents dead, the people regrouped listlessly.

He took his time, passing on information about the fates of the bands he encountered. The overall physical weakness and mental apathy of the Prairie People almost unnerved him. Blue Eye found several abandoned camps, with tipis blown over and the hides and corpses chewed by coyotes and wolves. He rode around these camps, not wanting to see the scattered robes, clothing and painted tipis representing months of patient work. Nothing could be done for the dead.

The poplar trees thinned as Blue Eye rode north and east from the prairie, replaced by spruce and fur. He had to choose his camps carefully so his horse would have enough grazing. The South Branch House appeared deserted as Blue Eye rode into the clearing. No sled dogs barked, no smoke rose from the chimney, and no canoes were beached on the riverbank. He tied his sorrel Runner to a tree and called out for his uncle.

"Anybody home?"

Only the sounds of the water rushing along the bank of the South Saskatchewan answered Blue Eye. The trading house door was not latched and Blue Eye pushed it open. The shelves and counters had been stripped of their neat stacks of trade goods. In the back, Firekeeper's bed waited, its blanket and buffalo robe carefully folded. On a small, low table by the bed, Firekeeper had set his valuable stone pipe and tobacco pouch.

He guessed Firekeeper may have already made up his mind about discontinuing the trading at the South Branch; otherwise, he would have an inventory of supplies on hand for the trappers preparing for winter. Blue Eye recalled his grandfather's partner kept meticulous records and always ordered enough supplies in the spring to completely fill the house and send a shipment to the Bow. He might have hidden this cache.

Blue Eye moved the sorrel Runner to a picket near the river and waited for his uncle to return. Without a concern whether his wait would last a night or a week, he made himself comfortable and slept soundly on his uncle's bed. In the morning he walked down the river to the other trading houses, finding them all empty. He spent the next two days repairing his riding gear, sleeping, and tending his horse. On the third morning, he shot a deer drinking at the river. Then his uncle arrived, and greeted him with typical good-natured teasing.

"I could smell your horse. Look at the mess he's made of the riverbank! You and your Piikani friends would bring your horses into the trading houses if we let you. I'm sure your grandfather does not let you picket your horse outside his trading house."

Blue Eye responded to his uncle's chiding with a quick reply. "Compared to the smell of a Cree fish supper, the smell of a Piikani horse is pleasant."

"Nahathaway, not Cree," his uncle reminded him. "You understand the difference, so don't talk like a white man."

They began debating about whether it was better to be Nahathaway or Piikani while they roasted chunks cut from Blue Eye's deer. Firekeeper ignored all of Blue Eye's questions about the empty shelves. Firekeeper looked older now, his face more lined, and he stooped a little when he walked.

"Your hair is almost as white as Alexander's," Blue Eye told him. "Maybe you're turning into a ghost!"

Firekeeper laughed. "What about your blue eye? Maybe you'll turn into a white man!"

When they had eaten, Blue Eye asked about the empty shelves. "What is your plan this year, uncle? I don't see any goods to trade." Firekeeper liked Blue Eye to call him uncle.

"I'm done with the South Branch," he replied slowly. "There will be no more trading for me. I'm going to return with you to the Bow and spend the rest of my time with my old friends Alexander and First Snow."

Blue Eye's breath shortened. Firekeeper had not been told about First Snow's death. He took his uncle's hand. "First Snow is dead, uncle. She died from smallpox this spring."

Firekeeper looked into his nephew's thin, dark face for a moment, and then left the house to sit on the steps overlooking the river. Blue Eye followed and waited for his uncle to speak. Finally, Firekeeper asked to be told about all The Family. He sat silently as Blue Eye explained.

"First Snow was the first Hannah placed on a scaffold in the poplars by the Bow. I'm sorry you did not hear this sooner. Many died. Grey Horse, too, is dead." Blue Eye described Grey Horse's death. Firekeeper said, "I always knew he had too much Piikani spirit and would not die peacefully."

Firekeeper stared into the river's current. Blue Eye sat by his side, and they watched the familiar eddies and waves fade, just as they had when he was a boy and his uncle had told him how he, Alexander and First Snow had built the trading house years ago.

"Now Alexander has nobody with him from the days at Hudson Bay," Firekeeper said as he stood up. "Tomorrow you and I will leave."

"But, uncle, what about the South Branch and all your trading? How can you leave now? You must have furs to collect this winter."

"Quit trying to figure everything out," Firekeeper answered. He returned to the trading house and fell asleep. Blue Eye sat on the steps, wondering how badly his uncle had been shaken by First Snow's death.

Early the next morning, Firekeeper was up and ready to go as the first light of the morning glistened off the river. When Blue Eye offered to let Firekeeper ride the horse, Firekeeper scornfully replied that he had walked, snowshoed, sledded and canoed all his life. He was not going to take up riding horses. Firekeeper slung his travelling bag over his back and handed Blue Eye two heavy packs to tie on either side of his horse. "Dried fish paste," he said proudly. "If you don't shoot any game along the way, we will eat fish."

Blue Eye disdainfully tied the packs of fish to his saddle. "Nahathaway food," he said with a weak grin. "Even my horse does not like the smell."

"It is good Nahathaway food. Alexander will be pleased to have it. He will be disappointed if we eat it ourselves along the way. Maybe we will have to eat your horse."

THE BOW, FALL, 1837. Firekeeper made the journey to Sun On The Mountains as easily as Blue Eye; and, as Alexander pointed out, could have continued if he had wanted. The sorrel Runner that Two Arrows had given Blue Eye broke its foreleg in a badger hole two days after they returned, and One Person shot it for Blue Eye.

Firekeeper waited until everybody was gathered in the trading house before opening his pack to distribute his gifts. Blue Eye glanced in the pack after the gifts were distributed. All that remained were a few pieces of clothing and Firekeeper's ledgers.

Stands Early, still not old enough to have specific responsibilities, took it upon herself to be Firekeeper's companion and, as a result, learned to speak a bit of Nahathaway. Firekeeper did not try to learn to speak Piikani. "I am too old," he told The Family. "I don't want to learn another language."

They all shared Alexander's pleasure in Firekeeper's decision to join The Family on the Bow. One Person had often thought about his own future and whether he and Long Fingers would rejoin one of the Piikani bands when they grew too old to travel on behalf of Sun On The

Mountains. He asked Firekeeper about his decision not to rejoin the Nahathaway. His question interested all The Family and they listened for Firekeeper's reply.

"Oh, I haven't given up being a Nahathaway," Firekeeper told them. "I'll always be a trader, and I'm not going to become a horse-riding Piikani like you. One night soon I'll make a pot of smoked fish stew for you, just so you will learn how much better a bowl of Nahathaway fish stew tastes than a bowl of buffalo stew."

The fish stew, Firekeeper promised, would be extra rich. The fish had been well-smoked and well-pounded before he had wrapped the paste in deer hide sacks. He would begin by soaking the sacks overnight, and then gently simmering the stew in a kettle all day. Even Stands Early, his most loyal companion, tried to dissuade him. "We have Piikani buffalo," the little girl boldly told him. "We are not starving. I would eat a gopher before I would eat a smelly fish." Although the adults tried to hush her, they hoped Firekeeper would guess they all shared her disgust at the thought of a fish stew. Hannah shook her head, wondering what Grey Horse would have thought of Firekeeper trying to turn The Family into Fisheaters.

When Firekeeper announced he would prepare the fish stew the next day, even Alexander tried to think of an excuse to be somewhere else. The oily smell drove everybody out of the trading house as he began soaking the deer hide sacks in pots by the fire. Long Fingers insisted he take the pots outside the house and keep them outside. Nevertheless, the next morning when the sacks had softened enough to remove the lumps of dry fish paste, he brought the pots back in the house and set them to simmer on the ledge inside the fireplace. Contentedly, he dozed on his pile of robes by the fire, occasionally stirring the stew and adding mysterious plants and roots he found by the riverbank. Stands Early claimed to have seen Firekeeper drop insects into the pot, and he overheard her remarks and banned her from helping him any longer. The Family moved into One Person and Long Finger's summer tipi and left Firekeeper alone with the nauseating stew.

"It is ready!" Firekeeper announced the next evening just before the sun slid behind the mountains. Alexander insisted the entire Family be present for the meal. If one person had to eat fish stew, then so did everybody! Firekeeper ceremoniously carried the kettle to the table, and held up a ladle full for them to see. The stew had a greyish tinge, and smelled strongly of decay. Stands Early stretched up beside the table and held her nose as she inspected the pot for grasshoppers and bees. "Very good!" Firekeeper announced, ignoring Stands Early as he sucked a lump of paste directly from the ladle. He swirled the pot vigorously and then, with his forefinger, scraped a ladle full of thick paste onto the wooden plates. A few clanks were heard as the scrapings dropped onto the plates. "Bones," Firekeeper declared.

The evening Silence lasted an unusually long time. "Go ahead," Firekeeper ordered. "Eat! You will be surprised."

One Person bravely poked his spoon into the pile on his plate, nudging the lumps cautiously aside until a small grey disk emerged from one side.

"What's this?" he said, hoping that whatever the slimy discovery turned out to be, it would be bad enough to end the meal.

Firekeeper jumped from his place and plucked the disk from One Person's plate. Carefully he rubbed it clean between his thumb and forefinger and held it up. "Well, this is a surprise. A British gold sovereign. Now how did that get in the stew?"

Instantly, everybody was poking their stew with spoons, searching for coins while Firekeeper laughed and laughed.

Finally, he stopped laughing long enough to tease Blue Eye. "I bet you wondered why your crazy old uncle wanted to carry sacks of smoked fish all the way across the prairies. Your old uncle knew no Piikani would try to steal a sack of smoked fish, or would even bother looking inside. There wasn't much fish in those sacks, Blue Eye, but there were a lot of gold sovereigns."

While Long Fingers simmered buffalo steaks, the others gathered around Firekeeper on the steps outside. He told them how he had sold all the furs and inventory from the South Branch for gold coins, giving a share of the coins to the Nahathaway families who had always helped him.

"The rest," he announced, "is ours!" He rinsed out the pot of fish stew and showed everybody the thick layer of gold coins at the bottom. "Sun On the Mountains gold!" The coins, he said with barely contained pride, were only part of what he had accumulated. Many thousand more coins were cached at the South Branch, waiting for The Family to bring them out.

Blue Eye stood at the edge of the excited gathering, his small pouch of coins from Fort McKenzie insignificant compared to Firekeeper's cache. Nevertheless, trading in gold, silver, horses and guns were not uppermost in Blue Eye's mind. "Maybe tonight I'll ask grandfather to tell me about his family in Philadelphia," he thought.

When Blue Eye asked, Alexander shook his head, no. "Tomorrow is coming so fast that anything you learn from my past will only hold you back. You must prepare for tomorrow."

Alexander continued with a comment that startled Blue Eye. "Sun On The Mountains will need a new leader soon. One Person and Long Fingers are content just to visit the Blackfoot bands and watch Stands Early grow. Firekeeper and I are old men. Hannah is only interested in managing the Runners. You are the right one to lead Sun On The Mountains now. You must begin to prepare yourself."

Although accustomed to his grandfather's straightforward ways, Blue Eye was taken aback by the enormity of the suggestion. Admittedly, he had ambitions for himself; he had been planning to ask for full responsibility for the trading on the Missouri.

In his journey from the South Branch, Blue Eye had thought carefully about the horse drive and he told Alexander he was still determined to see Fort Union.

"That's what I want to do," he concluded. "I'll see for myself. Until I do that, I cannot think about anything else. I found the beginning of my path when I went to the Missouri with Grey Horse. Now I must follow it to Fort Union. It may not end there."

"I cannot speak to you about your path," Alexander replied. "Only about your plans for the horse drive. I agree with the idea and I am sure the others will. But remember, whether the trading is successful or not depends upon many circumstances you cannot control. Many things can go wrong and how you handle them will be a test of your leadership. I accept you do not agree with my belief that the British and Americans will take the Piikani territory. This will give you an opportunity to see things for yourself. Perhaps when you return, you will be able to convince me that my concerns for the future of Sun On The Mountains are unfounded. Perhaps you will tell me the Americans are not our enemies."

"Perhaps," Blue Eye answered.

"Will Blue Eye be the only one from Sun On The Mountains making the drive to Fort Union?" Frances asked.

Alexander shrugged. "It is up to Blue Eye. He is responsible for the drive. If he needs help, he will ask."

Frances looked directly at Blue Eye. "Are you planning to ask anybody else to go?"

"It will be a long ride," he replied. "More than a month each way, maybe longer. We will have to cross Assiniboin and Crow territories."

"I'll come," Frances said with finality. "You will need help."

Alexander stood. Beginning with the drive, he said, the most important aspect of Blue Eye's trading duties would be learning all he could about developments that might affect the future of the Piikani and Sun On The Mountains.

"And when I am no longer able," Alexander concluded, "Blue Eye will lead Sun On The Mountains."

5 The Great Circle

THE LITTLE RED DEER RIVER, FALL, 1837. Sun On The Mountains arrived at the Great Circle as the leaves fell in the year of the smallpox and found the Piikani bands disorganized and subdued. For the first time, Alexander saw them without enthusiasm for life. The disease had passed through their land and all the survivors could talk of was getting enough meat and hides to last the winter. Even the buffalo cow hunt held no excitement for them.

The despondent tone of the Great Circle broke when Alexander led four grey Runners into the centre of the camp and announced the horses were gifts for Grey Horse's boyhood friends. As always, when gifts of importance were to be distributed the Piikani quickly gathered around, eager to see a display of generosity, an important sign of leadership and strength.

Hannah had painstakingly groomed the four matched Runners and painted their hips with a vermilion Sun On The Mountains symbol. Alexander, his white hair drifting on his shoulders, held the leads of the grey Runners in a silhouette framed by the warm hues of sky and the Rockies far to the west.

He began speaking, his voice steady and his language formal as he reminded the Piikani how Grey Horse had galloped through enemy territories with the horses that had brought the Piikani and Sun On The Mountains together as trading friends.

"The raising of the Runners is an honour shared by Sun On The Mountains and the Piikani," he said, generating a hush in the crowd before him.

"By riding fine horses, the Piikani show thanks to the Sun for the gifts of food and shelter. The Sun sees these horses, sees you are happy, and also sees that Sun On The Mountains has a place of peace by the Bow River.

"The gift of these four horses by Sun On The Mountains to the friends of Grey Horse," Alexander continued, "is a reminder of what Sun On The Mountains believes to be important.

"The horses are a reminder that Sun On The Mountains believes friendship is the greatest gift of life. Grey Horse had good friends. He had Stone Thrower and Fast Runner who rode with him on their first adventures; he had friends in all the Piikani bands who knew his word was true and he traded fairly for his horses; he had friends in Sun On The Mountains whose ways he followed.

"The horses are a reminder that Sun On The Mountains believes no person stands above another. We all have our own purpose and our own place. Look at these greys carefully. You cannot tell the fastest by only looking, or the one that will run the longest, or the one that will face the cold winds of winter. To know these things you must also see each horse's spirit. You must test them in adversity. You must start them far back from the buffalo chase and then see the ones with the heart to run to the front where the buffalo cows race. You must turn them into the winter wind and ask them to push through drifts to where the buffalo gather deep in the coulees. You must test them to see the best purpose for each of them, just as we test ourselves to find our best purpose.

"To Sun On The Mountains, all people are like these horses. We do not only see the clothes and necklaces you wear, the way you braid your hair, or the paints you use. We see your accomplishments. We see hearts that, like the brave Runners, are so filled with eagerness for life that the Sun shines outward from your eyes.

"The Sun burst with fire in Grey Horse's heart. The harshest test of life was placed before Grey Horse and he found a spirit within himself to overcome danger and fear. He showed us all that we are born with a powerful spirit in our hearts and we must celebrate it.

"Who cannot believe Grey Horse was a proud Piikani? Whose heart does not beat faster thinking of his speed as he galloped to Piikani territory?"

The crowd, warmed by the heroic image of Grey Horse racing ahead of the Cow and Assiniboin, began to stamp and clap with growing enthusiasm.

"Was not Grey Horse a true Piikani?" Alexander called out. The crowd cheered in agreement. For the first time since the commencement of the Great Circle, the people could feel their blood warming in the brotherhood of their tribe.

Alexander's voice rose above the excitement. "Are not the Piikani horses the fastest and bravest of all horses?"

When Alexander waved Stone Thrower and Fast Runner to his side, the crowd quieted, anxious to hear how he would distribute the horses.

"These horses now belong to two long-time friends of Grey Horse," Alexander shouted as he handed the leads to Stone Thrower and Fast Runner.

Alexander spread his arms above his shoulders. "The smallpox that brought death to our families is a test for Sun On The Mountains and for the Piikani. Do not let it be like rain that puts out the fire in your hearts.

"Just as Sun On The Mountains was sure Grey Horse would pass his test of courage and outrun the enemy, Sun On The Mountains is sure the Piikani medicine is too strong and too enduring to be defeated by the smallpox.

"To celebrate the victory over the smallpox, next summer Sun On The Mountains will drive a horse herd far into the territory of the Dakotas where the horses can be sold for the highest prices. We will return with packs piled high with trade goods.

"Sun On The Mountains will ride directly through the Assiniboin and Crow country, past the traders on the Missouri, and all the way to where many tribes meet to trade at Fort Union!"

The sudden silence of the awed crowd allowed Alexander to drop his voice to its former calm, quieting tone.

"Sun On The Mountains will need help from Grey Horse's Piikani friends to take this large herd without trouble through enemy territory. All who help will be rewarded. Sun On The Mountains will take many Piikani horses for trading. Blue Eye will lead the drive. Anybody with horses to trade must speak with him. You will have the winter to prepare. The herd must be ready to travel after the spring hunting of the bulls."

The instant Alexander concluded, the crowd pushed forward, anxious to hear more details about the drive. Alexander shook his head in response to their questions, saying Blue Eye would explain more to them before the end of the Great Circle. Frances and Hannah worked their way to his side and gradually they managed to return to the Sun On The Mountains tipis. Alexander seemed tired after his speech and asked to be left alone until the evening meal. Long Fingers, knowing Grey Horse would have been proud of Alexander's acknowledgement of his ride, sat in front of the tipi and refused to allow anybody to disturb Alexander's thoughts. Frances and Hannah went to find Blue Eye.

Most of the Piikani men had gathered around Blue Eye by the time Frances and Hannah found him tending the Sun On The Mountains pickets. Like his grandfather, Blue Eye used a slow, deliberately calm manner of speaking. It was the first time Frances had seen the Piikani filled with enthusiasm and when she mentioned the change in them, Hannah reminded her that the smallpox had been discouraging. Now, with the promise of an exciting journey ahead, Hannah assured her, the Piikani would regain their former arrogance and aggressiveness. "They see themselves as the most powerful people in the universe."

As Blue Eye answered the men's questions, he knew immediately they assumed the drive would be conducted as a warrior expedition. They were mostly concerned with the numbers of Assiniboin horse raiders they would be able to kill near the Cypress Hills, and the Crow and Sioux raiders they would be able to kill closer to Fort Union. To their disappointment, Blue Eye said he planned a trading journey, with no loss of lives, Piikani or enemy. He explained he was planning to head south-east through Blackfoot territory to the Milk River on the edge of Crow territory, and then along the Missouri to Fort Union.

Others were already talking about the drinking that would be done at Fort Union. Only a few of them had heard of Fort Union before Alexander proposed it as the destination. Nevertheless, they all believed an American fort would be more open to celebrating than Fort Edmonton where the British cautiously rationed the whiskey and locked out anybody who acted wildly.

"I was right," Blue Eye thought to himself as the talk around the campfires grew louder, "the drive to Fort Union is going to be difficult to complete safely and profitably."

Blue Eye told the men and women still listening it would take more than a month. To expect all the horses to remain sound for the journey without several days set aside regularly for rest was not reasonable. Blue Eye anticipated stopping to graze the herd for at least one full day in every five, depending upon whether the early summer grass remained green and healthy. As well, there would be the inevitable delays crossing rivers, and more delays caused by storms.

THE TRADING HOUSE, WINTER, 1837. After the Great Circle, a few Piikani men and women from the winter camps visited the trading house on the Bow to ask about the number of warriors, hunters, herders, scouts, and camp helpers that would be required. Their interest dwindled when word passed around that Blue Eye would not compromise; no warriors would accompany the herd. How could Sun On The Mountains drive three hundred horses across enemy territory without a warrior guard? Blue Eye could answer all their questions, except this one.

It was old Firekeeper who suggested the solution. "When Alexander and I set up the South Branch we had to earn a place for ourselves amongst the other traders, many of whom would have cut our throats rather than lose any business to us. We survived because we traded independently, and because we did not take advantage of anybody. First Snow and Alexander dressed plainly and quietly visited the Nahathaway families as friends, offering to trade high quality goods fairly and without whiskey. Then, at the end of the first season, we gave the other traders an opportunity to buy our furs at an auction, so they could send out their canoes completely filled. Everybody profited from our presence at South Branch and so we stayed there season after season.

"Alexander and First Snow did the same when they came to the Bow. Sun On The Mountains traded independently of the forts. They brought good horses and guns to the Piikani. Today, the Piikani have the finest horses and have kept the Sun On The Mountains territory free of outside traders. Sun On The Mountains have helped the Piikani, and the Piikani have helped Sun On The Mountains.

"Now, Blue Eye and Frances want to take horses to Fort Union to trade. Why change what Sun On The Mountains have always done? Why treat this trading journey any differently? Ride to Fort Union as you are, as Sun On The Mountains traders. Dress as you always dress, plainly. Speak as you always speak, plainly. Cross the enemy territories as traders. Don't choose sides in the old disputes. You are going to profit from the drive and those whose lands you cross deserve a share of the profits. When you offer to help others, there will be no fighting. I am sure of that."

Firekeeper's words were so thoughtfully prepared that everybody considered them fully and respectfully before commenting.

"I think Firekeeper's suggestion is good," One Person said. "Sun On The Mountains has maintained the horse herd and house on the Bow for almost fifty years now. The Piikani don't raid our herd, although they outnumber us almost five hundred to one. They permit us to stay because they can trust us as traders and as friends. We sell them horses at fair prices. We help them when we can and they help us. I think some Piikani will adopt Sun On The Mountains ways for this drive."

"What do you think, Alexander?" Hannah asked her father. "Do you think Blue Eye and Frances can make the drive without warriors?"

Alexander glanced briefly around the trading room, momentarily catching each person's eye.

"I think it will take all the Light we have to make the journey safely. Frances and Blue Eye can do it without warriors if each of you will share the strength of your spirit and send your Light with the horse herd."

Alexander gathered The Family together in the centre of the room where they formed a circle around Frances and Blue Eye. Connected to the other members of The Family through their hands, Alexander breathed deeply, his thoughts drifting into images just as they had done when he had sent Grey Horse to buy the Mandan horses.

To Frances, who had never before experienced the full spiritual power of Alexander, the trading room seemed to expand and contract with his deep breaths. With each breath, Frances could feel her own strength growing. All the remaining sadness from the death of her family at Fort McKenzie, all the sorrow from the smallpox deaths in the Blackfoot lands, and all her need to find a new home, sank below the strength flowing from the circle and onto her shoulders. For several minutes the entire world around Frances turned into stillness. She twisted her head slowly and looked at Alexander, One Person, Hannah, Long Fingers, and little Stands Early. A strange breeze as soft as a twilight mist swirled around her and Blue Eye. When the breeze stilled, the circle slipped apart. Everybody was laughing. Firekeeper hugged Frances. Part of Frances tried to describe the experience but couldn't. The place where words are formed had been replaced by the closeness she felt to The Family.

Later, when she sat alone on the cold porch and reflected upon all that had happened to her since Fort McKenzie, she could see the events moving in a continual progression towards this day; the meeting with Blue Eye when she had the irresistible urge to speak the truth about the trappers following Grey Horse up the hill; her father's perplexing recognition of Alexander James' name; Blue Eye taking her family from the fort and feeding them during the smallpox; the ride to the Bow; her sudden outburst of tears and the start of her friendship with Hannah and Long Fingers. All of these were events upon the single path that brought her to this day. Her path, at this moment, seemed so carefully laid out and vivid to her that she was sure she could never lose it. For the first time in her life, Frances understood what it meant to be strong.

Hannah chose to help her son in a practical way. She knew his poor skill as a rider would be a handicap for him on the long ride to Fort Union. There would likely be a time when he would need to ride hard, and she wanted him to be prepared. She began to look for a special horse for him.

THE FOOTHILLS, WINTER, 1837. When a deep snowfall concluded the season for hunting from horseback, Blue Eye and One Person rode from the trading house to begin their search for Piikani willing to join the horse drive to Fort Union. The January clouds hung low over the Bow River valley and fine snow fell softly as they guided their horses west. The horses' nostrils blew a fine mist of steam that slowly dissipated in the silence of the wooded groves. The river ice cracked with dull thuds. Less than five miles from the trading house, they could see the smoke from the tipis of the Broken Ribs. Heavy Shield, the Piikani tribal chief and the leader of Broken Ribs, had died from smallpox and the bands had chosen Sleeping Bird as their new chief.

Blue Eye was pleased his uncle had agreed to come with him to visit the winter camps. The Piikani leaders respected the old hunter and trader, and, although they would not expect him to speak for Blue Eye about the horse drive, they would interpret his presence as a sign that the proposal should be considered. For many years, One Person and Long Fingers had visited the bands, sharing news and delivering supplies, and they had become accepted as ambassadors of Sun On The Mountains' peaceful intentions. One Person had a quick sense of humour appreciated by the Piikani.

Sleeping Bird's tipi, made from sixteen new and still-white buffalo hides, was modestly painted with a narrow, dark red band along the bottom representing the earth, and a black band with small ovals along the top, representing the night sky and constellations. A black and white magpie, with closed eyes, was painted on the north side. Like all tipis in the prevailing westerly wind, the entrance and smoke flaps faced east. Outside the entrance a tidy stack of firewood had been gathered that impressed Blue Eye's orderly mind.

Sleeping Bird, heavyset and slow moving, greeted them warmly and immediately offered them strips of the fresh buffalo meat sizzling on skewers over the low fire. The interior of the tipi had a snugness — a hide tipi liner hung from the midpoint of the walls and thick buffalo robes lay on the floor — and made Blue Eye feel lazy as he leaned back comfortably while Sleeping Bird and One Person discussed hunting and the weather. Sleeping Bird's three wives, none of whom Blue Eye had met before, watched him in silence. The eldest of the wives, and obviously the leader, nudged the other two briefly and they left the tipi to return with armfuls of firewood. Sleeping Bird made no unnecessary effort, pointing to whatever he wanted his wives to hand him, or indicating when the smoke flaps of the tipi needed adjustment. After Sleeping Bird had finished eating, the wives added more sticks to the fire and the tipi became so warm that Blue Eye and One Person took off their jackets. More than an hour passed in idleness as Sleeping Bird asked Blue Eye inconsequential questions and appeared to think deeply about Blue Eye's casual answers. Several times Sleeping Bird nodded off and slept for a few minutes on the robes. Everybody waited without speaking for him to awake.

Eventually Sleeping Bird brought the conversation around to the horse drive by asking about the condition of the Sun On The Mountains horse herd.

"The herd is doing well," Blue Eye answered. "For most of the summer we grazed the horses higher up the Bow, saving the grass close by for winter. We have not had much trouble with them wandering. We have had more trouble with scrub stallions trying to steal mares."

Sleeping Bird looked intently at Blue Eye, his next question obviously important. "What have Sun On The Mountains been doing about those scrub stallions. They can be very troublesome and hard to drive away."

Blue Eye answered unhesitatingly. "We shoot them."

Sleeping Bird nodded. "*Aa.* I have heard about this. Don't the owners object and ask for compensation?"

"Occasionally. But nobody claims ownership of these stallions when they are running loose, so it is difficult for anybody to make a claim afterwards. If they have a real claim, we pay it."

"Why do you care about the stallions?" Sleeping Bird inquired, again with a purpose in mind. "Why not add them to your herd. They would make Sun On The Mountains even wealthier."

Blue Eye knew where these questions were leading and he answered in a way that would move the conversation more directly to the topic of the horse drive.

"Thank you for saying Sun On The Mountains is wealthy. It is a good compliment but not as true as most Piikani think. Yes, we have a large herd of horses but nothing else. The Piikani have horses but they also have the buffalo. Sun On The Mountains have no buffalo. We are dependent upon the Piikani. We have no hunters, only traders. We must trade our horses for meat or we will starve. The Broken Ribs in this way are a much wealthier band. That's why we must raise the finest horses. Otherwise the Broken Ribs and the other bands would not be interested in trading their meat, hides and furs to us. That's why we shoot the stallions. Every time one of our mares raises a foal that isn't good enough to become a fast buffalo runner, a racer or a riding horse, the Piikani are deprived of a good colt."

Sleeping Bird nodded in agreement, a hint of a smile on his fleshy lips and in the creases of his jowls. His eyelids drooped, deceptively covering the top portion of his eyes. His comments, unlike his lazy manner, were precise and carefully directed. "You speak very straightforwardly Blue Eye. You acknowledge the obligation between the Piikani and Sun On The Mountains. Many people don't think it worthy to acknowledge an obligation." He stopped for a moment to light his stone pipe with a small stick from the fire. He puffed several times then handed the pipe to Blue Eye. "Here. Smoke."

Blue Eye puffed and then handed the pipe back to Sleeping Bird who, after a few more puffs, handed it to One Person. While One Person smoked the last of the small bowl of tobacco, Sleeping Bird continued his observations.

"You are a strong-willed young man, Blue Eye. You proved your determination at the Sun Dance last fall. For a long time today you have been sitting with your uncle Nittsitapi and me, and listening as old men talked about the weather and hunting. All the time you wanted to talk about your horse drive. Not once did you try to interrupt. These things are noticed. Now, please tell me your thoughts on the horse drive."

Blue Eye had been anticipating this moment, the time when his skill as a leader would be first tested. If he could convince the tribal chief, Sleeping Bird, that Sun On The Mountains could take the herd through enemy territory without a warrior guard, then the bands would send their experienced herders and hunters.

"I have spent many days planning for this drive, Sleeping Bird. And you are the first Piikani that I am telling my plans to. I do this on the advice of my grandfather, Alexander. He remembers when he first came to Piikani territory and it was Heavy Shield who painted the first symbol on the Sun On The Mountains' door. I also am obligated to Heavy Shield who settled my dispute with Little Ears at the Sun Dance."

Sleeping Bird waved his hand, brushing aside further discussion of this matter. "I remember this dispute. It is settled. Forever."

Blue Eye continued. "I mentioned it because Sun On The Mountains believe that Sleeping Bird, like Heavy Shield, prefers peaceful agreements to fights and deaths, and will understand why we plan to ride to Fort Union without warriors."

Sleeping Bird did not comment and Blue Eye continued.

"Sun On The Mountains need Piikani help and that is the reason One Person and I came to seek Sleeping Bird's advice. We expect we will have difficulty crossing the enemy territories."

Sleeping Bird's earlier slumbering, half-alert manner vanished. As he listened to Blue Eye, his manner became animated. "That's a serious difficulty," he said.

Blue Eye nodded in agreement. "Yes. Sun On The Mountains will not risk any lives by bringing warriors to guard the horses as we travel through enemy territory."

Sleeping Bird scoffed. "To drive horses through enemy territory without weapons and without warriors is to risk lives. You will all be killed and the horses stolen."

One Person interrupted. "Listen to Blue Eye's plan. You may be surprised."

Sleeping Bird leaned back, feigning disinterest. "I will listen," he said dully. "Because of my respect for your uncle Nittsitapi, you may tell me your plan. Afterwards, I will know if my old friend who used to be a fine hunter has forgotten his Piikani ways."

Blue Eye began. "First, let me tell you what Sun On The Mountains believes will happen if Piikani warriors accompany the horses. Along the way the herd will be an open challenge to every band of horse raiders. Some men and women will certainly die defending the herd. This will come at a time when the Piikani have already lost many men to the smallpox. And certainly the enemies will capture some of the horses.

"After the drive, Sun On The Mountains will have to compensate the Piikani families for the deaths of the warriors on the drive. The cost of that compensation and the horses we lose will make the drive unprofitable. That's why Sun On The Mountains does not think it is a good plan. Sun On The Mountains has a better plan; one that is just as bold.

"Each Piikani rider accompanying the horse drive — each hunter, each herder, and each camp helper — will ride to Fort Union as a Sun On The Mountains trader, not as a Piikani. Each rider will wear Sun On The Mountains plain clothing and will ride horses painted with the Sun On The Mountains symbol. Each rider will carry only the weapons needed for hunting.

"A band of scouts will travel ahead of the herd and bring the enemy chiefs to me to negotiate an exchange of horses for the right to cross their territory."

Sleeping Bird leaned forward. "And if those enemy chiefs betray you? What if they allow you into their territory and then attack the herd? What can you do then?"

"They won't betray us. From each tribe we will accept a few men to join the drive. They will also bring horses to trade at Fort Union. They too will wear plain clothes and ride horses painted with Sun On The Mountains symbols. The enemy will no longer be an enemy. They will be Sun On The Mountains traders. These men will return to their tribes as wealthy as any Piikani that accompany us."

"You are a strong-willed young man, Blue Eye," Sleeping Bird repeated as he considered Blue Eye's plan. "I see much of Alexander in you."

One Person refilled the chief's pipe with tobacco from his own pouch and passed it around. After they had smoked, Blue Eye spoke again.

"I'm not strong-willed, Sleeping Bird. I know only one way, the way of the trader. I don't know the way of the warrior.

"Think how many horses the Broken Ribs have acquired by trade with Sun On The Mountains compared to the number of horses the Broken Ribs have captured in horse raids. As well, Sun On The Mountains' horses are much better than any you have captured. In trading with Sun On The Mountains, the Broken Ribs have not lost a single man. How many men have you lost in horse raids and war parties?"

Sleeping Bird shrugged noncommittally, and Blue Eye continued. "Sun On The Mountains is sure the tribes we meet on the way to Fort Union will see this truth. By being part of our trading, they will benefit much more than they would if they tried to capture our horses. Trading makes tribes wealthy, Sleeping Bird."

The next question Sleeping Bird asked indicated to Blue Eye that he had been convinced. "How many Piikani men will Sun On The Mountains need to help with the drive?"

"At least twenty, plus ten women and young people to help with the camps."

"What will be their reward for helping?"

"They will be paid with horses. They will also be able to bring horses of their own to trade at Fort Union. Sun On The Mountains will provide all the supplies and will make the agreements to cross enemy territories."

"Will the Broken Ribs return wealthy?"

"*Aa*. If they travel as traders, not as warriors. That will make them wealthy."

Sleeping Bird said he would talk the proposal over with the Broken Ribs, and that Blue Eye and One Person should return in two days to hear their answer. He would not use his influence as a tribal chief to encourage them to follow the Broken Ribs' decision. As Blue Eye and One Person mounted their horses for the ride back to the trading house, the wives of Sleeping Bird had already begun visiting the other tipis to share the news.

Blue Eye and One Person rode back in silence through the drifting snow. Blue Eye, barely eighteen, knew he had taken on a big responsibility in organizing the horse drive. There would probably be more than thirty people involved, possibly more if other tribes joined along the way, and for the first time Blue Eye sensed the faith others would need to have in his abilities to bring everybody home. For a moment, he thought perhaps he should have accepted the necessity of a warrior accompaniment, if only to take some of the burden off his own shoulders. With a warrior guard, enemy attacks would be expected and, in Piikani custom, the outcome could be considered the responsibility of the individuals, not the leader.

On the porch of the trading house, One Person held Blue Eye back for a moment. "You did well with Sleeping Bird. But don't be discouraged if he turns you down. There are many other bands to try."

Blue Eye shrugged. "I agree. I was pleased Sleeping Bird listened and asked questions. I think he was convinced, but you're right. He may not help us. There will be more opportunities with other bands. We have all winter to assemble the riders." One Person left Blue Eye and walked up the path to his tipi to tell Long Fingers about the visit to the Broken Ribs.

Inside the trading house the mood was muted. Hannah was out with the horse herd. Frances and Alexander were going through the ledgers. Firekeeper slept on a pile of buffalo robes by the fire. The trading house seemed crowded to Blue Eye since the arrival of Firekeeper; not because he took up room or was demanding, but because the winter weather kept everybody inside. During the warm months, The Family spent most of their time outside, only going into the house to eat and sleep. Now, they stayed in except to check the horses or to bring wood or meat from the cache on the outer, north wall of the house. Only Frances seemed used to spending hours indoors. Everybody else missed the opportunity to be alone for long hours with the horses, and to travel to the bands for trading.

Blue Eye rubbed his hands together beside the fire to warm his fingers. "We spent most of the day with Sleeping Bird in the Broken Ribs' camp," he said to Alexander and

Frances. "At first he was sceptical but he listened, mostly because of his friendship with One Person. When I explained my plan, he appeared interested. At least he didn't say 'no'. He invited us back in two days to hear his answer. By now his wives will have told the entire band about the plan. When we return, we should hear everybody's opinion."

"Be patient," Alexander answered. "This is a new idea for them. They are used to thinking that the only way to deal with other tribes is with violence. Give them time to mull it over. With 2500 Piikani between Fort Edmonton and the Missouri, I believe you will be able to find enough to accompany the drive."

"I think so," Blue Eye agreed. "When I told Sleeping Bird I thought everybody who participated would return wealthy — and safe — I could tell he began to appreciate our plan. The smallpox, I think, has tired the Piikani of death."

Frances stopped her work at the cutting board and turned to face Blue Eye. "I think if I were one of the Piikani wives, I would be happy if my husband were going on this journey. Considering how many lives have been lost on Piikani horse raids, I would prefer they tried this plan. In fact, I would not care if they returned wealthy, just that they returned."

Alexander chuckled. "You wait until you get to know some of the women better. They like the opportunity to show off a Crow scalp just as much as the men. Around us, they are quite subdued. Wait until you see them when a war party returns with captured horses and scalps. Ask Long Fingers about some of the celebrations she has seen. To tell you the truth, I would not be surprised if the women were more opposed to our plan than the men."

Just then Hannah pushed the door open and stamped her feet to shake the snow from her leather leggings. "If I were in a killing mood," she exclaimed vehemently, "I would take a gun and shoot some of the Piikani who let their scrub stallions run loose. I shot that troublesome white-faced stallion today and I would have liked to shoot its owner as well."

"Do you know who owned it?" Blue Eye asked.

"No! I sent word around last week that the stallion was loose and pestering our herds. Nobody claimed it. Today it started a fight. I shot it before it chewed up or injured one of our stallions. I suppose in a day or two somebody will ask for compensation."

Hannah brushed the snow from her rabbit skin hat. Her long, unbraided black hair fell loosely onto her shoulders. Her stocky build and round face with its wide smile always gave Frances the impression she had a placid nature. But at moments like this, when the welfare of the horse herd had been threatened, she revealed her aggressive side.

As she pulled her deerskin jacket from her shoulders and hung it on a peg by the door, she told Blue Eye she hoped his plans for the horse drive were progressing well. "I think the horse drive is the only way we are going to be able to clean out the scrub horses. I hope the traders in Fort Union are eager to buy pack horses because that's all most of them are good for. If we don't get rid of them, I think we should invite the Assiniboin to steal the whole lot. From what I have seen of their horses, this bunch of stone heads would fit right in."

Frances laughed, enjoying hearing Hannah's frustration. Too often, Frances believed, The Family kept their emotions controlled. The few words of anger or joy she heard were often cut short.

"Good for you Hannah," Frances called to her. "With you protecting our horses, The Family has no need to worry!"

Hannah brushed the last of the snow from her leggings and moved closer to the fire. "The horses are the entire Family's responsibility, Frances. They are just as much your responsibility as they are Blue Eye's or mine. I am their keeper for now, but the care of the horses is up to everybody." The admonishing tone in Hannah's voice cut through the room, its heat leaving nobody's skin untouched.

Hannah stood with her back to the fire, warming her legs. "I did not mean to sound so irritated," she added in a more gentle tone. "I don't like to have to shoot a horse, even a nuisance stallion. It is always difficult and today I wished another person could have pulled the trigger."

Frances turned again from the cutting board towards the fireplace. "I wish I knew more about the horses and everything else that happens here," she said, her words directed to The Family, not just Hannah. "I would like to take responsibility for something myself. I am in the opposite position of Hannah who has to make many decisions on her own. I don't make any."

Alexander, seated by the fire on a straight-backed chair he had made for himself the previous winter, looked at Frances inquiringly.

"Everything is changing for some reason this year," he said, purposefully not responding directly to her pointed remarks. "Between the smallpox, the horse drive, and the trading on the Missouri, I often wonder if Sun On The Mountains will ever find the peaceful days again we had in the years just after we built this trading house."

"I don't think so Grandfather," Blue Eye responded. "Besides, I'm enjoying the opportunities these changes bring, except for the smallpox. You had exciting times with Grey Horse and First Snow when you brought the Runners to the Bow. You enjoyed every day of it. One Person likes to tell me how you changed his life. He says if it hadn't been for Sun On The Mountains, he would probably be dead long ago, lying on a hillside with a Crow arrow in his side. You brought changes with you Grandfather. More changes are coming, beginning with this horse drive."

"I did not mean to start this discussion," Frances interjected. "I just wanted to say I would like more responsibilities – for anything."

"Do not worry, you will find your place here," Alexander assured her. "Try to remember you have been here less than a year. The rest of us have been here for many years. Before long you will find yourself too busy to be worrying about not having enough responsibility."

"But I would like to start now, not in years," Frances persisted.

"Why not begin by learning to speak Piikani," Hannah suggested. "Then you would be able to help more with the trading and on the horse drive."

A smile spread over Frances's face and she rushed over to Hannah and put her arms around her. "You always seem to have sensible answers, Hannah. Do you think Long Fingers would help me learn Piikani?"

Hannah, uncomfortable with Frances's physical display of affection, unwound the young woman's arms from her neck. "I cannot speak for Long Fingers," she answered solemnly. "But she would be the first person I would ask. She taught my mother to speak Piikani."

Frances could not hold her enthusiasm back. She quickly pulled on her jacket and almost ran out the door and up the path to Long Finger's tipi.

Alexander grinned as the door closed behind Frances. "From a girl who wouldn't speak when she came here during the smallpox, she certainly has changed. Now she has so much to say that she needs to learn another language."

"Yes," Hannah added. "Frances does not lack energy and she seems to have no fear. I'm sure she had ridden very little when she arrived here. Blue Eye had to lead her horse most of the way. Once she started riding with me to move the horse herds, she learned quickly. When she's riding her white pony, Feathers, she is sure she can go anywhere on her own."

"But what does she know about horse drives?" Blue Eye said in a perplexed tone. "I think the only reason she wants to come on the horse drive is so she can ride her pony. She says she loves her pony. Imagine giving your horse a name!"

"She wants to keep watch on you Blue Eye," Firekeeper muttered as he rolled over under his sleeping robes.

Hannah quickly covered her mouth to hide a smile as she saw her son's puzzled expression.

"I don't need to be watched," Blue Eye replied to Firekeeper's muttering. "I'll be leading the drive. I'll be the one doing the watching."

Firekeeper groaned loudly. "You are as slow-witted as your grandfather when it comes to understanding women. Ask your grandfather how long it took First Snow to catch him."

Understanding ran like hot water through Blue Eye. "You cannot be right. Frances? Me? I don't think that is possible. We are not at all alike. She is much too . . . " Blue Eye hesitated, fumbling for words while Firekeeper, Alexander and Hannah did their best not to laugh.

"Emotional!" Blue Eye blurted out. "She is always hugging and kissing. She cries just as easily as she laughs. I intend to marry somebody steadier."

Firekeeper rolled back under the robe. "White man!" he muttered loudly. "Just like your grandfather!"

Blue Eye pulled a ledger from the shelf near the window. "I have work to do. I have a horse drive to plan and I don't have time for this. If you want to tease somebody, try Stands Early. She is the right age to enjoy your idea of fun!" He opened the ledger and began to make notes, his back to The Family.

Hannah took over Frances' work at the cutting board, preparing the evening meal of buffalo roast. She tied a leather thong around the roast Frances had cut, and skewered it carefully on the short iron rods in the fireplace where it soon began to splutter and spit above the embers. Rushing from the house with the evening meal only half-prepared was typical of Frances, Hannah thought as she laid the wooden plates on the table. More impetuous, she decided, than emotional, as Blue Eye had suggested. She would be a good friend to Blue Eye who needed occasionally to be prodded into action. Hannah looked briefly over at her son who was absorbed in writing out another list of what he would need on the horse drive.

"What list are you working on, Blue Eye?" she asked. "Maybe we can help."

"I'm still making the list of the people I'll need. When we meet the other tribes we are going to need somebody to translate. I don't know anybody who speaks Crow, Assiniboin and Cree and would be a good hunter or herder on the drive. I'm wondering if it makes sense to bring somebody just to be a translator. The negotiations are a very important part of the plan and the wrong person could make mistakes. But what if something happens to the translator?"

"You cannot deal with every problem before it arises," Alexander pointed out. "Talk to One Person. He knows everybody. Why not ask him to help you find a translator. I would accept his judgement."

"That's a good suggestion. I think that's what I'll do."

"Why not go see him now. He loves company in the evenings."

"Good idea," Blue Eye answered, closing up the ledger. "By the way," he said as he placed the ledger carefully amongst the others on the shelf, "these ledgers are not being kept in the right order. I had to straighten them out yesterday."

Firekeeper called out from under his sleeping robes. "Be quiet. Go outside and straighten up the snowflakes. I think somebody has been mixing them up too."

"I'll keep some roast for your return," Hannah offered as Blue Eye opened the door to leave. "If you see Frances, tell her it would be safest if she walked back with you. It will be dark soon and she could lose her way."

Blue Eye shook his head. "Frances knows the path as well as anybody. You are making something out of nothing." He pulled the door closed a little harder than necessary as he left the trading house. As soon as Blue Eye stepped off the porch, Firekeeper lifted his head from the robes. "I hope Blue Eye is caught soon. Otherwise this house is going to be too confusing for me to get much sleep."

Frances and Blue Eye returned to the trading house in the dark with Long Fingers, One Person and Stands Early, stamping their feet noisily on the porch to shake off the snow. Once inside they were greeted by Hannah who told them she had left some roast warming by the edge of the fire.

"We ate with Long Fingers," Frances apologized. "Once Blue Eye arrived and began discussing the horse drive with One Person, Long Fingers said my Piikani lesson was over. The two men did not want to talk about anything else." From inside her dress she pulled out a small rawhide doll clothed in the blue cotton from Frances's former dress.

"Look at this. Stands Early made this for me. She said it looks just the way I was before I started wearing deerskin."

She handed the doll to Hannah who studied it carefully. "It does look a bit like you. Stands Early used the hair of a buffalo calf to match your hair. Everybody comments on your hair, Frances. It is very beautiful and unusual." Blue Eye purposefully avoided looking at his mother, although she glanced several times toward him as she spoke.

"I think we should sing," Frances announced cheerfully. "I'm feeling quite happy at the moment. When I was young, I loved to sing. I don't believe I have heard anybody sing for a long time. Except those sad chants of the Piikani. Who wants to sing something with me?"

There was a silence. "I'm sorry, Frances," Hannah said. "The Family does not sing."

"Oh don't worry," Frances replied blithely. "Lots of people can't sing. It doesn't matter if you're not musical. It's fun. Let's try a song."

Again, there was silence. "You misunderstood me, Frances," Hannah explained. "Sun On The Mountains chooses not to sing. We have our work and we have each other. That is enough pleasure for us. Singing is unnecessary."

Tears welled up in Frances's eyes. "But I have always enjoyed singing. It helps to brighten the day."

Alexander rose slowly from his chair. "I think we should at least let Frances sing one song. Perhaps something simple. After all, she has learned many of our ways without complaint. I think we should let her show us something of her ways. Hearing one song will certainly not take up too much of our time."

When there were no objections to Alexander's suggestion, he held out his hand to Frances and she moved to his side. "Now," he said, "you must show us how you sing. Would you rather sit or stand? Is there something we should be doing while you sing?"

Frances wiped the tears from her eyes and smiled thinly at The Family. "You truly don't know about singing. How odd. I thought you were poking fun at me. I can barely believe none of you has ever heard singing before."

"Alexander and I have," Firekeeper said, still lying on the robes. "In the canoes and in the camps at the South Branch. The paddlers sang. I must admit it helped to pass the time. But I haven't heard any singing since then."

"What about Fort Edmonton?" Frances asked. "Don't they sing there?"

"If there is singing at Fort Edmonton, we always leave because there is usually drinking," Blue Eye replied.

Frances arranged the chairs from the table in a semicircle in front of the fireplace and then stood to its right, beside Firekeeper's pile of robes. Frances explained she would sing a hymn, "Amazing Grace," she had learned on the steamboat from St. Louis. She took a deep breath and began.

The Family concentrated carefully, watching her movements with interest and listening intently to the music.

"Amazing grace — how sweet the sound,
that saved a wretch like me!
I once was lost but now am found,
was blind but now I see.
'Twas grace that taught my heart to fear,
and grace my fears relieved;
how precious did that grace appear
the hour I first believed.
The Lord has promised good to me,
his word my hope secures;
he will my shield and portion be,
as long as life endures.
Through many dangers, toils and snares

I have already come;
'tis grace hath brought me safe thus far,
and grace will lead me home.
When we've been there ten thousand years,
bright shining as the sun,
we've no less days to sing God's praise
than when we'd first begun."

As she finished, The Family sat hushed. "You liked it?" Frances asked eagerly. "Tell me, please, that you liked it." Her hazel eyes skipped around their faces searching for approval.

"I liked it," Hannah said.

"Very pleasing," Firekeeper said.

"I liked it," Alexander agreed, adding "especially the line about the sun."

They all looked at Blue Eye who seemed to be holding back. Finally he spoke. "Well, if this is the way Frances sings, I suggest we have more of it." Everybody laughed.

Alexander held up his hand. "One song is enough for tonight." Frances ran to Alexander and hugged him. "Thank you for letting me sing. I'm glad you liked it. I have learned lots more songs. I'm sure I have a hymnbook in my bags. If you didn't like that song especially, I could sing something different."

"Enough!" Alexander said, the black, searching pupils of his blue eyes catching her attention and interrupting her enthusiasm.

"Just one question," Hannah said softly to Frances. "Tell me, what type of people make these songs? I found this song tonight very moving. Are all songs like this one?"

Frances thought for a moment. "It's hard to describe songs. It's like my asking you about the horses. They are all very different. At first, most hymns, for example, probably sound much the same. But when you know them better you see how different the words are and how different the sounds. When I first saw your herd of horses, they all looked the same. Just different colours. Now Feathers is my favourite, but I wouldn't have known how to choose a horse when I first learned to ride. Music is the same. The more you hear it, the more interesting it becomes."

"Thank you," Hannah replied. "You are right about the horses. Each one is memorable to me, for one reason or another. They each respond to you differently when you ride them. Some are nervous and shy. Some are bold. Some steady. Others you cannot trust."

"They are like music, then," Frances concluded. "Songs suit different moods, different circumstances. If you like, next time I'll sing one that is easy to learn and you can try."

The next morning Blue Eye and his uncle, One Person, rode to the camp of Sleeping Bird and the Broken Ribs. The weather continued low and heavy, with light snow falling as they followed the trail along the Bow. Neither spoke after they left the trading house and had urged their horses forward into the cold westerly breeze.

Sleeping Bird again took his time getting around to discussing the purpose of the visit. His three wives sat expressionless while the men smoked a little and One Person inquired about the latest results of the hunting. Blue Eye patiently ate and smoked while Sleeping Bird and One Person talked. Sleeping Bird gave no indication of how the talks about the drive had gone and, with an indifference that Blue Eye knew disguised a perceptive mind, drifted into sleep when the conversation lagged. Finally, the chief turned his full attention to Blue Eye.

"How are the plans for the Sun On The Mountains horse drive progressing?" Sleeping Bird asked with a sudden, intent look. "Have you talked with the other bands since you last visited the Broken Ribs?"

"My answer is no to both your questions. Our plans have not changed and we have not discussed this with any other bands," Blue Eye answered. "We are waiting to hear Sleeping Bird's response."

Sleeping Bird's heavy eyelids drooped. Blue Eye, fearing the chief would fall asleep asked, "Has the band reached a decision about joining the drive?"

"*Aa,*" Sleeping Bird responded, fully alert. "The decision has been made. We do not think the horse drive can be successful without warriors. There will be too many opportunities for the enemies of the Blackfoot to outnumber you. The chiefs of the Assiniboin and Crow may agree to take a payment for allowing you to cross their territories, but that won't be enough to stop their warriors from trying to capture a few horses. People will always do what they want. No chief can make a promise that everybody will keep.

"The Broken Ribs think the herd will be too tempting a prize for the chiefs to be able to stop every warrior. You were right when you said lives would certainly be lost and some horses stolen. The Broken Ribs think all of your lives will be lost if there are no warriors to defend the herd.

"If the Assiniboin were to bring a herd through our territory, that is what would happen. Our leaders may agree, but that would not stop some of our warriors from trying to capture the horses."

Blue Eye purposefully kept his face expressionless as he listened. "I'm disappointed by this," he replied evenly. "I had hoped the Broken Ribs would want to sell some of their horses for a good price at Fort Union. I have a few questions to ask." Sleeping Bird nodded to indicate he would answer Blue Eye's questions.

"If some Broken Ribs disagreed with the band's decision, would they be permitted to join the drive on their own?"

Sleeping Bird shrugged. "This drive is not like the buffalo hunt. The band police can enforce regulations during the buffalo hunt because its success depends upon everybody following the orders of the leaders.

"The success of the horse drive does not affect all the Broken Ribs. For that reason, individuals may make their own decisions."

"Then the Broken Ribs would not discourage anybody who wanted to join?" Blue Eye asked.

"We would think them foolish to risk their lives but we would not stop them. In my opinion I think you would be better trying the other bands. The Broken Ribs have made their decision and many would not want you persuading the young men to risk their lives in the drive."

Sleeping Bird leaned back on his robes. "The smallpox took many Broken Ribs. Most of us are content now to hunt buffalo and live peacefully. Nobody is interested in travelling through the enemies' territories. We need all our young men and women for hunting."

Blue Eye pulled a short coil of tobacco from his jacket. "We will honour your decision and not look for men and women in the Broken Ribs to ride with us to Fort Union. We will look for riders in the other bands." He handed the tobacco to Sleeping Bird.

"Sun On The Mountains thanks Sleeping Bird for considering our plan. If any riders care to join, tell them the rendezvous will be at the Bow. We will meet at the first full moon following the bloom of the golden buffalo beans."

Sleeping Bird smiled at Blue Eye, tucked the tobacco into his pouch, and then leaned forward and whispered so his wives could not hear. "If I were young, I would go to Fort Union with you. But I am too old. However, there is one Broken Rib who will go. He will find you soon."

"Thank you," Blue Eye replied. "When the horse drive leaves, Sun On The Mountains is sure the Broken Ribs will be wishing for our success."

The snow continued to fall lightly as Blue Eye and One Person rode along the trail to the trading house. One Person rode in the lead. Both men's thoughts were on the Broken Ribs' decision not to participate. Although the Broken Ribs would not stop members from joining the drive, Blue Eye had been hoping for a strong endorsement of the plan, one that would show the other bands the Broken Ribs believed the drive would be a success under his leadership. Blue Eye was pleased, however, that Sleeping Bird had privately endorsed the drive. He wondered who Sleeping Bird would send.

Even One Person was startled when a tall Piikani, about two years older than Blue Eye, stepped suddenly on the trail in front of their horses.

"*Oki*," the Piikani said with a serious expression. "I would like to talk with you about the horse drive."

"*Oki*. You surprised us," One Person responded as he dismounted. "Even our horses did not notice you."

The young man smiled briefly. "You did not see or hear me because you were thinking too loudly about the decision of the Broken Ribs not to send riders on the horse drive to Fort Union. Did you forget my father said one Broken Rib would go with you to Fort Union?"

"Your father?" Blue Eye replied in surprise. "Your father is Sleeping Bird?"

"*Aa*. Sleeping Bird is my father. My name is Thinks Like A Woman."

One Person and Blue Eye exchanged a quick glance.

"Thinks Like A Woman." One Person repeated. "You are Lightning And Thunder. I have heard of you. Didn't you leave the Broken Ribs band before the smallpox?"

"*Aa*. I came back to the Broken Ribs after the smallpox to visit my father and mother. I was too late. My mother had already died. I have talked with my father several times but I don't live with the Broken Ribs."

"Is Lightning and Thunder your band now?" Blue Eye asked.

Thinks Like A Woman laughed. "No. It's not a band. It's who we are. We don't belong to any band. I ride with my friend, Never Seen. We keep to ourselves." He pointed up the bank to a young man wearing a brightly beaded jacket and riding a small dark horse with red and black feathers hanging in its mane and forelock. He held the reins of a chestnut.

"Never Seen does not like to talk. Maybe later he will come closer." Thinks Like A Woman smiled at Blue Eye. "Perhaps Otssko Moapsspiksi thinks I am handsome. I find his blue eye very pleasing."

Blue Eye suppressed a smile as he caught Thinks Like A Woman's intent. "You are handsome and charming," he answered, "But I am not like you."

"What did you want to talk to us about?" One Person asked, changing the topic. "Do you want to know about the horse drive?"

"Yes," Thinks Like A Woman answered with a brevity that impressed Blue Eye. "Never Seen and I may help you."

"We need help," Blue Eye acknowledged. "How would you help?"

"You will need scouts to ride ahead of the herd. To find grazing, to find buffalo."

"And to find the enemy?" One Person interjected. "Blue Eye needs scouts to meet the enemy chiefs. Can you do that?"

Thinks Like A Woman returned One Person's pointed question with a hard stare. "We can do that. Never Seen and

I have ridden several times to Fort Union. We had no trouble with the tribes you call the enemy."

"You have been to Fort Union?" Blue Eye said, his tone rising into a question. "Why did you ride to Fort Union?"

Thinks Like A Woman shook his head. "That's our business. You don't need to know the why of everything. All that's important for you to know is that we can cross through the territories of the Assiniboin and Crow without trouble."

The snow began to chill One Person's feet. He stamped them and said it was too cold to stand and talk. "We should build a fire if we are going to talk longer. Or would you and Never Seen come to The Sun On The Mountains trading house?"

Thinks Like A Woman answered without hesitation. "I'll come to the trading house. Never Seen will wait where he can watch the house. You go ahead. When he sees I am alone, he will bring my horse and we will follow your trail."

One Person and Blue Eye rode ahead, as Thinks like a Woman suggested, and at the first clearing where they could ride beside each other Blue Eye asked One Person what he knew about the young man.

"Most of the Piikani know him and Never Seen," One Person answered. "Lightning And Thunder have their own ways. There are a few in all the tribes."

Blue Eye rode in thought for a few minutes, and then turned to One Person who was smiling broadly.

"Don't worry," One Person laughingly answered Blue Eye's questioning look. "They are not dress-wearing Two Spirits. These men are some of the best Piikani horsemen. They are hunters and warriors. Grey Horse told me he watched Thinks Like A Woman and Never Seen kill two Assiniboin horse raiders by the Red Deer River. Grey Horse never told me, but I think Lightning And Thunder protected the Runners."

"You know all the Piikani, uncle. I'm fortunate to have your help," Blue Eye replied. "I admit Thinks Like A Woman surprised me, the way he suddenly appeared on the trail. Do you believe he has been to Fort Union?"

"If I were you, I would believe everything he told me. He and Never Seen often disappear for a long time, and then show up without any explanation. He appears open but he is very careful in what he says. Did you notice how he cut you short when you asked about his reason for going to Fort Union? He kept a lot to himself. I've heard Never Seen isn't Piikani."

THE TRADING HOUSE, WINTER 1838. One Person and Blue Eye called The Family together to prepare them for the arrival of Thinks Like A Woman and Never Seen. Frances, seeing everybody else accept the two unusual visitors unquestioningly, resolved to keep her opinions to herself, although she wondered if she would have been as reserved if she were expecting visitors like this in a drawing room in London.

The Family waited for the men, but it wasn't until Blue Eye opened the door onto the porch to see if they were nearby outside that Thinks Like A Woman stepped forward from the brush. Blue Eye couldn't see their horses, or Never Seen, but guessed he kept watch.

Frances studied the tall, lithely built visitor and could not help admiring his handsome face and graceful movements. Even his effortless manner as brushed the snow from his leggings showed a sense of natural fluidity. His hair flowed, untied, around his face. She wondered if the Piikani women found him this attractive. Thinks Like A Woman shook his long hair clear of his shoulders, giving Frances a quick smile, as if guessing her thoughts. A row of white ermine tails tipped with black decorated the front of his jacket. He was slim-hipped with long but slightly bowed legs that gave him a rocking motion as he walked towards the fireplace to warm his hands.

Thinks Like A Woman looked directly at Alexander. "You must be the one Sleeping Bird calls The White-Haired Piikani," he said. "I met your friend Grey Horse several times. He often spoke of your powerful medicine."

"Grey Horse and I were good friends," Alexander said. "He died last spring on the Missouri."

"I heard. He was a great horseman. The best horse I owned I bought from him. It was a Runner. A Crow killed that horse and I killed the Crow. I would rather have kept the horse."

Frances lifted a pot of stewed ribs from the fireplace. "Please have something to eat with us," she said to Thinks Like A Woman. She ladled the ribs into bowls and Stands Early handed them around the table. Thinks Like A Woman sat silently with everybody before they ate. When Stands Early offered him a spoon, he smiled and flicked his wrist. A short-bladed knife suddenly appeared in his hand. When she laughed at this trick, he showed her another. Balancing the knife on his finger, he flipped it high in the air and stretched out his arm. The knife slid, handle first, into the sleeve of his jacket. Under Stands Early's continued scrutiny, he began to eat with the spoon.

Frances pushed her chair back abruptly. "I forgot about your friend outside," she exclaimed to Thinks Like A Woman. "He is standing in the snow outside while we are eating in here. Do you think he would come in if I asked him?"

"I think he would prefer to be outside. He may come in another time."

"I can at least take him something to eat."

"If he sees you, he will stay hidden."

"That's foolish. I'm taking him some ribs. I'll find him!" Frances hurriedly filled another bowl and pulled on a jacket. "Nobody is going to come to the Sun On The Mountains trading house and tell their friends they left hungry!"

Thinks Like A Woman grinned, his large, black eyes flashing with a charming amusement. Hannah shook her head at Thinks Like A Woman. "Let her go. She does what she wants."

"She is wearing men's leggings. This will be interesting."

"We all wear men's leggings in the winter," Hannah pointed out. "Riding in a dress isn't very practical."

Frances stood on the porch for a few moments and then followed Thinks Like A Woman's tracks towards the bush where she stopped and called out in Piikani, "*Oki. Oki.*" Inside the trading house, they could hear her high-pitched voice.

"At least Never Seen will tell from her voice that she is a woman," Thinks Like A Woman said. "He won't come out of the brush. Not even for a bowl of hot ribs."

Frances waited, holding the bowl of ribs with steam rising from it. "I can wait as long as he can," she said to herself. "We'll see if he can stay in the bush longer than I can stand here."

Snow fell lightly in large flakes and she wished she had taken the trouble to put on a hat. Her resolve was rewarded in a few minutes when Never Seen stepped into the clearing and, from about twenty yards, pointed to the ground, indicating Frances should set the bowl down.

Frances shook her head, smiled, and waved back to him, indicating he should come to her. He shook his head in return, indicating he would not come closer.

"Then I'll come to you," Frances said under her breath. Never Seen smiled at her boldness and walked forward to meet her.

"Do you speak English?" Frances asked as she handed him the bowl of stew.

"No English," Never Seen said softly, his face half-hidden as he sucked the meat from the small bones. Frances looked over his clothing while he ate. He was dressed like a typical Piikani in tall winter moccasins, thick leggings, a jacket and a round cap with long earflaps. But, Frances noticed, unlike most Piikani who rarely adorned their winter clothing, Never Seen had detailed bead embroidery on his jacket, gloves and hat as well as coloured, notched feathers hanging from the shoulders and neck of his jacket. Long Fingers had explained to Frances that notched feathers represented accomplishments, mostly related to encounters with an enemy. She found it hard to believe this sweet-faced, smooth-skinned young man could have earned so many notches.

Never Seen sipped the last of the broth and handed the bowl back to Frances with a nod of his head. "Good." Carefully he wiped his hands on the lower part of his leggings and pulled on his gloves.

Frances tapped herself on the chest. "Frances. My name is Frances."

"Fran — ces," he repeated slowly.

"And you are . . . ?" she asked, pointing to him. "What is your name?"

"Nev — er Seen," he replied in English. He spoke softly and cautiously, repeating the English syllables that Thinks Like A Woman had taught him.

She pointed to the trading house. "Come," she said, using a Piikani word from her first lessons with Long Fingers. He shook his head and turned back to the bush. After a few steps he halted and turned back. "Fran – ces." He spoke carefully. She smiled and he smiled. He turned and was quickly gone.

Inside the trading house, everybody looked inquiringly at her as she pulled off her hat, mitts and jacket. "He is a polite young man," she said, shaking the snow from her auburn curls. "We talked a little. He said the ribs were good."

Thinks Like A Woman laughed. Winding a few locks of his straight hair around his finger, he said, "I think he liked your curls more than the ribs."

Thinks Like A Woman's teasing of Frances reminded Alexander of Empty Hand, First Snow's father. His old friend's ability to generate warmth through humour had been important in holding his Nahathaway band together.

Thinks Like A Woman's likeable manner put him instantly at ease in the company of The Family. This man, Alexander concluded, was a natural leader, yet he had chosen to forego the social life of a band.

Frances cleared the bowls from the table and Firekeeper handed around his pipe, keeping it filled with tobacco. Everybody except Frances and Stands Early smoked. Smoking was always done leisurely. It could not be hurried without overheating the pipe bowl. The atmosphere in the trading house became calm as they waited their turns with the pipe.

"What have you heard about our plans to drive a herd of horses to Fort Union?" Blue Eye asked as the last puffs on the pipe were taken.

Thinks Like A Woman answered nonchalantly. "I saw my father, Sleeping Bird, yesterday and he told me you were against taking a warrior guard with you. Everybody thinks your herd will be too tempting a target. Even a small party of raiders would have a good chance of running off a few horses."

"He is right," Blue Eye answered. "There will always be some men ready to risk their lives to capture even a couple of horses. All they would have to do is startle the herd into running. At least one or two horses would be easy to cut out. We don't disagree with the Broken Ribs' opinion about that."

Thinks Like A Woman nodded in agreement. "Sleeping Bird said you planned to trade for safe passage across the enemy territories. When he told me that, I said it might work."

"Do you think you might join us?" Blue Eye asked, placing the most important question directly in front of Thinks Like A Woman.

Thinks Like A Woman glanced sharply at Blue Eye. "I see you follow the Piikani tradition of taking your time before discussing the most important things. My answer is yes. But I will not come if you take a warrior guard. No matter how many warriors you bring, the Assiniboin will bring more. A warrior guard would be a challenge to the Assiniboin. They would be pleased to accept your challenge."

"That's a good reason not to bring warriors," Blue Eye acknowledged. "But it is not our reason. Sun On The Mountains doesn't believe men should kill their enemies."

"I have heard that about Sun On The Mountains. They say you are Quakers. You have beliefs that are difficult to follow in Piikani territory. All Piikani take pride in the death of their enemies. We are proud of our war trophies."

Alexander and Hannah exchanged a quick glance when their guest used the word Quaker. "Where did you hear we were Quakers?" Alexander asked. "We are known as Sun On The Mountains."

Thinks Like A Woman smiled, his dark eyes full of laughter. "I pick my friends carefully," he said purposefully turning toward Blue Eye.

"But it doesn't matter to me what you believe," he continued. "What you do, is all that matters. Never Seen and I are interested in making a good trade at Fort Union for the horses we will bring. Your plan will work and we will help. Now you know that, we can talk as friends. I will shake your hand." He reached his left hand to the centre of the table where he grasped Blue Eye's hand. "Tell me the rest of your plan and what help you need."

Firekeeper, whose drawing skills were the best, drew a pictograph for Thinks Like A Woman representing the number of scouts, hunters, herders and camp helpers Blue Eye believed would be needed to herd three hundred horses to Fort Union.

"All of us will dress plainly," Blue Eye explained. "Nobody will wear beads or hair decorations or paint their horses with signs that will identify them as anything but Sun On the Mountains traders. That is very important. It will reduce the suspicion of the Assiniboin and the Crow if we don't dress as Piikani. Second, it will encourage everybody to work together on the way to Fort Union."

"Never Seen won't like that!" Thinks Like A Woman laughed, giving Frances an innocent look. "Never Seen likes clothing with a lot of decoration."

Frances raised her eyebrows in mock surprise. "I didn't notice. He had very little beadwork and feathers on his clothing."

"No matter," Blue Eye pointed out, ignoring the quick exchange between Frances and Thinks Like A Woman. "Never Seen will have to dress plainly like everybody else."

Thinks Like A Woman returned his attention to the pictograph. "You won't need this many scouts," he said confidently. "You will need only two."

"Two? Two won't be enough to cover the territory ahead of the herd."

"Two will be enough," Thinks Like A Woman insisted. "Never Seen and I will be enough."

One Person interrupted. "Just you two? I think they should take at least five."

"Don't worry," Thinks Like A Woman replied. "There will be more scouts helping us. Never Seen and I know many Lightning And Thunder living with the Assiniboin and the Crow. You will have enough scouts."

Blue Eye paused. "You have friends in the Assiniboin and Cree camps? Can you trust them?"

Thinks Like A Woman's reply caught Blue Eye unawares. "Can you trust Frances?"

Hannah and Alexander, seated opposite at the table, laughed aloud. "Very good," Hannah said. "I think your Lightning And Thunder friends will make the drive interesting."

"I need to be careful," Blue Eye said authoritatively. "I'm the leader of the drive. The others on the drive may not want to rely solely upon Thinks Like A Woman and Never Seen."

"Are you the leader . . . or are you the worrier?" Thinks Like A Woman said lightly. "You let me know if any of the Piikani worry about our abilities as scouts. Tell them I'll slip into their tipis at night and cut their throats. Then they will not have any worries."

For a moment, The Family held its breath. Seeing their concern, Thinks Like A Woman shook his head. "*Sa*. I won't cut anybody's throat. I have said I will join Sun On The Mountains and, until the drive is over, I will refrain from . . . " He drew his finger dramatically across his throat. "Maybe I'll become polite and serious like Blue Eye. Who knows?"

One Person leaned toward Thinks Like A Woman. "Be careful what you say about the future. Sun On The Mountains has a powerful medicine that changes men's hearts. You may find a new path to follow when you return from Fort Union."

"Perhaps," Thinks Like A Woman answered. "If Blue Eye and Frances can convince Never Seen to dress plainly, it is possible they can convince me of Sun On The Mountains' medicine. But for now, Never Seen and I must make a visit to our Assiniboin and Crow friends. You would like them, One Person. They are very sociable."

Thinks Like A Woman stood. "We will return before all the riders meet here this spring."

"Wait," Blue Eye said. "I'm not sure if it is wise to tell the enemy about this drive until closer to the day we leave."

Alexander reached over to rest his hand gently on his grandson's shoulder. "It will be better if they are prepared. Let Thinks Like A Woman talk with his friends. They will spread the word and by the time the herd arrives, everybody will be anxious to hear what you propose."

"Your grandfather is right," One Person added. "If there is going to be trouble, we will know about it sooner this way."

Before Thinks Like A Woman left the trading house, he held Frances' hands and looked deeply into her eyes. "You are a very pretty girl," he said seriously. "And I see you have a way of capturing men's hearts. But I must tell you that you won't get far hunting Never Seen. He is mine."

Frances blushed and drew in a long breath. "I'm not hunting Never Seen!" she replied sharply.

While The Family all laughed at Thinks Like A Woman's teasing of Frances, Hannah and Firekeeper exchanged a quick look that Thinks Like A Woman noticed.

"Thank you, Frances," Thinks Like A Woman continued with pretended relief. "I'm glad to hear you will be hunting in other territories." He looked meaningfully over his shoulder at Blue Eye who was attaching the pictograph to a ledger.

"I envy you," Thinks Like A Woman whispered to Frances. "I, too, like a smart man."

Frances pushed the Piikani toward the door. "Go! Get Out!" Stumbling as he pulled on his knee-high moccasins, Thinks Like A Woman could not resist one parting jest. "I know some nice Assiniboin men. Wear a dress this summer instead of men's leggings and I'll introduce you. Look for me at the rendezvous!"

Frances slammed the door. "That man talks too much," she said in disgust while The Family stared in disbelief at her unrestrained emotions. Hannah caught Firekeeper with a stern glance just before he was about to continue teasing Frances and he checked his remark.

"Come," Hannah said to Frances. "You and I will walk with Long Fingers and Stands Early to the tipi. Then we will move the horses."

Blue Eye, Firekeeper, Alexander and One Person talked briefly about Thinks Like A Woman, agreeing that his experience with the enemy, his reputation amongst the Prairie People, and his knowledge of the route to Fort Union made him a good choice to lead the scouts.

"I think you have also found your translator," One Person added. "If he has friends in the Assiniboin, and Crow camps he must be able to speak their languages."

"I shouldn't have overlooked asking him that," Blue Eye said. "Even so, I think we should have more than one translator. Negotiating the passage through the territories will be too important for us to rely entirely upon a single person. I would also like to have a translator who could stay with the herd. Have you found anybody else?"

"Not yet. As soon as the weather clears, we will visit more bands. We still need to find at least twenty riders. Firekeeper's drawing was good. If we had more of them, we could show them to the other bands and everybody would understand."

Firekeeper agreed to tear a few more sheets from his ledgers to make the drawings. "You will have to buy more ledgers in Fort Union," he told Blue Eye. "Can you remember to bring them for me, or shall I tear out a few more pages for another list?"

Blue Eye quickly replied, "If I bring you anything from Fort Union, Firekeeper, I will make sure it is wrapped in a stinking old fish."

Alexander smiled as he leaned back on the bed he had built for First Snow. He smiled not at Blue Eye and Firekeeper's exchange, but at the small signs he was seeing in Blue Eye who was finally beginning to temper his seriousness with occasional light heartedness. Firekeeper had been the one who had shown Blue Eye that it was fine to be serious, but he could also be easier going. Now, after meeting Thinks Like A Woman, Alexander felt his own optimism and enthusiasm rekindling after burning low following the deaths of First Snow and Grey Horse. He missed Grey Horse's delight in the Runners, and his excitement when one of the young horses proved to be fast and sure-footed in a buffalo chase. He thought of how First Snow had left her Nahathaway life at Hudson Bay without regret or complaint and had learned the life of a trader. He could often imagine her riding at his side from the North Saskatchewan to the Bow. Other moments he could see her making tipis with Long Fingers, or tending young Hannah and later Blue Eye. Most often, he could feel her moving closer at night under the robes, putting her arm over his shoulders and whispering.

Now, with The Family preparing for the horse drive, their actions working together for a common purpose, Alexander felt the renewal of Sun On The Mountains. The Light,

Alexander was sure, had begun to shine with a clear purpose in his grandson. The horse drive would be a success. Blue Eye would prove to be the new leader, the one who would find a way to deal with the Piikani, the Americans and the British. From Long Fingers and Hannah, Frances would learn to control her energy and, like the west winds that brought the Chinooks to melt the winter snow, she would shine her Light on Sun On The Mountains. And little Stands Early would become a woman and bring more life to The Family. Like the current of the Bow River that increased as each tributary joined the main stream, he could see the power of Sun On The Mountains grow as the strong Lights of strong people were gathering by the Bow.

But only Blue Eye, Alexander knew, could defend Sun On The Mountains and the Piikani from their still-hidden enemies. Blue Eye had encountered the Americans only once and had left the body of Grey Horse high in the poplar trees on the banks of the Missouri. He had returned to the Bow to find his grandmother dying from smallpox. And still he was willing to face the Americans again, this time driving a herd of horses to Fort Union.

With all his heart, Alexander longed to be a shield for his grandson, to stand before him, protecting him when the onslaught began. But Blue Eye's life and the Sun On The Mountains' trade that would be their target, just as it had been his father's life and the family's Philadelphia bank during the Revolution.

Almost asleep on the big bed, Alexander barely heard One Person leaving the trading house, and Firekeeper's steady, deep breathing by the fire. Just as Alexander fell asleep, he heard Blue Eye softly humming Amazing Grace as he opened a ledger.

6 Visiting the Winter Camps

THE FOOTHILLS, WINTER, 1838. The days of the new year were just beginning to lengthen when Blue Eye and One Person began their journey south along the foothills of the Rockies to find the wintering Piikani bands. A pack horse carried their sleeping robes and gifts of ammunition, tobacco, needles, metal cups, and knives. The foothills provided protection for the bands camped along the many rivers and streams flowing east from the mountains. The bands moved their winter camps irregularly, prompted by the need to provide forage for their horses.

It had been snowing lightly for several days, covering the trails along the riverbanks where One Person led his horse as he searched for the paths where the bands brought their herds to water. Although the horses could survive eating snow, the Piikani broke holes in the ice so the horses could drink their fill. One Person and Blue Eye had been following the eastern edge of the foothills, stopping whenever they found a frozen stream crossing from the west. Today, they stopped riding as soon as the sun began to touch the tips of the mountain peaks to the south-west.

One Person turned his horse. "There were some deer tracks across our trail not too far back. I'll hunt there until it begins to get dark."

"I'll set up the camp," Blue Eye said. He pulled off his gloves and began the cold work of untying the packs, picketing the horses and building a fire and a shelter. As soon he heard the crack of One Person's gun, he added bigger branches to the fire to build a blaze that would burn down to coals by the time his uncle returned.

The next morning three Piikani hunters, one a woman, rode into the camp as Blue Eye finished loading the pack horse. All were dressed in dirty, ragged winter leggings and jackets. The men carried guns and bows. The woman had no weapon. Their horses were thin, nervous and head shy, signs of having been treated harshly by their owners.

"We heard a gun last night," one of the hunters said. He ignored Blue Eye, and spoke directly to One Person. "We have a winter camp over there," he said, pointing south to the end of an easterly running ridge.

Blue Eye blew onto the last coals of the morning fire as they talked. The two men continued to ignore him. They pushed their lower lips out in approval while sliding their hands admiringly over the Runners' legs. When he had flames built up a little, Blue Eye asked if they would like tea. "*Aa*," the woman answered, speaking for the first time. The two men just nodded. Blue Eye pulled the lid off the kettle and filled it with snow before setting it on the edge of the fire. As the snow melted he added more until the kettle was filled with hot water. He untied a corner of a pack and drew out a small pouch of tea leaves and a cup.

The woman stood by the fire, most of her face surrounded by a close-fitting fur hat. An ugly purple scar ran diagonally from the corner of her right eye, over the edge of her nose and to her lip — the traditional punishment for infidelity. Blue Eye gave the scar a brief glance and waited for the tea.

One Person brought the two men closer to the fire.

"This is Wounded Foot, and Horse One Spot," he said. "She is Left Alone," he said, pointing to the woman. "They belong to the Big River band. They have just started hunting today. I said we would give them a meal from the deer I shot."

When the tea was made, Blue Eye handed a cup around and they took turns sipping from it. Horse One Spot pulled the cup from Left Alone's hand before she could drink and handed it to Wounded Foot. "You wait until we are finished," he growled at her. Blue Eye's anger rose and he had to steady himself. The ill treatment of Left Alone was not his concern. Nevertheless, he made sure he kept enough tea in the kettle to give her a full cup at the end. He sliced the venison and broiled strips for the hunters.

"I have heard of Sun On The Mountains," Wounded Foot boasted. "I have heard that you don't raid for horses and you don't take scalps."

Horse One Spot sniffed loudly and drew his sleeve over his nose. Dissatisfied with the result he probed his nostril with his finger. "We are good horse raiders," he said arrogantly. "We are true Piikani. We have taken many scalps." He grinned and Blue Eye saw he had no upper front teeth, the sign of a man who liked to fight.

"Wounded Foot and I have so many Crow and Assiniboin scalps that we are going to make a tipi from them." Horse One Spot threw his head back and laughed into the sky, his eyes rolling. "Wouldn't that be a sight? A tipi made from scalps." Then, reaching over, he jerked Left Alone's hat off and held his knife against her forehead.

"Too bad we don't know if she is Piikani or Crow. If she is Crow, we could scalp her." He laughed loudly as he pulled her hair roughly, and then pushed her into the snow. "Ha Ha Ha!" he laughed again. Saliva from his gap-toothed grin sprayed onto the fire.

One Person ignored Horse One Spot's cruelty. "We would like to visit the Big River camp," he said evenly. "We are looking for hunters and horse herders in the Piikani winter camps to help us make a trading journey after the early bull season."

Wounded Foot said they would be welcomed in the Big River camp but he would not lead them there. "We must continue hunting. We are not interested in going on a trading journey unless you bring back whiskey."

"We will not be bringing back whiskey," Blue Eye said.

"Then no real Piikani hunters will go with you." Horse One Spot spat in disgust. He looked toward the Runners. "If you are in the camp when we return, we will talk about trading for your horses."

"These horses are not for trading," Blue Eye answered firmly.

Horse One Spot scoffed. "You said you were traders! All horses and women are for trading."

Wounded Foot stood up quickly. "We will hunt for two, maybe three days," he said. "Not far from here." He jerked Left Alone to her feet. "Bring me my horse," he ordered. She gave him an angry look but obeyed. As she left the fire, Wounded Foot said, "She is a stupid woman but she carries good luck to the hunt. That's why we bring her. We hunted for two days without her and saw nothing. Today we brought her. She says she can hear the animals speaking."

"She was lost when she was a child," Horse One Spot added. "She says the animals spoke to her, telling her where her camp was. If she isn't good luck for us, we will take her scalp and feed her to the wolves!" His amused laugh carried into the trees.

Wounded Foot and Horse One Spot pulled their reins from Left Alone's hand. "Get on," Horse One Spot ordered her. "If you don't find us a deer today, I will put an arrow into you." He laughed raucously again.

Left Alone swung onto her horse with surprising ease. "I will find three deer today," she answered flatly. "Be sure not to miss this time."

Horse One Spot scowled. "She's a stupid woman," he said to One Person. "I will kill her one day." He kicked his horse hard and the hunters cantered back down the trail.

One Person and Blue Eye put out the fire and saddled their horses with a sense of foreboding. If these rough-mannered hunters were representative of the Big River band, it would be very unlikely that they would find any riders in the camp suitable for the horse drive. The trail of the three hunters was clear as Blue Eye and One Person continued south towards the low ridge that Wounded Foot had told them would lead to the Big River camp. At the end of the ridge, they found a stream. There, the three hunters' tracks headed toward open country. Blue Eye and his uncle turned upstream, following the well-used horse trail leading to the camp. One Person said he expected the camp would be small, perhaps as few as ten tipis. When they could see smoke rising above the fir and poplar trees, they met two boys riding beside a herd of twelve horses they were taking to water. One of the boys pointed out the trail to the camp, telling them the chief, Black Bear, could be found in the largest tipi.

The camp was almost silent except for one tipi near the edge where loud crying and shouting indicated someone had died recently. They stopped in front of the largest tipi and called out a greeting. A thin arm pushed aside the entrance flap and Black Bear, a haggard, middle-aged man wearing a summer deerskin jacket and leggings, peered at them for a moment.

"Oki," One Person greeted him, and explained they were from Sun On The Mountains and wanted to meet with the band about plans for a trading journey.

Black Bear replied with a relieved voice. "*Aa*. Naato'si Otatsmiistakists. We have many friends who have traded at your house. You are welcome in the Big River camp but our hospitality can only be small. A man died last night."

"Don't be concerned about hospitality," One Person replied courteously. "We will be stopping only a short time." Black Bear pointed to a grove of trees where they could tie their horses. Other horses had already pawed the snow in the clearing and there were no cottonwood bark bundles nearby for feed. As One Person tied his horse, he stroked its neck and assured it that he would find it some grazing soon. Blue Eye noted the untidy condition of the camp with deer bones, pieces of hide, pack equipment and horse droppings strewn between the tipis. The Big River band, he concluded, would have to move before the spring melt, or the stench would be overwhelming.

One Person pushed aside the oval tipi flap and Black Bear, sitting cross-legged by the fire, gestured for them to enter. A solemn-faced woman sat by his side. He introduced her simply as his wife and did not give her name.

"You will have to pardon us," Black Bear began. "Everybody is preoccupied with mourning." He did not seem inclined to elaborate and, as was the custom, One Person allowed the chief to direct the conversation to the weather, hunting, travelling conditions and news from the other bands. Black Bear's wife did not offer any food, nor did Black Bear bring out a pipe.

After One Person described the conditions at other camps, he mentioned the encounter with the three Big River hunters.

"We met two hunters this morning, Wounded Foot and Horse One Spot. They rode with a woman named Left Alone who they said would bring them luck."

Black Bear asked the direction the hunters were travelling. "East," One Person replied. Black Bear and his wife exchanged a relieved look. "Left Alone is a bad woman," the wife said, speaking for the first time. "Maybe she will not come back to this camp."

One Person looked at her questioningly and then ran a forefinger diagonally from the corner of his eye to his mouth, indicating Left Alone's scar.

The woman nodded. "That was done by her husband, Horse One Spot. She said he was too poor a hunter to take care of her. She often hunted with other men. He believed she was unfaithful. She left his tipi after he cut her face."

Black Bear took over the story. "She then lived with our best hunter, Little Knife, and his sister. Not as a wife but as a hunter. She and Little Knife brought meat to all the camp. Then, two days ago, Little Knife's sister found him dead, stabbed. Left Alone, Wounded Foot and Horse One Spot had disappeared."

"Do you think Left Alone travels willingly with Wounded Foot and Horse One Spot?" One Person asked.

The mention of Left Alone prompted the woman to speak again. "What does it matter?" she spat. "She is his wife. Nobody else wants her. We have too many women in this camp. She claims she has powerful medicine. I say she is not Piikani." Her vindictiveness surprised Blue Eye.

"Before Horse One Spot married her he was a good hunter," she continued, "then he became too lazy to hunt. All he wanted was to go to the Missouri to drink. Now he and Wounded Foot brag all the time about the Crow they have killed on the Missouri. We think most of the scalps are from Piikani they have robbed."

Black Bear lowered his eyes in shame. "They are dangerous."

"You must have enough men in the camp to deal with Wounded Foot and Horse One Spot," Blue Eye pointed out. "They are just two men and you are many."

Blue Eye's observation yielded a small, resigned shrug from Black Bear. "The shame is that I am the leader of the band and I do nothing. Horse One Spot is my son."

Black Bear's next comment, muttered lowly, barely carried across the fire. "They don't care who they kill. That's how they get horses and robes to trade on the Missouri. Everything they can steal from our band and other Piikani, they take south to trade for whiskey."

"Maybe when the Great Circle meets in the summer, you will receive help in dealing with these two," Blue Eye suggested. "If what you have said is right, they are probably travelling to the Missouri now. Your band will be safe for a while. There is no shame in asking for help at the Great Circle."

The despondency clouding Black Bear's eyes touched Blue Eye and he knew the situation in the camp would continue to worsen. Under the protection of Black Bear, Horse One Spot and Wounded Foot were safe from reprisals. Without a strong band leader to resolve the problem, the other Big River men could only hope the two men would eventually go away. Nobody would take responsibility for killing Wounded Foot and Horse One Spot in an ambush, and the two men were probably too wily to be tempted into a straightforward confrontation.

Blue Eye explained the purpose of their visit, giving Black Bear and his wife most of the details of the drive; but he could see they were uninterested. Their own problems had so completely taken over their lives that, until they were solved, other matters would not be given much consideration.

Black Bear promised to tell the band about the drive and the rendezvous on the Bow. Judging from his tone, Blue Eye expected the telling would be done unenthusiastically and that they should not expect to see any riders from The Big River band. Before noon, Blue Eye and One Person were again on their horses.

Before they left the camp, Blue Eye pulled a quarter of the deer from their packs and dropped it beside the tipi entrance for Little Knife's sister.

The afternoon sun shone brightly making the ice crystals in the air sparkle as Blue Eye and One Person rode toward the end of the ridge, heading almost directly into the sun. It was fine weather for riding and Blue Eye expected they would make good distance. However, One Person suggested they make camp.

"This is a good big clearing," he said. "The horses could do with a little extra grazing. Would you mind if we stopped early?"

"Of course not, Uncle. The snow isn't deep and there's good grass underneath."

"There is trouble all around us, Blue Eye, and I don't think we should travel without a supply of fresh meat. I'll try to find another deer in the morning."

Blue Eye wondered why his uncle planned to hunt the next morning, instead of this evening, but didn't ask for an explanation. He swung off his horse, and unsaddled and picketed his horse on a small sapling. "You make a big fire," he called out cheerfully to his uncle, "and I'll take care of the pack horse."

After Blue Eye neatly arranged the camp, with the shelter open to the fire and a good heap of dry wood gathered, he checked the pickets. One Person stretched out in the shelter, his feet facing the fire, and chewed the meat Blue Eye broiled on poplar skewers.

"Black Bear is in a difficult situation," Blue Eye said as he arranged the skewers. "Because of his son, he cannot perform his responsibilities as leader of the band."

"He knows Horse One Spot won't change. It is too late."

"All men can change, Uncle. There is hope for everybody."

His uncle sat up and looked straight at him. "What about all the Piikani he and Wounded Foot will kill? What hope is there for them?"

Blue Eye sighed. "There's no answer to that question. I don't think even Grandfather could answer it."

One Person reflected for a moment. "You will be a good leader of Sun On The Mountains, Blue Eye. You think carefully about responsibilities. Most important, you already know the problems you can solve and the ones you can't. At the Big River camp, I could see you wished to help Black Bear but you kept back. It would not have helped them or us if we had become involved."

"I thought about the horse drive," Blue Eye explained. "I told myself that was where my responsibilities lay."

"Good words, David James," One Person said.

"David James! I never use that name. Did you know Grandfather's friend?"

"No. But Firekeeper did. Your grandmother and grandfather travelled with David Thompson on their first journey to the Bow. He has never returned. Your grandfather often heard traders talk about his travels and the routes he found for them."

"Am I Blue Eye or am I David James?" The question slipped spontaneously from Blue Eye. "What do you think, Uncle? Am I Blue Eye, or am I David James?"

One Person shook his head with amusement. "What does it matter who you are? Thinks Like A Woman is right. All that matters, is what you do."

"That is what Grandfather says. There is nothing in talking about truth, only in living it."

"That sounds good. But this is too much talking for me. Let's rest."

Blue Eye tried to sleep but it was too early. He placed another robe over his uncle who had fallen asleep. He built up the fire, thinking his uncle would like a cup of tea and some hot strips of meat when he woke. The mountains to the west almost hid the sun, and an evening chill had set in when One Person rolled over and spoke.

"What have you been doing while I slept?" he asked.

"Thinking about my first ride with you. Do you remember riding with me to the Broken Ribs when I was small?"

"How could I forget? You were a terrible rider. You held onto your horse's mane all the way."

"I was afraid you would start trotting and I would fall off. I didn't want to have to walk back to the trading house."

"Didn't I promise we would go slowly?"

"Yes. You promised. And you kept your word. You were a good uncle."

"You weren't a good rider. But you were determined," One Person acknowledged. "I liked that about you. I still do."

Blue Eye handed his uncle the cup of tea to drink. "I was lucky to have you to teach me. We went on some long rides, didn't we?"

"Yes. Some very long rides. We brought many bands to trade at Sun On The Mountains. That's why many Piikani know Blue Eye."

Blue Eye stirred the fire with a stick, taking care not to raise any sparks. Then, with his back to his uncle, he asked, "This is another long ride, isn't it?"

"Life is a long ride." One Person murmured. "That is what Alexander said to me when we first met. Life is a long ride. He was right."

Soon afterwards, they pulled their robes over their chins. Despite all his concerns about the Big River camp, Blue Eye slept soundly. In the morning, One Person arose first, kindled the fire and scouted for tracks in the poplars around the clearing. Returning to the fire, he ate a handful of dried meat and began saddling his horse.

"I'm going hunting," One Person said when his horse's nickering woke Blue Eye. "I'll return at noon. Keep the horses close by while I'm gone."

Blue Eye had just finished repicketing the horses when he heard One Person's first shot. Judging by the loudness of the shot, he guessed One Person would be back before noon.

He sat by the campfire, constantly alert to any movement in the poplars or any unusual sounds. He heard a second shot, much closer than the first one. A few minutes later he heard a third shot. It was not like One Person to miss. But killing two deer didn't make sense. They could not carry that much meat.

One Person rode into the clearing a short time later and dismounted, his teeth chattering from the cold, his left hand bare, and a thin bloodstain frozen on his thigh.

"What happened?" Blue Eye asked, keeping his alarm under control.

"I missed the first deer. Then I slipped and my gun misfired when I dismounted to stalk the second deer. I missed that deer, too," One Person answered as he hobbled to the fire to warm his hand.

"How badly is your leg hurt?" Blue Eye asked.

"It's nothing. It barely bled. We will have a look as soon as I get warm."

Blue Eye made fresh tea and handed a cup to his uncle before unsaddling the horse. "I heard three shots," he said when he returned to the fire.

One Person nodded. Blue Eye pulled a robe from the shelter and laid it over his shoulders. Then he helped him pull the legging from his wounded leg. The wound was slight, just a nick, and the cold had already stopped the bleeding. Blue Eye kept the kettle boiling all afternoon, slowly adding small bits of fresh meat until he had made his uncle a thick soup that would be digested more easily than tough strips roasted above the fire. One Person slept on and off and slowly regained his energy.

The loss of his Uncle's left mitt concerned Blue Eye more than the small wound. Late in the afternoon, he began to make a replacement that, although not as good as the original, would be just as warm. At the next Piikani camp, he would be able to trade for a new pair.

By evening One Person had regained his strength and was walking with only a slight stiffness in his leg which, he said, would take care of itself as soon as he began riding the next day. Because they had rested all afternoon, neither was in a hurry to go to sleep and they sat by the campfire talking aimlessly about small things while watching the half-moon rise in the east.

"There are certainly many stars," One Person said for no reason.

"Yes," Blue Eye answered.

"I killed two men today."

"I know. You never miss. Nor are you careless with your gun. What happened to the woman, Left Alone?"

"She is fine. She says she will lead the Sun On The Mountains hunters on the horse drive to Fort Union."

"Thank you."

"It was a problem you could not solve."

7 The Rendezvous

THE BOW, SPRING, 1838. The river's ice broke out in early April. Blue Eye estimated there would be two months when the river would remain low and clear before the ice and snow melted in the mountains upstream and the rivers flooded. The full moon shone in late April and Piikani from the south reported seeing the blooms of the golden buffalo beans. Blue Eye noted the sightings in his ledger and began counting the days until the next full moon when the rendezvous would take place.

"Come with me," Hannah said to her son one morning as he was about to take out his ledgers again to review his preparations for the drive. "I have something to show you."

Standing untied near the porch was a nondescript, lightly built, bay Runner. When Hannah softly called out, "Quaker," the gelding trotted to the railing and nuzzled her.

"This will be your new horse," she explained. "Grey Horse showed me how to train a horse to belong to just one rider. Now I will show you. This horse will take you to Fort Union and back and I won't have to worry." Blue Eye looked dubiously at the small bay.

"I named him Quaker," his mother said, "because Alexander says white people usually don't notice a Quaker. It is only when there is trouble that a Quaker is noticed. Your horse will be the same. Nobody will notice him. Nobody will know what we have taught him. But one day, you might need his help, and he will help you. You will be able to rely upon him, just as you can always rely upon the Sun On The Mountains way."

Blue Eye asked Hannah not to tell anybody she had named the horse. Piikani never gave their horses names; they simply referred to them by their colour, such as the bay with the white hind sock. Hannah smiled at Blue Eye's pride and promised to keep the horse's name a secret.

Every afternoon for the next month, Blue Eye and Hannah worked with Quaker. By the end of the month, Blue Eye could ride without a rein. Hannah worked hard with Blue Eye, teaching him to shift his balance to tell his horse to slow down or speed up. Together, they taught Quaker to stay nearby without being tied but to shy away if anybody but Blue Eye or Hannah approached. Hannah wanted to be sure it would be almost impossible for anybody to steal the horse. He would gallop from the centre of the herd when Blue Eye whistled or clapped his hands.

They only tested Quaker's speed once, in a race against one of Hannah's Runners. Quaker won easily and Blue Eye, for the first time, had the opportunity to tease his mother about her horse.

"Never brag," she cautioned him. "You keep Quaker's abilities to yourself. Never let others know what he can do."

As Hannah sat talking with her son, she wanted to ask him if he ever felt as she did, so filled with life that she could split apart. There was so much, and she contained it all. How could she be as immense as this land, and yet so small? How could she fill the sky with each breath? How could she show her son the Light that shone in everything and everyone?

She said nothing. To understand it, he had to know it for himself. There were no words, and so she never talked with him.

The golden buffalo beans bloomed by the river ten days before the next full moon, the day planned for the rendezvous of the riders. Blue Eye selected a meadow on the bank of the Bow, south of the trading house, to set up the tipis. At Hannah's suggestion, the meadow had remained ungrazed, heavy with spring grass to welcome the Piikani riders. He bought a twenty-hide tipi and four smaller ones and Frances painted them with Sun On The Mountains symbols. She and Blue Eye erected the tipis in the meadow, built a small fire hearth of river stones in each, and piled clean, sleeping robes inside.

"If the drive is to be successful," Blue Eye told Frances as they dragged firewood to the camp, "everybody must become part of Sun On The Mountains. If they sleep in Sun On The Mountains tipis and live together during the rendezvous, when we start on the drive everybody will be thinking like Sun On The Mountains."

Although Thinks Like A Woman and Never Seen had returned once to Sun On The Mountains to assure Blue Eye that their Lightning And Thunder friends knew of the horse drive, he had not seen the pair since, nor had any of the Piikani he asked. Blue Eye confided in Frances that he had begun to have doubts about their suitability. "They are too used to acting on their own. They are going to find it difficult to cooperate with everybody on the drive."

"I think they will be fine," Frances answered optimistically. "One Person says they are different, and that's what makes them the best scouts. If your uncle isn't concerned, neither should you be."

Blue Eye shook his head. "If they are not here for the rendezvous, I may have to choose somebody else. But I agree they would be the best. If they can travel freely in the Assiniboin and Crow territories, they will find water and grazing, and will anticipate complications with the tribes ahead. We don't want any surprises."

Blue Eye didn't mention his concern to anybody else, but each time riders approached the trading house, he quietly asked if they had seen Thinks Like A Woman and Never Seen. It was if the two scouts had disappeared.

A ragged teenage boy and girl, twins from the Elk Seeker band, rode an old horse into the clearing five days before the new moon. They shared the horse, they told Blue Eye, taking turns riding and walking or running. The boy, Born On A Horse, and the girl, Always Running, confidently announced they would be going with the horse drive to Fort Union. Blue Eye told them nothing would be decided until the rendezvous. He introduced them to Alexander and Firekeeper, the only ones home. They told Alexander they had traded their other horse for a summer's supply of meat for their mother. She still owned one good horse to pack her tipi and belongings. They had been helping their mother all their lives and this was the first time they had left her. Their father, Yellow Shield, had died when they were young.

Blue Eye's heart jumped at the name Yellow Shield. That was his father's name, believed to have died more than fifteen years ago. He looked across at Alexander who had a rare, surprised look.

"There was a Yellow Shield with Sun On The Mountains many years ago," Alexander said to the twins. "We heard he died shortly after he left the trading house. Do you know about this Yellow Shield?"

"He was our father," the boy answered. "After he left Sun On The Mountains, he joined the Elk Seekers. He died many years ago on a buffalo hunt."

"Yellow Shield was also my father," Blue Eye said without emotion.

The twins grinned. "We knew that!" Always Running said with a bright smile. "That's why we are sure you will choose us to go with you."

"We will see," he replied, "To decide now would not be the Sun On The Mountains way."

"The Sun On The Mountains way?" the twins asked. "What is that?"

"It is the way of doing things so they will work out the best for everybody. If I choose you because we have the same father, then I am not doing everything I can to make sure the drive will be a success. When I choose, I will choose the ones most suited to the drive."

"Then you will choose us," Always Running replied without hesitation. "Wait here while we get our bows. We will show you how well we shoot!"

The twins ran back to their horse and returned with their bows and a quiver of arrows. "Pick a target," Always Running demanded. "I'll hit it first shot!"

An old cottonwood tree stood about twenty yards away and Blue Eye pointed it out.

Without appearing to aim, Always Running lifted her bow and shot an arrow in one motion. The arrow skimmed the right edge of the tree. "If that had been a deer or buffalo, it would be dead. I only missed by this much," she said, indicating a barely visible gap between her thumb and forefinger.

Born On A Horse raised his bow and sighted.

"Hurry up!" his sister called out. "That deer is going to move before you shoot." Undeterred by this pestering, Born On A Horse took his time, holding the bent bow without any sign of effort as he steadied his aim. "Hurry!" his sister urged.

Still holding the bow, Born On A Horse twisted his head to look at Blue Eye. "Look at the tree," he said when Blue

Eye met his gaze. Before Blue Eye could focus on the tree, Born On A Horse released the arrow and it thunked into the centre of the cottonwood.

"Your shot only scored because you took so long to aim," Always Running insisted. "I could have shot two arrows in that time."

"You both shot well," Blue Eye said, "But it is only a tree and you were both standing. Next summer I'll need hunters who can shoot buffalo from a galloping horse. Will you be able to do that?"

"We could if we had good horses," Born On A Horse claimed.

"Then, come and meet my mother and Frances," Blue Eye said. "They will talk all you want about good horses."

They found Hannah by the river and, when she heard their story, she gave them each a brief hug.

The twins assured her they expected to go to Fort Union. Hannah looked them over. "Well, your father was a horseman. If you can ride like him, I am sure you would both be helpful."

"The twins want to see the horse herd," Blue Eye said to change the topic. "Where's Frances? I want her to meet my sister and brother."

They followed Hannah farther up the riverbank to the prairie where the herd of Runners grazed, scattered from horizon to horizon. "My day herders will gather them before evening," she told the twins. "Two herders watch them at night."

"Are these the horses you will be sending to Fort Union?" Born On A Horse asked. "There are more than four hundred horses in this herd."

"We are only sending two hundred of these Runners. We have one hundred riding horses to sell that are being raised with the bands for shares of the colts, and another hundred that are of poor quality in a separate herd. They will be sold as pack horses."

Born On A Horse asked a practical question. "What about stallions? Will you be sending any stallions from this herd, or will you geld them first?"

Hannah nodded in acknowledgement of the boy's interest. "Good question. The answer is no. We won't send any stallions, only geldings. We keep the best stallions ourselves so we can control the bloodlines. All the others are gelded. The best horses to buy at Fort Union will be the three and four-year-old geldings."

Hannah led them down the hillside to a wide flat by the river's edge where three boys were training young horses to be taken on the drive. Frances, on her white pony, Feathers, was holding a small herd close to where the boys were working. The twins, unlike most young Piikani, seemed to be at ease with Frances' fair skin and they shook her left hand as Blue Eye explained to Frances that the twins had arrived early hoping to be part of the horse drive.

"*Oki*," she said to the twins in her beginner's Piikani, "I am learning to speak Piikani. You are welcome here."

Always Running began to talk rapidly about how they had been waiting all winter to come to the Bow. Her brother nudged her, saying Frances did not understand.

Frances smiled as Always Running apologized. "Speak slowly," Frances replied. "I'm learning."

Hannah took over the conversation and told the twins to watch how one of the boys passed a small square of hide over the grey's back, the first step in preparing the horse to accept a rider.

"Why not just ride the horse into the river where it cannot buck too long," Always Running interjected. "That's the way we do it."

Hannah replied that the Runners learned much more quickly if they were treated gently. "They are more excitable than most horses and if they are not started slowly, they don't become good buffalo runners.

"How many horses will you start this way?" Born On A Horse asked.

"We will have this whole herd started in ten days," Hannah answered. "Before Blue Eye departs with the horse drive, these boys will have ridden seventy-five of our two-year-olds and will have more than fifty of our three-year-olds ready to be finished by a skilled rider. They will know how to turn with a rein, or by a shift in the rider's weight, or with a tap of the heels. The riders who buy them can teach them their own way of chasing buffalo."

"How much for a three-year-old?" Always Running asked. "One that is ready to ride."

Hannah shrugged. "That depends if it is just a riding horse, or a buffalo runner. We get from ten to twelve robes for an average riding horse and thirty or more robes for a buffalo runner."

"Thirty robes!" Always Running exclaimed. "Thirty buffalo robes! The most I have ever heard is fifteen robes. Who would pay thirty?"

"Hunters who want the best will pay thirty," Hannah answered.

"What about the grey gelding?" Born On A Horse asked while his sister continued to shake her head at the thought of paying thirty robes for a horse.

"A grey like that one, just started, would be about fifteen robes," Hannah said. "Grey horses are our favourites and we probably won't sell this one until we see how he progresses. Why? Do you like him?"

"Yes. I can see he is learning without trouble. He is paying attention to the boy and thinking about what is happening. I like horses that pay attention."

"Not me," Always Running bragged. "I like fast horses. One day I'll have the fastest horse in the buffalo hunts. I'll bring down five cows in one run."

Hannah thought for a moment. "I need help getting these horses ready for the drive and since you're here early, maybe you two would like to work for me."

"I would rather hunt," Always Running replied, too quickly for Hannah's liking. She turned to Born On A Horse.

"Could I earn a horse?" he asked Hannah.

"Yes." She pointed to the boy working the grey. "He will earn the grey before the drive departs. You could do the same."

"What would I have to do?" Born On A Horse asked.

"First I would have to teach you our way. Then you would choose ten horses to train. When you can ride each one quietly from here to the trading house, one of the ten will be yours."

Born On A Horse held up his hands, palm forward and his fingers spread. "Ten horses. One would be mine."

Hannah nodded, yes.

"I will try."

Hannah looked to the other twin. "And you? Would you like to earn a horse?"

Always Running declined. "I'll bring you fifteen buffalo robes in trade."

"That would not buy you a Runner that is ready to hunt buffalo," Hannah warned. "You will need thirty robes."

"Then I'll bring thirty," she said with a hint of disdain. "Thirty buffalo robes by the end of the bull season."

"I'll make it easier for you," Hannah replied. "When you bring me fifteen robes, I'll let you choose a horse. If Blue

Eye accepts you on the drive, you can pay me the other fifteen robes when you return."

Hannah told Born On A Horse to ride with her to the herd where they would pick out ten horses for him to train. "We will start today," she said, leaning from her horse to gather a handful of rawhide leads from the branch of a tree. With these looped on her arm, she waved twice, sending a signal to the herder to the west. "I'm telling him we are going to ride through the herd," she explained to Born On A Horse.

They rode through the herd, exchanging comments, until Hannah said it was time for Born On A Horse to choose the horses he would train.

"I already know the ones I want," Born On A Horse replied. He picked two pintos, a grey, two sorrels, three bays and two chestnuts — one with distinctive white front socks and a blaze.

"Very good," Hannah said. "You must have listened carefully to what I had to say. You chose all the horses I liked."

"Who would know better than you?"

Hannah smiled. "I think the chestnut with the socks and a blaze is the one you want for yourself."

"I'll decide when I am finished. But today he is my favourite."

Alexander spoke before the Silence at the evening meal, thanking the twins for coming to Sun On The Mountains, and acknowledging their blood relationship with The Family. Although the twins did not respond with words, their constant smiles told everybody of their pleasure. Blue Eye watched them, intrigued by the way they displayed their emotions so openly. It was obvious they expected to be chosen for the drive.

Aware that the twins had never eaten at a table before, nor used a fork and knife, Blue Eye explained the basics of their use and the twins did their best, laughing at their own clumsiness, and when they had to use their fingers. Soon they had the entire Family watching, including Firekeeper to whom Piikani humour usually seemed to be too forward and without subtlety. However, he couldn't resist the unpretentious twins who found no shame in being playful. Always Running hunched over the table to shorten the distance her fork would have to travel to her mouth, and her braids dangled in the gravy on her plate. When she slurped the gravy from the ends of her braids, Stands Early couldn't control her laughter.

After the meal, Frances volunteered to sing and brought out a rectangular wooden box that she called a thumb piano. The box was made of thin wood, about six inches by eight inches, with a sound-hole cut into the top. Eight metal tongues of different lengths were screwed to a fret and Frances flipped these softly over the sound-hole with her thumbs to produce notes.

"My father bought this for me in St. Louis," she explained. "A man was playing it and my father traded him some coins for it. It is very simple compared to the violins my father and I played in London. They would have been too fragile for us to bring to the Missouri. Perhaps in Fort Union I will be able to buy a violin."

As Frances spoke, Hannah translated for the twins.

"Play for us," Alexander urged, settling back in his chair.

"First," Frances explained, "I have to tune it." Using the end of blunt knife to loosen the screw on the fret, Frances tuned the tongues by adjusting the amount each protruded from the fret, humming to herself. The tongues produced a high, bee-like buzz.

"I'll play the hymn I sang last week," she said.

Her audience waited, avoiding making any sounds that would disturb Frances' concentration.

Frances shook her head in amusement. "Relax, this is meant to be enjoyed. It isn't painful! You look like you're about to be attacked by Crow. The music won't hurt you."

It wasn't until she had completed the second verse of the hymn that her audience began to respond with slight nods and taps in time to the hymn's rhythm.

"The first verse repeats," she said, still playing the box. "I'll say the words and then anybody who wants to, can sing along."

"Amazing Grace, how sweet the sound," she called out.

Stands Early was the first to join Frances, timidly at first but then with more confidence on the second line.

"That saved a wretch like me."

Hannah and Blue Eye joined in for the third line. "I once was lost but now am found."

Alexander joined in on the fourth line. "Was blind but now I see."

Frances sang two more verses and then returned to the first verse. The Family stood up and joined her, remembering the words without prompting. When the song ended, they all looked at each other in surprise, then, with cheers and laughs, urged Frances to play more. She played two faster hymns before putting the thumb piano aside.

"Well, Alexander," she asked, "did you enjoy the music?"

Alexander could not help but share everybody's pleasure. "I never thought I would sing a hymn. I admit it caught me by surprise. I wish my mother and father could hear this. They would have enjoyed your song." He looked around the trading room and saw the bright faces of his family.

"Look around, Frances," he added after a moment's reflection. "In this room we have Firekeeper, a Nahathaway from Hudson Bay; Blue Eye and Hannah who are Nahathaway, American and Piikani; One Person, Long

Fingers, Stands Early, and the twins who are Piikani; you, a British girl; and me . . . an old Philadelphian Quaker. We speak three languages and thought we could talk with anybody. You have shown us another way, Frances. Thank you. If everyone agrees, I think Sun On The Mountains should welcome Frances' music into The Family."

Frances curtseyed, acknowledging The Family's acceptance. Her gesture brought curious looks from everybody except Alexander. "It is a respectful way of saying thank you," she said, blushing as she saw a hint of old Quaker sternness in Alexander's eyes.

"Saying thank you is enough," he said. "We do not need to bow and curtsey."

Blue Eye brought Always Running to One Person's side. "My sister needs thirty buffalo robes to buy a Runner from Hannah. Are there any bands nearby that are hunting?"

One Person shook his head. "Impossible! Thirty buffalo robes before the drive leaves! Even if you could bring that many down, the robes could not be prepared in time."

"Hannah says she will take fifteen now, and fifteen after I return from the drive," Always Running countered.

"If you go on the drive," Blue Eye added, giving her a stern glance.

"Blue Eye says you can make a fast shot," One Person said. "If Hannah would agree to lend you a Runner, you can try. The Broken Ribs always welcome a good hunter who does not want meat. You may get your fifteen robes if one of the families will take your meat in exchange for preparing the hides."

Always Running liked One Person's plan.

"Tomorrow, I will introduce you to Sleeping Bird," One Person offered.

The next morning, Alexander waited outside the trading house for Frances. "Until you came to Sun On The

Mountains," he said, "I did not realize how many of my old Quaker ways I continued to follow. Your music is good. Thank you." Frances rested her head on his broad chest and hugged him, feeling his immense, reassuring inner force. The whole world could lean on him, she thought, and he would not mind.

The weeks leading up to the rendezvous did not bring any more riders to the trading house. Blue Eye suspected the riders were hanging back, watching to see who would be first to join. His suspicion proved correct. Left Alone arrived first, followed by two Elk Seekers. From a short distance, Blue Eye didn't recognize Left Alone; she looked much thinner than he remembered. When she was close enough for him to see her penalty scar, he recognized her and hoped she had come to lead the hunters. Her eerie ability to find game would attract other riders to the drive.

The two Elk Seeker hunters accompanying Left Alone told Blue Eye they rode only with her. If she were one of the hunters on the drive, they would participate.

The Broken Ribs arrived the next morning, led, to Blue Eye's surprise, by Sleeping Bird. "I am pleased to see you," Blue Eye said, greeting the chief. "I see you have brought eight well-mounted riders with you. Bringing them yourself is an honour for Sun On The Mountains. You must believe the drive will be a success."

Sleeping Bird replied. "Don't attribute too much to my coming to your rendezvous. I am only here out of curiosity. You should thank your fast-shooting sister, Always Running, for these eight riders. When she has not been hunting buffalo, she has been talking incessantly about the horse drive. She has convinced these men they will be wealthy heroes if they ride with Sun On The Mountains. I am only here to observe and to advise the Broken Ribs."

Despite the admonishing tone in Sleeping Bird's voice when he mentioned Always Running, Blue Eye guessed the girl's unceasing enthusiasm for adventure must have influenced the sombre chief.

"Sun On The Mountains does not expect anybody to be a hero," Blue Eye said. "We are traders. I will lead the riders to Fort Union and I will return with all of them to the Bow."

Sleeping Bird shrugged. "We will soon see what kind of a leader you are, Otssko Moapsspiksi. Talk does not make a leader. Action does."

"*Aa,*" Blue Eye agreed. "Tomorrow we will discuss the drive. Tonight, One Person and Long Fingers will be roasting meat for everybody. That will give you an opportunity to meet the riders."

He pointed to the four tipis painted with Sun On The Mountains symbols. "These tipis will be shared by all the riders. As is the Sun On The Mountains custom, there is no preference given to any person. In this camp we live as equals."

Sleeping Bird pointed to the large twenty-hide tipi and said, "I will sleep in there. The others can sleep in the smaller tipis." He pulled his belongings from his horse and carried them to the large tipi. Just as he was about to enter, Left Alone pushed aside the flap from the inside, almost bumping into him. He stared hard at her, wondering how best to handle the awkward situation of sharing a tipi with the scarred woman known for her strange power of hearing animals speak.

Left Alone solved the problem for him. With a slight smile that lifted only the unscarred right side of her face, she held open the tipi flap for Sleeping Bird. "I have not chosen a place yet for my belongings," she said. "We can decide together how to arrange the robes."

Blue Eye could tell Left Alone's small gesture startled Sleeping Bird. The incident, although minor, was noticed by the others and set the tone in the camp that Blue Eye wanted.

By evening more than thirty men and women had arrived, of whom Blue Eye estimated twenty were potential riders, the others being children and older observers, such as Sleeping Bird, who would deliver reports later to their bands. Before dusk, the Sun On The Mountains' tipis were full and more had been erected. The mixing of the men and women from several bands established a familiarity amongst the riders as they arranged the robes in the tipis.

One Person and Long Fingers had been roasting buffalo all afternoon and serving the meat to any hungry rider or observer. When everybody had eaten, Long Fingers hung a pot of bubbling stew by the fire. Late arrivals could help themselves to all they wanted. Just before dusk the riders made a final check of their horse pickets, and then Blue Eye addressed the camp.

"Sun On The Mountains welcomes everybody to this camp. You have all heard the horse drive will leave at the next moon. The season of the bulls will be almost over and the rivers low enough to cross. Sun On The Mountains will take three hundred horses to trade at Fort Union. We will also be taking about one hundred horses from the Piikani bands to trade.

"We will not return before the Great Circle. We will cross Assiniboin, Crow and possibly Sioux territory. This evening is set aside to talk amongst ourselves about the dangers and for you to tell me your suggestions. Tomorrow morning I will announce the final plans for the drive. Afterwards, we will have demonstrations to show each other our riding and hunting skills."

This last comment brought a loud, enthusiastic rumble of approval from the riders. "Do you have any of those skills?" a young Elk Seeker called out to Blue Eye and the crowd all laughed. Blue Eye shook his head. "We will see," he replied in a good-natured tone.

Soon afterward, the camp settled down for the night, but not before Always Running had gathered a lot of attention by bragging about her and her brother's prowess with their bows. The older riders listened. They silently resolved to teach the twins a lesson.

The Family joined the camp in the morning. The night had been cold and a light frost glistened on the grass.

The riders and the onlookers gathered by the fire where One Person and Long Fingers served the morning meal of broiled meat and baked prairie turnips. The riders had their bows by their sides. Blue Eye knew they were more interested in the demonstrations than they were in hearing him discuss the plans for the horse drive. By now, he told himself, they would all have discussed the Sun On The Mountains proposal, particularly the exclusion of any warriors. He walked through the crowd to the fire, disappointed not to find Thinks Like A Woman and Never Seen. As he looked across the Piikani faces, men and women and children, he felt himself falter, then he remembered his grandfather's words, speak to the Light in everyone, and he began. The Piikani stopped talking and listened.

"I am going to talk about the drive and then I will answer your questions. As Sun On The Mountains, I am obliged to speak plainly. I will hold nothing back. I expect there will be times when you will not all agree with my plans and we will have to make decisions together. But there is one part of my plan I will not change." He paused to let the crowd speculate on his thoughts.

"The most important thing I have to say is that everybody who leaves with Sun On The Mountains will return with

Sun On The Mountains. If you ride with us to Fort Union, I promise that you will return with us.

"I will not change my mind on this. I will bring everybody home safely from Fort Union. There are no horses so valuable I would be willing to lose one life for them."

Blue Eye paused again, letting the murmurs from the riders and onlookers subside.

"This will be a trading party. Not a war party. We are going to Fort Union for profit. We will return from Fort Union with supplies your families want. We will not return with one stolen horse, one prisoner or one scalp. We will only bring back what we have traded for.

"Our scouts will ride ahead of the herd to find grazing and water. When we approach the enemy's territory, our scouts will bring their chiefs to our herd. We will negotiate the right to travel across their territory. All the agreements will be made by Sun On The Mountains. None of you will be asked to contribute.

"We will need hunters to keep the camps supplied with meat. We will need herders for the horses, and we will need camp helpers to cook and set up tipis. Everybody will be paid equally. The pay for each rider will be the same: whether you ride as a scout, a hunter, a herder or a camp helper. We will need at least two scouts, ten herders, ten hunters and five camp helpers. If more riders come, we will bring more horses."

Immediately, Blue Eye could hear grumbling from the riders about the payments. The hunters thought they should be the highest paid.

"Everybody is taking the same risk," he replied. "The payments will be the same for everybody. The total will be one hundred good horses, shared equally. The fewer who come, the more each will earn. If all of you decide to participate, you will each earn at least three horses."

The grumbling began again. "Wait! See the horses for yourselves," he called out as he signalled to Frances. She lifted her gun and fired a shot over the river. Moments later, Hannah, Born On A Horse and the two young herders trotted one hundred Runners through a clearing and into the river.

"See for yourselves," Blue Eye said as the crowd stood to watch the horses swim the river. "They are Sun On The Mountains horses, all bred to be fast buffalo runners. They will be shared by all those who participate in the drive."

The herd of horses clamoured up the bank and into the meadow. The sight of the dripping, dancing horses drew a hush from the crowd. The alert, finely-limbed horses would have stopped the heart of any horseman and Blue Eye was sure the effect would not be wasted on the riders, many of whom had dreamed of the day they would be able to afford a Sun On The Mountains Runner.

"In addition to these horses,' Blue Eye told them, "We will provide you with suitable mounts for the journey to and from Fort Union. Also, anybody who wants to trade for themselves at Fort Union is welcome to bring up to three horses.

"Riders must accept Sun On The Mountains ways for the entire journey," he continued. "This means you will dress plainly and wear your hair in braids. All riders must treat the tribes we meet with respect — as friends, not as enemies."

A Badger asked the first question. "What if the enemy chiefs don't honour the negotiations or can't control their warriors? What will we do if we are attacked?"

"Then we will defend ourselves."

"Can thirty riders defend three or four hundred horses?" one of the tall, Elk Seekers challenged. Blue Eye recalled he rode with Left Alone.

"Thirty Sun On The Mountains riders can defend a thousand horses," Blue Eye replied, focusing his attention on the hunter who had asked the question. "The Sun On The Mountains medicine will give us the strength to resist those who would steal from us.

"Remember, you, too, will be Sun On The Mountains. If you did not already believe in the power of Sun On The Mountains, if you thought the drive was foolish, you would have not come here today. You already know we will not be attacked. By coming here today, you have already shown that the power of Sun On The Mountains has entered your hearts."

The Elk Seeker hunter did not appear convinced. "I am an Elk Seeker. Not a Sun On The Mountains. Sun On The Mountains can not protect me with words about strong hearts. Only arrows will stop the Assiniboin and Crow from killing everybody and capturing the horses."

"If you believe that, then leave now."

The Elk Seeker scowled. "I have not decided. I will hear more. This afternoon I will see the skills of those who ride to Fort Union. Then I will decide."

Blue Eye turned his attention to the rest of the crowd, his attention travelling across their faces. "You do not have to believe my words," he told them. "You only have to believe the one hundred horses standing before you. If Sun On The Mountains did not have medicine, would it have all these Runners to give to you?

"If Sun On The Mountains did not have medicine, why haven't the powerful tribes of the Prairie People raided our small trading house and captured our horses and killed us?"

Blue Eye's cool composure as he posed the questions calmed the crowd, many of whom had often asked the same questions around their campfires.

"Sun On The Mountains medicine," Blue Eye said with certainty in his voice, "is our Way. That is all. The Prairie People know if they come to Sun On The Mountains, they will leave satisfied with their trade. We will make a fair trade to cross the territory of the Assiniboin and Cree. They will recognize that a fair trade is better than men dying.

"We will show them it is better to trade for one horse, than to die for two horses."

The next question, from the other Elk Seeker hunter, was the one that Blue Eye had hoped would not be asked. "We were told Thinks Like A Woman and Never Seen have already been chosen as scouts. They are not here. That proves the lightning and thunder are unreliable."

Blue Eye scanned the crowd. All he saw was frowns. This question was Blue Eye's first real test. This was a question about his ability to judge men, and was much more important than all his lists of supplies and riders. He took his time answering.

"Thinks Like A Woman and Never Seen will be ready when they are needed. Thinks Like A Woman shook my hand. I accepted. They will be here. That is all I expect from them or from anybody. If you say to me you are coming to Fort Union, I expect you to be here the day we leave, ready to go."

"No good!" the Elk Seeker shot back. "If Thinks Like A Woman and Never Seen are not here now, then we should choose new scouts."

"They are here!" One Person's well-known voice echoed from the back of the crowd. Everybody turned their attention from Blue Eye to One Person. With a broad grin, he pointed out two, stooped old men, one dressed in torn, dirty buckskin, and the other covered by a blanket high over his shoulders. "The scouts have been here the whole time and nobody recognized them."

Thinks Like A Woman straightened up, pulling off his old jacket to reveal his muscular chest and shoulders. Never Seen, his face mostly hidden by a blanket, drew the blanket aside to reveal his heavily embroidered buckskin shirt.

Frances, watching as the two men rubbed the grime from their faces, clapped in relief and delight at the cleverness of their disguises. She had been unable to follow most of what Blue Eye had been saying but she had known that the crowd placed a great importance on Blue Eye's answer to the Elk Seeker's question about the scouts.

As Thinks Like A Woman waved to the gathering, Frances noticed he had two sets of Sun Dance scars on his chest. She had seen Blue Eye's and One Person's single scars and she wondered if the two sets had a particular significance.

One Person spoke, taking advantage of the attention he received for revealing the presence of the two men. "I apologize to Blue Eye for this trick. I recognized Thinks Like A Woman and Never Seen early this morning but said nothing. I told the Elk Seekers to question Blue Eye about the scouts."

One Person led the two Elk Seeker hunters forward. "These are good men and will be valuable hunters on the horse drive," he added.

Thinks Like A Woman stepped beside Blue Eye and, taking his face in his hands, kissed him loudly on the cheek. The crowd laughed as Blue Eye pushed Thinks Like A Woman away.

Sleeping Bird stood up and thumped his tall lance. "I have listened to Otssko Moapsspiksi speak today. I am convinced. If I were a young man I would go with him to trade at Fort Union and I would accept Sun On The Mountains ways.

"But I am old and Blue Eye is young, too young I once thought, but I see for myself he has the medicine of his grandfather, Alexander, and the strong will of his mother, Hannah, and the cleverness of his uncle, Nittsitapi." He paused dramatically. "I'm also glad he does not have his uncle's terrible sense of humour!" The crowd clapped and laughed.

"When Blue Eye spoke, his words went to my heart. I was impressed when Blue Eye said, 'Everybody who leaves with Sun On The Mountains will return with Sun On The Mountains.' Those are the words of a leader who values the lives of his friends. They are words all Piikani should hear.

"As leader of the Broken Ribs, I say that any Broken Ribs who become Sun On The Mountains for the drive will be welcomed home by the Broken Ribs at the end of the journey.

"As leader of the Broken Ribs, I pledge today I will sponsor a Horse Dance for all those who will ride to Fort Union."

A hush followed Sleeping Bird's speech. A Horse Dance was not undertaken lightly and to hold one to protect a trading journey was noteworthy. The Horse Dance would be held secretly, and anyone not taking part in the ride to Fort Union would not be told where or when it would be. Blue Eye glanced over to where Alexander, Long Fingers, and Stands Early were seated on the grass. Alexander nodded approvingly at Blue Eye.

Blue Eye returned his attention to the riders, telling them they should bring their horses, guns and bows to the flat behind the camp where they could demonstrate their skills.

Before Thinks Like A Woman and Never Seen slipped away, Frances caught up to them and thanked them for coming. "Blue Eye was not sure if you would be here," she added.

"We are now Quakers," Thinks Like A Woman responded with a slight smile. "We keep our word."

Frances hesitated, then asked, "Tell me why you have two Sun Dance scars. I couldn't help noticing them."

Thinks Like A Woman looked down at his chest. "This is from the Dance when I found my Piikani spirit," he said pointing to the top scar. "And this is from the Dance when I found my other spirit."

Frances puzzled over this explanation, and Thinks Like A Woman waited for her to understand. Then the answer came to her. "The spirit of Lightning And Thunder."

"Yes."

The spring sunshine had warmed the air by noon. The demonstration of skills by the riders promised to be exciting. The entire camp followed the riders to the flat where they stood by their horses in preparation for the contests. Born On A Horse and Always Running both rode Sun On The Mountains horses that attracted attention from the other riders, much to Always Running's pleasure. The teenagers, although several years younger than the other riders who were mostly in their twenties, were determined to make a good showing. They expected, however, that they would have difficulty besting the other riders in horsemanship as the others had all brought favourite horses to the rendezvous.

Frances and Blue Eye set up the contest, a row of ten, soft poplar logs evenly placed down the meadow. The riders were told to gallop in pairs beside the row and fire as many arrows as possible into the logs. The two Elk Seekers rode first, galloping full speed on each side of the logs and releasing a barrage of arrows. At the other end, they slid their horses to a stop, and galloped back.

"Eight hits each," Blue Eye announced and called out two Round Robes next. These two riders had planned their run and they serpentined through the logs, one turning left and the other right. They guided their galloping horses with their legs and released their arrows from close range, over and under their horses' necks. One scored seven hits, the other six.

The twins rode last. Just before their start, Born On A Horse slipped off his horse and jumped on behind his sister. They galloped full speed to the centre log, and slid to a halt. Using her legs, Always Running pivoted the horse in a tight circle as they fired their arrows. Their first arrows hit the closest logs and, with each spin of the horse, they fired at progressively further logs. Neither twin hit the furthest logs, almost seventy-five yards away. Nevertheless, it was obvious the twins could control the horse well and shoot accurately.

"Six hits for Always Running, five for Born On A Horse," Blue Eye called out. The twins were disappointed with their results but knew they had done the best they could using a horse Always Running had only been riding for a few days.

After the demonstration with the bows, the riders demonstrated high-speed riding by picking up men from the ground and carrying them to safety. Blue Eye, who had not taken part in the first demonstration, fell off while trying to pick up Born On A Horse. "Now we see why you're not a warrior!" an Elk Seeker called out as Blue Eye limped back to the laughing crowd. Blue Eye, calling back, promised not to fall off during the horse drive. He gave Quaker a gentle stroke on his neck and smiled as the crowd continued to tease him.

"Is that the best horse you've got?" another rider called out. "Or is it the only one quiet enough for you to ride?"

Again, the twins showed themselves to be competent but did not shine as much they had hoped. Blue Eye, sensing their disappointment, held a marksmanship demonstration as an opportunity for them to show their skills without horses. He set up two targets for the demonstration, with speed and accuracy counting.

Always Running could not help herself and challenged the two Elk Seekers, saying she would shoot her ten arrows into her target before they could shoot five each. Blue Eye tried to discourage her, but could not. Always Running released eight arrows and hit with seven before the two men scored with their five arrows.

Born On A Horse launched nine arrows before his competitor, a Big River hunter, had launched seven. Holding his bow fully drawn with the tenth arrow, he turned to the crowd and asked them to tell him when his arrow was aimed on the target. Higher, lower, left, right, they called in jest. Meanwhile his competitor shot two more arrows, happy to take advantage of Born On A Horse's foolishness. Born On A Horse turned his head from the crowd and looked over his bow as his competitor's tenth shot skimmed wide of the target. "That's one buffalo that won't get away from us," Born On A Horse called out. Without sighting, he released his arrow. It hit the centre of his competitor's target. "Meat for everybody," he said to his competitor who clapped in admiration and thanked him for helping bring down the last buffalo.

"We won't go hungry with your shooting," Always Running cheered for her brother.

A proposal to shoot the guns drew only a lukewarm response and the demonstrations ended, although several men organized horse races.

"Tonight, after we eat, each one of you must decide if you are coming with Sun On The Mountains to Fort Union," Blue Eye called out before the riders began betting on the races.

Born On A Horse and Always Running rushed to Blue Eye's side. "Does this mean we are chosen? Can we go to Fort Union?"

"Of course," Blue Eye answered. "You were show-offs today, but nobody minded. There is no doubt you can ride and shoot well enough." He paused, then continued, "You are going to earn three or four horses each on the drive. Do you still want to keep your agreements with Hannah about the horses you can earn before the drive leaves? Hannah will understand if you have changed your minds."

Blue Eye had talked to Hannah earlier about this, and she had agreed to release the twins from their obligation if they asked, but admitted she would be disappointed if they did. The Family had always been firm in its Quaker belief that agreements were unbreakable; once they had given their word, they were obligated to fulfil their commitment. Horse trading was always difficult, and Hannah had encountered almost every excuse imaginable, including the discouraging situation of someone lying about an agreement.

The twins looked at each other, and nodded in quick agreement. "We'll do what we promised," Born On A Horse said. "Hannah made a fair trade with us."

"Good," Blue Eye said. As Always Running hurried back to where the riders were preparing for the horse races, "She already knows who she is," he said to himself. Then, as Born On A Horse galloped toward the herd where Hannah waited, he added, "Now Hannah will have someone to teach everything she learned from Grey Horse."

For the rest of the afternoon the riders raced their horses, tested each other's bows and, as Blue Eye had anticipated, became friends. In the evening when the horses were picketed for the night and everybody had eaten, Blue Eye asked if any of them had decided against participating in the trading journey.

"I counted twenty-eight riders today," he began. "There is not one of you I won't welcome on the drive. Sun On The Mountains will increase the size of the payment so each of you will receive four horses."

A Big River hunter stood up and said he had changed his mind. He wanted to go but had recently married. He had agreed with his wife that he would not go if she could not accompany him. Blue Eye responded by saying that they needed camp helpers. "We would welcome her," he added. "She will receive four horses of her own."

"Then we will come," the hunter answered.

Three single women stood up. They had formed a friendship in the camp. "We will go," they said almost in unison and then one blurted, "Maybe there will be some handsome men at Fort Union."

Frances then stood and, using basic Piikani, said she, too, would go. Although everybody had assumed she would go, this gesture and her use of Piikani showed she did not expect special treatment.

"Good," Blue Eye said to the five women. "Each of you, too, will receive four horses. I will give Frances my list of supplies tomorrow. You must tell me if there is something you want that I have not included."

The women nodded, hardly able to believe they would be given four horses just for looking after the camp supplies. They waved to Frances who walked along the edge of the crowd to join them.

"Who will be hunters and who will ride with the herd?" one of the Round Robes asked.

"Does anybody want only to be a hunter or a herder?" Blue Eye responded.

The twins stood up. "I want to hunt," Always Running said with certainty.

"And I want to ride with the herd," her brother said with equal certainty.

"Then that is what you will do," Blue Eye promised. "Is there anybody else with a preference?"

"We can only be hunters," Left Alone said with the two Elk Seekers standing at her side.

Four of the Broken Ribs stood. "If Left Alone is directing the hunt, we will be hunters."

"Then that is what you will be," Blue Eye repeated.

As the rest of the riders stated their preference, the split worked out well; twelve hunters and sixteen herders.

"It is decided," Blue Eye said after the choices had been made. "However, there may be days when the hunters will have to help with the herd, especially when we start and the herd will want to spread out.

"Tomorrow you will choose one horse from the herd to ride and train in preparation for the drive."

The riders were pleased at the trust shown by Blue Eye in giving them a horse each before the drive. The twins exchanged excited looks, thrilled they would have good horses of their own. In all their lives, they had never thought they would be this wealthy.

Blue Eye, just as Alexander had done at the Great Circle, stood with the Piikani Sun and the mountains to his back as he addressed the riders.

"The evening sun is caught on the mountains now," he said. "This would be a good time for us to pledge ourselves to the safe completion of our trading journey." Blue Eye pledged first, giving the riders an example to follow.

"Blue Eye," he began as he faced the twilight to the west, "promises he will bring his friends home safely."

Left Alone stood next. "Left Alone promises she will bring her friends home safely."

One by one the other riders followed, standing, saying their name, and repeating the pledge.

"From now until we return from Fort Union," Blue Eye called out when they had finished, "you are no longer Badgers, Broken Ribs, Elk Seekers, or Round Robes. You are all Friends . . . Friends of Sun On The Mountains."

"Friends!" the riders cheered. "Friends! That is what we will call ourselves."

"Good," Blue Eye concluded. "Tomorrow you will return to your bands to prepare. In thirty days we will meet again in this meadow as Friends ready to begin our journey. Tonight we will have our first celebration as Friends of Sun On The Mountains."

8

The Horse Drive to Fort Union

THE CYPRESS HILLS, SUMMER, 1838. As they promised, all the Friends had returned for the drive after the season of the bulls. As well, five more riders asked to join, and Blue Eye accepted them. The Friends' faithfulness and their belief that the journey would be profitable pleased Blue Eye, but it had brought him an unexpected problem. Instead of bringing a few extra horses to trade on their own account at Fort Union, all the Friends had brought their full allotment of three horses each, adding another hundred horses to the herd of two hundred Runners, the one hundred riding horses, and the one hundred pack and scrub horses belonging to the Piikani bands. Blue Eye kept an accurate count of the horses and their owners in a ledger, anticipating disagreements later.

"Five hundred horses!" One Person had exclaimed when he learned of the new total. "With only thirty-three riders, you will be kept busy," he had warned. "Perhaps you should find more help."

Blue Eye had considered One Person's suggestion but was sure that any Piikani he could persuade at the last minute to join would have been only partially convinced of the trading journey's success and would quit or be uncooperative if trouble arose.

The next change in Blue Eye's plans arose because the Piikani bands wanted a guarantee they would be paid for their one hundred scrubs and pack horses, even if the animals did not arrive at Fort Union, the outcome the Piikani thought most likely. Blue Eye had wanted to return the horses to the Piikani bands rather than guarantee to pay for them, but Hannah was resolute in her determination to weed these low-grade horses from the herds. She bought them on the spot, paying the Piikani in guns and other trade goods. The Piikani griped about the prices but Hannah refused to barter, saying she was paying a fair price for horses on the Bow. If they wanted Fort Union prices, they had to take the same risk as everybody else. The Piikani, still griping, had taken the guns and goods. Blue Eye predicted this trade would not turn out well, particularly if the horses brought high prices at Fort Union. Inevitably, the bands would claim they had been swindled by Sun On The Mountains and should be paid the higher price. After Hannah paid for the hundred horses, the bands arrived with another hundred pack and riding horses and asked to be paid for them as well. Hannah agreed, pleased to see more low quality horses leaving the territory. The herd increased to six hundred horses.

Blue Eye had to make his first important decision the evening before the herd was scheduled to leave. Thinks Like

A Woman had ridden into the camp late in the afternoon and suggested the herd should travel east to the Cypress Hills and into Assiniboin territory, and then south-east to Fort Union. The herd, he had said, should be kept as far north of the Missouri as long as possible. Blue Eye had anticipated driving the herd south to Fort McKenzie first and then east along the north bank of the Missouri to Fort Union.

"There are too many Crow and Sioux raiding parties along the Missouri," Thinks Like A Woman had responded. "North of the Missouri is still Blackfoot territory, but it is easy for raiders to slip across the river for a few days." Thinks Like A Woman's serious tone was unusual. Normally, he took advantage of every opportunity to tease and flirt with the solemn Blue Eye.

"We could make a fast drive along the Missouri with a small number of horses," he had continued, "but six hundred horses are too many to outrun any horse-raiders. With six hundred horses we would have to stand and fight, and you won't do that unless you have no other choice. If we go through the Assiniboin territory, we can negotiate with the Assiniboin chiefs and they will control all their warriors. The Assiniboin chiefs can control the Cree north of the Cypress Hills. If you can get the Assiniboin chiefs to agree to your proposal, they might be able to keep all the horse raiders under control and we will pass through without a fight to Fort Union. There may be Crow closer to Fort Union. We will have to deal with them later."

Blue Eye had studied his scout for a few moments. "I trust your judgement. We will head for the Cypress Hills."

"Good," the scout had replied with a grin. "But don't think your difficulties will be over when you get to Fort Union. Don't forget, my blue-eyed friend, we will be returning with much more in trade goods than many

American traders would dare to transport. Six hundred horses are going to buy you a lot of attention at Fort Union!"

Blue Eye had then told the riders the new route. They would drive the herd east, downstream along the north side of the Bow River to where it joined the South Saskatchewan. From there, they would turn south-east to the Cypress Hills — the entrance to Assiniboin territory. If they could make an agreement with the Assiniboin, they would cross the hills and then veer south-east for about twenty days to Fort Union. If the Assiniboin weren't agreeable to a Sun On The Mountains' proposal, they would have to backtrack to the original route. The backtracking, Thinks Like A Woman estimated, would add six or seven days to the journey.

"Have you decided what you will offer the Assiniboin?" he asked Blue Eye.

"No," Blue Eye admitted. "And I know I should decide. It would be a mistake to leave it too long."

Thinks Like A Woman laughed. "I never expected to see you without a plan," he said. "Maybe you'll surprise me and do something unexpected!"

Blue Eye considered the remark, then answered, "Yes. That is a good decision, to do something unexpected."

Thinks Like A Woman and Never Seen had slipped away from the trading house ahead of the herd just before a thunderstorm clogged the entire Bow valley. Rain poured down all night. At dawn, with the rain continuing, Blue Eye had postponed the start of the drive. The camp became a bog of sloppy, criss-crossed horse trails. Blue Eye waited for two days, looking each morning for any break in the weather that would permit the tipis to be dried and packed. Each day he waited, he knew Thinks Like A Woman and Never Seen would be one day closer to the Assiniboin.

The Friends, as they had agreed, had trimmed or plaited their hair in braids, and were dressed as plainly as Blue Eye.

Here and there he had seen small Sun On The Mountains symbols embroidered in beads on their shirts. On the surface, it looked as if they all were ardent Sun On The Mountains Friends. However, he suspected some of them were hiding feathers and medicine bundles under their shirts. The rain showed Blue Eye their aggressive personalities dwelled only slightly below the surface. A pair of Long Buffalo Robe hunters had argued over the ownership of a horse and had threatened each other with knives. With nothing better to do, a crowd gathered in the rain and began to take sides. Blue Eye stepped between the men and told them they could let the matter be settled by others, or they could leave the camp. Sullenly, the men sheathed their knives and walked away, leaving the decision about the horse to Blue Eye who chose to add it to the herd for trading at Fort Union. He made up his mind that night to start the horses on the trail the next day. The tipis would be packed, wet or dry.

The herd had been unruly at the start, wanting to split into smaller bunches, galloping without warning, and scattering into the brush for shelter when thunder boomed. Blue Eye called the hunters back after the first day, requesting they stay close until the horses settled down. On the third day, when the showers cleared, the herd became difficult to move from the fresh, green grass. They began to travel together on the fourth day, following the lead of a reliable, old dark bay broodmare with a small white spot on her neck. Her inclusion had been Hannah's idea. She had watched the mare dominate the breeding mares and thought she would likely fight her way to the top of this herd.

Only Frances's continual optimism held the camp helpers together during the first, muddy days on the trail when it always took longer than expected to load and unload the wet packs. Necessity and wet rawhide ropes taught Frances more of the Piikani language than the hours she had spent in Long Fingers' tipi. As exhausted as she was, she refused to be discouraged by the difficult conditions.

"Be cheerful," she reminded herself, repeating Alexander's favourite advice when difficulties arose. "Be a good Quaker. Be cheerful."

As they made each camp, the women established a routine and showed Frances the secrets of setting up and dismantling the small, travelling tipis. Frances rode Feathers hard and pushed herself harder to keep the pack horses together. The wet packs galled the horses' backs and the women redistributed the packs each day. The sight of Frances trotting her white pony amongst the pack horses assured the riders ahead that all was well with the camp helpers. When the sky cleared and the women could set up the tipis on dry ground, the entire camp relaxed and the work seemed easier for everybody.

When the horses began to stay together, Left Alone and the hunters rode ahead, searching for game along the Bow River. Blue Eye and two Big River riders stayed at the rear of the herd, followed by the loaded pack horses. Six riders followed the river bank, and the rest kept the herd from spreading out on the prairie. Born On A Horse and a Badger watched the lead.

The journey's first casualty came on the fourth day. A gelding broke its foreleg during one of the many squabbles as the herd established its pecking order. Blue Eye shot the gelding, noting in his ledger it had been a scrub from the Big River band.

On the twelfth afternoon, they arrived at the foot of the Cypress Hills. There was no sign of Thinks Like A Woman and Never Seen.

Blue Eye controlled his impatience to continue moving, accepting that the wait at the Cypress Hills would rest the herd and the Friends. The first blustery days along the trail had, in fact, brought the Friends closer together. They joked now as they lounged by the campfire, kidding each other about their slips and falls in the mud, the cold food and the soaked sleeping robes. Several asked him about how he planned to deal with the Assiniboin, and he replied that he didn't have a plan. Nobody believed him.

The Friends did not care if they had to wait for weeks for the scouts. The hunting was good and there was fresh water. Their exposure to a raiding party concerned them slightly. From their own adventures, they believed a direct, frontal attack would be unlikely. They expected a stealthy approach at night by two or three Assiniboin or Cree raiders who would halter as many horses as they could handle and gallop them into the darkness. Their best defence against this type of raid, the Friends agreed, was the instincts of Left Alone, leader of the hunters. She rode herd each night and recommended half the herders and hunters also ride at night, unpredictably moving around and through the herd while looking for nervous horses, the most revealing sign of a raid. Left Alone slept during the day, the two, watchful Elk Seeker hunters always by her side.

The Friends allowed the horses to spread over the west flanks of the Cypress Hills while they waited for Thinks Like A Woman and Never Seen to return. The hunters had been having good luck in the hills, bringing antelope and deer to camp on each of the previous two evenings. Today, with Left Alone leading the way, the hunters had gone south in search of buffalo cows.

Each day of waiting at the Cypress Hills had made Blue Eye more uneasy. When Thinks Like A Woman and Never Seen had ridden ahead, they had insisted Blue Eye stop at the western edge of the hills and hold it there until arrangements had been made to meet the Assiniboin chiefs. "Do not cross into Assiniboin territory until we return," Thinks Like A Woman had warned.

All morning Blue Eye had been watching the hilltops for the two scouts. Although he trusted Thinks Like A Woman's decision to take the shorter route through the hills, he could not settle his uneasiness, sometimes thinking it would have been better to take the herd south along the Missouri, a longer route but more within Confederacy territory.

"Be patient," Blue Eye told himself. "You made a choice and whatever problems arise, you will find a way to solve them." Riding Quaker high onto the hillside, he intended to keep a close watch on the surrounding hilltops, but he could not help his thoughts from wandering back to the early morning when Frances had given him a warm hug.

"Isn't this exciting?" she had said, leaning her head on his chest. "I never guessed my life would be like this. I should be worrying about being close to Assiniboin territory. But I don't. I'm loving every minute of this journey." Her show of affection caught Blue Eye by surprise, although he was able to cover up any outward sign of its effect. The enigma of Frances had been strumming in an empty corner of Blue Eye's thoughts like the beat to the cheerful little songs she sometimes hummed around the trading house.

Now, the enigma played a little more loudly. That hug had contained more than sisterly feelings and its warmth had been appealing. He told himself to concentrate on the safety of the Friends and the horses, that this was a poor time to be thinking about Frances.

As Blue Eye directed his attention back to the horses, the herd inexplicably began to drift down the hills, as if it were time to return home to the Bow. Before Blue Eye could signal the herders to turn the herd, Born On A Horse, always alert, swung his buckskin gelding down from the north and eased him into a rolling canter to intercept the leaders. The leaders slowed, stopped, gazed at Born On A Horse with their unique Runner intensity, and then resumed grazing.

Without realizing it, Blue Eye had been looking over his shoulder since they had left the Bow, used to having the Rocky Mountains to the west as a landmark. Here, on the grassland, he had to reorient himself with the sun, making note through the day where it was shining on his shoulders. The grasslands felt eerie to him, without the distinctive features of the foothills. Here, unless a rider paid careful attention, he could get turned around, lost. It must be terrible in the winter, Blue Eye concluded, with no trees for fires, and nothing to break the almost constant wind.

Simple hand signals between the herders had been evolving since the first day of the drive, reducing the need to shout over the noise of the herd and the wind. Only a few signals had been pre-arranged; an abrupt vertical wave of either arm signalled immediate danger, and the inappropriate removal of clothing, such as taking off one's jacket on an overcast day, alerted everybody to approaching riders. A bare chest warned everybody to be alert but to remain in place.

Blue Eye enjoyed watching Born On A Horse's skill with the buckskin. Since Hannah had given him the buckskin to ride on the drive, Born On A Horse had lived continuously with the herd.

Today, as he surveyed the hills to the east again, Blue Eye thought about the three day delay at the trading house. Would the scouts expect the herd to be this late? Was it possible Thinks Like A Woman and Never Seen had already brought the Assiniboin chiefs to the Cypress Hills and they had left? The chiefs would have waited for at least two days. Be patient, he repeated to himself.

Several of the Runners nearby lifted their heads and stared up the hill past Blue Eye, shifting their feet as their instinct to flee from danger tightened their muscles. Blue Eye looked up the hill but could see nothing unusual. "Blue Eye," a voice whispered from the tall grass just behind him. He turned. "Don't look for me. Just listen," the voice whispered. "It is Never Seen. Thinks Like A Woman is bringing the Assiniboin and Cree chiefs. They are not far. Go to the camp and prepare for them."

Blue Eye walked his horse down the hill toward the camp, slowly removing his jacket and shirt. None of the Friends responded. But, during the next few minutes, knives were loosened in belts, and bows untied to hang loosely from riders' shoulders. In the camp, women began noting the locations of the loaded guns and slipping ammunition bags and powder into their pockets. To anybody watching from the hills, the only possible hint of unusual preparations was Blue Eye's slow ride towards the camp.

"Never Seen is on the hillside," he said to the women. "Thinks Like A Woman is close by with the Assiniboin and Cree chiefs." He did not have to tell them they were being watched. Nor did he have to tell them to continue with their work. They knew what to do.

From the north, one of the Elk Seeker hunters rode along the base of the hill, his chest bared. He rode toward the camp, responding with a wave as the herders called out their usual, offhand greetings. Blue Eye wondered if the hunter had seen the Assiniboin or had been warned by Never Seen. A few moments later three Round Robe hunters rode into sight, following the Elk Seeker's path. Blue Eye willed himself to stay calm as he scanned the horizon. It would be best if the other hunters and herders stayed away from the camp; otherwise, it might appear to the arriving chiefs that the Friends were assembling for trouble.

Thinks Like A Woman rode into view and waved from high up on the hillside to the east, followed moments later by ten riders. The scout rode down the hill, leading the riders past the few horses on the hillside and then straight through the centre of the herd to the camp where he slipped off his horse. The riders stayed mounted.

Blue Eye recognized two riders as Cree, and eight as Assiniboin chiefs. The Assiniboin were impressively dressed, wearing clean leather jackets and fringed leggings, and with their hair precisely parted on both sides to emphasize a broad, centred swath combed straight forward to the tops of their eyes. Some had beads tied into their swaths, others small feathers. Red and blue streamers fluttered from their lances. The chiefs were tall and lean, and their legs hung far below the girths of their painted horses. Several of the chiefs had beaded circles on the fronts of the jackets and one carried a hide shield painted black with small green circles. The two Cree, probably hunters who happened to be nearby, wore dirty leggings and sleeveless shirts and were much shorter and heavier than the Assiniboin. They fingered their bows nervously. The Assiniboin chiefs waited for Thinks Like A Woman to make the introductions.

"*Oki*. The herd looks well, One Eye Like A Star," Thinks Like A Woman said to Blue Eye with a grin the chiefs could not see. "Was your ride pleasant?"

"*Aa*. We enjoyed riding through mud and sleeping in wet robes," Blue Eye answered as he walked forward to greet the chiefs. "Would the chiefs like to smoke our pipe?"

Thinks Like A Woman translated the request. As the chiefs dismounted, the women took their reins and led the horses to the picket pegs beside the camp. Under his breath, Thinks Like A Woman spoke to Blue Eye. "Be generous, handsome leader. This is the first time the Assiniboin have seen horses like these Runners." He frowned toward Quaker who stood half-asleep, untied, by Blue Eye's side. "They asked why a wealthy person like you would ride an old woman's horse."

Thinks Like A Woman began the introductions. Blue Eye shook each chief's left hand. "Did Thinks Like A Woman warn you that I am Sun On The Mountains and I have customs you will find strange?" he asked. The chiefs looked intently at Blue Eye as Thinks Like A Woman translated his question. The chiefs nodded in understanding and then pointed to Blue Eye's black-flecked, blue iris. "They want to know if your shining eye can see into their hearts," Thinks Like A Woman said with a straight face. Blue Eye ignored the scout's humour and indicated that everyone should be seated. Frances handed Blue Eye a pipe and tobacco. When the chiefs had taken two or three long whiffs each, Frances passed around a pot of warm meat chunks and cups of sugared tea.

Before Blue Eye spoke, Thinks Like A Woman said he had made a promise to the chiefs. "I agreed to sit in the middle of the chiefs," he told Blue Eye as he got up and moved to the other side of the fire. "They trust me to translate but they wish to talk amongst themselves during the negotiations and they don't want me to tell you their conversations."

"Tell the chiefs it is not the Sun On The Mountains way," Blue Eye replied. "Sun On the Mountains has no secrets. Tell him we want you to tell the chiefs everything we say amongst ourselves."

As the comment was translated, a dark look passed between the chiefs. Blue Eye continued. "The Friends speak openly. That is our way." He waved his hand across the camp and the horse herd. "We are Sun On The Mountains Friends. We hide nothing from each other or from those we meet."

The Assiniboin and Cree looked inquiringly at Thinks Like A Woman who simply shrugged his shoulders, as if it were pointless to ask Blue Eye to follow traditional negotiating etiquette.

The eldest Assiniboin chief, Fast Walker, gave Blue Eye a hard, direct look. "We all have something we wish to hide."

"We all have something we wish to share," Blue Eye countered and, as Thinks Like A Woman translated, the Assiniboin chief chuckled in admiration of Blue Eye's quick response.

"Because you have come to our camp as guests," Blue Eye continued, "I will speak first. You have come because Thinks Like A Woman has explained our plan to take this herd to Fort Union to trade."

Thinks Like A Woman translated and the men nodded, indicating they understood.

"Do you think it is a good plan?" Blue Eye asked. The chiefs' faces remained stern, not revealing any sign of approval. They didn't answer.

"Do you think we have valuable horses?" Blue Eye then asked. "You have seen them. Do you think they will fetch a high price in trade?"

The men looked at each other and whispered. "They are good horses," a Cree replied. Blue Eye detected the barest hint of a smile from Fast Walker when the Cree replied, the corners of the chief's mouth curling upward. When the other chiefs looked to Fast Walker for a comment, Blue Eye decided to continue focussing his attention on Fast Walker.

"Yes, they are good horses," Blue Eye said. "Sun On The Mountains Friends will be welcomed in Fort Union for bringing good horses like these to trade." Again, the chiefs shrugged.

"Have you been to Fort Union?" Blue Eye asked.

Finally, Fast Walker answered one of Blue Eye's questions. "Once," he said. "There is too much fighting and drinking at Fort Union. The Assiniboin killed many

Blackfoot but have traded there very little since that day. We will not return. We don't need to go to Fort Union to kill Blackfoot." The Friends standing nearby nudged each other as Thinks Like A Woman translated this last remark.

"Killing is not the Sun On The Mountains way," Blue Eye replied. "We are traders. That is why we have many horses and are many Friends."

The chiefs frowned. "We have heard Sun On The Mountains are Piikani. Is that true?"

"No. Sun On The Mountains lives with the Piikani, but are not Piikani." Blue Eye pointed to the small symbols on the shirts of the women. "See, Sun On The Mountains."

The men whispered again. "Thinks Like A Woman is Piikani and he rides with you," Fast Walker pointed out.

"No, he rides as Sun On The Mountains," Blue Eye said. "Would a Piikani cut his hair short? Would a Piikani sit with Assiniboin chiefs and talk about trade? Would a Piikani bring six hundred horses to the edge of Assiniboin territory and not carry war medicine?" He leaned forward and grasped the neck of Thinks Like A Woman's shirt.

"Look for yourselves. You will see this Friend does not wear a war medicine bundle. He is Sun On The Mountains."

Blue Eye took a deep breath, hoped for the best, and pulled open Thinks Like A Woman's shirt. No medicine bundle hung from his neck.

Blue Eye let the drama of the moment make its impression on the chiefs who began whispering amongst themselves.

"How do you protect yourselves without medicine?" Fast Walker asked.

Blue Eye returned the chief's inquiring look. "When you live the path of Sun On The Mountains, all things are medicine, all things are holy. Life is our medicine."

Fast Walker listened, without responding. Blue Eye, sensing the chief understood this belief but was not interested in discussing it, let the topic drop.

"That is talk for another time," Blue Eye said. "Today we will talk about horses. Would you be willing to negotiate a price to take the herd across your territory to Fort Union?"

He put the question as bluntly as he could, directing it toward Fast Walker.

Again, the men whispered. "How many horses?" Fast Walker asked.

"Fifty," Blue Eye responded without hesitation.

The men whispered again, this time for several minutes. Blue Eye sat unmoving.

"Good horses?" Fast Walker asked.

"Yes, only good horses."

"Sixty horses," a Cree interjected, thumping his fist on his knee for effect.

"Fifty is enough," Blue Eye replied.

"Fifty would be agreeable," Fast Walker said without further whispering. "Thinks Like A Woman said you had already decided on a payment and would not negotiate." He smiled at Blue Eye. "You are a bold young man. I would like to see what you carry in your medicine bundle makes you so sure of yourself." The chiefs laughed.

"Now show us the fifty horses," Fast Walker said, rising from the ground.

"No," Blue Eye said without rising to his feet. "You show us the fifty good horses you will pay Sun On The Mountains."

The chiefs whispered angrily and Fast Walker again sat down to speak. "We will not pay you fifty horses. You will pay us fifty horses to cross our territory."

"No," Blue Eye repeated. "Tomorrow, you will bring us fifty good horses and five riders. The riders will become Sun

On The Mountains Friends and will journey with us to Fort Union. We will trade your horses profitably there."

The Cree scowled. "This is foolish!" they protested. "We will not give you anything. You will give us fifty horses or you will ride back to Blackfoot lands." The Assiniboin chiefs whispered before Fast Walker spoke again.

"We could take all the horses from you now," Fast Walker pointed out, choosing his words slowly and allowing Thinks Like A Woman time to translate. "We might have warriors close by ready to run off the herd. You would be outnumbered."

"Yes. That is possible." Blue Eye replied with equal care. "And some Assiniboin and some Friends will die. Afterwards, parents and children in all the camps will mourn. They will slash their arms and legs, cut off their fingers and cry for days. Some men might only be wounded in the battle. They will be fortunate because, while they limp, they can brag about the battle. They will not be able to hunt or provide for their families, but they will be able to brag about all the horses they captured and scalps they took. Their families will be hungry but proud. Is that how a chief looks after his people? Do the Assiniboin and Cree think our horses are more valuable than the lives of their men and women?"

The chiefs scowled as Thinks Like A Woman translated. Blue Eye continued before Fast Walker could speak. "By raiding our herd, you would not capture the most valuable possession of Sun On The Mountains."

The chiefs looked around the camp. "You have nothing here of value but the horses. Maybe a few things in your packs."

Blue Eye shook his head in disagreement. "What your riders will learn from trading with Sun On The Mountains at Fort Union is more valuable than fifty horses. From Sun

On The Mountains, your riders will learn to acquire all they want through trade. They will learn how to visit the forts and return alive.

"They will learn it is better to trade for one horse than to die for two horses. A man can capture many horses from his enemies. But the more often he raids, the sooner he will be killed. If a person learns to trade, he can acquire for himself as many horses as Sun On The Mountains. He and his friends and his family will grow old together. That is what the Friends who ride with us believe."

Blue Eye looked directly at Fast Walker who appeared unconvinced. Blue Eye continued, the challenging tone of his voice requiring little translation.

"Fast Walker has no reason to believe Sun On The Mountains words. Deeds, not words, reveal the truth. We have offered to take fifty Assiniboin horses and five Assiniboin riders with us to Fort Union. You must decide now if you will take that offer or will watch us turn the herd south to the Missouri."

Fast Walker's creased, sombre face slackened and he rolled onto his back laughing. "Anybody who expects to be paid fifty horses to ride across Assiniboin territory deserves a chance to prove himself. Tomorrow we will send you fifty horses and five riders."

After Fast Walker accepted the arrangement, the Cree left, whipping their horses into a gallop. The Assiniboin were amused by the Crees' haughty departure.

"Those Cree wanted us to join them in a raid against the Blackfoot," Fast Walker explained. "They are inconsequential leaders of two small bands from the north. They wear old clothing and have no pride. We would not have given them any of the fifty horses."

The Assiniboin relaxed after the Cree rode off. Blue Eye asked Thinks Like A Woman to introduce the chiefs to the

Friends who had gathered around during the negotiations. Several of the hunters and herders showed obvious concern about meeting the Assiniboin chiefs, but with good grace shook their left hands in friendship.

As the Friends and the Assiniboin exchanged greetings, Thinks Like A Woman took Blue Eye aside. "Thank you. I enjoyed sitting between the chiefs and wondering if they were going to kill us. Is that the Quaker way? To go to the Assiniboin without knives and bows and ask them to kill us? Was that your plan?"

"That wasn't planned," Blue Eye admitted. "I even surprised myself."

"And that is the only reason it worked."

With the greetings exchanged and more than twenty men and women gathered in the camp, Fast Walker asked Blue Eye to describe how he would conduct the trading at Fort Union. "Are you going to ask them to give you fifty horses?"

Everybody laughed as the chief's question spread through the riders.

Blue Eye smiled, accepting the remark as an acknowledgment, and began to explain how the herd had been graded into pack horses, riding horses, and Runners, and pointed to various Sun On The Mountains horses nearby, indicating the grade of each. The Assiniboin chiefs commented upon the Runners with their much finer heads, alert expressions and nimble movements.

"The pack animals," Blue Eye continued, "will be sold mostly to poorer people and we will accept furs and buffalo robes in exchange. We will be glad to get rid of them. They are the culls from the Piikani herds on the Bow. They don't represent the beauty of our herd. We may get six or seven robes for each of them.

"The riding horses will attract wealthier buyers and we will accept no less than twenty head and tail buffalo robes for them."

"That's a high price for a riding horse," Fast Walker commented. "We would not pay that."

Blue Eye shrugged. "That's our price. There will be many travellers and Indians at Fort Union who have not seen finer riding horses. They will pay our price."

"And the Runners?" Fast Walker asked. The chiefs leaned forward, very interested in the price for the Runners.

"The Runners will start at thirty robes," Blue Eye said. The chiefs shook their heads. "Too much!"

"We will only accept thirty robes in silver and gold coins for the Runners," Blue Eye added, unsure whether the Assiniboin would understand the value of the coins that were the accepted currency on the Missouri. Frances handed Blue Eye a small bag and he poured out a few coins.

"These are dollar coins," he said handing one to Fast Walker. "The Americans on the Missouri use them to trade. Americans will trade four coins for one head and tail robe. You can trade the coins for any guns or goods you want." He held a handful of coins in front of the chiefs.

"I'll show you. Suppose you want to buy a pack horse worth five robes. How would you do that?"

The chiefs and many of the Friends who were watching had puzzled expressions as they looked at the coins in Blue Eye's hand. Blue Eye asked Frances to get his ledger from the packs. Opening the ledger to a blank page, he sketched a horse with five buffalo robes to the right. Below each robe he sketched four coins.

He laid the ledger open on the ground so everyone could see his sketches. Without a second thought the Assiniboin chiefs and the Friends edged closer, shoulder-to-shoulder, forgetting their tribal differences as they listened to Blue Eye's explanation.

"Four coins for one hide. Five hides would be this many coins." He reached over, took Fast Walker's and Frances' hands, and spread out their fingers. Then, pointing one by one to each of the twenty coins sketched beside the five hides, he showed the relationship between the coins and the twenty fingers held up by Fast Walker and Frances.

Fast Walker understood. "One horse, five hides, twenty coins. All the same!"

For the next hour, Blue Eye continued explaining the relationship between the coins and hides, horses, guns, knives, and other trade goods. The most difficult part for Blue Eye concerned the Indians' doubts about the practical value of the coins compared to the value of a knife or a gun.

One of the Assiniboin interrupted Blue Eye to display the half dozen coins he had strung between bear claws on his necklace. He said he had acquired the coins in Fort Union several years earlier. Frances admired the coin and claw necklace, and all the women hurried over to inspect the necklace on the pleased Assiniboin's chest.

Soon afterwards, the sun began to drift toward the horizon and the Assiniboin mounted their horses to depart. "I would like you to bring me some coins from Fort Union," Fast Walker told Blue Eye. "Bring me ten coins," he added, displaying all his fingers.

"What about guns and knives and kettles?" Blue Eye asked.

"Bring those too."

The Friends discussed until dark their arrangement with the Assiniboin and the likelihood of the Assiniboin chiefs delivering the fifty horses and five riders the next day. Several of the Friends half-hoped the Assiniboin would back out, proving their suspicions right. Thinks Like A Woman defended the Assiniboin, saying he had known Fast Walker for many years and did not have any reason to doubt his word.

"I would be more concerned," Thinks Like A Woman pointed out, "with our being able to keep our promise and show them we can make a good trade at Fort Union. If we come back with too little, then we will have a big reason to be worried!"

The next morning, five Assiniboin arrived with the promised fifty horses. While this impressed the Friends, they appreciated the Assiniboin's immediate adoption of the Friends' plain clothing and hairstyles. After the introductions were made and the route planned to Fort Union, Blue Eye suggested each Assiniboin be paired with a Friend until everybody learned their riding assignments and the herd accepted the fifty new horses.

Laughing Boy, the gregarious, handsome son of Fast Walker, asked to be paired with Blue Eye, a request that seemed to bring great amusement to Thinks Like A Woman.

"*Oki*," Blue Eye said as Thinks Like A Woman introduced him to Laughing Boy.

"Lightning And Thunder?" Laughing Boy asked in Assiniboin.

Blue Eye looked at Thinks Like A Woman.

"He's asking if you're Lightning And Thunder," Thinks Like A Woman explained.

Blue Eye caught the humorous glances being exchanged by the two men and realized he was being teased. "No, not Lightning And Thunder," he said in Piikani. "I am a Cheerful Spirit." Laughing Boy turned his mouth down in feigned disappointment.

The route Laughing Boy and Thinks Like A Woman suggested would take the herd across the Cypress Hills, then south along the Whitemud River to the Milk River and then downstream to the Missouri and on to Fort Union. This route, although slightly longer than going directly southeast from the Hills, would keep the herd within Assiniboin territory and away from the Crow territory below the Milk River.

The Assiniboin had chosen Laughing Boy to be their spokesman because he spoke Piikani that he said he had learned from Thinks Like A Woman. He urged the Friends to be watchful for Cree. He believed the two Cree had returned to their camps to recruit warriors willing to risk their lives to capture a few Runners from the herd.

"My father has sent warriors to find those Cree and escort them out of our territory," Laughing Boy said, "but they may slip back before our men find them. The Cree were not pleased to see the Assiniboin making an agreement with Sun On The Mountains. Capturing a few of the horses would help break that agreement. They could blame the raid on the Assiniboin."

The easy acceptance by the Assiniboin chiefs of the Friends' drive across their territory did not trouble Blue Eye. He had made up his mind to trust the likeable Fast Walker and was impressed by his sending his son, Laughing Boy, with the Friends to Fort Union. But, like Laughing Boy, Blue Eye did not trust the Cree.

When the hunters returned to the camp at noon, Left Alone called Blue Eye aside, giving support to his suspicions about the Cree. "The animals are restless," she said. "I sense men watching the herd. I know the presence of the Assiniboin. These watchers are not Assiniboin."

"Stay close by the herd this afternoon," Blue Eye ordered. "There is no time to call the hunters in." He peeled off his jacket to give the warning sign and resumed his position at the back of the herd with Laughing Boy.

With no sign of any concern at the prospect of a raid, Laughing Boy continued riding beside Blue Eye. "The Cree are fools," he told Blue Eye. "If they capture some horses, we will catch them within a day and scalp them all." He had a light-hearted, easygoing manner and when Blue Eye told him that nobody, including Cree horse raiders, would be scalped on the drive, Laughing Boy began to ask questions about the Piikani riders, the trading house, and then told several amusing stories about his own encounters with the Blackfoot tribes.

He and Thinks Like A Woman had ridden together for many years, he added. "He taught me to speak Piikani and Crow . . . and some other skills." He looked toward Blue Eye who shook his head and answered the look with, "No," he assured him again, "I'm not the same as Thinks Like A Woman."

"Nobody is the same as Thinks Like A Woman," Laughing Boy replied.

Thinks like A Woman stopped the herd early that day on a large flat surrounded by low, eroded hills and a few coulees. There, with open sight lines in all directions, raiders would find it difficult to ride unobserved within striking distance of the herd. Thinks Like A Woman and Laughing Boy had a suggestion that the Friends agreed would give them the best chance of stopping a raid before any horses were captured or lives lost.

"Most likely," Laughing Boy explained, "the Cree will try to run off a small herd. They will think there are too few of us to chase them and we will not want to risk leaving the herd unprotected." Twenty pack horses, he suggested, should be allowed to gather into a separate herd and drift away from the other horses. In the darkness, the Cree would not be able to identify the more valuable horses and would assume the smaller herd contained several Runners. Two or three Friends would hide inside the herd, holding the reins of their riding horses.

Never Seen, Thinks Like A Woman and Laughing Boy volunteered to spend the night in the pack horse herd. However, as Frances pointed out, the Friends could not risk losing all three as they were the only translators. Always Running pushed forward and volunteered to take the place of Thinks Like A Woman who smiled at Never Seen and Laughing Boy.

"Stay close to the men," he told the girl who shook her head scornfully and answered, "I can look after myself!"

Left Alone continued to sense the watchers all through the late afternoon and early evening. She told Blue Eye the antelope were nervous and did not want to feed. Whether it was his own imagination or Left Alone's perception, Blue Eye noted an unusual calm in the air.

Always Running returned to the camp just before dusk and told her more cautious twin she would be spending all night hidden in the herd with Never Seen and Laughing Boy. "Those Cree will get a surprise if they attack tonight!" she boasted.

"Your sister will be fine," Blue Eye assured Born On A Horse after she had left. "She will have two good, experienced men with her if the Cree attack. You cannot always be her protector. You ride herd tonight on the buckskin. If there's trouble, I'll be expecting you to be riding a fast horse and holding the herd together. I need you to be focussed on your responsibilities if something happens." Born On A Horse gave Blue Eye a curious glance, half anger and half appreciation, and went to catch his buckskin gelding.

The moon had just risen behind the camp when Left Alone spotted the Cree raiders edging their horses single file down the hillside to the north, staying in the shelter of a narrow coulee. She elbowed Blue Eye and pointed to the coulee. Blue Eye shook his head. He couldn't see the Cree raiders. Left Alone dropped a large rock into the fire. The crack of the rock hitting the hearthstones could be heard across the flat. Instantly the Cree stopped their horses and stood motionless.

Again Left Alone pointed to the coulee. "They will move soon." When the Cree rode forward again, Blue Eye noticed the movement and counted four riders. Their path to the pack horses would take them to where Born On A Horse sat on the buckskin, his back to the approaching Cree riders. Without a word, Left Alone slipped from the campfire and, crouching low, disappeared into the middle of the herd. Blue Eye watched as the Cree moved from the coulee onto the flat, exposing themselves fully for the first time. Their approach had been cleverly planned, Blue Eye thought. With the moon on the opposite side of the camp, their silhouettes could barely be seen against the dark sky.

The four Cree were no more than a hundred yards from Born On A Horse when Blue Eye saw him turn the buckskin to circle the pack horses, riding the horse away from the path of the Cree. From somewhere in the herd, Left Alone had warned him.

The Cree now had an open path to the herd and, with fifty yards remaining, they charged at a gallop, shouting at the startled pack horses, driving them across the flat and north into the prairie where other Cree might be waiting to speed them away to a hidden camp. The pack horses had just broken into in a lumbering gallop, urged on by the shouting Cree, when Never Seen, Laughing Boy, and Always Running swung onto their faster horses and pushed their way to the front of the herd.

In the darkness, the Cree could see the figures galloping ahead but had no opportunity to lift their bows as their horses twisted, jumped and dodged to avoid the moonlit gopher holes and rocks. The three Friends drifted to the left edge of the pack horses and began to urge the herd to the right, turning them in a long circle and up a small hill that would slow them and eventually turn them back to the camp. An unexpected gully, which the horses jumped blindly, almost unseated the three Friends. The four Cree, gaining ground by cutting across the circle, charged straight to the gully. Three of the horses jumped it cleanly. The fourth stumbled, sending the rider tumbling over his shoulder to land with a sharp crack. The pack horses, now circling back to the camp, streamed past the fallen rider. His horse galloped into the middle of the herd, its long rein dragging. One of the Cree stopped to look for his fallen comrade. When he saw the Friends bearing down, their figures outlined by the moon, he turned and galloped away.

Never Seen, Laughing Boy, and Always Running stopped their horses as soon as the three Cree fled into the darkness. They walked their excited horses back to the gully and the fallen Cree rider. After a few minutes searching they found him, facedown, and unmoving. Never Seen approached the Cree, prepared to jump clear at the first hint of movement. He prodded him with his bow and then with the tip of an arrow. "Roll him over," Laughing Boy suggested. "Let's hope he's dead."

Never Seen, knife in one hand, tugged on the Cree's shoulder until the Cree flopped over onto his back. Never Seen held his hand over the Cree's mouth, checking for breath. "He is alive. What should we do?"

"Can you carry him back to camp?" Laughing Boy asked. "That would be the Sun On The Mountains way. Care for your enemies." There was a pause and Laughing Boy said, his voice still filled with light-heartedness, "Too bad he isn't dead. It would be easier if you only had to carry his scalp back to camp."

"He is small. A young boy," Never Seen replied. Born On A Horse rode to their side, dismounted, and looked down at the boy. "Never Seen and I can bring him to the camp. We will let Blue Eye decide what to do." Never Seen stooped over and lifted the boy, then suddenly set him down. "You should carry him," Never Seen said emphatically to Born On A Horse.

"What's wrong?" the boy asked. "He doesn't look heavy."

"He's a girl!" Never Seen answered with a shudder, pushing Born On A Horse toward the limp figure.

Born On A Horse lifted the girl into his arms, tucked her arms by her sides, and walked through the night towards the flickering campfire on the far side of the flat. She trembled as he walked but her eyes stayed closed. By the time he reached the campfire, Laughing Boy had already told the Friends about the girl. Frances and the women carried her into a tipi. The men gave her little thought as they discussed the defeat of the Cree raiders. Blue Eye cut short their congratulations by suggesting that the herd should not be left unguarded.

"She was light," Born On A Horse said to his sister as they rode back to the herd. Always Running didn't want to talk about the girl. She wanted to talk about how she had vaulted onto her horse and ridden almost to the lead as soon as the Cree galloped the pack horses. "I was right behind Laughing Boy," she said. "Nobody could have seen the gully we jumped. I'm surprised more riders didn't fall. I only stayed on because I saw Laughing Boy clear the gully."

"How old do you think she is?" Born On A Horse asked.

"The girl? What does it matter?"

"She couldn't be more than a year or two older than Stands Early," Born On A Horse continued. "Ten or twelve.

Maybe she fell off because her horse was bumped as it jumped the gully."

That night Frances slept with a rawhide rope tied from her wrist to the girl's ankle. During the night the girl tossed and turned, waking Frances several times. In the morning, Frances untied the rope and went to find Blue Eye.

"She is still not awake," she said to him. "What can we do with her? She is a child. I cannot believe the Cree would take such a young girl on a raiding party."

Blue Eye spoke flatly, unconcerned. "Who knows? She may have been somebody's sister, or even wife, and refused to stay behind. They may have brought her to help make their camps. The Piikani often take boys on raids to help in camp and to hold the horses. Why not take a girl?"

Their conversation drew a crowd of men and women, all with opinions on how to deal with the girl. The most practical suggestion was to simply leave her with some food and water and hope the Cree would return for her. Others suggested taking her with them until they met other Cree or Assiniboin who would take her, although they pointed out that the girl, without family, would likely become a camp slave or be sold to the Crow.

In general, the Friends were of the opinion the girl would be a burden on the drive, especially if she did not regain consciousness soon. Until she woke, she would have to be strapped to a travois.

Left Alone, who normally did not take part in discussions that did not involve hunting, spoke strongly. "I know what it is like to be left behind," she said. "I remember waking in the night and being alone. It had rained and I could not see any trails. I could not remember if I had been sleeping. Maybe I was like this Cree girl and had fallen from my horse. I can remember nothing before that night. Maybe I'm not Piikani. I don't know who I am."

The men tried to ignore Left Alone but she insisted upon being heard. "The girl should be taken back to her family. She must become a woman with the Cree. If you decide to leave her here, I'll stay with her until she wakes. Then I'll take her myself to her Cree family."

Left Alone's resolute tone took the Friends aback and they found her ultimatum unreasonable. It did not make sense, they told her, to stop the herd halfway to Fort Union just to look after an injured Cree girl. Nor could they afford to travel without Left Alone. Her warning about the Cree raid had proved her importance.

Left Alone shook her head. She would not change her mind. She would not leave until the girl was awake and could be returned to her family.

"But you aren't sure the Cree we saw were part of her family," Laughing Boy said. "Maybe she won't want to go back to them."

"Then we will stay here until she can tell us what she wants." Left Alone refused to argue. She had made up her mind.

Blue Eye knew he had a serious problem to solve. The herd should be moving again soon. The grass was already low along the flat and soon the herd would wander in search of fresh grazing. However, if they brought the girl with them on a travois, they would be taking her further and further away from her family, something that Left Alone would not accept.

"We must sit in Silence until the solution is visible," Blue Eye told the Friends. "That is the Sun On The Mountains way."

The Friends had never participated in a Sun On The Mountains Silence and were reluctant to waste time sitting. Blue Eye persisted and soon had most of the Friends sitting cross-legged along the perimeter of a square he had marked on the prairie as the first streaks of deep red morning sky began to light the horizon.

"We will sit and think about the girl until the answer comes. Anybody who has an inspiration should stand, say their thoughts, and then sit again. We will know when we hear the right answer."

At first the Friends felt foolish, sitting half-asleep on the grass and saying nothing. Then, as their thoughts settled, they began to enjoy the peacefulness of the square and they let the presence of the injured Cree girl enter their private thoughts. The herders, spread far across the flat with the horses, felt the medicine of the Friends on the square. Blue Eye began to see the girl not as a problem but as a gift to be understood. He stood up.

"I think the Cree girl has been sent to show us we have only been thinking of ourselves on this journey. We have only been thinking of how much we are going to profit from trading these horses. The girl is sent to tell us the profits from this trading journey can be used to help others, not only ourselves." He sat down.

One of the Assiniboin stood. "I have a daughter. If she were lost, I would want her found. I would pray that Sun On The Mountains Friends would be the ones to find her."

As the Assiniboin sat down, everybody turned as the wind blew open the flap of the tipi. The Cree girl walked out, holding her head in pain and crying. Never Seen rose to his feet. While the rest of the Friends watched, he softly spoke a few Cree words to the girl. She looked up as Never Seen put his hand over her shoulder and guided her towards the square. She sat, sobbing, beside Never Seen, holding her aching head between her hands. Left Alone brought her horse to her side, and handed its rein to Never Seen. "Tell her she does not need to be afraid. Tell her we have kept her horse safe for her to ride home when she is ready." Never

Seen spoke to the girl again in Cree and the girl nodded her head. "She understands," Never Seen said.

Left Alone spoke to the Friends. "Our answer has walked from the Sun On The Mountains' tipi. We will know her wishes by tonight. If she wants to return to her family, someone will take her." As soon as Left Alone finished speaking, the Friends simultaneously stood up and went back to their duties, content the drive would resume the next morning and that Left Alone was amenable to 'someone' taking the girl back to her family.

Frances hurried to Never Seen who stood awkwardly with the girl at his side. "Thank you," she said. Never Seen, his shy eyes focused on the ground, whispered again to the girl in Cree. The girl looked up at him without expression. He whispered again and this time gave her a slight nudge towards Frances.

"I told her that she is safe. I told her she could trust you."

Never Seen returned to tend his horses. The other women, including Left Alone, followed Frances and the girl into the tipi. A few minutes later, Left Alone went in search of Laughing Boy to act as their translator. Later in the afternoon, Laughing Boy explained to the Friends that the girl wanted to find her family. She said her head ached but she would be able to ride her horse.

Always Running and Never Seen offered to help find the girl's family and return her to them. Laughing Boy suggested the Friends also send an Assiniboin, White Snake, to assure any Cree and Assiniboin they met that this was a peaceful mission. Never Seen agreed to the suggestion.

As the three riders prepared to leave with the girl the next morning, Blue Eye led a white-faced bay gelding to them. "Tell the girl this horse is for her, a gift to thank her for reminding the Friends there are many reasons we follow the path to Fort Union."

Blue Eye glanced over the four members of the party and restrained a smile. "A Cree girl, a Piikani who doesn't speak to women, a Piikani who speaks too boldly, and an Assiniboin. You should enjoy each other's company!"

As soon as the men and the Cree girl were mounted, Left Alone rode beside them. "Tell the girl she will never be left behind again," she said. "Tell her this medicine was mine but I no longer need it." The girl stared at Left Alone's deep scar. Left Alone pressed a small leather bundle into the girl's hand and trotted off.

Frances, seeing Left Alone's rare smile, called out to her as she set a pack on top of a travois. "You made a generous gift, Left Alone."

Left Alone stopped her horse and turned back to Frances. "Found," she said, patting herself on the chest and pointing to the herd and the riders. "I am found." She touched her heels to the horse and galloped to catch the hunters leaving the camp.

Born On A Horse could feel the loneliness in his stomach as he watched his sister riding into enemy territory. The twins had never before been separated for more than a few days. He expected that his sister might be gone for a long time. After the riders found the girl's family, they would have to ride hard to catch the herd before it arrived at Fort Union. He cantered the buckskin up the hillside to where he could watch and wave as long as possible to his sister. The previous evening he had quizzed Always Running to make sure she knew the rivers the herd would follow to Fort Union. Always Running described the route once and then refused to repeat it. "Don't worry so much," she said. "We will be at Fort Union with you."

Although Born On A Horse waved from the hilltop as the riders led the Cree girl north from the herd, Always Running looked back and waved only once.

As much as Born On A Horse wanted to be like Blue Eye who always appeared to be confident that he could handle every problem, Born On A Horse could not stop imagining all the dangers his sister would have to overcome. He knew he would not be able to stop worrying until he saw his sister again. If he saw her again.

He galloped recklessly down the hillside, telling himself the strong prairie breeze caused the tears in his eyes. Minutes later he resumed his position near the lead of the herd, and concentrated as well as he could on keeping the lead mare walking at an even pace.

The Assiniboin chiefs kept their promise and the Friends drove the herd without another incident south along the White Mud River, and east along the Milk River to where it joined the Missouri. These rivers formed the northern border of the Crow territory. Laughing Boy assured the Friends that he and Thinks Like A Woman had cautioned the Crow to stay well away from the herd. "There are a few Crow who are Lightning And Thunder," was all he would add when Blue Eye asked him to explain his confidence.

Always Running, Never Seen, and White Snake caught up to the herd at the junction of the Milk and Missouri rivers. "It was a good idea to bring White Snake with us," Always Running told the Friends. "It took us three days of searching to find the girl's band. When we approached their camp, seven or eight warriors mounted their horses to attack. The girl wouldn't call out to them. If White Snake hadn't been with us, we would have had to retreat. When the Cree saw White Snake was an Assiniboin, they let us approach. Afterwards, we discovered the Cree horses were weak and slow. We could have outrun the Cree, but the girl might not have found her family.

"Even after White Snake told her family we had ridden all the way from the Cypress Hills to return the girl to them, they treated us impolitely, not giving us anything to eat. I'm sure the girl's father took the white-faced bay gelding for himself as soon as we left. We tried to find out why the girl had been on the raid but nobody would talk about it. The girl never spoke, and her father and mother did not seem pleased to see her.

"White Snake says the Cree are very angry about our bringing horses through Assiniboin territory. The Cree are sure the Assiniboin are being paid and they want to be paid too. We left as soon as the girl was with her parents. We rode as hard as we could to catch you, and to stay ahead of the Cree. They followed us for one day."

As Always Running spoke, her brother's anxiety subsided. None of what he had worried about had come to pass. His sister had delivered the girl to the Cree, and had returned unharmed. Always Running had made a good impression on White Snake who was now telling the other Assiniboin about how fast they rode after they left the Cree. "Always Running rode fast. She almost kept up to me!" White Snake bragged. "Never Seen could barely keep up. We had to wait for him several times."

"Maybe Never Seen was the reason the Cree gave up chasing you," Laughing Boy remarked. Everybody knew what he meant.

The Friends continued to trail the herd toward Fort Union and, with the three riders returned from the Cree camps, they stopped looking over their shoulders and concentrated upon following the Missouri. Left Alone, her good humour continuing, led the hunters to a small herd of buffalo where they killed three cows, taking enough of the best meat to last the Friends for the final ride to Fort Union.

Left Alone used her spare time to investigate the valleys of the Missouri tributaries, not sure what she was searching for but content to follow her impulses. On the second day after the men returned from the Cree camp, she sighted the girl following the herd's broad trail and riding the white-faced bay gelding. She circled behind the girl, looking for Cree riders who might be using her as bait to lure the Friends from the herd. By dusk, Left Alone was sure the girl rode alone. When she made a camp, Left Alone approached her, calling out from a hillside far enough away that the girl wouldn't be startled. They camped together, sharing the chunks of dry meat Left Alone always carried. From the way the girl swallowed the chunks without chewing, Left Alone guessed she had not eaten for several days. She wore Left Alone's medicine bundle on a thong around her neck. In the morning, Left Alone led her to the herd.

In the Friends' camp the girl talked openly for the first time. She spoke with a slight stutter. Her name was Crooked Smile. She had not been born a Cree, but an Assiniboin. The Cree captured her in a raid three years ago and that was when her jaw had been broken. After she had fallen from her horse in the raid on the Friends' herd, her head had ached and she felt confused. When the Friends brought her back to the Cree camp she had tried to say she didn't want to return to the Cree, but couldn't explain what she wanted. A day after the Friends left her in the Cree camp, her stepfather had taken the gift horse for himself, and she made up her mind she would steal it back, run from the Cree and find the Friends. The white-faced gelding with the small girl aboard had been too fast for the Cree horses and her stepfather gave up the chase after a few hours.

"I will stay with the Friends," she stuttered, not attempting to hide her crooked smile.

Laughing Boy translated for the Friends, adding that he would be willing to take the girl back to the Assiniboin camps and find her birth family after the herd had been sold at Fort Union.

Blue Eye thought for a moment before answering. "That will be fine. In the meantime, she can help with the camp and with the herding. She must be a good rider to have outridden her stepfather. There will be a lot of horse work for everybody when we get to Fort Union."

FORT UNION, SUMMER, 1838. While the Friends crossed the Cypress Hills, Frances and Thinks Like A Woman had ridden ahead to Fort Union to watch the trading and learn the prices for horses, guns and buffalo robes. When they returned, they brought news that pleased Blue Eye. "The traders and the Indians have already heard about our horses," Thinks Like A Woman said. "We are expected. I think a few Assiniboin must have ridden ahead of us, telling them about our herd. The Sioux and the Crow are already bringing their tipis to the fort. They intend to buy many horses."

"That's very good news," Blue Eye replied. "The more buyers there are from different tribes, the better the prices."

Here, Frances and Thinks Like A Woman exchanged a quick glance. Blue Eye noticed and asked, "What about prices? How much for robes? How much for a well-trained riding horse?"

Frances answered. "The hunting to the south has been good. The Indians have extra robes to trade for horses. We saw a small herd of poor quality riding horses sell as high as twenty robes each. Packhorses are scarcer than we thought and are bringing up to ten robes. There are a lot of Crow at the fort. They are already talking about the Runners."

"We should be able to do well," Blue Eye commented. "What about the Runners? What is the minimum price we should set?"

"That is difficult," Frances said. "Perhaps fifty robes. Maybe more. But the Indians we talked to said they would only trade robes for horses. They didn't have many coins."

"What about the men in the fort? Do they have coins?"

"Some, but I don't think they have enough. We heard they almost always trade for robes and furs with the Indians. Sometimes they will trade a little in coins with the white trappers and independent traders who come to the fort."

"Then they will have to get some," Blue Eye said. "We cannot carry goods worth six hundred horses all the way back to the Bow. We would need to buy back half the horses to pack the goods."

9 THE AUCTION

FORT UNION, SUMMER, 1838. The Friends drove the horses into a valley about an hour's ride from the fort and began sorting them into three herds; pack horses, riding horses and Runners. After almost two months on the trail, the horses were hard-muscled and lean. The camp helpers set up the tipis by a stream and searched the prairie ravines for firewood and buffalo chips. The days and evenings were too warm for fires other than for cooking and the scarcity of fuel was not a problem.

The Friends had talked often during the journey about the prices for the horses and were anxious to see if Blue Eye could live up to his promises.

"We must sell the horses together, as Sun On The Mountains Friends," he told them. "Not as Piikani or Assiniboin. We must not compete against each other and lower our prices. These are good horses, better horses than these buyers will get anywhere else, and we deserve to be paid well.

"That's why the sale will be an auction, like the one Grey Horse and I held at Fort McKenzie.

"This afternoon, we will show some of our Runners around the fort to attract the buyers. We will build up our prices by offering the pack horses first and then the riding horses. On the day we sell the Runners, the buyers will be prepared to pay a high price.

"Expect to see a lot of Indians and white traders coming here to examine our horses. Tell everybody to come back for the auctions. Don't discuss prices or agree to sell any horse — no matter what you are offered."

Fort Union's two military-style stone bastions hung over the fort's high picket walls, glaring at the Missouri to the south-east and the river flat to the northwest where hundreds of Crow, Sioux, Assiniboin, and Blackfoot tipis sprawled across the neutral ground. A steamboat, tied on the riverbank in front of the fort, swayed in the Missouri current. When Blue Eye, Thinks Like A Woman, White Snake, Born On A Horse, and Left Alone rode onto the flat leading five Runners, the tipis emptied and an excited crowd gathered. Several Assiniboin known to White Snake greeted him, teasing him about his plain dress and hair.

"I may not be handsome, but these Runners are," he retorted, silencing the men. "Too bad you cannot afford to ride a beautiful horse like this," he called out, holding high the lead rein of the dark grey Runner skittering beside him.

Thinks Like A Woman led the five riders to the principal camps of each tribe. As they stopped at each chief's tipi to explain how the horses would be auctioned, the chiefs asked if the Runners could be purchased beforehand.

"No," the Friends replied. "We want everybody to have an equal opportunity to bid. That's the fairest."

The chiefs understood the sale procedure but were shocked when the Friends told them the minimum bid for a Runner would be two hundred dollars, in silver or gold coins, the equivalent of fifty robes. Blue Eye warned them the Friends would not accept paper money, only coins.

The use of dollars evoked long discussions ending with the prospective buyers anxious to acquire coins from the fort. "Don't expect the fort to have enough coins for everybody," he added. "You may have to trade robes at the forts further south to acquire the coins. We will delay the sales until you have time to trade for the coins you will need."

As the Friends moved between the tribal camps, they encouraged spectators to visit the Sun On The Mountains' camp. "You are all welcome," they said, "to come to our camp and see the horses before the sales begin."

Several buyers tried to ridicule the Friends' high prices for the Runners. White Snake, who enjoyed the attention and the bantering, replied to the loud remarks made by a Sarcee hunter travelling with a Blackfoot band. "Yes. It is a high price," White Snake called back. "A poor hunter like you should come to the earlier sales. Maybe you can afford to ride one of our pack horses."

Blue Eye gave White Snake a sharp glance when the remark brought a stormy scowl to the Sarcee's face.

"Don't brag too much," Blue Eye cautioned. "We are here to sell horses, not to start arguments. Be agreeable. We are here for a reason." Thinks Like A Woman laughed at Blue Eye's calculating attitude. "You plot like an Assiniboin!"

The fort sent an emissary, a stocky, middle-aged Negro wearing a smart, grey jacket, to invite the Friends to the fort for an inspection of the horses. Blue Eye shook his head. "Thank you for the invitation," he answered in English, startling the emissary who hadn't expected an Indian to speak the fort's language so fluently. "We have brought only a few of our horses here today," Blue Eye added. "Please invite the men from the fort to visit our camp tomorrow to inspect all of our horses."

The emissary laughed. "Men from the fort do not visit Indian camps to trade. The Indians come to the fort."

Blue Eye nodded. "Sun On The Mountains treats all people equally. The men from the fort can come to the flat now to see these five Runners, just like these other men are doing, or they can accept our invitation to visit our camp tomorrow with everybody else."

The emissary raised his eyebrows in amusement. "It will be interesting to pass that message along. But don't expect anybody from the fort to take up your invitation."

In the morning, Sioux, Crow, Assiniboin and Blackfoot rambled between the fort and the Sun On The Mountains' camp, arguing amongst themselves about the value of the horses. In the afternoon, the men from the fort arrived in military style with the head trader, George Lively, following the emissary who carried an American Fur Company red white and blue banner. Three armed men followed behind Lively.

Lively, a tall, fair-haired man with an autocratic manner that irritated the Friends, stayed mounted on his horse and demanded a tour of the herds. He spoke in a long, drawn-out way that Blue Eye had never heard at Fort McKenzie or at Fort Edmonton. Frances, welcoming the opportunity to speak English, offered to show Lively the herd.

"No," Lively insisted, dismissing her with an abrupt wave. "I understand there is an Indian here with an unusual blue eye who speaks English." His 'I' sounded more like 'Ahh' to Blue Eye. When Blue Eye stepped forward to speak to Lively, the trader interrupted him. "You are the chief, aren't you? My emissary said you spoke English. I want you to escort me. I will not be led by a woman."

For a moment, Blue Eye's temper rose. "I am not the chief. We are all equal. We are Sun On The Mountains Friends. Frances is a Sun On The Mountains Friend and she can show you the horses as well as anybody. If you need help valuing the horses, then I will assist you."

Lively's pale skin turned crimson at the subtle insult. His three armed escorts and the emissary grinned behind his back. "I can do my own damn valuing," Lively growled.

Frances mounted Feathers. "Which do you prefer to be shown first; the pack horses, the riding horses, or the Runners?"

"I want to see all of them," Lively replied. "I will give my opinion soon."

When Frances returned with Lively and his followers an hour later, Lively glared hard at Blue Eye. "I don't know what manner of men you and your tribe are. Sun On The Mountains Friends means nothing to me. I have never heard of you. However, I offer my compliments on your horse herd, particularly the Runners. The pack animals are of no special value. Most of the riding horses are above average and a few look to be outstanding. However, I have not seen any buffalo horses at the fort to match the Runners."

"Thank you," Blue Eye replied. "As regards the Sun On The Mountains Friends, it does not matter who or what we are. All that matters is that we are here to sell horses. We bring good, sound horses and we expect fair prices. There is nothing else about us that should interest you."

"Is that so? I disagree. There is much about you that interests me." Lively pursed his lips. "You speak in a way I have not heard for years. I have one question, however. The woman told me you would only sell the Runners for gold and silver coins, at a minimum of two hundred dollars per horse." Blue Eye nodded in agreement, and then Lively continued.

"I do not doubt the horses are fair value, but with two hundred Runners to sell, you are asking for $40,000. It's an enormous sum, even for the American Fur Company. Last year we only stocked $30,000 in goods at Fort McKenzie. I don't think there is $40,000 in silver and gold within three hundred miles of the fort. You cannot expect to sell all the Runners for cash."

"Cash? Is that another word for coins?"

"My word, you are a different soul. You know enough to sell horses for $40,000 but you don't know the word cash. That is a word for coins, and for paper money. "

"We will only take coins," Blue Eye replied, ignoring Lively's references to his soul. "The British traders will not accept American paper money. Your company will have to supply the coins for the Indians. You have a steamboat at your dock. I suggest you send it down the Missouri to bring back coins from your other forts. In the meantime, the Indians will gather their robes and furs to trade for coins when the steamboat returns. You will benefit from the extra trade, the Indians will be able to buy the horses, and the Sun On The Mountains Friends will be paid."

Blue Eye imagined Lively's fingers twitching as he calculated his profits on the $40,000 in robes and furs the Indians would trade at the fort to acquire coins.

"How old are you?" Lively asked.

"Eighteen," Blue Eye answered.

"You already have the way of the world about you," Lively replied.

"I have the Sun On The Mountains way," Blue Eye countered.

"Perhaps one day you will tell me about your way. In the meantime, we have an agreement. Your plan to bring coins here from the other forts will work."

"But only if you trade fairly with the Indians for the coins," Blue Eye interjected. "You will have the only large supply of coins in the area and it will be a temptation for you to take advantage of the situation. Of course, no coins or robes will be traded for whiskey."

Lively returned Blue Eye's steady, direct look without flinching. "Interesting thoughts," he said, more to himself than to Blue Eye. "I agree. You will have to delay the sale of the Runners until the steamboat can make the trip down the river and return with the coins."

"We will tell everybody the auction of the Runners will take place two days after the steamboat returns," Blue Eye assured him. "That will give all the Indians the time to bring their robes and furs to the fort. To keep everybody's interest, we will auction the pack horses five days from today, and the riding horses three days later."

Blue Eye continued. "Sun On The Mountains would welcome the opportunity to learn how trading takes place in Fort Union. When the steamboat returns, will you take three Friends into the fort and show them how you trade the coins for the robes and furs?"

Lively stiffened. To have Indians observing firsthand how he calculated trade values would be troublesome, and to have the company's trade in illegal whiskey halted would be even more stifling. Nevertheless, the profits on $40,000 in robes would more than compensate him for the terms Blue Eye imposed.

"Of course," Lively replied. "The presence of your men in the fort is acceptable."

"I did not say men," Blue Eye pointed out. "I said Friends. Men and women."

"Oh! My mistake," Lively apologized. "Perhaps one or two of my people from the fort could stay in your camp?"

"Of course," Blue Eye responded. "Men or women?"

"A Negro," Lively answered, pointing to his emissary, "His name is Henry. I will also send a clerk."

Blue Eye walked to the side of Lively's horse. "I will explain to the chiefs how they will be able to exchange their robes and furs and anything else of value for coins," Lively said as Henry handed him his horse's reins.

"Tell me," Blue Eye asked Lively in a low voice, "do you know about music?"

Music, Lively answered with sincerity, was what he missed most while living in the fort. He had not heard an orchestra play since he had left St. Louis. He whistled several bars of a bright tune.

"Those are sounds I have never heard before," Blue Eye said when Lively finished. "Is that a song?"

"That's only part of a song," Lively answered. "A long song that brings back many memories for me." Lively's square shoulders softened and his voice carried a weariness Blue Eye had not expected the trader to reveal.

"I have learned part of a song," Blue Eye said. "Amazing Grace."

Lively gave Blue Eye a dark, inquiring look. "That's a song you won't hear south of here."

"Frances taught it to me. She said she learned it on a steamboat."

"Well, your Frances should know better. That is a song many claim was written by abolitionists — against slavery."

When Blue Eye asked about slavery, Lively said it was too complicated to discuss in a short time. "Another time, possibly."

"Perhaps you could help me with something else," Blue Eye said. "Frances told me she had a violin in England. I would like to buy one for her. Could you help me find a violin?"

Lively said he would have the steamboat captain make inquiries along the Missouri.

"Thank you," Blue Eye said. "I want to surprise Frances after we sell the horses."

As Lively led his men back to the fort, Blue Eye wondered if he had made a friend or an enemy in the exchange.

Five days later, the Friends drove the pack horses to the fort's corral for the first auction. Born On A Horse led the horses into the sale corral, and Frances noted in a ledger the price each brought. The Piikani on the Bow, she knew, would insist upon being told the sale price for each of their horses, even though they had sold them to Sun On The Mountains at the start of the trading journey.

The Crow came to the auction with the best supply of furs and robes. The bidding became confused at the start when different combinations of furs and robes were offered in exchange for the horses. After fifteen horses had been auctioned, Thinks Like A Woman halted the bidding to work out a better system. Within a few minutes he and the buyers had worked out a rate of exchange and the sale continued, with the pack horses selling for as high as twelve robes each. The Crow bought one hundred and fifty-five of the one hundred and ninety horses offered, the Friends holding back nine horses to pack the trade goods home. The Crow enjoyed outbidding their enemies and rarely bid against each other.

The prices were almost double what Hannah had paid the Piikani bands for these culls. Blue Eye could already hear the grumbling starting.

Not taking any chances on the neutrality of the territory around the fort, the Crow left immediately with their purchases.

The fort and the tipis on the flat emptied during the sale of the two hundred Sun On The Mountains and fifty

Assiniboin riding horses. This time, the Crow had to bid hard against the determined Sioux who, anticipating the Crow's willingness to pay a high price, came prepared to outbid their enemies. Blue Eye kept back the old, dark bay broodmare with the small white spot on her neck that had led the herd from the Bow. Frances smiled at his sentiment as she watched him tie the mare by their tipi. The twins and White Snake demonstrated the training level of each horse during the bidding. The sale of the first three horses set a minimum price of twenty robes per horse. The Sioux bid strongest for geldings; the Crow favoured mares; the Assiniboin preferred younger horses; and the Blackfoot showed no preference, picking individual favourites and bidding relentlessly on them. The competition, however, was not only between the tribes. Members from the same tribe bid against each other. The men from the fort, too, bid but seemed to have an agreed upon an upper limit of thirty robes. They bought four older horses for a lesser price, but were outbid on younger and well-trained horses.

Frances kept the ledger so there would be no misunderstanding about the values attributable to the fifty Assiniboin horses. That night the five Assiniboin could barely believe six of their horses had been sold for over forty robes each and not one sold for less than thirty robes.

"Your trading isn't over," Blue Eye cautioned Laughing Boy. "You cannot take these robes back to your camps. I don't think Fast Walker and the other chiefs will be impressed if all you bring back is robes. You must exchange the robes for trade goods and coins when the steamboat returns."

"But the fifty horses were a payment to the Friends," Laughing Boy argued. "The robes are yours. That was what the chiefs agreed to at the Cypress Hills."

"The Assiniboin joined the drive as Friends," Blue Eye countered. "All the Friends ride for profits. We will not let anybody return without a share of what they have earned. Fast Walker said he would not pay more than twenty robes for a riding horse. We will keep twenty robes for each horse as our payment. You will take him the profits above twenty robes for each of the fifty horses. Frances has a record in the ledger."

"You are generous," Laughing Boy said.

"No. I am not generous. I do what I believe to be right. Nothing more, nothing less."

The Friends all speculated on what prices the Runners would bring, with guesses ranging up to $500. From the sale of their pack and riding horses, the Friends had accumulated over 8600 robes, a huge pile worth at least $34,000 that had to be covered and stored until they could be loaded on the steamboat. The Friends were thankful they had decided not to accept robes or furs for the Runners. "We would have to hire our own steamboat to deliver all the robes to the buyers in St. Louis," Frances joked.

"We could do that," Blue Eye said, taking her suggestion seriously. "Tomorrow I'll talk with George Lively and inquire about taking these robes and furs to St. Louis ourselves and bringing back trade goods."

The others looked at him in astonishment. "Steamboats are for whites," Thinks Like A Woman asserted. "Indians bring furs and robes to the forts to trade. White men load them into steamboats and take them away."

"We are not Indians and we are not whites," Blue Eye replied. "We are Sun On The Mountains." He spoke so resolutely that nobody wanted to discuss the matter further, believing that it would be best for Lively to show Blue Eye the flaw in his plan. Early in the morning, Blue Eye rode to the fort to visit Lively.

"Use our steamboat!" Lively exploded. "What kind of Indian are you? First you persuaded me to send to the other forts for $40,000 in cash and now that isn't enough. Now you have 8600 robes you want to sell yourselves in St. Louis and you want to use our steamboat to take them there." He laughed. "I cannot do that for you, even if I wanted to. If I supplied a steamboat to take your robes to St. Louis, I would be giving up my own profits. I cannot help you compete against my employer."

"Perhaps . . . " Blue Eye began.

"Perhaps nothing!" Lively spluttered. "Forget this idea. I will pay you a better price for your robes than you would receive from any fort on the Missouri above St. Louis."

"We need trade goods to take back to the Piikani and Assiniboin," Blue Eye argued. "Will you be able to supply trade goods for all the robes?"

Lively shook his head. "I seem to be getting deeper and deeper into this with you. Come back tomorrow and I will have a list prepared for you of all the trade goods I have ordered to be brought on the steamboat with the coins. We will make a fair trade. You will have the list tomorrow, as soon as Henry can copy it." Lively paused. "I suppose you can read."

"Yes," Blue Eye answered.

"I suspected that. What's your English name?"

"David James."

Lively stood up from his desk. "I am not going to mention any more in my reports than I have to about my trading with Sun On The Mountains. Somehow I don't think it will do me much good to say a Piikani teenager drove six hundred horses through Assiniboin territory and showed me how to make more money in one season than other company traders have made in five seasons. I would like to take a little glory myself, if that's all right with you."

Blue Eye found Lively's motives intriguing. "Yes. It is all right with me," he said. "You take the glory and I'll take the trade goods and coins." He reached over Lively's desk and shook his right hand.

As they shook hands, Lively noticed the thick Sun Dance scars on Blue Eye's narrow chest.

"There is much more to you than meets the eye," he said.

Blue Eye smiled and turned to leave. Just as he reached the door, he looked back and said, "If you look in the right place, you'll see everything."

As soon as Blue Eye returned to the camp Thinks Like A Woman asked, "Did you get your steamboat?"

"No. You were right. I should have thought it through a bit more. Lively pointed out that we would be taking away his business if he let us use his steamboats."

"What are we going to do with all these robes?" Thinks Like A Woman asked.

"Lively will trade them for the goods he has ordered from the other forts. He will tell me tomorrow what he expects will be on the steamboat. We can decide then what we want to take back to the Bow."

While Thinks Like A Woman went to tell the Friends about the goods arriving on the steamboat, Blue Eye sat by himself, his back resting on a tipi pole. Until Frances had suggested the idea of going to St. Louis with the robes, he had never wondered what a large city of white people would be like. Frances had told him about the different types of stores and the large houses in St. Louis and it hadn't interested him at the time. Now it did. Perhaps one day he and Frances would ride the steamboat to St. Louis and she would show him the houses and the carriages. Mostly he wanted to see where all the buffalo robes went. Just then Frances turned the corner of the tipi.

"Where do they all go? The thousands and thousands of buffalo robes? Why do people in St. Louis need so many?" he asked her.

Frances set down the pack she was carrying and spent the rest of the morning explaining how buyers came from all over the country to St. Louis to buy robes and deliver them to cities like Boston and New York where fashionable people would wear them over their feet in carriages or make them into coats.

"Some will be sent as far as Europe. Just like you bought and sold these robes, others will buy and sell them. The robes will travel further and further away from here."

"I would like to see Philadelphia one day," Blue Eye said. "I would like to see where Alexander lived. I would like to see everything you have told me about."

Frances laughed. "That's far too much for one person to see."

The Friends, with little to do until the steamboat arrived with the trade goods and the coins, lolled about the horse camp for two days, taking turns tending the Runners and occasionally visiting the other camps. Inevitably, with everybody having time on their hands, the proposition of a horse race spread and a challenge arrived from the Crow. Blue Eye refused to consider the proposal, saying horse races between tribes always led to trouble.

Thinks Like A Woman and Laughing Boy argued that they should agree to a race — not to gamble, but to show the speed of the Runners to the best advantage. "It would bring more buyers to the auction," Laughing Boy asserted. "And if we don't participate, they will think we don't believe our horses are fast enough to win. We will look bad if we don't race."

Blue Eye knew the Friends were determined to take up the challenge of the Crow and that, whether he agreed or not, the horse race would take place. "All right," he conceded. "But the race must be held to show our Runners to their best advantage, not for the Friends to gamble away our profits."

Born On A Horse had a unique idea for the race, an idea all the Friends agreed would generate enormous enthusiasm for the auction. Thinks Like A Woman and Laughing Boy rode to the Crow camp and made a proposal that the Crow, tossing their heads back in derisive laughter, accepted after only a few questions

The race would take place in two days. Sun On The Mountains would race five Runners against five Crow horses. The owner of any Crow horse that beat a Sun On The Mountains horse would be able to keep the Sun On The Mountains horse. However, any Sun On The Mountains horse that finished ahead of a Crow horse would be ridden through the auction by a Crow. The race would only be a demonstration, the Friends said, and they would offer no other prizes or accept any wagers.

For two days, the men and women from the fort and the camps studied the herd of Runners, trying to determine the ones the Friends would pick to race. The Crow sent riders hurrying south to bring back the fastest Crow horses for the race. Because the race would be long, from the fort to the top of the furthest visible hill and back, the Crow asked that only horses with stamina be sent.

The Friends decided to first choose the riders for the race and then let the riders choose their own mounts. Always Running, now well-known for her bold, fast riding, was a unanimous first choice and she, in turn, suggested White Snake who had led all the way when they had raced back to the herd from the camp of Crooked Smile's stepfather. Born On A Horse, although as good a rider as his sister, was considered too cautious to race against the Crow who would not hesitate to risk the life of a horse to win a race. Both Elk Seeker hunters declined to race, saying their skills were not suited to racing. However, in a suggestion that showed how they had begun to believe in the equality of the Friends, they asked for Left Alone to be selected.

As soon as the Friends selected Left Alone, Crooked Smile stepped forward. "I will race, too." Then the discussions began. No one doubted the slightly built, young girl's ability to ride but they had all seen or heard of the Crow's ruthless tactics in a horse race and were sure they would purposefully injure Crooked Smile to win her horse.

"I'm not scared," she replied. "I can stay away from the Crow just as well as I can stay away from the Cree." Her stutter had diminished since she had joined the drive.

"If she wants to, let her ride," Blue Eye said. "If nothing else, she'll make the Crow overconfident. If she loses, it is only one horse."

Frances looked questioningly at Blue Eye as he agreed to the choice of the young girl.

The suggestion for the fifth rider, Never Seen, surprised everyone. Everybody had assumed he would be reluctant to attend such a public event as he had stayed well away from the auctions.

"There won't be a Crow rider who will get near Crooked Smile if Never Seen is racing!" Thinks Like A Woman answered, half in jest, having noticed Never Seen's protective interest in the girl. "And if she wins, it will be more glorious for him than taking a Crow scalp."

Never Seen looked down, as usual, as he agreed to race.

Born On A Horse selected a black gelding for his sister, and wanted to give Crooked Smile his buckskin. Blue Eye, however, insisted that she ride his horse, Quaker. When the riders protested at this choice, Blue Eye replied that it was the only way he could be sure she would be safe. Never

Seen, Left Alone and White Snake chose greys. Having heard the legend of Grey Horse riding the first grey mare to the Bow, the Friends believed a grey would always be the fastest. While the others went to prepare for the race, Blue Eye took Crooked Smile aside and showed her how he rode Quaker. Just as Hannah had done, Blue Eye showed her how Quaker would follow her balance. With uncanny quickness, Crooked Smile soon had Quaker responding to her commands and was galloping around the camp scattering horses and riders. Thinks Like A Woman noticed Quaker's unusually alert attitude, and knew Blue Eye was not a man to be underestimated.

The riders inspected every saddle until they found the best ones for racing, light but with solid girths and the best leather and poplar stirrups. The Runners, in peak condition from the long drive, were rested and eager for exercise. While all the Friends watched, the riders trotted and cantered their mounts around the camp.

George Lively nominated himself as starter and as finish judge. He sent his clerks and Henry to stand at the turnaround point to ensure all riders completed the full circuit. Although Blue Eye had grown up watching Grey Horse and Hannah race against the Piikani, the gambling this race generated between the tribes surpassed any he had ever seen. Horses, tipis, clothing, and even captured slaves were wagered. It made little sense to Blue Eye that anyone would bet so heavily that they would be impoverished if they lost. Indians from all the tribes piled their wagers on either side of the finish line. The sophistication of the bets on the race varied from predicting the number of winning Crow horses, to predicting the order of finish.

By entering three women in the race and only two men, the Friends had made a mistake, according to the gamblers who favoured the Crow in the belief that the skill and tactics of the riders in such a dangerous race would be a bigger factor than the speed of the horses.

Interference of any kind in a race was permitted, individually or collectively. Two riders, for instance, could pull another rider from a horse. The Friends gave Crooked Smile last minute orders not to race near any Crow rider. "It is better to lose than to be hurt," they told her. Frances could not help but notice the concern the Friends now had for the girl they once considered abandoning by the Cypress Hills.

The curious crowd watched as the Friends tightened their cinches, intending to ride the race with saddles and stirrups. Even George Lively looked unsure about this strategy.

"They will race better with stirrups," Blue Eye explained to Lively. "They will be able to balance their weight above their horses' backs and their horses will run faster. The extra speed more than makes up for the extra weight of the saddles."

At the starting line, the Crow stripped all the blankets and pads from their horses. One of the Crow rode a vicious, one-eared pinto that kicked and bit at any horse that came near. The ten horses at the start plunged and reared in eagerness. Lively fired his pistol and the horses leapt forward. As predicted by Blue Eye, all the Sun On The Mountains horses and riders got a smooth start while three of the Crow, their hand wrapped in their horses' manes as the only means of hanging on during the first accelerating strides, were almost unseated.

The Runners added to their lead, galloping over the flat and up the three tiring hills leading to the turn. Always Running kept to the front, followed closely by Crooked Smile. Left Alone and White Snake rode side by side. Never Seen rode ten lengths behind. Only two Crow horses had kept up, the one-eared pinto and a bay.

As they completed the turnaround, Always Running guessed the Crow's plan to capture the horse of Crooked Smile, the weakest rider. Always Running rode straight at the Crow on the bay. He swung his whip hard at her horse. It screamed and reared, throwing her. She jumped to her feet in time to see Crooked Smile galloping down the hill with the Crow on the one-eared pinto close behind.

"Help her," Always Running shouted to Never Seen as he raced by on the grey. The Crow began swinging his long lash, trying to catch the girl and pull her from her horse. Quaker galloped easily but would not increase his speed. Blue Eye, seeing the Crow closing on Crooked Smile, whistled as loudly as he could. Quaker's ears flickered and he lengthened his stride.

The Crow turned and saw Never Seen bearing down and swung his whip toward him. Just as the Crow swung his whip a second time, Never Seen stretched out, grabbed it with both hands, and jumped from the grey. The Crow, his wrist caught in the whip's handle, flipped backwards off the pinto.

The Crow could only watch and listen as the crowd cheered as Crooked Smile and Quaker crossed the finish line. The Crow racers took their defeat with equanimity. They had suspected the Runners would be faster and had planned their tactics ahead, hoping to capture at least one horse. Instead of seeing their defeat as a disgrace, the Crow used it to increase their determination to buy as many Runners as possible. At the finish line, they offered to buy the Friends' saddles. Born On A Horse and Always Running sought out the Crow who had whipped her, and were ready to fight. The Crow, with Thinks Like A Woman translating, congratulated the Friends, commenting particularly on Always Running's skillful battle sense and bravery. "You were very daring to push me away from the other riders and put only yourself in danger. You had a fierce look. I made a mistake. I did not expect you to be such a good rider," the Crow admitted. Always Running grinned at the Crow's praise.

"Show me the Runners," the Crow requested, acting as if he and the twins were now close comrades. "I'm going to buy one for myself. I want your advice."

Rarely would a Crow ask for a stranger for advice concerning a horse purchase, and even Born On A Horse's anger subsided as the Crow made his request. He saw the Crow had done his best to win the race, using the ruthless tactics he would expect anyone to use in a battle or a horse race. "Choose a grey gelding," Born On A Horse advised the Crow. "If you buy a mare you might get a good colt. But a grey gelding will be fast. When you ride it, don't use a whip. He will run his fastest without it."

The race added to the reputation of the Runners and drew in more buyers every day. As soon as the steamboat docked, Frances and Laughing Boy moved to the fort to observe the exchange of the furs and robes for the coins.

"The boat went as far as south as it could in the time it had," Lively told Blue Eye. "I hoped it would make it to St. Louis and back. All the captain could bring back was $23,000, not enough to supply everybody. I promised the Crow and Sioux more coins than that. To make matters worse, because of the race the Indians are now prepared to pay unheard of prices for the Runners. The Friends are going to be wealthy when they leave Fort Union."

"I'm not concerned about that," Blue Eye said. "I'm more concerned with your not having enough coins for everybody. It would not be right to only let those who have coins bid on the horses. Many of the Indians have been waiting at the fort for ten days for the coins to arrive."

"There is nothing I can do now," Lively replied. "$23,000 is all I could get. Our forts are not set up to handle a big transaction like this. We normally trade a few hundred robes at a time. Not thousands."

"We can't delay the sale any longer," Blue Eye said. "The word has been out about the coins for long enough now that the Indians may have found some for themselves south of the fort. But we can't rely on that. We will have to accept buffalo robes, furs and coins for the horses. After the auction, you will buy the robes and furs from Sun On The Mountains."

"But how can I pay Sun On The Mountains? You want to be paid in coins, not trade goods."

"The American Fur Company will sell the robes and furs for us in St. Louis after the auction and have the coins delivered here before the end of the summer. Some of the Friends will return before the first snowfall to collect them."

Lively cleared his throat. "I admire your trust, David. So I will tell you this clearly. If the company cannot deliver the coins in the fall, what will you be able to do about it? The company could sell your robes and furs and keep the coins. It would be the company's word against yours. Who do you think would win?"

"The company," Blue Eye agreed. "But next year, what will the company do when the herds are auctioned further up the river and the Sioux and Crow and Assiniboin meet there? Next year, we will not need the fort or the American Fur Company. Next year, the Indians will be prepared with cash ahead of the auction and your company will wonder why its trading became so poor after a good year like this.

"It is your choice, Mr. Lively. Deliver the coins this fall and Sun On The Mountains will trade here for many more years. If you don't deliver the coins, Sun On The Mountains will trade somewhere else."

Lively leaned back in his chair, his hands clasped behind his head. "The coins will be delivered," he promised. For the first time since he had met the Sun On The Mountains Friends, Lively smiled. He called out to Henry in the next room. "Play the present for Frances."

"Do you know that sound?" Lively asked Blue Eye as they listened as Henry plucked a stringed instrument.

"No. Is it a violin?"

"It is better than a violin. It is a guitar," Lively said with satisfaction. "The steamboat captain couldn't find a violin. Frances will like this guitar better than a violin. Take my word for it; nobody would want to sing accompanied by a violin."

Henry entered the room, the guitar cradled in his hands.

"Would you mind if it was my surprise for Frances?" Lively asked. "I was rude to her the first day I met her. I would like to make amends. She has told me quite a lot about Sun On The Mountains and how your grandfather came to set up the trading house."

"Alexander is an unusual person," Blue Eye said. "He and Frances are fond of each other. It would be a good idea for you to give her the guitar. She will tell Alexander you can be trusted. He has some doubts about the intent of the Americans along the Missouri."

"I'm sure he does," Lively agreed. "I have an idea. Why don't I invite the Sun On The Mountains Friends to be my guests at a celebration in the fort? That's when I will give the guitar to Frances."

Henry stepped back in astonishment. "A celebration in the fort!" he blurted in disbelief.

"Yes, a celebration in the fort," the head trader responded. "I think we should invite the Friends to the fort to thank them for trading here."

Blue Eye stood up. "We'll come to the fort after the sale of the Runners." He glanced again at the guitar. "I hope Frances will like her guitar. It looks fragile. We will have to pack it carefully."

Henry set the guitar on a table and said he was ready to go with Blue Eye as part of the exchange with Frances and Laughing Boy who would watch the trading in the fort.

As soon as Blue Eye arrived back at the Sun On The Mountains' camp, he told Thinks Like A Woman about the limited number of coins. "We will have to accept some robes and furs. Anything of value, I suppose. Lively will take everything we receive and pay us with coins in the fall."

"You are taking a risk," Thinks Like A Woman noted.

"*Aa*. I wish I had time to talk to all the Friends before I agreed to this. First I have to make sure we can make our payment to Fast Walker and the Friends from the Bow, even if Lively doesn't deliver the coins. After that, I will pay the Friends. Then only Sun On The Mountains will have something to lose."

Thinks Like A Woman disagreed. "No. All the Friends and all the tribes have something to lose. If Lively doesn't pay, the Piikani won't trust the American traders again. I think the Assiniboin, too, won't trade here. Remember when you told Fast Walker that 'Everybody has something to share?'"

"Yes."

"Now everybody has something to lose."

"That's why I would have preferred to talk this over before I accepted the arrangement with Lively."

Thinks Like A Woman replied swiftly. "You are the leader. You made a decision and if it does not prove right, the Friends will accept it. You listened to their advice whenever you could. This time you didn't have time. Don't think about it anymore."

Blue Eye agreed. He had no choice but to take robes and furs from the buyers who couldn't find coins. The decision had been made, and it was the only way he could live up to his promise that everybody would have a fair chance to buy a Runner. That was what he had promised everybody the first day, and that is what would happen, even if it meant a loss to Sun On The Mountains.

The success of the final auction astounded even the most hopeful of the Friends. The auction began with a parade of Runners ridden by the five Crow. The Crow who had whipped Always Running pulled a cougar skin blanket from his one-eared pinto. "A gift for the fastest rider of all!" he called to the crowd as he handed the blanket over the fence to Crooked Smile. With a knowing look at Blue Eye, the Crow whistled. Quaker, standing by Blue Eye, lifted his head. "Your sleepy horse is more courageous than he looks," the Crow said in a low voice as he rode by. "He looks like Lightning And Thunder to me."

Two of the older mares brought the lowest price, $250 each, but young, fast geldings brought up to $500. The Crow who rode the pinto stopped bidding at $350 on a grey gelding, then, prompted by a subtle nod from Born On A Horse, bid again and again to buy the grey for $550. The auction ended at dusk.

"I'm thankful we are finished the sales," Laughing Boy said with a sigh. "I was sure there would be an attempt to steal the horses before we could sell them. Now that the Crow and Sioux have Runners, they will be busier than before stealing from each other. They will be happy!"

The camp without a herd seemed eerie to the Friends. After more than a month of travelling with over six hundred horses, the Friends now owned less than seventy-five riding and pack horses.

Blue Eye had been correct; the Indians had gathered more coins from the traders and forts along the Missouri. The next morning the Friends packed all the robes and furs, as well as the clothing and tipi covers accepted in the auction of the Runners, and took the loads into the fort for sorting and counting. By early afternoon, Frances and Laughing Boy returned with a reckoning of the value of all the additional robes and furs; $21,000.

Frances announced a total of $60,500 for the Runners. She added it to the $34,000 received for the pack horses and riding horses. "That's $94,500. We will be leaving with $39,500 in coins and $15,000 in trade goods. George Lively will pay us $40,000 in coins this fall."

The $39,500 in silver and gold coins, weighing over 1000 pounds, was distributed in all the packs for transporting back to the Bow and the Assiniboin camps. Three additional pack horses to carry more trade goods had to be bought from the Crow who happily charged the Friends fifteen robes per horse. After the loads were assigned, the Friends rode to the fort to spend the evening celebrating with George Lively and his men.

Never Seen, Crooked Smile and the two Elk Seekers stayed in the camp with the horses and supplies. All the others, taking along the packs with the coins, visited the fort. For most of the Friends, this visit was the first time they had been allowed inside a fort. George Lively, Henry and the clerks welcomed them, showing them the stone bastions, the storerooms where the furs and robes from the sales had already been pressed into bales, the living quarters, and Lively's large, framed house where they would be eating.

Lively had spent considerable time preparing for the Friends and, as Henry had pointed out to him before the Friends arrived, never before had the fort been opened to such a large band of Indians.

"The Friends are different," Lively had explained to Henry. "They have been here for over a fortnight and they haven't been involved in one fight or argument. They traded fairly with us, and with everybody else. We can trust them. Besides, they are trusting us with $40,000 in robes and furs."

"Which the company will sell for $50,000 in St. Louis," Henry had pointed out.

Lively had shrugged. "That's why we are here. But who would believe Blue Eye and the Friends would take in almost $100,000 for those horses? There probably isn't an independent white trader north of St. Louis with that kind of capital."

"Did you give them an IOU or a written note for the $40,000?" Henry had asked. "Or is Blue Eye going to take your word?"

"He is willing to take my word. But he has taught me a few things about trading I never knew before. I have guessed the reason he accepted my offer to pay him the $40,000 in the fall. He said he had promised the buyers an even chance to buy the Runners. But he knew if he only accepted coins, half the buyers would not have been able to bid. At first I thought he would risk a loss himself rather than fail to do what he promised. But, as it turned out, he attracted more buyers with robes and furs to the auction and they pushed up the prices. He is a very clever young man.

"Now I would like to show him something about trading — how a written note will give him security if anything should happen to me. A note from me will be honoured by The American Fur Company. That's the least I can do for him."

That evening Lively led the Friends into the dining room where ten of them could sit at the long rectangular table. The other Friends would have to make themselves comfortable in chairs or on the floor. Lively apologized for the few places at the table. "We have never had so many visitors before." Blue Eye insisted upon sitting on the floor, rather than at the table where Lively had set a place of honour for him, as the leader of the Friends.

"I serve the Friends by leading this trading journey," he said to Lively. "Born On A Horse leads the herd, Thinks Like A Woman leads the Scouts, Left Alone leads the hunters. We all serve. The honour is in the serving, not the leading."

As a compromise, Lively and Henry moved the table and chairs outside so everybody, Lively included, could sit on the floor.

"Before eating, may the Friends have a moment of Silence?" Blue Eye asked.

Lively assured him a prayer would be welcomed and then watched in surprise as the Friends stayed where they were, seated or standing, in Silence for an unusually long moment. Frances ended the Silence, saying she had enjoyed her few days in the fort counting robes and coins with the clerks. Lively, still wondering if a prayer was going to be said, thanked her for her compliment on the fort's hospitality. The Friends began to eat, using their own knives to cut the buffalo meat. They tried the white bread that Henry passed around. Some enjoyed it. Others took a bite then handed the remains of the slice back to Henry.

"Get your plate and join us," Frances called to Henry after everybody had started to eat.

An embarrassed silence passed between Henry and Lively. "Henry eats in the kitchen," Lively pointed out. "This room is for me and guests."

"Then we will join him in the kitchen," Frances exclaimed as she rose and, plate in hand, began to walk to the kitchen.

Lively's head shook. "Henry is a Negro, Frances. Negroes live separately from us."

"I don't agree with that!" Frances retorted, her hazel eyes shimmering as she turned and continued to the kitchen.

"Wait," Blue Eye said. "Henry has been working with us in our camp and in the fort. Why doesn't he eat with us?"

Lively looked around the room and realized he had become the centre of attention. Although only a handful of the Friends spoke English, they had all recognized the conversation concerned Henry. "You don't know about Henry, do you Blue Eye? Frances hasn't told you about Negroes."

Blue Eye shrugged. "I know Henry is a Negro. What else is there to know?"

Lively waved Henry back from the entrance to the kitchen. "Bring your meal in here, Henry."

As they finished their meal, Lively explained to the Friends that Henry was his slave; he had bought him far down the Missouri River, far past St. Louis. He owned Henry, just as other Americans owned many Negroes. The Friends understood slavery, having seen captured enemies working in camps, but could not understand why Henry did not appear to be held in the fort under threats, as were captured slaves.

"There is no better place for Henry to go," Lively explained. "His family are far to the south. If he returned there as a runaway, he would be captured and forced to work in the fields. He is better off here, helping me as my clerk."

"Mr. Lively is right," Henry added. "Mr. Lively treats me well. I have learned to read, write, and clerk for Mr. Lively. I am his emissary when tribes come to the fort."

"Henry knows all my business," Lively added. "I pay him wages and each year he earns a bit of my profits. One day Henry will earn enough to start trading on his own. Until then, he will stay with me."

"I think slavery is wrong," Frances said.

"Perhaps it is," Lively responded. "I sometimes wonder myself. But it is the American law. There is nothing that can be done. I own Henry. There is no alternative for him. I could give him his freedom today, but it would not change anything. Nobody else would pay him as fairly as I do and there would always be the possibility he would be mistaken, purposefully or not, for a runaway. Bounty hunters might take him to a city on the Missouri to be sold again. With me, he is safe."

Frances, not able to argue with Lively's explanation, finished her meal sitting beside Henry. Lively passed around a large tin of loose tobacco, urging everybody to fill their pipes. After everybody enjoyed their first smoke of the evening, Lively stood to thank the Friends for bringing their fine horses to the fort. Although only a few of the Friends understood English, they all understood Lively's intention. Henry and the clerks brought out two wooden crates and handed each of the Friends a sharp steel knife, a twist of tobacco, and a bag containing sewing needles and threads. Thinks Like A Woman stood and thanked Henry and the clerks.

"I have a special gift for Frances," Lively announced. Henry went into Lively's room and returned with the guitar. He handed it to her. "It is all tuned, Miss Frances, and ready to play," he said with a broad smile.

With tears in her eyes, Frances strummed the strings. "I must learn a little before I play," she said. "I have never owned a guitar. It will take me a while." She gave Lively and Henry a fond hug. "Thank you. It is a very thoughtful gift."

"I have to admit it was not my idea," Lively said. "I think you can guess who suggested it."

Frances ran to Blue Eye and gave him a hug as well. "I will play a song very soon for you," she whispered.

Lively, however, was not finished. "I have something else," he called out. "This is for all the Sun On The Mountains Friends. I will speak slowly so Thinks Like A Woman can translate for everyone.

"The Sun On The Mountains Friends have done well in trading their horses and we are anxious for them to return next year. The Sun On The Mountains Friends are very wealthy. They have sold many horses and now their packs are filled with trade goods and coins.

"As a sign of their trust in me, the Friends are leaving behind valuable buffalo robes to be delivered to St. Louis. Before the first snowfall, I will return with coins in payment for these robes. The Friends have not asked me for a guarantee or pledge. They have accepted my word.

"As a sign of my good intentions, I prepared a paper today that the Friends can take to any fort of The American Fur Company and be paid the coins. The company will honour this paper. It will bear my mark and my clerk's.

"I give this paper to the Friends, not because my word is not strong. I give this paper to the Friends so all the traders along the Missouri will know the Friends are careful and honest in their dealings. When the coins are paid, this paper will be marked by the Friends to show the agreement has been completed."

A clerk handed Lively a square of paper and a quill pen. He signed the note and handed the pen to Henry who also signed.

"Now, who amongst the Friends should hold this paper until payment is made?"

The Friends urged Blue Eye forward to receive the paper from Lively. Blue Eye looked it over, noting Lively had written it as a letter addressed to David James. Lively, seeing Blue Eye's hesitation over this, urged him to accept it. "If something should happen to me," he said, "you would have a much better chance of receiving payment than would one of the Piikani or Assiniboin." Blue Eye signed, then folded the paper and tucked it into his jacket pocket.

A thunder of pounding on the entrance gate brought the solemnity of the moment to a halt. Seconds later, two sentries burst through the door into the dining room.

"Sorry to interrupt, Mr. Lively," one of the sentries explained anxiously. "There are two Crow at the gate asking for help. One looks to be seriously injured."

Lively, Blue Eye, and Thinks Like A Woman hurried to the gate where the guards stood by a Crow kneeling by another bleeding from his right shoulder. The Friends recognized the wounded Crow as the one who had given Crooked Smile the cougar skin blanket. Thinks Like A Woman bent down and asked what happened. The wounded Crow, too weak to answer, gestured for the other to answer. He and Thinks Like A Woman talked briefly.

"He says they were bringing gifts to the fort for Born On A Horse and Always Running when somebody shot at them. It was dark and they don't know who it was. His friend thinks whoever shot him, did it to steal the grey Runner he bought at the auction. The horse is gone, along with two hunting bows that were gifts for the twins."

"Bring both men inside," Lively ordered. Blue Eye and Thinks Like A Woman lifted the wounded Crow. The other Crow followed them into the dining room. There, they laid the wounded man on the floor where Blue Eye cut away his bloody shirt to inspect the bubbling wound. A bloody stub of an arrowhead protruded from the wound. Blue Eye pressed a piece of the shirt over the wound to stop the bleeding while Frances and Henry cut a long bandage that Blue Eye tied around the Crow's chest to hold the temporary dressing in place. The other Crow paced around his friend, gesturing with his knife in anger. Thinks Like A Woman spoke sharply to the Crow, telling him to put his knife away. The Crow glared back, but before he could reply the sentry returned to the room.

"Now there is a little girl at the gate, Mr. Lively. All she will say is 'Blue Eye'. She refuses to leave."

"I'll talk to her," Frances said waving the others aside. "It must be Crooked Smile. I hope nothing has happened at the camp!"

Frances returned moments later, followed by Crooked Smile who went to the wounded Crow and stared down at him. Everybody watched as she knelt and ran her small hands over the bandages. Standing up again, she gestured that she wanted the Friends to form a square around her.

"She wants us to sit the same way we were when she awoke at the Cypress Hills," Thinks Like A Woman said. The Friends stepped back and sat along the walls of the dining room. Lively, Henry and the uninjured Crow stood beside the wounded Crow until Thinks Like A Woman pushed them to a wall where they sat, elbow to elbow, amongst the Friends.

Crooked Smile walked around the Crow as if looking for an entrance. Twice she walked around without stopping. The third time she stopped behind his head, knelt, and straightened his left arm so it lay perpendicular to his body. Then she drew his right arm out, stopping when the bandage pinched his shoulder. From her waist she drew her knife and cut the bandage loose. Blood trickled from the wound when she pulled his right arm straight.

Crooked Smile crossed her hands, locking her right thumb under the palm of her left hand and pressed hard around the wound. She looked up at the Friends opposite her, and then closed her eyes. George Lively, to her right, watched carefully, and then was distracted by the flickering of the candles in the room as a gust of night breeze blew into the room. He looked to see who had opened the door. The door was closed. When he returned his attention to Crooked Smile, she lay unconscious beside the Crow.

The Friends did not move until the Crow began to sit up. Then they rushed forward. Frances lifted the small girl's head and stroked her forehead. Crooked Smile opened her eyes. Seeing Frances, she reached up and clasped her arms around her neck. The arrowhead fell from her hand.

A few minutes later the Crow and Crooked Smile were on their feet. Crooked Smile, gripping Frances's hand, could not recall how or why she had come to the fort. The Crow only remembered falling from his horse and, as he touched his shoulder, seemed surprised that everyone had been so concerned about his slight wound. "See. It almost already healed. Whoever shot at me must have had a weak bow."

The other Crow showed him the blood soaked bandages and arrowhead to convince him he had been seriously hurt. The injured Crow refused to believe Crooked Smile had healed him. To the Friends, he appeared to be much more concerned by the loss of the grey Runner and the two hunting bows. The other Crow, however, continued to point in amazement at the wound.

Blue Eye and Thinks Like A Woman were the last Friends to leave the fort. At the gate, Lively shook Blue Eye's right hand.

"I will see you again," Lively said. Then, as they parted, he added, "My Quaker friend."

10 Returning to the Bow

THE TRADING HOUSE, LATE SUMMER, 1838.

Firekeeper was not in a hurry to die, although death approached quickly. Curiosity kept him alive. He had made up his mind he would not die until he could see Blue Eye again and hear how the trading went at Fort Union. Some nights, his coughing kept everybody awake. It had started in the dry days of July, and now it wouldn't stop. Walking to the porch exhausted him and so he lay most of the day on his buffalo robes by the fireplace and waited for Blue Eye to return.

Firekeeper believed Blue Eye would be the one most likely to carry on his tradition of efficient trading. Blue Eye had the orderly mind needed to run a profitable trading house. Alexander had the determination and the instincts needed to set up a trading operation but he found the day-to-day record keeping and planning to be tedious. Hannah loved the Runners and, while she helped with packing, she could not stay away from the horses for long. One Person was a wanderer, and Long Fingers a homemaker who cheerfully rode with One Person whenever he felt the urge to visit the Blackfoot bands. When they had heavy packs to deliver, Stands Early went with them.

Frances, Firekeeper believed, had the intelligence and the energy to be a trader but she did not have the patience to wait and let the trading season unfold. Frances was too impulsive, although her impulsiveness provided a nice counter to Blue Eye's careful thinking. Sometimes a trader needed to move quickly and take a risk that would pay off later. If Blue Eye had a weakness, that was it. He didn't like to act quickly. Firekeeper believed Frances and Blue Eye made a good team.

The profits of the horse drive to Fort Union did not interest Firekeeper as much as whether the drive would show the compatibility of Frances and Blue Eye. If they worked well together, they should become married. Alexander and First Snow had proven to Firekeeper the effectiveness of a husband and wife willing to pool their energies to achieve what neither could achieve alone.

From his pile of buffalo robes by the fireplace, Firekeeper could hear the movements of visitors and Friends around the trading house. Listening was easy; he could listen with his eyes closed, concentrating whenever he heard the horse drive mentioned. Although he could understand only a few Piikani words, he was sure Stands Early would tell him as soon as anybody heard from the riders. Whenever Stands Early became bored, she walked to the trading house and sat by his side.

Firekeeper was aware serious trouble continued to erupt between the Piikani and the traders at Fort McKenzie, although Alexander said little about this conflict. If it had not been serious, Alexander would have been sending more robes south. Instead, as Firekeeper observed, Alexander had been sending robes north to Fort Edmonton along with regular deliveries of pemmican and furs.

"Firekeeper, wake up," Stands Early said rubbing his shoulder late one afternoon just after three Badger hunters had dropped by the trading house to sell the last of their bull hides. "Wake up," she urged again. "There is news."

Firekeeper rolled over, his grey hair falling across his temples. "Slow down," he said in Nahathaway. "What is it?"

"Blue Eye. Frances. Friends. Many more. Soon."

"Blue Eye! Frances!" Firekeeper exclaimed as he understood her meaning. He brushed his hair from his face and sat up on the robes. "Get Alexander!"

By the time Stands Early had found Alexander and brought him into the trading house, Firekeeper had moved to a chair at the table. "Is it true? Blue Eye and Frances will be here soon?" he asked.

Alexander replied, "Yes. Some hunters met them yesterday. They said the Friends were travelling slowly. They expected to be here tomorrow."

"Tomorrow. Good."

Stands Early stayed with Firekeeper the rest of the afternoon, making him a meal of soft, boiled meat, and airing out his sleeping robes on the sunny porch. Long before the low light of evening stretched long shadows across the porch, Firekeeper fell asleep, building up as much strength as possible for the arrival of the riders. He awoke early in the morning and Stands Early brought him water and more soft, boiled meat with thin slices of fried prairie turnip soaked in gravy.

Firekeeper awoke at noon, and again Stands Early brought him food. This time he sat on the porch to eat and watch. The Friends arrived in mid-afternoon and Firekeeper, unable to leave the porch, had to wait until everybody else had greeted Frances and Blue Eye before they could make their way to him. Frances hugged him and when she released her hold, he remarked in Nahathaway to Blue Eye how much she had changed.

"He says you have changed," Blue Eye told her. "He says he would have mistaken you for a Piikani the way you rode Feather to the trading house."

Frances laughed, and Firekeeper could see the happiness in her hazel eyes. He held onto Blue Eye's hand as they talked and, seeing the easiness of the relationship between his nephew and Frances, knew the inevitable would happen. Firekeeper coughed hard, the spasms bending him over. "Don't worry," he said to Blue Eye and Frances as he caught his breath. "I'm just tired. Take care of the riders. We'll talk later."

Blue Eye brought the riders to the front of the trading house late in the afternoon, so Firekeeper could see him make the final settlements. When he finished, Blue Eye asked, "Are there any Friends who believe they have not been treated fairly? If there are, now is the time to speak."

The Friends all shook their heads, eager to be on their way to show their families the results of the trading at Fort Union and to tell them about their encounters with the Assiniboin and Crow.

"That's good," Blue Eye concluded. "You have kept your promises. Sun On The Mountains has also done as it promised. Everybody that left with Sun On The Mountains has returned with Sun On The Mountains. We had a successful journey."

"And Blue Eye never fell off his horse!" Thinks Like A Woman called out, raising a cheer from the Friends. As they left, the Friends would have enjoyed galloping off in Piikani style but their loaded pack horses could only walk.

Crooked Smile, who had chosen to ride with Left Alone rather than return with Laughing Boy to the Assiniboin, asked Blue Eye if she and Left Alone could camp by Sun On The Mountains until they decided where to go next.

"You are always welcome at Sun On The Mountains," he said. "Stands Early will want to meet you."

The only sad parting was between Born On A Horse and his sister, Always Running. Born On A Horse, still riding the buckskin, had decided to stay with Sun On The Mountains and continue training young horses for Hannah.

This was the first time the twins had contemplated going different ways. As often as they had talked about it during the ride from the Assiniboin territory to the Bow, until this minute the finality of their decision had appeared distant. Now, the parting dragged at their feet and neither could move.

"I will always remember the way my sister rode raced against the Crow," Born On A Horse said, "and how you turned the Crow rider aside even though he whipped your horse's face. I will remember my sister as Rides Fearlessly."

Always Running responded by wrapping her arms around herself in the Piikani gesture signifying the capture of a new name, and then opened her arms to release her old name.

"I will always remember your steady hand upon a bow and the way you can look away with a smile as you release the arrow," she said to her brother. "I will remember my brother as Shoots With A Smile."

Blue Eye, who had stood near by the twins as they parted, thought about his own parting from Two Arrows.

Rides Fearlessly swung onto her horse and rode away, giving the horses and goods she had earned to her brother.

As the shadows darkened the porch, Long Fingers called everybody inside for the evening meal. Frances, wearing a deerskin dress borrowed from Long Fingers, showed them her guitar and promised to play a few of the songs she had learned on the way back from Fort Union. Blue Eye brought Left Alone and Crooked Smile into the trading house and introduced them to Firekeeper, One Person, Long Fingers and Stands Early. The two girls were about the same age. Stands Early, taller and more talkative, took charge of

Crooked Smile and led her to Firekeeper's robes to eat their meal.

Alexander, whose flowing white hair and deep blue eyes made Left Alone uneasy, began the meal by requesting the discussions of the value of the goods and coins from Fort Union be saved until after the meal. "I think we would rather hear about the Assiniboin and the traders at Fort Union."

After the Silence, Blue Eye told the highlights of the journey, making the observation that the quality of the Runners convinced the Assiniboin and the tribes at Fort Union that Sun On The Mountains intended to establish its presence as peaceful horse traders in the region.

"We all kept to Sun On The Mountains ways, and that convinced the Assiniboin we only wanted to pass through their territory as traders."

Frances interrupted, "Don't be too modest, Blue Eye. Tell everybody what agreement you negotiated with the Assiniboin chiefs."

Blue Eye, after a few words of encouragement, explained how he turned down the request for a payment of fifty horses and instead asked the Assiniboin to send fifty horses and five riders of their own with Sun On The Mountains.

"I admit I was relieved when we rode into Fast Walker's camp on our return journey and Laughing Boy surprised his father with a gift of ten coins made into a necklace. Later, Fast Walker told us he had not expected to receive anything from his horses at the sale in Fort Union. He told me Sun On The Mountains will always be welcome in Assiniboin territory."

"That is the real value of the journey," Alexander added. "You have shown them that trade benefits both parties, Assiniboin and Sun On The Mountains. From now on, they might be more willing to trade. Maybe you have shown them an alternative to horse raiding."

"Maybe," Blue Eye said.

The stories from the journey, especially the story of the horse race and the gift of the cougar skin to Crooked Smile by the Crow rider, continued well past the completion of the meal. Finally, Firekeeper insisted they tell him the results of the trading.

Blue Eye told him the prices for the pack horses, the riding horses and the Runners.

Hannah gasped. "You sold Runners for one hundred and forty robes! We have never sold a horse for more than forty robes before."

Firekeeper left the table and, on his way to his sleeping robes, whispered to Alexander, "Everything is going smoothly. Now I need to sleep."

Over the summer, Left Alone and Crooked Smile began to hunt further and further from Sun On The Mountains. One evening they returned with a Badger boy, shot in the back. Crooked Smile pressed her hands on the boy and drew out the bullet, but fell unconscious herself. After that, Left Alone would not allow her to heal others, saying she needed to grow older and stronger before she could heal without endangering her own life.

Shoots With A Smile trained horses with Hannah, and everybody assumed he would eventually take over her responsibilities, as she had taken over from Grey Horse. He often heard of his much-discussed sister from visitors but didn't see her again that summer.

Thinks Like A Woman and Never Seen made another trip to Fort Union to visit the Lightning And Thunder they had met at the auction. They told Blue Eye the Piikani were killing any white traders and trappers north of the Missouri. Sleeping Bird told Blue Eye he had a premonition and had seen the prairie strewn with buffalo bones.

Firekeeper died before the Piikani gathered for the Great Circle, and The Family placed his body in a scaffold close to the river. Blue Eye sat by the river all afternoon. When Frances joined him, he told her about the summer he had spent on the South Saskatchewan with his uncle and the loans he had made to the Nahathaway trappers. "He told me that helping was his way."

11 RETURNING TO FORT UNION

THE MISSOURI, FALL, 1838. All summer the Piikani bands by the Bow had discussed the unexpected success of the Friends trading journey to Fort Union. For the first time, many of the Friends found they were treated with the same respect at the Great Circle as the Piikani with noteworthy hunting or warrior accomplishments. Many Friends continued to wear their hair without ribbons and feathers, and to paint small, vermilion Sun On The Mountains symbols on their jackets and shirts.

Blue Eye kept to himself during the Great Circle celebrations, quietly insisting that, for him, the trading journey would not be completed until George Lively paid Sun On The Mountains the $40,000 in coins he still owed for the robes and furs sold at Fort Union. Only when the coins were paid would Blue Eye accept any congratulations.

Blue Eye, Frances, Thinks Like A Woman and Never Seen rode for Fort Union as soon as the bands dispersed, intending to buy pack horses at Fort Union to carry the coins and supplies back to the Bow River.

As the riders pulled up on the ridge above the Missouri, they saw nothing below to remind them of the excitement and arrogance they had seen swirling around Fort Union in the spring. The red, white and blue banners that had snapped above the fort's stone bastions and picket walls hung in tatters. A few, thin ponies grazed on the dry, fall grass where hundreds of Crow, Sioux, Assiniboin, and Blackfoot tipis had sprawled in the summer sun. A thin stem of smoke trickled from the fort, the only sign of occupation.

The riders glanced at each other. Without a word, they urged their Runners down the ridge. They rode unnoticed past the grazing ponies and to the gates. It wasn't until Blue Eye dismounted and battered on the planking with a rock that their presence drew attention.

Three men, all drunk, their clothes dishevelled and filthy, pushed the gate open just far enough for them to poke their rifles through and order the riders to leave.

"No trading. Closed!" the drunkest of the men spat out, gesturing with his rifle for Blue Eye to back away from the gate. The man swayed, and then braced an arm against the man to his left. They both stumbled to their knees, their rifles waving towards Blue Eye's midsection.

"We are here to see George Lively," Blue Eye replied in a polite tone. "Please tell him he has visitors." The men lowered their rifles, surprised by Blue Eye's educated English.

"Watchya want Lively fer?" the third man demanded. He sized up Blue Eye and saw only a slightly built, troublesome young half-breed wearing leather leggings and shirt, and with his hair in a single braid.

Before Blue Eye could answer, a fourth, potbellied man pushed forward, shoved the others aside, and glared at Blue Eye. He was not as drunk as they were, but drunk enough to be quarrelsome. He wore a bowler hat pulled low over his brow. A greasy fringe of grey hair poked out all around. The stubble around his mouth was streaked with traces of white fat and spittle. He wiped his mouth with the back of his hand, spreading the mess across his fat cheek. His left eye had no pupil and wandered in its scarred socket. His right eye stared at Blue Eye for a moment then ran over Frances, Never Seen and Thinks Like A Woman.

"I'm in charge here," he said, his hands now thrust into his pockets to keep his pants up. "Anythin' ya wanna talk to Lively 'bout, ya talk to me."

"I am here to see George Lively," Blue Eye replied.

"Ya can't see him. He run off with the company's money and a slave."

Blue Eye took a deep breath before continuing in an even, polite tone. "Are you with the American Fur Company?"

"Damn rights I am. I'm the head trader at this here fort 'till Lively's replacement shows up. And I ain't doing no trading with nobody till I's ready." He paused, looked over the Runners and the riders, and then slurred, "Whatchya wanna trade? Horses or women?"

"I am not here to trade," Blue Eye replied. "I am here to collect what is owed to me." He reached inside his shirt and pulled out the agreement from Lively that promised the American Fur Company would pay $40,000 in the fall. He handed it to the trader.

"What the hell's this?" the trader jeered to the men at his side. "Don't tell me this blue-eyed breed's got some writin' to show us." The trader read, his lips moving with each word. Two men crowded against him until he pushed them aside. The third man, paying no attention to the letter, unbuttoned his pants and urinated beside Blue Eye's feet.

"This letter don't mean nothing to me," the trader said, shaking his head. He threw the letter on the ground at Blue Eye's feet, near the pool of urine. "There ain't no money and you ain't no David James. You're just a Goddammed breed. Get the hell out of here."

Blue Eye picked the letter up, brushed off the dirt, and tucked it back in his shirt as the traders pushed the gate closed. As Blue Eye mounted Quaker, the gate creaked open again and the potbellied trader stepped through the gap. He looked first at Quaker, then at the Runners, then at Blue Eye.

"Wanna trade one of them other horses for some whiskey?"

Blue Eye turned Quaker away without answering. A drunken white like this had killed Grey Horse at Fort McKenzie. The best thing to do was leave. They camped further up the Missouri that night.

Frances, voicing her practical thoughts, pointed out that they should not consider the whole trading venture a failure just because Lively had failed to live up to his end of the bargain. "The Friends who brought horses to Fort Union have all been paid. The Assiniboin have been paid. Only Sun On The Mountains have lost," Frances said as they built a fire. "You took a chance and trusted George Lively. You are learning not everybody you trust is worthy of your trust," she said. "You have the scars on your chest to prove it. Next time, you will handle it differently."

"Yes," Blue Eye agreed. "But I am responsible. I wanted to profit too much from the trading. I have learned a hard lesson."

"No!" Frances insisted. "You did not want more than what was right. You sold the horses and robes fairly. I'm sure the Crow and Sioux are pleased with the horses they purchased. You trusted the wrong man with your money. That's all."

Thinks Like A Woman shook his head in frustration. "You act as if there is nothing to do. Don't your ways allow you to collect what is yours? I think we should find out for ourselves what happened to Lively. The slobbering trader at the fort is a fool. I don't believe him." Thinks Like A

Woman pulled Never Seen to his side and began to stagger, mimicking the drunken trader.

"See. I'm a drunken white trader. Why would you listen to me?" He and Never Seen lurched around the camp, stumbling and clutching at each other.

"Wanna trade this woman for whiskey," Thinks Like A Woman slurred while poking his fingers into Never Seen's ribs. When Never Seen pulled away, Thinks Like A Woman turned a leering grin towards Blue Eye and grabbed his elbow.

"How 'bout tradin' fer this half-Indjun. He worth just a little whiskey. Falls off horse too much. Believe anything. Make good woman for fat white trader."

Blue Eye smiled, realizing Thinks Like A Woman was showing him he had been too quick to accept the trader's version of Lively's disappearance. "Tomorrow we will find out for ourselves what happened to Lively," he promised. They didn't talk again that evening about the missing money.

After eating, they watered and picketed the Runners and then stretched out on their sleeping robes by the fire. Thinks Like A Woman and Never Seen were soon asleep. Blue Eye, leaning back, told Frances how the day reminded him of the day drunken trappers at Fort McKenzie killed Grey Horse.

"Grey Horse had been drinking," she reminded him. "Come, put your robe next to mine for the night," she said with a smile. "I'll put my arms around you and give you something more pleasant to think about."

The sun had already begun to shine over the tops of the brush around the camp when Blue Eye woke. Frances sat by the fire brewing tea. Thinks Like A Woman's and Never Seen's Runners were gone.

"Where did they go?" Blue Eye asked Frances.

"I don't know. They were gone when I woke up."

Minutes later Thinks Like A Woman and Never Seen rode up the bank and to the camp, their Runners wet to the withers from crossing the river.

"We had a visitor last night," Thinks Like A Woman said. "A Crow." He led Blue Eye and Frances to the willows by the bank and pointed to the curved prints of a Crow moccasin in the mud. "I heard him. I pretended to be asleep. He looked over our Runners and left. This morning Never Seen and I followed his tracks. He's in a camp below that steep hill," he said pointing across the river.

Just then, a Crow rode a grey horse into view on the opposite bank and, after waving his bow and gun above his head, dropped them on the bank, tied his shirt and leggings in a bundle on his back, and rode into the river. Never Seen slipped into the poplars behind the camp.

Blue Eye recognized the Crow's horse. "That's a Runner," he said to Thinks Like A Woman as the Crow neared the bank.

"Yes. And the Crow is the one who rode the one-eared pinto in the race at Fort Union. Don't you remember him? Crooked Smile healed him in the fort. He gave her the cougar skin." Blue Eye looked carefully at the Crow who had put his shirt and leggings on and was now scrambling up the muddy bank.

The Crow's brilliant face paint and elaborate hairstyle were so dominating that Blue Eye could not be sure he was the one who had been wounded at the fort. Thick braids hung evenly above his ears. A single, black-tipped feather clipped with one death notch hung from his left braid. The hair from the centre of his head fell straight back over his neck and hung halfway down his back. Most dramatically, he had painted his entire face black with alternating thin stripes of red and yellow running from his forehead to his jaw line.

When the Crow dismounted by the campfire, The Crow kissed Thinks Like A Woman on the cheek and wanted to kiss Blue Eye as well. Blue Eye pulled back and shook his head. Thinks Like A Woman reached over and tugged the Crow's shirt away from his right shoulder to show Blue Eye a narrow scar, all that remained of the arrow wound. The Crow ignored Frances. Never Seen stayed well back in the willows.

The Crow and Thinks Like A Woman talked in Crow for a few minutes. "He is named Two Lives, because of his death at the fort. He wants you to know he owes the Friends this life," Thinks Like A Woman said. He pointed to the notched feather in Two Lives' hair. "He recaptured the grey Runner that was taken from him at the fort."

Blue Eye nodded, acknowledging the Crow custom of retaliation. "We thought it was the best Runner we sold."

Thinks Like A Woman continued. "He says George Lively and his slave are living in the Crow camp. He has been watching for us and wants to take us to see them."

Blue Eye shook his head. "Lively is probably cheating the Crow now. I don't want to get mixed up with the Crow. Ask him if Lively has our coins."

After a brief conversation with Two Lives, Thinks Like A Woman said the Crow had helped Lively. He had been a prisoner in the fort. He says you must go with him to talk with Lively."

"Do you think it's safe for you to ride into a Crow camp?" Blue Eye asked Thinks Like A Woman who grinned, saying, "Always a doubter, aren't you? I've been in Crow camps before. Some of the Crow are very handsome." He told Two Lives they would ride to the camp. The Crow held up two fingers, saying a few curt phrases that Thinks Like A Woman translated.

"He says only two of us should go. He wants us to leave our wives on this side of the river. He says the Crow women don't want them near their men."

Frances spoke decisively. "Tell him I am not anybody's wife and that I am coming with you."

Thinks Like A Woman translated France's insistence to the Crow who frowned but didn't argue.

"Be careful with this Crow," Blue Eye warned Thinks Like A Woman.

"I'm always careful," Thinks Like A Woman replied.

Two Lives crossed the river and returned to his camp while the Sun On The Mountains riders finished their meal and packed their belongings.

On the riverbank, Frances, without hesitation, undressed and tied her shirt and leggings high on her saddle and crossed the Missouri like the men, swimming with one hand in her horse's mane. After months of driving horse herds with The Friends and riding with Blue Eye and the Piikani horsemen, any reserve she once possessed had long been set aside in the expediency of plains travel. The riders arrived at the Crow camp and, followed by the hard-eyed stares of the Crow men and women, and curious, hidden glances of the children, were led by Two Lives toward a large tipi painted with a red eagle, its wings outstretched and talons ready to strike.

"Sun On The Mountains," Two Lives repeatedly called out when the men in the camp pointed to Thinks Like A Woman who smiled at them and waved in return.

Two Lives entered the red eagle tipi and brought out George Lively and Henry. Lively no longer wore his dark blue company suit and was dressed instead in black rough wool trousers and a clean, much-mended white linen shirt. His moustache was trimmed and his blonde hair combed. Henry wore his smart, grey clerking jacket.

"Hello, Quaker," Lively said as he greeted Blue Eye. When they had parted after the trading in the spring, he had called Blue Eye a Quaker and Blue Eye had smiled. This time he did not.

"We hoped to meet with you before you went to the fort," Lively continued. "I expect they told you quite a story."

"Yes. They said you had run off with the company's money and a slave. They would not honour the debt owed to Sun On The Mountains."

"Did you think I would break my promise to you?" Lively asked, a slight smile wrinkling the corners of his eyes. Blue Eye still found Lively's slow rolling accent difficult to follow.

"Last night I believed Sun On The Mountains would not receive its $40, 000," Blue Eye replied. "I believed I had trusted the wrong man. Perhaps I was wrong."

"You trusted the right man," Lively asserted. "Show him the coins, Henry."

Henry opened the entrance flap of the tipi and pointed to a neat row of packs along the back wall. "$39,150 in silver and gold coins," he said. "We owe you $850."

Blue Eye reached out his left hand, first to Henry and then to Lively. "I apologize for doubting you," he said.

"You shook my left hand," Lively commented. "Are we Piikani now?"

"No," Blue Eye replied, "You're an American and I'm Sun On The Mountains. We trust each other."

Frances asked why $850 was missing. "The amount seems trifling compared to $40,000, but I'm curious."

Instead of answering directly, Lively suggested they make themselves comfortable in the shade on the north side of the tipi. They settled on the grass and, as they talked, Thinks Like A Woman translated the conversation for Two Lives.

"I am going to tell you the whole truth," Lively began. "I should have told you everything before, but I did not want to involve you." He paused, and then continued, directing his talk to Blue Eye.

"I am from South Carolina but I am not a slave owner. I am an abolitionist. I had slaves until five years ago when I heard the abolitionist, Henry Garrison, speak in Boston. My heart changed and I could no longer own slaves. I freed the family I owned and sent them north. I purchased the freedom of a few more slaves using my own money.

"It did not take long for my neighbours to take advantage of my beliefs and soon my money and property were gone. Before I left Carolina, I helped Henry escape and brought him with me to Fort Union as my clerk. I did my best to appear as a firm believer in slavery, to convince others I owned Henry legitimately.

"Bounty hunters found us six weeks ago and I had to pay them the reward, $850, to leave without Henry. As soon as the company heard of my abolitionist beliefs they sent the men you saw at the fort to watch me. They told me I must not pay you. I hid the coins, and they arrested Henry and me and were going to send us to St. Louis. Two Lives captured three company officers and exchanged them for us."

Blue Eye took his time before replying. "I'm pleased you and Henry are safe. The matter ends here for Sun On The Mountains. We will take our coins and go back to the Bow." He stood up.

"Please, listen, there is more," Henry interrupted passionately, rising to his feet and taking Blue Eye's arm.

"What is it?" Blue Eye said, surprised by Henry's intensity.

"My girls are still slaves in the South. I must bring them here, with me. And their families. My grandchildren."

Blue Eye, sitting down again, looked questioningly at Frances. "I don't understand all this."

Frances turned from Blue Eye to Henry. "Tell us what you need," she said. "We will help you if we can."

Henry explained that his two daughters, their husbands and children might be able to escape but they would not make it to the Northern States without help from the Quakers who operated a guarded movement to assist runaway slaves. "It is very dangerous," Henry continued.

"Your grandfather, Alexander, would have known what happens to Quakers who help slaves," Lively added. "George Washington owned slaves, and he did not agree with the Quaker beliefs."

"If you had the money, could you buy the families?" Blue Eye asked. "Wouldn't that be better than helping them escape? Money is what you really need, isn't it?"

"Yes," Lively answered for Henry. "But it would take at least $15,000 to buy all of Henry's family and bring them to the North."

"Would you sit with us?" Blue Eye asked. "I cannot answer your request alone. Do you remember how we sat in the fort?"

Lively and Henry nodded as they recalled the Friends sitting in a square on the floor of the dining room at Fort Union. Thinks Like A Woman spoke to Two Lives and they moved to make up the side of the square opposite Lively and Henry. Blue Eye and Frances faced each other, forming the other two sides. Lively's attention slipped as a brief gust of wind shook the smoke flap of the tipi. He looked up to see if the flap had broken loose. His thoughts wandered. When his attention returned to the square, Blue Eye was speaking.

"Take all the money, Henry," he said. "That is our answer to you. Just buying your family's freedom isn't enough.

Settlers need horses and wagons and tools. Your families must also have those things. Without supplies, they will not have their freedom."

"But $40,000?" Lively exclaimed.

Frances interrupted Lively. "At the Bow, One Person told us we had more coins than we could use, that there weren't enough furs and robes for us to buy in the entire Blackfoot territory. Now the coins will have a use. Take them."

"We will pay you back," Henry promised.

"Perhaps," Blue Eye answered. "But Sun On The Mountains would not expect that. Sun On The Mountains would rather you found ways to use the money to help others."

Henry and Lively had already discussed many times how Henry's girls and their families could be brought north. Lively would travel to South Carolina alone and return with the families and the documents needed for them to travel. Henry would stay hidden with the Crow until the families arrived. "I cannot buy Henry's freedom," Lively explained. "He is too valuable. He will never be free. Other bounty hunters will search for him."

"What about you?" Frances asked. "Won't the company arrest you again?"

"They can't. Not if David James signs the agreement I gave him, acknowledging the money has been paid to him."

Blue Eye drew the letter from his jacket. Henry sharpened a feather and made ink from one of Two Lives' paints. Blue Eye as David James. Underneath, as a witness, Frances signed as Frances Watson.

Two Lives made a suggestion. "In Crow territory there are many trails the whites are following to the west. Henry can stay with us until the families arrive. I will take the families across Crow territory to Piikani territory. Then a

Piikani will have to take them to Oregon." He gave Thinks Like A Woman a questioning look.

"Perhaps," Thinks Like A Woman said with a grin. "But I am not Piikani. I am Sun On The Mountains."

Lively agreed with Two Lives' plan on the route west, saying he had heard of some settlers following the Santa Fe Trail southwest from Independence, Missouri. Other settlers had talked of heading northwest towards the Oregon territory where the Methodists had established missions. "My father had hoped to go to Oregon one day," Frances said. "Henry can go where my father couldn't."

"Whatever you decide to do," Blue Eye told Lively and Henry, "is up to you. We came here to get our coins and return to the Bow. The coins are now yours. We are going home."

On the way back to the river, Two Lives asked Thinks Like A Woman about the twin Piikani who had raced at Fort Union. "She was as brave as a Crow," Two Lives said. "She would have run her black horse right over me if I had not turned aside." Thinks Like A Woman told him the girl now lived as a warrior, adding, "She is Blue Eye's sister."

"Good!" Two Lives cheered. "Then she is a warrior for Sun On The Mountains. She's too good a rider to be a trader."

Just as the Friends reached the riverbank, Never Seen rode out from the brush, startling Two Lives.

A knife spun into Two Lives' hand. Just as quickly, Thinks Like A Woman reached over and held his arm.

"She was supposed to stay on the other side!" Two Lives exclaimed in Crow. "If she were not your camp woman I would beat her!"

"She?" Thinks Like A Woman asked. "Don't you recognize Never Seen from the race?"

Never Seen dismounted and took off his beaded jacket and leggings to swim the river, watching the Crow's expression. After a few moments, Two Lives laughed and pointed his bow at Frances. "What about that woman? I look forward to finding out more about her the next time we meet."

With a brief salute of his bow toward Frances, Two Lives reined his grey Runner around and galloped back to the Crow camp.

Thinks Like A Woman did not translate Two Lives' comments. When they had swum to the other side of the Missouri, Frances asked him to explain why the Crow had pointed at her with his bow.

"Two Lives wanted to know if you were a man, too."

Blue Eye laughed for the first time since they had left the Bow.

Nobody commented when Blue Eye and Frances stood before The Family when they returned to Sun On The Mountains and, in the Quaker manner, announced their intention to become man and wife. Their only child, William, a dark-haired, dark-eyed boy had an adventuresome personality that would draw him irresistibly to the horse herds.

12 A Proposal

THE TRADING HOUSE, SPRING, 1850. Alexander did not travel far from the Sun On The Mountains trading house in the twelve years after the death of Firekeeper. On warm nights he slept in One Person and Long Fingers' tipi. His strength and presence did not lessen as he entered his eighty-eighth year, but he talked less and less. Hannah knew her father had something on his mind and assumed it had to do with Philadelphia; otherwise he would have discussed it with her. His concern for the Piikani never dwindled and, as more traders moved closer to the Bow, she began to accept that her father had been right about the future of the Piikani territory.

While Shoots With A Smile had found his own path managing the herd, his sister, Rides Fearlessly, had never found a peaceful path, only the path that led her on clandestine raids against the white traders on the Missouri. After the horse drive to Fort Union, she had not rejoined the Elk Seeker band, wandering instead in and out of several camps. Although she could not raid the traditional Piikani enemies after riding with Laughing Boy and White Snake of the Assiniboin and meeting the Crow at Fort Union, she found new enemies. Two disastrous trips to the new forts on the Missouri where she lost comrades set her heart against all whiskey traders and she began harassing any she found north of the Missouri. Several times she had returned wounded to Sun On The Mountains. Each time, Shoots With A Smile had tried to persuade her to stay far away from the Missouri.

Thinks Like A Woman was the only one with any ability to caution the volatile Rides Fearlessly about the ultimate end of her path. His warnings, however, did not stay with Rides Fearlessly long. After recovering from her wounds, Rides Fearlessly would disappear again. She continued to wear, and was known for, her plain Sun On The Mountains clothing.

At age four, William, Blue Eye and Frances' dark-haired son, had sought out the horses on his own and Hannah had found him clinging to the rails of the corral by the trading house. The horses had poked their noses through the rails at him and he was petting them without concern. William's outrage at being carried back to the trading house had not surprised Hannah.

"William will be gone from Sun On The Mountains before he is sixteen," she had told Alexander. "Blue Eye and Frances will never make a trader of him. He already has the same look about him as Yellow Shield, and Blue Eye's reckless sister, Rides Fearlessly.

"And," she had warned, "if William follows Rides Fearlessly's path, the entire Missouri River may find itself in trouble."

Alexander had suggested Hannah take William under her care. "At least he will learn to be a good horseman," he said. "Later, he may make good use of what you teach him and find a more peaceful path. Blue Eye and Frances will understand."

When Frances and Blue Eye had insisted their son spend a little time in the trading house each day learning to read and write, William had crept out the window and ran to the corral.

Realizing they faced an impasse with William, his parents agreed to Hannah's and Shoots With A Smile's proposal to make him the best horseman possible. Although this path was hard for Blue Eye and Frances to accept, they were rewarded by their son's startling progress.

"He reminds me of Two Arrows when he was a boy helping Hannah train our horses," Alexander told them. "When I look at William, I see another of God's horsemen. William is very fortunate. He is born into a life where there are horses and a prairie to ride. Let God enjoy William's pleasure."

Stands Early, in her early twenties, had continued to spend her spare time in the trading house, and didn't leave the counter when young Piikani men made transparent excuses to visit her. The only man she had shown an interest in was Shoots With A Smile and, in the fall of 1847, they had told The Family of their intent to marry.

Today, as the warm spring winds melted the last of the ice along the river, One Person and Long Fingers admitted to Alexander that they were concerned Rides Fearlessly seemed destined to draw trouble to The Family.

"We are getting old and we worry too much," Alexander said. "We should be content to sit here on the porch of the trading house and enjoy the sunset over the mountains. There are always young warriors like Rides Fearlessly around. They must find their own path. If Grey Horse had been a young man today, we would have thought him just as unconcerned for his life."

"Sikssikapii," One Person whispered to himself. "I have not thought of him for years." He grasped Alexander's shoulder.

"He certainly made our lives exciting," Alexander said. Soon they were laughing as they recalled their adventures. They were still leaning against the log wall of the house and enjoying the Piikani Sun and their memories when Blue Eye and Frances approached them.

"We have a proposal we would like to make to The Family," Frances said. She explained that for several years she and Blue Eye had noticed new people passing through Blackfoot territory. Missionaries, for example, had been travelling south from Fort Edmonton.

"Missionaries," Alexander scowled. "I have heard of their visits to the Prairie People. These men say nobody can reach God's kingdom without their help. How can these missionaries claim to know so much more of God than the Prairie People?"

Alexander's intensity did not alarm Frances. She had often heard Alexander say the Light could be experienced directly by everyone, that the clergy stood between an individual and God. She had argued with him several times, sure her father's Methodist ministry had helped many of his congregation.

Blue Eye continued the discussion, moving it away from the topic of missionaries. "In the south, American traders are bringing in as much whiskey as trade goods."

"Rides Fearlessly seems to think she can stop them," One Person said with a slight smile.

"Yes. That is what she thinks," Blue Eye agreed. "But there are too many. They will cross the Missouri soon and build more forts."

"Probably," Alexander acknowledged.

"And at Fort Edmonton," Blue Eye went on, "the Cree and Assiniboin fight after they've been drinking."

Alexander leaned forward. "All this is not unexpected," he said, "I talked about this before you went to Fort Union. It is inevitable. The Prairie People are losing control of their territory. They cannot hold the whites out forever. The question is, what should Sun On The Mountains do? Should we fight the Cree, the Americans, the British and the missionaries until we are killed ourselves? Do you have a suggestion?"

"No. Not now," Blue Eye answered, his hand still in Alexander's. "We know some of the Assiniboin, Kootenay and Crow and Sioux. But we don't know what is beyond their territories. We have been to Fort Union, Fort McKenzie and Fort Edmonton. At each of these places we have learned that the furs, robes, and money are sent east. We want to go east to the cities. That is where we will see the future of the Piikani territory. We want to go to London and learn more about the British."

One Person, Long Fingers and Alexander glanced at each other, knowing without talking what each other was thinking. Alexander urged his grandson to continue. "Go on," he said. "Tell me what you propose."

Frances spoke. "I left London fourteen years ago," she said. "I'm sure I can find my father and mother's friends again. With their help, we will learn all we can.

"We can travel by steamboat down the Missouri to St. Louis, then to Boston and by steamboat over the ocean to London. The Family would have to take care of William for us while we are gone."

Alexander took a deep breath and released the couple's hands. "A journey to London is a big decision."

"Almost as big a decision as asking the Piikani for permission to build a trading house on the Bow," One Person commented. "And almost as big as sending Blue Eye and a herd of six hundred horses to Fort Union without any warriors."

Alexander acknowledged One Person's comments and agreed to think about the proposal. The Family would talk about it after the evening Silence. When Blue Eye and Frances had left the porch, Alexander hinted at his concerns.

"I know Blue Eye and Frances can handle danger," he said to One Person and Long Fingers. "I am more concerned about the temptation they will face in London." When One Person and Long Fingers questioned Alexander, "They will decide for themselves," was all he would say.

"They will see for themselves and they will decide for themselves. I don't want to influence them."

When The Family agreed that Blue Eye and Frances' journey to London would benefit everybody, Alexander handed Blue Eye the envelope he had received from his mother after the American Revolution.

"I have never opened this. Perhaps one day you might. While you are in London, if you are curious about the James family, look for the bank that sent this to Hudson Bay." He pointed to the seal in the top left corner of the envelope, a pilgrim carrying a walking staff. "That is the bank's mark."

"Is there no address?" Frances asked.

"No," Alexander replied. "The bank was a collection of Quakers. If the bank wanted to find a person, it could. But nobody could find the bank unless the bank intended them to."

Blue Eye took the envelope. "I will try. But I won't hurry. Grandmother said life explains itself slowly."

"Yes," Alexander agreed with a smile. "But she did not have your curiosity."

Frances and Blue Eye, assured by Hannah that she would watch William carefully, left the Bow in mid-summer, riding to Fort Union where they boarded a steamboat for St. Louis.

In St. Louis, Frances bought new clothes; summer dresses for herself, and light suits for Blue Eye. Blue Eye had his hair cut short, like the other men. Except for his dark skin, no darker than many others, he appeared to be little different than anyone on the crowded sidewalks of St. Louis. Many people noticed his blue eye and gave him the same sideways glance as the Piikani had when he was a boy.

13 THE CRYSTAL PALACE

LONDON, FALL, 1851. Blue Eye maintained a cool distance from the passengers he and Frances met on the decks of the wooden Cunard steamship during their twenty-five day crossing from Boston to Liverpool. His meticulous mind absorbed information about The United States and Britain, the two powerful countries whose territories he would be exploring. The men and women Blue Eye met appeared confident that their progressive thinking, ingenuity and hard work made them superior to all other people in the world. He remained uninvolved. Just as he had done in the trading room as a boy, he noted the diversity of the people he met, their clothing, their interests, and their variety of accents. He planned to return to the Bow with a complete record of what he had done and seen, a record The Family could use as the basis for a good decision about the future of Sun On The Mountains.

The traffic, noise and smoke of London did not trouble Blue Eye as much as the starches and sugars that accompanied English meals, making them difficult for him to digest and as uninteresting to him as the slabs of fatty beef. He missed lean buffalo meat. Frances, sure he would soon adjust to the food, worried more that her husband was overwhelmed by the immensity of London. When she questioned him, he replied that, despite the generosity of Frances' friends and cousins in London, he had no understanding of life in London.

"It isn't because I'm Sun On The Mountains," he assured her. "I see all these people working hard but I don't see their path. Until I understand their path, I will never know the future of the Piikani, and that is why I'm here."

They rented a flat large enough for entertaining the families in London who had known Frances' parents, the Watsons, and shared their devotion to the Methodist Church. Blue Eye, polite, unusual, and intriguingly distant, became the centre of attention and the couple was invited to many dinners. The Sun On The Mountains ways, as described by Frances, sparked long conversations, although her friends could not believe she knew Piikani men who carried scalps and captured horses from their enemies. Blue Eye showed the most interest when Frances showed him the life in London her family had exchanged for their ill-fated journey up the Missouri. Frances missed their son, William, and worried about him. Blue Eye assured her that Hannah and the rest of The Family would be taking good care of him.

Several times Frances suggested that Blue Eye try to find the bank with the pilgrim seal. "I will," he replied. "But it can wait a while longer. That letter was written almost seventy years ago," he said. "Finding out about Alexander's past will not help me now. I came here to learn what I can about what lies ahead. When that is done, then I can concern myself with the past." Nor did Blue Eye have an interest in finding any of Alexander's relatives. Blue Eye was as bored in London as his father, Yellow Shield, had been in the trading house on the Bow.

Blue Eye found what he was looking for on a bright June morning in London when he and Frances bought tickets to The Great Exhibition of 1851. The instant he passed through the, enormous, intricately laced, cast iron gates of the Exhibition, Blue Eye knew this was what he had been searching for.

Only days later, as his mind comprehended the enormity of the Exhibition, did he read in a brochure that the gates he had passed through had been forged in the Coalbrookdale foundries of the Darby family, Quakers whose ingenuity had made them wealthy and famous, notably as the inventors of coke smelting, the mass production of intricate brass fittings used in steam engines, and as the constructors of the world's first iron bridge.

The Crystal Palace, as the breathtaking three-storey glass halls of the international exhibition came to be known, fascinated Blue Eye. He returned every day for a month to explore the eight miles of galleries. No river valley, no mountain pass and no prairie coulee had called out to him as strongly as the galleries of The Great Exhibition. For the first time since he had left the Bow, Blue Eye allowed himself to be assimilated by his surroundings. The details of each exhibit poured, unimpeded, into his mind. Instead of counting robes, coins, guns, bags of pemmican and trade goods, Blue Eye's mind assembled the complicated puzzle presented by the art, invention and manufacturing exhibits from around the world.

Nothing in the Exhibition escaped Blue Eye's attention: the huge, locomotives; the tiny porcelain dolls; the ceaseless water fountains; the tall elm trees growing in the entranceway; the howdah on top of the stuffed elephant; the Colt pistols; the Canadian canoe and moose heads; the steam-powered cotton jennies; the model of the Liverpool docks complete with 1600 rigged ships; the shackles, chains and cuffs forged in Birmingham for the American slave owners; the artificial legs and teeth; and the musical instruments.

Blue Eye's appetite for the Exhibition was voracious. He stopped strangers in the galleries, asked them what they had seen and what they enjoyed the most. He talked to exhibitors and then wandered on, always aware of how much more he could learn. Blue Eye began to eat his evening meals in a hurry, anxious to return to the Exhibition. He brought along as many of Frances's friends and family as he could persuade.

"The Exhibition is the Great Circle of your world," he told Frances and her cousins at dinner. "Just as the Prairie People gather each summer to hunt and to exchange gifts, here your people have gathered to share their knowledge."

Queen Victoria and her husband Albert revelled in the attention the Exhibition brought to the British Empire, and to themselves as the Exhibition's patrons. Albert, a serious-minded German, had been involved with the Exhibition since its conception and had purchased the first season ticket. He and Victoria, often accompanied by their son, the future Edward VII, were regular visitors.

Albert and Blue Eye met one morning at the Moving Machinery Hall. Blue Eye, on his back to inspect the gears beneath a steam-driven press, noticed the feet of the crowd moving. He crawled out, and almost bumped into Albert whose aides had cleared the area of spectators.

"Do you know the purpose of this?" Blue Eye asked, pointing to a gear on the steam-driven printing press he had been inspecting. "I can't see what it operates." Albert, taken aback by Blue Eye's sudden appearance, relaxed when he realized that Blue Eye was only interested in learning about the machinery. Albert called over the exhibitor's representative who explained the gear's importance.

"Thank you," Blue Eye said as the representative finished his explanation. Then, turning to Albert, he held out his right hand. "Blue Eye," he said as he shook Albert's hand. "And you are Albert. I've noticed you come almost as often as I do. You should be proud of the Exhibition."

Albert, as everybody else in London had done, commented on Blue Eye's name. "Most unusual. Of course, it is a nickname . . . because of your eye."

Blue Eye shrugged. "My birth name is David James. But on the Bow River I have always been known as Blue Eye, Otssko Moapsspiksi."

"The Bow River?" Albert's interest was aroused and he extracted the story of Blue Eye and Frances' journey to London. Albert leaned on a lever of the press while he and Blue Eye's conversation lengthened into a discussion of Alexander and First Snow's arrival on the Bow River. Albert had been informed of many of the details of The Hudson's Bay Company's activities. The future of its charter had been under discussion for several years in parliament, he told Blue Eye. Their conversation then turned to the recent encroachment by traders into the Prairie People's territory.

"The Prairie People?" Albert inquired. Blue Eye explained that Europeans referred to them as the Blackfoot Confederacy.

"So you are here to discover the British Empire's plans for the Prairie People's land," Albert concluded when Blue Eye finished his explanation.

Blue Eye laughed. "I have already discovered it! The British Empire's intentions are on display here, in the Crystal Palace. The British Empire has no secret plans. The future of the prairie and life at the Bow is as clear as the glass above us. I don't think it likely that the British Empire intends to travel by horseback and live in a tipi on the prairie. I think it is more likely the Prairie People will soon be travelling by railroad and living in houses."

Albert then asked a question that surprised Blue Eye. "Tell me, if the Piikani were to resist, to fight for their territory, what do you think would be the outcome?"

"Alexander says they would lose. It would be a hard fight, but they would lose. He says the Piikani are the best horsemen he has ever seen. He says the best one hundred men from the British and the Revolutionary armies could not ride against the best one hundred Piikani."

"If they are so formidable, why would they be defeated?" Albert inquired.

Blue Eye explained about the Piikani's skill with horses, how they managed their horses on the open prairie, how they were able to train them without corrals and fences, and how they could ride through herds of buffalo at full speed, their hands free to fire their bows. "Imagine what would happen if the Prairie People were to organise their mounted warriors into a cavalry," he concluded.

"Why don't they organize a cavalry?" Albert asked.

"Because they think first as hunters, then as warriors. Hunters like to live in small bands. A small band can hunt close by its camp. If a band gets too big, the game close by doesn't last and the hunters have to begin travelling further. Small bands are more effective. And that is the way the Prairie People raid their enemies — in small bands, or as individuals. They don't think in terms of organized war."

"But even as raiders they could be effective," Albert noted.

"No," Blue Eye replied. "It is hundreds of years too late for that." He pointed toward the machinery along the hall of the Crystal Palace. "My grandfather says the enemy the Prairie People face today cannot be defeated by men on horses."

"Your grandfather is most likely right," Albert added after a moment of careful thought. "Although I do not like to hear that he calls The British Empire the enemy of the Prairie People."

Albert's frankness encouraged Blue Eye to show him Alexander's unopened envelope. "My grandfather said if I was interested in learning about my family, I should go to this bank," he said pointing to the small pilgrim seal. "Would you know anything about it?"

Albert looked over the blue envelope. "1785. This is dated well before my time. Most of what I know about Britain I have learned in the past ten years, since my marriage to Victoria. To be honest, I know more about German history."

Albert called an aide over and told him to take down the particulars of Blue Eye's inquiry. As Albert parted, he suggested Blue Eye view the Model Dwelling House. "I designed it myself," Albert said, "and had it constructed on the grounds outside the Exhibition hall. You may build a house like it by the Bow one day." With an amused, narrow smile, he reached forward to shake Blue Eye's hand. Blue Eye smiled and reached out with his left hand. "Sun On The Mountains," he said. Albert shook Blue Eye's left hand and then told his entourage he was ready to move on. Blue Eye resumed his inspection of the exhibits in the Moving Machinery Hall.

As pleased as she and her friends were when they heard about Blue Eye's meeting with Albert, Frances placed more importance on his showing Alexander's envelope to Albert. Just as Blue Eye's inexhaustible curiosity had brought him to England, she was sure it would to send him further, in search of information about his grandfather.

Much to Frances's surprise, an answer to Blue Eye's inquiry was at their door a week later.

Blue Eye recognized their visitor as one of Albert's aides, the one who had taken down the information concerning the letter. "A friend has sent you a note," the aide said, handing Blue Eye a handaddressed envelope, "To Be Delivered To Blue Eye Only".

"Thank you," Blue Eye replied taking the envelope. "Who is this friend?"

"I do not know, sir." The aide answered, his face expressionless.

"Is there something else?" Blue Eye prompted as the aide made no sign of leaving.

"Well, sir, if you do not mind my saying so, I think it would be best if you destroyed the contents of this envelope as soon as possible." The aide turned and left.

Blue Eye slit open the envelope and pulled out a small folded card. It, too, was plain, with no name, just an address.

Blue Eye read aloud. "Number 15 Acheson Street."

He handed the note and the envelope to Frances who inspected them.

"I recognized the man who delivered this," Blue Eye said. "He was with Albert at The Exhibition."

"Shall we go to Acheson Street?" Frances asked. "This must have something to do with your showing the envelope to Albert."

"Most likely. But it doesn't seem clear. If Albert didn't want me to know the note came from him, he would have sent an aide I wouldn't have recognized. I think Albert wanted me to know he sent the note."

They talked more about it over supper and agreed they would go to Acheson Street in the morning.

14

Number 15 Acheson Street

LONDON, WINTER, 1851. To Blue Eye, Number 15 Acheson Street looked almost indistinguishable from the others in the row of Victorian, two-story, business houses. They all had wrought iron railings leading from the street to their doors where engraved brass plaques described the nature of the business conducted within; importers, shipping consultants, and manufacturers' representatives. Number 15 had no brass plaque.

Blue Eye knocked. His eyes caught a slight movement in an upstairs window and moments later the door opened and a tall, pale, grey-haired woman gestured for them to enter. She closed the door slowly, as if it were heavy.

"My name is Elizabeth," she said in a youthful voice. "You must be David and Frances."

"Yes," Frances replied. "We came in response to this note." She handed Elizabeth the envelope. Elizabeth read the card with deliberation. "Thank you for coming," she said.

Elizabeth led the way into the drawing room beside the entrance where a low coal fire glowed in a grate. "It is warm," she explained. "I keep the curtains drawn for privacy. I miss the sunshine." She left them sitting on a small couch by the window while she made tea. She returned with a tray and set it on a low table between the couch and her winged-back chair.

"I know you can sit quietly," she said as she settled into the chair. Without another word, she rested her forearms on the chair. Nobody spoke for several minutes. Finally, she leaned forward. "The tea should be ready. Would you pour for us Frances?"

As Frances poured the tea, Elizabeth said, "David. Tell me about Alexander. How is he?"

"Please, call me Blue Eye. Even Grandfather does. He is well. He was sad when his wife, First Snow, died from the smallpox. And was sad when Grey Horse died and when Firekeeper died. But he has my mother, Hannah, and many others in The Family for company and he keeps busy in the trading house."

"Naato'si Otatsmiistakists?" Elizabeth asked. "Sun On The Mountains. That is its name, isn't it?"

"Yes," Blue Eye answered, impressed by Elizabeth's knowledge and interest. "Grandfather built it and The Family all live there, including Frances and me."

"That would be One Person, Long Fingers, Stands Early and Shoots With A Smile." Elizabeth said. "Tell me, how does Rides Fearlessly survive? I believe she must have some of Alexander's invincibility. She is taking on the whiskey traders just as he took on Washington's army."

"How do you know all this?" Blue Eye asked. "Who are you?"

Elizabeth smiled as her eyes pinned Blue Eye with a familiar, concentrated gaze. Elizabeth's eyes were deep blue and flecked with fine black bolts.

"You are Alexander's sister, aren't you?" he guessed aloud.

"Yes," she answered. "I do my best to keep track of my brother and his family. You are dear to me, and I do not want to lose sight of you. I have the help of several business acquaintances in the Hudson's Bay Company, and in the fur companies on the Missouri. Few people forget meeting my brother."

"Tell us about him," Frances requested. "He never talks about his life before Hudson Bay."

"That is for him to tell." She reached beside her chair and pulled forward an iron strongbox, about one foot square with a brass hasp and heavy padlock. She withdrew a ledger from the box and set it on her lap. "But there are a few things I can discuss because they concern you today.

"Our parents, Richard and Alice James, owned a Quaker bank in Philadelphia. They had three children, Alexander, Thomas and me. This is my accounting of their estate. Neither Thomas nor Alexander has claimed a share. I have managed the money on their behalf. As Alexander's family, you and the others at Sun On The Mountains will inherit his share of the estate."

She handed the ledgers to Blue Eye. "These are the records of how I have continued operating Richard and Alice's bank. Read for yourself what I have done with Alexander's share. I will answer any questions I can."

Blue Eye skimmed through them, and then read some of the pages in detail. "What does this mean 'Disbursement'?" he asked pointing to several entries.

"Just that. Money going out. If there is no notation accompanying the entry, then I will not explain it. Anonymity makes charity possible."

Blue Eye continued reading. "Returns?" Blue Eye asked. "What are those?"

"The opposite of Disbursements. Money coming back. Again, no explanation."

Frances and Blue Eye leaned back on the couch, astounded.

As Blue Eye returned the ledgers to Elizabeth, she guessed his thoughts. "Two million pounds is a lot of money," she said. "The James have done well."

"Yes," Frances agreed. "Does one third belong to Alexander?"

"By law it is mine. But by what is right, it belongs to Alexander and his family — all seven hundred thousand pounds. That would be about three million American dollars, depending upon the exchange rate you can negotiate."

Elizabeth chuckled. "I must admit I've often thought about this day. I always wondered if I would live long enough to meet my brother's family and show them how well we had invested their inheritance."

As Blue Eye returned the ledgers to her, she said, "This makes the $40,000 you gave to George Lively and Henry a bit easier to overlook, doesn't it? The Friends — and the Assiniboin — took incredible risks to drive the Runners to Fort Union. And you gave almost half of the profits to help a family of slaves. Why did you do that?"

Blue Eye glanced at the ledgers in the strongbox. "A disbursement. Money going out," he said. "No explanation."

"A sense of humour!" Elizabeth said. "You are a surprise."

She thought for a moment. "I understand you have an envelope with the pilgrim seal." Blue Eye handed it to her.

Elizabeth looked it over carefully. "I wonder why Alexander never chose to open this. Yet he has kept it all these years. I remember my mother writing it. We wondered if he ever received it. He wouldn't have given it to you if he didn't want you to open it. Why don't you read it?" She handed the envelope back to Blue Eye.

"My grandmother told me life explains itself slowly. It is what we learn along the way that is important. I am in no hurry to read about something that happened sixty-six years ago." He replaced the envelope in his pocket.

"In that case, we will return to business matters," Elizabeth said. "Although Alexander does not want his inheritance, that does not mean you cannot have it now, if you want it. I can give it to whomever I want. All you have to do is ask, and it will be yours."

Blue Eye took hold of Frances's hand firmly. "We came to London to learn what we could for Sun On The Mountains and the Piikani, not to bring back money. Money will not do The Family as much good as what I have learned these past weeks at The Crystal Palace."

"Ah. The Crystal Palace. And you are the mysterious, dark man with one blue eye who insists upon examining everything." Elizabeth arched her brows. "Have you learned all the secrets of the Empire? Have you seen Albert's house?"

Blue Eye laughed. "You know a lot about us. Alexander will be surprised when I tell him you knew we were here and kept watch on us the entire time!"

"I keep watch on many people," Elizabeth replied with a faint smile. "Even Methodists who swim naked in the rivers," she said, turning her attention to Frances.

Frances raised her hand to cover her mouth and conceal her amusement at Elizabeth's knowledge.

"Oh, don't act as if I might be shocked," Elizabeth said. "Nakedness is not a sin, and even if it were, crossing the Missouri in your clothes would be foolish, and foolishness is a sin."

She turned her attention to Blue Eye. "Would you excuse an old woman's curiosity about a personal matter?"

"Of course," Blue Eye answered. "What is it?"

"Of all I have heard about the Piikani, I am most curious about the Sun Dance. How fortunate they are to know their Sun so directly. Would you show me your ceremonial scars?"

"They are not very Quaker," he replied, "but I'll show them to you." He unbuttoned his shirt.

"I cannot imagine how you endured that," she said.

Blue Eye smiled. "It wasn't something to be endured. It was something to be experienced."

After he closed his shirt, Elizabeth said, "Now, back to business. Tell me, what do you two intend to do?"

"Frances and I cannot return to the Bow with Alexander's inheritance," Blue Eye said. "Keep the money, Elizabeth. From what I have seen in the ledgers, you have found a good purpose for it."

Elizabeth nodded. "Alexander did right in sending you here." From the side of her chair, she pulled out the note that had brought them to Acheson Street. "This is of no further use to you," she said as she ripped it in half and dropped the pieces into the fire. "Even royalty respects a Quaker's silence. Perhaps one day they will respect our equality."

Frances, who had become accustomed to The Family's containment of their emotions, was not surprised by the practical tone of Elizabeth's conversation. Not once had Elizabeth shown a trace of excitement at meeting her brother's grandson. Elizabeth, it seemed to Frances, treated Blue Eye as a customer she had investigated before allowing him to enter her mysterious bank. Elizabeth had revealed little more of herself than what was in the ledgers.

"Before you go," Elizabeth continued, "I can tell you one thing you should be aware of. The British Government is watching how The Hudson's Bay Company governs their territory. Little is being done or said openly. But soon, I think the Government will buy The Company's charter. This will happen before your son, William, is grown." She tapped the strongbox. "There is enough in here for you to buy their charter before the British Government does. The Government will not pay more than five hundred thousand pounds. You could use this money to buy it and negotiate a better settlement for the Blackfoot Confederacy. Think about this suggestion."

She stood up, signalling the end of the visit. "If you need help, I will hear of it and will do all I can."

She held out her right hand for Blue Eye to shake. Seeing him hesitate, she said, "Today we talked business." Blue Eye took the offered hand, wondering if she knew the Piikani custom of shaking left hands. Frances moved forward to embrace Elizabeth who stepped back and held out her hand for Frances.

A week later they booked a passage to Philadelphia. When the agent delivered their tickets, inside the folder they found a bill of lading showing that two grey, thoroughbred mares, purchased two days earlier from the Royal Stables, would be on their boat for delivery at the docks of Philadelphia. The consignee was simply, A Friend.

15 PHILADELPHIA

PHILADELPHIA, SPRING, 1852. While Blue Eye led the two thoroughbred mares down the gangplank at Philadelphia, Frances gathered the baggage. She had done her best to turn down most of the cutlery, place settings, clothing, and jewellery her friends in London had tried to persuade her to accept, but still had accumulated two full trunks. Her London friends could not understand the difficulty of shipping the trunks by steamboat to Fort Union, then packing them by horse to the Bow.

Now, with fall setting in, and with two mares to transport to the Missouri and then up the river to Fort Union, Frances thought of how easily they had made the journey from west to east, arriving in London with only the few clothes they had bought in St. Louis. Most of the clothing she returned with she planned to give to Long Fingers who would distribute it to women in the bands.

She had just collected their trunks and bags and was about to search for Blue Eye and the mares when a woman in her early sixties interrupted her thoughts.

"Excuse me," the woman said, "but I am hoping you are Frances James."

The woman, dressed in expensive but dark, plain clothing and wearing a broad bonnet that shaded her pale blue-grey eyes, held out her right hand. "My name is

Rebecca James. Alexander, your husband's grandfather, is my uncle."

When Frances gave her a puzzled look, Rebecca explained, "Blue Eye is my cousin."

"Are you Elizabeth's daughter?" Frances asked after a moment. "We met her in London."

Rebecca shook her head, revealing glimpses of her skin, pale in the afternoon sunlight. "No. My father is Thomas, Alexander's brother. Elizabeth is their sister."

"Excuse my confusion," Frances said. "But Elizabeth didn't tell us Blue Eye had a cousin."

"Probably not," Rebecca said. "Elizabeth does not like to talk about anything to do with Philadelphia."

Before Rebecca could reply, Frances saw Blue Eye leading the mares through the crowd. "There are our horses. How we are going to transport the horses, the baggage and ourselves to the Missouri River is a mystery. Please, would you mind watching the baggage while I tell Blue Eye you are here?" Without waiting for Rebecca's answer, Frances pushed her way through the crowd to where she had last seen the mares.

She returned a few minutes later with Blue Eye and introduced him to his cousin.

"Welcome to Philadelphia, The City of Brotherly Love," Rebecca responded with cheerful formality, "and the home of the James family from the day it was founded — except for a brief spell during a revolution."

Blue Eye and Frances felt charmed by Rebecca's open warmth and her ironic humour.

Rebecca continued, "Aunt Elizabeth sent me a letter with the ship's captain saying you and the horses were on this ship. I am relieved I arrived in time. I feared you may have already unloaded the horses and raced for the Bow."

"The horses were the last cargo to be unloaded. Otherwise we would have left early this morning," Blue Eye replied.

"That is understandable. You have probably had all you want of civilization. But please, would you stay a few days with me. I have a home by the Schuylkill River and a stable. Your horses have not had any exercise since they left Liverpool. They will need a chance to run in a field for a few days before you go west. Stay with me until your horses are ready to travel."

Blue Eye and Frances agreed and in a few hours were at Rebecca's home. "I am sure you have thousands of questions," Rebecca said as she led them up the stairs to their room. "And I will answer them all — if I can — this evening. You may make yourselves comfortable and rest until then. I have a few business matters to attend to this afternoon. Look around all you want."

Blue Eye explored the house, taking advantage of Rebecca's offer. The house appeared much too big for one woman but he could not see any signs of other occupants. All the bedrooms on the second floor were tidy, and the halls, dining room and sitting rooms looked unlived-in. The walls held oil portraits and landscapes, none of interest to Blue Eye, although he did recognize a portrait of Rebecca, painted perhaps thirty years earlier.

In the dining room he found a family portrait showing three children sitting with their parents in front of a house that might be Rebecca's, although the trees and bushes that now covered the grounds made it impossible for him to be sure. He studied the children in the portrait and, seeing a boy with blonde hair, guessed the children were Alexander, Thomas and Elizabeth, and the parents were Richard and Alice. He had never been able to imagine his grandfather as a boy, and this portrait seemed inaccurate, as if the artist had not seen the strength that must have always been in his grandfather.

In London, Elizabeth had avoided discussing the James family but here, in Philadelphia, where Alexander, Thomas and Elizabeth had been raised, he hoped Rebecca would be more forthcoming.

Rebecca returned to the house late in the afternoon and found Blue Eye and Frances at the stables, watching the horses graze on their first green grass since leaving London.

"We hope they are in foal," Blue Eye said to Rebecca. "That way, we will have four horses to start breeding."

They talked the rest of the afternoon about themselves, the trading house on the Bow, the Piikani, the Runners, and all the members of The Family and the Friends, including Thinks Like A Woman and Never Seen. Rebecca listened, controlling her surprise at what must have seemed to her a semi-barbaric life. Frances reassured her, saying that before she met Blue Eye at Fort McKenzie, she, too, would have thought life at Sun On The Mountains to be intolerable.

"Now, it is just everyday," she added. "I have to admit I found life in London difficult."

Rebecca raised her eyebrows. "Well, I would agree. Aunt Elizabeth is always inviting me to London but it does not appeal to me. I prefer Philadelphia." She paused and gave the couple an astute look. "I suppose you are politely listening to me and wondering if I am going to answer some of your questions." she said.

"Come with me into the kitchen. We will eat supper and I will do the talking."

She led them to the kitchen where she sliced a cold roast and passed them plates, cutlery and a plate of sliced vegetables.They sat at a square table.

"I know you can sit quietly," she said, just as Elizabeth had. The Silence was short, ended by Rebecca. "I am alone so much that I do not spend too long in Silence," she explained.

Rebecca pointed to a thick envelope on the counter. "After Aunt Elizabeth met you in London, she wrote me saying you should be trusted. She is very cautious. You'll understand why after I tell you about our family. But she and I have become close, as close as anybody can become with Elizabeth.

"She asked me to tell you the entire story of our family." Rebecca paused. "Would you like to hear about the James?"

Blue Eye nodded. "Yes. I would like to know about the family."

"Good," Rebecca said. Her story was long, and much of it perplexing to Blue Eye who had learned very little history.

"First," she began, "I will tell you about your great-grandparents, Richard and Alice James. They were born in Philadelphia more than one hundred years ago.

"Richard and James owned The James Bank and loaned money to anybody they thought was honest and hard-working. That thinking made them wealthy.

"They had three children; Thomas, Elizabeth and Alexander. They were all in their teens when the War of Independence began.

"When the war started, Richard and Alice were among the most outspoken of the Quakers. The Revolutionaries tried to persuade them to support the war, and help pay for the army. Of course, they wouldn't. At first, no Quakers would fight or pay war taxes, but then a few began to change their minds. Any Quakers who changed their minds, or had sons who fought, were disavowed by the others. So you can imagine how disheartened Richard and Alice were when George Washington persuaded their son, Thomas, to join his army. As soon as the family was disavowed, people who had loans with our bank refused to repay them. Even some

Quakers, people we had known all their lives, refused. Not soon after Thomas left Philadelphia to fight with the Revolutionaries, a farmer murdered Richard, just to get out of a debt. Nobody was arrested, and Alice was offered no help.

"She was forced out of her home and had to take Elizabeth and Alexander to New York where they thought they would be safe. That was when Alexander disappeared. He was only 15. By the end of the war, Alexander had been declared a traitor and George Washington offered a reward for his capture. Alice and Elizabeth took all the money they could recover and moved to London to begin a new bank. They never heard from Alexander again, although they knew he had been at Hudson Bay.

"When my father, Thomas, returned to Philadelphia after the war," Rebecca continued, "he believed his enlistment in the Revolutionary army had caused his family's downfall. He devoted his life to recovering his family's losses; the money, the land, the home on the river, and acceptance by the Quakers.

"Alice and Aunt Elizabeth could not forgive the Quakers in Philadelphia," Rebecca said. "They became very secretive about their affairs. They believed what had happened in Philadelphia could happen again.

"Alice died ten years after the war. Aunt Elizabeth never married. I am Thomas' only child. That makes you and your family my heirs."

Blue Eye and Frances sat back in their chairs, overwhelmed by all the information they were receiving.

"Don't you want to know how my father fared when he made up his mind to regain all that Richard and Alice had lost?" Rebecca asked with a slight smile. "Aren't you curious?"

Blue Eye thought for a moment. "If you want to tell us," he said.

"Thomas left me over two million dollars, plus this house and more land. I've more than doubled it. The James problem, you must have noticed, is not making money, it is finding a use for it."

"Yes," Frances agreed. "But can't you give some away?"

"No. We do not give anybody anything. We are still The James Bank. We invest in honest people who work hard. Work makes us all strong. Work creates wealth, and wealth creates work. Elizabeth says you understand this." She held up Elizabeth's letter for emphasis.

"Like you, I do not always expect the return of my investment. I have been using some of the money to free slaves. I've paid for the release of some. And I've paid to help others escape. Elizabeth told me about how you helped the slave family at Fort Union.

"She said if you were being charitable, you would have forgiven the $850 Lively paid for Henry's reward. If you were being generous, you would have given them $15,000 to free the families. Instead, you gave them the entire $40,000 — so they could invest in supplies and land and earn their livings. That is beyond charity and beyond generosity. That is our way."

"Did Elizabeth also tell you that we have no need for Alexander's inheritance?" Frances asked.

"Yes. But she asked me to point out that the Piikani and Sun On The Mountains will not be able to live on the Bow forever. You saw that for yourselves at The Great Exhibition. Perhaps you should think about how Alexander's inheritance could be used. Would you consider using the money to buy the land in their name, and making it theirs with a British land title?"

Blue Eye thought for a moment. "We have discussed that, but it wouldn't be right. They have the same right to decide their path as we do, whatever it might be. They have to make this decision themselves. Only if the Piikani ask, would we help."

Rebecca's blue-grey eyes steadied themselves onto Blue Eye. "I see you are no longer a seeker," she said in a quiet tone. "Now you not only know how to speak to the Light in everyone, you also know how to answer the Light in everyone."

"Yes," he replied. "I know."

16
Opportunities

THE TRADING HOUSE, SUMMER, 1852. William raced his horse across the clearing in front of Sun On The Mountains, cheering as his parents rode up the path. He waved to them as he slowed and circled behind the tall, grey thoroughbred mares trotting up the path.

As soon as his parents reached the corrals, he jumped from his horse and ran to his mother, wrapping his arms around her neck. "You're home!" He had grown several inches in the past year and now she realized he was almost as tall as her. William turned to his father. "Everybody missed you! Especially me." As he leaned against his father, he whispered to him, "I even worked on my books while you were gone! You can ask Hannah, she'll tell you."

"You're a good boy, William," Blue Eye replied. "And I hope you had enough time to ride the horses with all the reading you must have done!"

William laughed. "I sure did. We went everywhere, to all the camps, to see everybody. And they all asked about you. They all wanted to know where you had gone."

He pulled his father back toward the corral fence. "Tell me about these horses. They're big, aren't they? Are they fast? What are we going to do with them?"

Blue Eye shrugged. "Maybe we'll eat them. They are big enough for a few meals, don't you think?"

"No," William laughed. "Tell me really what we are going to do."

"Well, we have thought about raising horses for the settlers on the Missouri. We thought if we could find somebody who wanted to raise some colts and train them to . . . "

"I will!" William interrupted. "Let me do that."

"Well, first we'll have to see what your grandmother and Shoots With a Smile think about them. They may say they are too big for Runners."

"They'll keep them, I know that for sure," William said as he climbed over the corral rails.

"Use the gate, William," Hannah called out as he swung over the top rail. She stood beside Blue Eye and Frances to watch William and the mares. "Welcome home," she said. "Your son has grown." Frances put her arm around Hannah's waist.

"Thank you for taking care of him for us," Frances said. "We missed, him but we knew we didn't have to worry."

"He missed you. He has a lot of energy. Too much sometimes." She moved closer to the corral. "Tell me about these horses."

By late afternoon, William was riding the mares in front of the trading house while The Family watched from the porch.

"I picked out something special for you at the Crystal Palace," Frances told Alexander. She had rested her hands on his shoulders as he sat in his chair by the step and, as she spoke, she could feel a ripple of tension dart through his muscles.

"It was a model of a steam engine," she said. "But Blue Eye misplaced it and now we have nothing to show you."

Alexander reached up and held her hand against his shoulder. "I have seen enough," he assured her.

"But," Blue Eye interrupted, "we did bring you some news from London and Philadelphia." He reached into his jacket pocket and pulled out the blue envelope. "We met your sister, Elizabeth, in London and your niece, Rebecca, in Philadelphia." Alexander took the envelope, looked into his grandson's eyes, and without a word, handed it to Hannah. "Put this somewhere safe," he said. He listened without interrupting as Blue Eye told him about his family, the other people they had met and what they had seen.

In the evening, Hannah and William returned to the corrals, watching the new mares trot like long-legged dancers next to the graceful, but smaller Runners. She wondered what Grey Horse would have thought of the new mares. Would he have thought they were too fragile to survive a prairie winter?

Hannah checked the gate again and walked back to the trading house. As much as she loved William, he was almost a teenager and becoming too independent for her to be able to watch. Hannah enjoyed having him at her side on the days she rode to the herds. But now he was more interested in riding further from the trading house, with Shoots With A Smile to the Piikani camps where he could be with boys his own age.

Stands Early supervised William as much as she could, insisting he practice his reading and arithmetic each evening. To encourage him, Stands Early agreed to speak with him in Piikani, the language he loved. For his part, he would read to her in English from the books that Blue Eye had read as a boy. Now that Blue Eye and Frances had returned to the Bow, Hannah admitted to herself that she felt relieved they would be with William in the evenings.

Frances and Blue Eye's return from London brought a new sense of purpose to The Family. After the couple had explained all they had learned in London, with Blue Eye emphasizing the exhibits of machines and tools he had seen at The Crystal Palace, The Family agreed they had no choice but to prepare for the arrival of more white traders and settlers in the Prairie People's territory.

The success of the horse drive to Fort Union and the couple's journey to London convinced the Piikani members of The Family that Blue Eye and Frances had a special ability to understand and anticipate white people's actions. If Blue Eye and Frances said the white people were gathering just over the horizon and would soon take the Prairie People's territory, then that is what would happen.

Alexander knew Blue Eye and Frances were right, that the machines of The Great Exhibition were coming. Now he wondered if he would live to see the changes. A British flag had never flown at the Sun On The Mountains trading house and no church services had been held. He hoped he would not see either.

For Hannah, the ominous news that her son and Frances had brought from London seemed impossible to believe. All her life she had known the prairie to the east, the mountains to the west, and the rivers to the north and south. Inside the perimeter the Prairie People maintained control, and deep inside their territory, like a spring leaf buried inside a poplar bud, lived the Piikani, Sun On The Mountains and the

Runners. She reflected for several days before she reached a conclusion.

"I have been thinking," she said to The Family one evening, "about what Blue Eye and Frances have been telling us of their journey to London. I believe they are right. But I don't believe the changes will mean the end of Sun On The Mountains. I believe the changes will be the beginning of a long, green season. Sun On The Mountains will outgrow its home on the Bow. The end of the Blackfoot territory will bring new opportunities for everybody, even the Piikani."

She sat down and The Family remained silent. Hannah rarely stood up to speak at the table. Even more rare was for her to say what she had been thinking.

17 The First Missionary

THE TRADING HOUSE, SPRING, 1853. On the spring afternoon in 1853 when the first black-robed missionary from Fort Edmonton arrived at Sun On The Mountains, Alexander and Stands Early were the only ones home. They invited the missionary to stay overnight, as they would any guest. He sat with Alexander and Stands Early on the porch while waiting for the rest of The Family to return in the evening. Alexander explained about how he and The Family lived at the trading house.

"Are you Christians?" the missionary asked.

"Yes. We are Christians."

Looking at the new log house The Family had built for Blue Eye, Frances and William, the missionary asked Alexander, "Have you built a church for prayer?"

"Yes. We have a church."

"Very good. Could I see it?" asked the missionary

"You are looking at it."

The missionary replied, "I don't see a church."

"We live in it."

The missionary thought for a moment. "Interesting," he said. "A church you live in."

"Yes," Alexander answered. "We live in our church."

"How often do you hold your services?" the missionary asked Alexander.

"Every day."

"Every day! That is wonderful. You must be very devout."

"Very."

"How many of you attend your services?"

"We all see the Light."

"Impressive!"

Alexander, Stands Early and the missionary sat for several minutes, enjoying the late day sun.

The missionary spoke first. "We have had little success at Fort Edmonton converting the Indians to Catholicism. Tell me about your experiences."

Alexander replied. "Poor. We have not converted a single one."

The missionary's surprised look was directed more at Stands Early than at Alexander. "But you claim this Indian woman is a Christian. Who converted her?"

"She has always been a Christian."

"How could she be born a Christian? These people have not accepted Jesus into their lives. They have not been baptized. They do not take the sacraments."

The missionary's response had an argumentative tone and Alexander replied, "The Creator gave them buffalo, not bread."

The missionary stood up. "There is only one true faith," he insisted. "It is the duty of all Christians to bring their fellow man into its fold."

Alexander could tell the missionary was becoming angry and might leave, and he wanted the missionary to stay so The Family could hear his expression of faith.

"We can differ, you and I," Alexander countered in a conciliatory tone. "We have good reason to differ. Sun On The Mountains, Blackfoot, Assiniboin, British, American, Catholics, Methodists, Protestants. We are not the same. Nevertheless, there are many paths through life. Life is a long ride. We can all complete the journey."

The missionary resumed his seat and began questioning Alexander and Stands Early about the Piikani who had joined Sun On The Mountains.

"The Piikani have accepted Sun On The Mountains," Alexander explained, "and we live and trade with them, that is all. They have their ways and we have ours. They see for themselves how we live. We have chosen to follow some of their ways, and a few Piikani have chosen some of ours."

Alexander gave Stands Early a warm rub on her upper back as he spoke. "Stands Early and her husband, Shoots With A Smile, live with us. And so do her parents, One Person and Long Fingers. They are Piikani and also Sun On The Mountains. They have Piikani ways and they have Sun On The Mountains ways. Others come and go from our trading house. Rides Fearlessly wears our plain clothing, although she follows the Piikani way with a special diligence."

Rides Fearlessly intrigued the missionary and he asked, "Is she one of their medicine women?"

Stands Early laughed at the thought of Rides Fearlessly leading a ceremony. "No," she answered. "The Piikani way that Rides Fearlessly follows is that of a warrior. She and a few others are determined to kill any white people who come uninvited into Blackfoot territory."

"She would kill a white man!" the missionary exclaimed. "And your door is open to her?"

"It is her way," Alexander repeated. "It is her path. Perhaps one day, she will live another."

The conversation ended as Shoots With A Smile and William rode to the trading house and dismounted. The missionary scrutinized William.

"William is my great-grandson," Alexander said as he introduced him to the missionary. "He's almost fourteen years old."

"My name is Big Horse," William added with confidence. "I ride the big horses."

"The big horses," the missionary said. "What big horses do you ride?"

"The Sun On The Mountains horses. They are the biggest horses anywhere."

Alexander described the thoroughbred mares Blue Eye and Frances had brought from London and their breeding program to raise horses for the American settlers moving into Oregon.

"We will always have the Runners," he added, "for the buffalo hunt. But we cross some of the Runners with the thoroughbreds. My daughter, Hannah, and Shoots With A Smile are in charge of the herd. William is learning from them."

"He is going to be the best Sun On The Mountains rider," Shoots With A Smile said, his hand on William's shoulder.

William nodded. "I always ride. Except when they make me do my lessons in the house."

"Can you read?" the missionary asked.

"I don't like it. I would rather ride."

The missionary's interest in William became apparent with his next question. "And do you know about Jesus?"

William replied to the question with disinterest. "He is the Light we share."

"Have you read about him in your Bible?" the missionary asked.

"Bible?" William repeated the word. "Bible? What is that?"

"How can this boy know about Jesus but not know about the Bible?" The missionary asked, looking at Alexander.

"The Bible is other people's stories. We have our own experiences," Alexander replied.

The missionary bristled. "You may call yourself Christian but you are not giving your family a Christian education."

"Yes," Alexander agreed. "They are fortunate. But, please, everybody will be here soon and then you can tell all of us the redeeming value of your Christian education."

When The Family gathered at the table for the meal, the missionary mistook the beginning of the Silence as a cue for him to bless the meal. As the missionary began his blessing, "Dear Lord," William stared in open astonishment.

When the missionary finished and they began to eat, Alexander asked him to explain the blessing.

"We must thank the Lord for giving us food each day," the missionary explained.

"The Piikani do the same thing," Stands Early added. "They ask for help in making their hunting successful and they offer prayers of thanks."

"That is not the same," the missionary replied. The evening progressed with discussions about the missionary's religious practices and the way they compared to Sun On The Mountains and the Piikani. The missionary spent the night in the house, sleeping on Firekeeper's former bed by the fireplace. In the morning, he watched as The Family returned to their chores with the horses and with the preparation of the trade packs.

"I would like to speak frankly with you," he said drawing Alexander to the side of the porch. "Your great-grandson, William, has a remarkable personality. I would like him to come to Fort Edmonton to receive a truly Christian education. He is at the age where he can be shaped to become a servant of the Lord. But he must come soon. Already he has chosen an Indian name, Big Horse, and follows the Piikani man who looks after your horses. It would be a shame to see a fine boy like him devote his life to training horses when he could become a leader and train his people in the way of The Church."

Alexander shook his head. "You do not know William. William learns only what William wishes to learn. We have taught him to read and write, but we cannot teach him his path. William will not stay long with Sun On The Mountains. He stays close to Shoots With A Smile because he is sure to be visited by his aunt, Rides Fearlessly. That is the path William will follow."

"The woman who would kill a white man? Surely you will use your authority to ensure he avoids that mistake."

"I have no authority. The obstacles of life cannot be avoided. Our path will lead us where it will. But that does not mean you cannot learn from William. Visit us again and perhaps William will tell you what he knows about horses. I cannot speak for him."

"He is just a boy. You must speak for him. If William were to come to the fort," the missionary said with carefully chosen words, "your family would be welcome to visit. I am sure the Factor would always be generous with William's family. Perhaps he could help you expand your trading."

"Perhaps the Factor would not like Sun On The Mountains to expand its trading," Alexander said as he helped the missionary onto his horse. The missionary left, wondering what it would take to tempt Alexander to bring his family to The Church.

That evening, Alexander told The Family about the missionary's offer to speak to the traders at Fort Edmonton on behalf of Sun On The Mountains. William thought poorly of the missionary, basing his opinion on the tired condition of the missionary's horse. Blue Eye and Frances thought it would be worthwhile to learn more from the missionary.

"The missionary is not God's messenger or his guide," Blue Eye added. "He is the scout for those who make plans for Blackfoot territory."

"Yes," Alexander agreed. "Perhaps the missionary is also a trader, bargaining for Piikani souls! It is interesting that he comes to us from Fort Edmonton and returns to Fort Edmonton." Alexander shook his white hair.

The missionary visited several times during the next years and continued his sparring with Alexander over matters of faith. William, or Big Horse as he insisted on being called, scoffed at the idea of living in the fort with the missionary.

THE TRADING HOUSE, WINTER, 1858. The year Alexander turned ninety-six he lost some of his ability to focus his mind. His conversations wandered. The missionary visited more often, believing he could reconcile a weakened Alexander to The Church. The missionary's last visit was memorable for The Family.

Alexander lay on his bed half-asleep, the missionary in his dark robes standing on his right, as Crooked Smile and Left Alone entered. Crooked Smile, now with a reputation as a healer, moved to the left side of the bed, across from the missionary and took hold of Alexander's hand. She held it for several minutes, her eyes closed.

"He isn't ready to die," she announced. "There is still more for him to experience before he can die."

Alexander opened his eyes. "You are being foolish, Alexander," she said with a directness that caused the missionary to stiffen. "You know you cannot die before you reach the end of your path."

Crooked Smile locked her hands together and pressed on Alexander's chest. She pulled back and held out an open hand towards Alexander. "Give it to me," she ordered.

Alexander reached under the buffalo robes and withdrew the blue, unopened envelope from his mother.

"You must decide, old man," she said pointing to the envelope. "You have carried this since you came to the Bow." She turned, and left the trading house. Left Alone stayed behind to see the outcome.

Alexander lay on the bed for half an hour, ignoring the others in the trading house. As soon as he had made up his mind, he rolled out of the bed and stood up, weakly, but not holding anything for support.

He handed the envelope to Blue Eye. "Read it aloud, so everybody will know."

Blue Eye slit the envelope with the point of his knife. The letter, a folded handwritten page, fell open.

London, England
September 1, 1785

My dear Alexander:

Elizabeth and I read in The Hudson's Bay Company reports of the bitterly cold winters at York Factory, and how the men with you are suffering terrible hardships. We share a cheerful moment as we learn of these adversities, knowing our Alexander faces them with the same fortitude that stopped Washington's soldiers in Philadelphia.

We hear only gossip, and of no gratitude for the lives of the slaves and the free men you held safe during the war. We expect the truth will remain untold. For the telling we care little, but will remain always grateful that your life was spared, though you imperilled it willingly so others would live, and were cast out.

As John says, "Greater love hath no man than this, that he lay down his life for his friends."

Your courage and strength are God's gift. Use them to answer to the Light in all people.

With love, always.

Your mother,
Alice James

"It is not what I expected," Blue Eye said to his grandfather.

"Why did you expect anything?" Alexander asked. "What question could be answered in a letter? It is only a letter from my mother."

The missionary interrupted. "You were a servant of God's mercy," he said to Alexander. "You must believe He will acknowledge your deed of honour."

As Alexander turned directly to the missionary, his black pupils opened and his blue irises shrunk until all the missionary could see were two steady centres of darkness.

"And for my Piikani friend, Grey Horse, what will be his acknowledgement?" he said.

Alexander heard about, but never saw, the Palliser Expedition of 1859 that claimed to make the first scientific survey of the Blackfoot Territory. When he died in 1862, The Family bound his body and placed it on a scaffold by the Bow.

FORT EDMONTON, FALL, 1863. Blue Eye and Stands Early tied their horses to the railing outside the trading house at Fort Edmonton and began to loosen the ropes on their cart of buffalo robes.

"Blue Eye!" a Hudson's Bay Company clerk leaning against the doorway called out. "This is a surprise. We thought you were doing all your trading on the Missouri these days."

"A lot of it," Blue Eye replied. "But not all of it." He began to pile the robes by the doorway.

"There's a letter for you in the trader's house," the clerk said while he watched Blue Eye and Stands Early unload.

"A letter?" Blue Eye replied with interest. "I'll pick it up when I finish here. We need a few supplies. Stands Early has the list." She handed the clerk the list she had printed.

Blue Eye went to the trader's house, knocked, and asked for his mail. The servant reached over to a narrow shelf beside the door and sorted through a bundle of packages and papers. He handed a small, blue envelope to Blue Eye.

It was addressed in precise script; 'Blue Eye James, C/O Fort Edmonton. Please Hold.' In the upper left corner was the pilgrim seal. Blue Eye turned it over and read the return address. 'R. James, Philadelphia.'

Sitting on the empty cart, he read the letter.

July 16, 1863

Dear Blue Eye:

I trust this letter finds all The Family in good health. Please pass along my condolences on the death of Alexander, your grandfather and my uncle.

I write in response to your letter of November last, that I am just now in receipt, and am able to inform you of two important developments.

First, Elizabeth died December 22, and so The Family's sorrow is doubled. The consequence is that you are now the ultimate heir of the large package she showed you in London and that I will keep safe until I receive instructions for its delivery. I have also made arrangements for a similar package in Philadelphia to be kept safe awaiting your directions.

Second, you may have heard already that the entire Hudson's Bay Company is to be sold to the International Finance Group for £1,500,000; one million pounds more than you could have bought it for ten years ago. This group is associated with Barings, a bank with whom we rarely deal. However, Elizabeth made special mention in her last days that you were to be informed should this transaction be finalized, as it now appears will happen.

The war in America goes poorly for the Union. Lincoln's Emancipation Proclamation has weakened his position. Until this conflict ends, please route correspondence to me through The Society in London. I am sure I am watched.

With love,
I remain, a Friend,
Awaiting your instructions.
Rebecca.

Blue Eye did not consider Rebecca's brevity unusual. Since their meeting twelve years earlier, they had corresponded yearly and Rebecca's letters had always been purposeful and unadorned with conversation. This letter, although shorter than most, had Rebecca's typical evenness in all matters. Whether it was Elizabeth's death or the sale of a company, she considered events to be no more than news. Blue Eye tucked the letter in his pocket, wondering if the men at the fort had been told of The Company's change of ownership. He looked in the trading house to see if Stands Early needed help carrying out the supplies. He would read the letter aloud after the evening meal. Frances, as was her style, would write a lengthy reply.

18

BIG HORSE

THE TRADING HOUSE, FALL, 1870. The Piikani believed he was a son of the Sky Spirit who gave the Prairie People their first horses. When Big Horse rode, he and his horse were transformed into one inseparable animal. Big Horse, one common story ran, could sleep on his horse at night, travelling when others had to dismount to rest. The night before a race the other riders moved their pickets as far as possible from Big Horse's camp. They believed he knew how to persuade their horses to run slowly against his.

Big Horse had been born with the perfect combination of physical and mental traits for horsemanship. He had a short, supple upper body that balanced above a horse's back. His long legs could grip a horse's barrel tightly and still communicate gently. From his grandmother, Hannah, he inherited a soft touch in his hands that could calm and relax a horse; from his grandfather, Yellow Shield, a recklessness that, once set in motion, convinced his horses that no obstacle was insurmountable; from Blue Eye, a calculating coolness and thoughtful generosity; and from Frances a charm that recognized no distinctions.

Blue Eye and Frances gave up their last expectation that William would become a Sun On The Mountains trader, when, as a fifteen-year-old, he had ridden into Assiniboin territory with Rides Fearlessly and won five geldings in a single horse race. Laughing Boy, who had become a chief in Fast Walker's band, had sent a message back to Blue Eye: "The Assiniboin had better luck better trading at Fort Union with you than they had racing against your son. Next summer we will win!"

Everybody loved Big Horse. To all the Sun On The Mountains, all the Blackfoot tribes, and even to the Assiniboin, Crow and Cree who raced against him, Big Horse's open charm proved irresistible. The missionaries, as much as they shook their heads in disapproval at his lack of interest in the Church and its sacred beliefs, could not help but be warmed by Big Horse's ever-present cheerfulness, generosity and competitiveness. The traders at the forts on the North Saskatchewan and the Missouri cheered when Big Horse and Rides Fearlessly trotted in, confident they could count upon their arrival as the start of an exciting a week of horse racing and memorable, good times. Few realized Rides Fearlessly was his aunt.

Even those who lost races against Big Horse and his Sun On The Mountains horses became admirers rather than enemies. Just to have raced against Big Horse became a mark of distinction. A win against Big Horse surpassed the honour of killing an enemy.

While his parents found it hard to reconcile their Sun On The Mountains ways and their son's daring races, they knew they had to accept where Big Horse chose to direct his considerable natural abilities. When Big Horse first proposed to The Family that he would travel with Rides Fearlessly and race the thoroughbred and Runner crosses against horses from all the tribes on the plains, Frances had been the first to see how Sun On The Mountains would benefit from Big Horse's plan.

"Big Horse is determined to do this," she had told The Family. "We cannot change that. Nor can there be doubt about the speed of his horses. The crossbreeding of the London mares with the Runners has given them a longer stride and endurance." This observation, of course, was not news to The Family who had watched Hannah and Shoots With A Smile select the best horses each year for the breeding program.

Frances had turned to Blue Eye. "Think back to when you drove six hundred horses through Assiniboin territory to Fort Union. Would you have been content then to stay in the trading house with Alexander?

"You are The Family's leader today and you will live a long life like your grandfather. You will still be trading in another forty years. Is it right to ask Big Horse to stay by your side and wait his turn for another forty years? Let Big Horse follow his path. Let him have his day. He is willing to ride as a Friend to the forts and camps. He will race as a Friend; fairly, and to win."

She paused, letting The Family think about her words.

"What better way for Sun On The Mountains to know what is happening in the Blackfoot territory than to have Big Horse welcomed wherever he goes? Who will hear more news than Big Horse? Here, on the Bow, all we will learn is what the plodding traders and sad missionaries are willing to share. Horse racing is where the hot blood runs. From Big Horse we will learn many things those close to us don't wish us to learn. Already, he has brought us news they haven't heard at Fort Edmonton — that the Montana whiskey traders have moved north from the Missouri."

Blue Eye stood. "I agree. Big Horse can bring us news we would not hear otherwise. Of course, we are reluctant to see our son leave the trading house. But he has a path to follow. When the Friends drove the horse herd to Fort Union, we did not lose one life. I don't think horse racing is different than horse trading. They can both be done without loss of life."

Big Horse stood. "I am Sun On The Mountains and I am a horseman. This is who I am, and this is what I will be." He smiled with self-assurance and tugged open the top of his deerskin shirt to reveal a string of blue beads. "Alexander gave me these. He said they belonged to Grey Horse. He said they would remind me that when I ride, I ride for Sun On The Mountains. I will not forget. " It was a long speech For Big Horse.

The meeting had ended and the next morning Hannah, Big Horse, Shoots With A Smile and Rides Fearlessly chose their fastest horses and began training them to race. Blue Eye, Frances and Stands Early made a trip to Fort Edmonton to show the traders the Colt revolvers and Spencer rifles with rim-fire cartridges that Big Horse had won from Civil War veterans drinking on the Missouri.

The Spencer rifles could fire seven shots in less than twenty seconds. Buffalo hunting was becoming a slaughter as the repeating rifles spread across the plains. While Blue Eye was curious to see the British traders' reaction to the new guns, he was just as interested to see their reaction to the news that Montana whiskey traders were now openly operating Fort Whoop-Up on the Canadian side of the border. The Company traders and the missionaries had always assured Sun On The Mountains the boundary between the British land and the American land would be maintained, particularly with respect to the illegal trading of whiskey. Blue Eye was aware, however, that The Company traders resented the enforcement of the laws that made whiskey trading illegal, while their counterparts in Montana could operate illegally but openly and without penalty.

Now, in the late summer of 1870, as Blue Eye listened to Rides Fearlessly describe bloody fights between the Piikani and the Cree and Assiniboin, and bloody fights at the whiskey posts, Blue Eye knew another year of death was coming. The smallpox had killed two thirds of the Prairie People thirty years earlier. How many would survive the whiskey traders?

Several times, Blue Eye asked himself if Sun On The Mountains would be able to remain neutral in the conflict between the Piikani and the whiskey traders.

It was a time of confusion on the prairies, Rides Fearlessly told him. The Piikani, she said, were losing territory to the Assiniboin and the Cree, whose lands were being overtaken by whites and Métis from the east. The whiskey traders were taking control in the south.

Big Horse and Rides Fearlessly left soon afterward for races on the Red Deer River, wearing their plain Sun On The Mountains clothing and leading five of their best horses. Blue Eye, with Frances by his side, could not help but smile at the high value the two placed on those five horses. "What would they think if we told them Rebecca held over $4 million dollars for Sun On The Mountains in British and American banks?" he said to Frances as the riders gave the horses a last drink at the Bow.

"They would still be riding with those five horses to the Red Deer," Frances answered.

"You are right," Blue Eye agreed. "William is never going to become a Sun On The Mountains trader."

When Big Horse returned from the Red Deer River, he brought more discouraging news. Scarlet fever and smallpox were killing hundreds of Piikani, and the whiskey traders could not be stopped. Worse, in Big Horse's opinion, the Piikani horse herds were declining in number and in quality. The Piikani had been losing their best horses in raids or by selling them too cheaply, usually to the Americans.

"There are not many Piikani horses left that can race against us," Big Horse told Blue Eye. "On the Red Deer, I had to give their horses a head start and even then I won." Rides Fearlessly agreed with Big Horse, adding, "The soldiers on the Missouri have the good horses. Too many of the Piikani still believe owning five poor horses makes a man wealthier than a man who owns one good horse."

Blue Eye became sure the Piikani's future was threatened when he heard the Hudson's Bay Company lands were now controlled by the Dominion of Canada. He had no doubt the steam engines he had seen at The Great Exhibition would soon be crossing the prairie.

Before Sun On The Mountains left for the Great Circle, Blue Eye made a plan he thought might help the Piikani retain their territory. Thinks Like A Woman and Never Seen met them along the way and they rode to the Great Circle together, leading the horses that were their traditional gift to the Piikani.

THE LITTLE RED DEER, FALL, 1870. The celebrations had already begun at the Great Circle when Sun On The Mountains arrived. But, instead of being greeted with excitement, they were greeted by Death. Death controlled the perimeter of the Great Circle, wearing many faces and having many names. In some tipis, Death's face grimaced behind running smallpox sores; in other tipis, Death's face squinted beneath the jagged slashes of enemy's knives; in others, Death's face wore the feathers of a Cree or Assiniboin raiding party; in others, Death's breath stank of whiskey. As Sun on the Mountains rode through the perimeter and saw the slashed forearms, the bleeding thighs and calves, and were waved at by hands with fingers chopped to stumps, they could only hold their breath and regret they had not brought more food, horses and guns.

But from the centre of the camp, one voice defied Death, clamouring above the wailing of the men and women mourning the brothers and sisters whose journey had taken them to the Sandhills. That voice was the defiant Three Eagles, the twenty-eight year-old leader of The Fifteen Dead Warriors Society.

Three Eagles and The Fifteen Dead Warriors, some of whom looked to Blue Eye to be no more than twelve-years-old, held themselves in the background when the Piikani greeted the Sun On The Mountains' arrival.

Three Eagles, his face and bare chest streaked with a blue, earthy chalk, had short hair cut even with his jaw and tied with a black headband. The other Warriors had painted themselves with red ochre as well as the blue chalk, and wore their hair in side braids tied with black feathers and red leather thongs.

Each of the fifteen young men wore fringed deerskin shirts with black and red stars painted on the backs. Each red star represented a Cree or an Assiniboin killed by a warrior, each black star a white killed by a warrior. The stars were small, leaving room on the shirts for more stars to be added.

By the camps of the old chiefs that evening, Blue Eye asked only a few questions about the small number of tipis in The Circle, and did not mention, although he could not help but notice, the small servings of gristly buffalo forequarters at the evening meal.

Blue Eye stood with his back to the setting sun as he praised the spirit of the Piikani before he made gifts of horses and guns. This was how his grandfather had always stood at the Great Circle, and how Blue Eye had stood to speak to the Piikani at the rendezvous before the drive to Fort Union, thirty-one years earlier.

The older chiefs responded with praise for Sun On The Mountains, saying The Family had always been generous in their gifts at the Great Circle.

Blue Eye replied formally, saying he recognized that the Piikani had traded with Sun On The Mountains with fairness and respect since the time of his grandparents, Alexander, The White-Haired Piikani, and First Snow, the Nahathaway woman. He spoke lengthily, mentioning One Person, Long Fingers, Thinks Like A Woman, Never Seen, and giving special attention to Grey Horse and his race through enemy territory to bring the Runners to the Piikani. He mentioned times when the Piikani and Sun On The Mountains had helped each other, such as the journey to Fort Union.

"Sun On The Mountains has always been grateful to the Piikani for permitting us to trade on the Bow and to graze our horses on Piikani grass," he concluded.

"It is good you acknowledge this obligation of friendship," Buffalo Tails, the oldest leader of the Broken Ribs said.

Blue Eye continued with carefully chosen words, "For many years, the Piikani have sheltered Sun On The Mountains from Crow, Kootenay, Cree and Assiniboin raiders. We know we could not have maintained our horse herds without Piikani protection. Inside the Great Circle of the Piikani, Sun On The Mountains has prospered."

The Piikani murmured, pleased with this recognition of their strength.

"I will speak plainly," Blue Eye continued. "The Piikani have seen the numbers of white traders and missionaries on the Missouri and the North Saskatchewan. Every year more of them come up the rivers, and behind them are many more. All around the Piikani territory, the white people are gathering.

"The Piikani cannot hold out them out of this territory much longer."

The Piikani murmured, many disagreeing with Blue Eye's opinion of their capability to defend their territory.

"I tell you only what I know to be true," Blue Eye said, responding to their scepticism. "Three summers ago, the white leaders made an agreement to take all the land for themselves. They call this land The Dominion Of Canada. This agreement is made with their laws and they will use those laws to take your territory. Soon they will come and tell you how they will divide the Piikani territory.

"This is what Alexander told me would happen. This is what I have seen in my journeys to the east. This is what I have learned from the white people. This is what I know to be the truth.

"I am telling you today the Piikani cannot fight the white traders with the weapons the Piikani have fought the Crow and the Assiniboin. The Piikani must fight the white traders with white traders' laws.

"Sun On The Mountains knows the white laws and can make an agreement to keep the white traders out of Piikani lands. Sun On The Mountains can help the Piikani. If you claim the lands from the Red Deer River in the north to the

Oldman River in the south, and from the mountains in the west to the Cypress Hills, Sun On The Mountains will help you."

The Piikani chiefs talked amongst themselves. "Would this agreement keep the Crow and Assiniboin from Piikani territory?" Buffalo Tails asked.

"Yes," Blue Eye replied. "It would make this territory only Piikani. The hunting would be yours, the rivers would be yours, and the grass would be yours."

"And what about the other Prairie People?" Buffalo Tails asked.

"Sun On The Mountains would help them, too, to make their own agreements. But first we must act for the Piikani. Then we will help the others."

The chiefs talked amongst themselves. Blue Eye and the rest of Sun On The Mountains waited, not taking part in the discussions. It soon became obvious that only a few chiefs sided with the Sun On The Mountains proposal. Worse, Sun On The Mountains was becoming the focus of much of the Piikani animosity toward every white person.

Rides Fearlessly, overhearing a derogatory remark about Frances, could not restrain herself and pushed into the Piikani surrounding Buffalo Tails. Her pushing led to a retaliatory push and then a scuffle began between Rides Fearlessly and one of The Fifteen Dead Warriors. Big Horse flew into the Warriors, shoving them aside as he forced his way to where Rides Fearlessly had pinned a young warrior face down on the ground.

Big Horse pulled Rides Fearlessly aside. Buffalo Tails held the young warrior, now fuming in humiliation.

"We did not come to the Great Circle to fight," Blue Eye said, his eyes focused upon Buffalo Tails. "Sun On The Mountains does not fight. We will leave in the morning."

The Fifteen Dead Warriors jeered, hoping to taunt Big Horse into retaliation. Big Horse controlled his temper.

"Say what you want," he said, shrugging aside their insults. "It is easy for Warriors to be brave when you know Sun On The Mountains will not retaliate. You remind me of the Cree."

The sting of this remark almost gave the Warrior the strength to pull himself from Buffalo Tails' grasp and strike at Big Horse.

"Look at you!" Big Horse said to The Fifteen Dead Warriors. "You are ready to fight with those who came here as your allies. You talk bravely now because your real enemies are not nearby. If a Crow band were outside your camp now, they would steal your scrub horses and ride away laughing. You could not catch them unless you borrowed Sun On The Mountains horses. Your horses are pitiful."

The Warriors responded as Big Horse anticipated, in proud defence of their horses. Big Horse and Rides Fearlessly fuelled The Warriors' boasts with frequent interjections of disbelief.

"Fifteen Dead Warriors!" Rides Fearlessly called out. "At one time Piikani horses used to be fast but now they are only fit to drag tipi poles."

Within minutes, Big Horse and Rides Fearlessly had what they wanted; a challenge to a horse race. The Warriors and Sun On The Mountains parted in the dark, agreeing to let Buffalo Tails set the terms for the race in the morning.

Inside their tipi, The Family met to discuss the horse race. "Big Horse and I have done this before," Rides Fearlessly explained. "A horse race is the best way to stop a fight. Nobody will be injured or killed. After the race, both sides will accept the outcome." Blue Eye and Frances agreed, having seen how the Piikani, especially The Fifteen Dead Warriors, had escalated the fighting.

Blue Eye acknowledged he was disappointed that the Piikani were likely to turn down the offer to help claim their land, but he still hoped to reach a partial agreement. Thinks Like A Woman disagreed. "The Piikani will never believe they need to claim ownership of the land. They don't believe the land can be taken if they don't claim it. They believe it is theirs already." He proposed an alternative to Blue Eye's proposal.

"Let us ask the Piikani to help Sun On The Mountains by giving a treaty for the land by the Bow. If Sun On The Mountains has a treaty with the Piikani for the land on the Bow, then you could show that treaty to the white people and it would prove the Piikani owned the land."

"You negotiate like a white trader," Blue Eye said as he realized how well Thinks Like A Woman understood the white system and the way it could be used to the Piikani's advantage.

"It is a good idea," Blue Eye added, "but I don't think the chiefs are going to be able to convince the bands to do anything that would benefit Sun On The Mountains."

"There is a way," Thinks Like A Woman said. "There is always a way. The Piikani will want a prize awarded for the race. We could offer some horses to the Piikani if they win. If we win, the Piikani must agree to sign our treaty. The race could be a simple way to settle this."

"That's too much like gambling," Blue Eye countered. "I would not like to own land I had won betting on a horse race."

"You could be helping the Piikani," Frances pointed out. "This is the best chance we have to show the government the Piikani own the land."

The Fifteen Dead Warriors were not as angry in the morning as Blue Eye thought they might be. While Big Horse and Rides Fearlessly prepared for the race, the Warriors stood behind the chiefs as they listened to Blue Eye's offer of a prize for the winner of the race.

"Sun On The Mountains will give ten Runners to the winner of the race."

"Ten Runners!" Buffalo Tails exclaimed. "That's a generous prize." Without giving Blue Eye an opportunity to respond, Buffalo Tails continued, "I know Sun On The Mountains. The Piikani must have something you want to justify your offering ten Runners."

"No," Blue Eye answered. "We came to the Great Circle to be with our long-time friends, the Piikani, and to make an offer to help them make a treaty. That is all. The Piikani have told us they do not need our help. That is decided. Now we offer ten Runners to the winner of the race. Let your best rider to try to win them from us. Whether they are successful or not, Sun On The Mountains hopes the trust between us will be restored."

Buffalo Tails listened then said, "The Piikani thank you for your offer of help, and now that matter is closed."

"Yes," Blue Eye answered. "The matter is closed. We know if the Piikani want our help, they will ask."

Buffalo Tails smiled at Blue Eye's recognition of the Piikani pride. "Continue, Blue Eye. You have more to say. We know you are a clever man."

Blue Eye nodded his head. "Sun On The Mountains needs Piikani help. Sun On The Mountains needs Piikani protection for the territory on the Bow where we have our trading house and graze our horses. We need a paper to show the white traders that the Piikani permit Sun On The Mountains to remain there."

Buffalo Tails looked to the other chiefs who nodded in approval. "The Piikani will help Sun On The Mountains. We will say to the white traders that the Piikani permit Sun On The Mountains to trade on the Bow."

Blue Eye looked into Buffalo Tails' tired face but could see no hint of the reason for this agreement without the usual negotiations. "Sun On The Mountains thanks you," Blue Eye said. "Sun On The Mountains will make an agreement this winter and bring it for all the band leaders to make their marks."

"This paper will be the sign of the friendship between Sun On The Mountains and the Piikani," Buffalo Tails added.

It was Crooked Smile who later explained Buffalo Tails' quick decision. "Buffalo Tails knows what I know; he sees what I see. The Piikani are dying." She spoke without emotion, as if her pronouncements were facts. "Their hunting is poor. They have few horses. Too many young men and women are drinking whiskey. Buffalo Tails sees this and knows that Piikani medicine cannot change this path. Buffalo Tails believes Blue Eye has a medicine that can see the path ahead."

The consequences of the race concerned Frances. "What will happen when Sun On The Mountains wins the race? The Warriors have only their pride."

"Big Horse won't win," Crooked Smile said in a flat tone. "The Fifteen Dead Warriors own a grey Runner that will win. Big Horse will see himself fall off."

Rides Fearlessly glanced up and everybody expected her to argue that the black thoroughbred-cross ridden by Big Horse would be unbeatable. Instead, she accepted Crooked Smile's prediction. "If Crooked Smile says the Piikani horse will win, that is what will happen." She shrugged and walked away.

That afternoon The Fifteen Dead Warriors led their grey Runner from behind their tipis with two long ropes tied to either side of its bridle. The grey, anticipating the race, reared and plunged between the ropes.

Shoots With A Smile recognized the horse. "We sold that gelding last year to Laughing Boy. Hannah thought it was uncontrollable but Laughing Boy turned it into a racer. I wonder how Three Eagles got it from Laughing Boy."

"Laughing Boy would help him," Thinks Like A Woman said. "Three Eagles is Lightning And Thunder. The whiskey traders should stay away from him."

"And the others?" Blue Eye asked. "Are they Lightning And Thunder?"

"No."

Buffalo Tails had laid out the racecourse. It started along the south bank of the Red Deer River and headed east to where Thinks Like A Woman and a Piikani chief had marked the turning point. There, the racers would swim the river, race west along the north bank and then swim the river back to the camp. The first rider up the bank to the camp would be the winner.

"Is the grey faster than the black?" Frances asked Rides Fearlessly.

"If Crooked Smile says it will win, then it will win."

Big Horse watched the Warriors saddle the grey, an unusual strategy for the Piikani who preferred to race bareback. With Warriors still holding the long lead ropes, Three Eagles handed his starred jacket to a Warrior, swung onto the horse and gave Big Horse a challenging nod.

As soon as Buffalo Tails fired his gun, the Warriors slipped the leads from the grey and the race began. Big Horse took the lead and let the thoroughbred stretch its long legs into a comfortable gallop. The grey Runner knew how to race. Most horses would naturally surge ahead as they caught the lead horse, or waste energy fighting their riders if they were held back. The grey, however, kept its place, galloping just far enough behind to avoid the dirt and stones kicked up by the black. All the way to the turn, Big Horse tried his best tactics to break the grey's strategy. He slowed to a rolling canter, daring the grey to try to pass, but the grey hung back.

Big Horse had just started the first swim across the river when the grey splashed in behind. The strong thoroughbred swam through the current and clambered up the bank with the grey still close behind. Big Horse glanced back and Three Eagles acknowledged the glance with another challenging nod.

They raced along the bank, heading into the late afternoon sun. Big Horse then realized Three Eagles' strategy. Racing into the sun, Big Horse could only raise his eyes high enough to see a short distance before the glare blinded him. His horse, too, dropped his head, to avoid the glare. Behind them, Three Eagles and the grey Runner could follow the heels of the black.

Big Horse could hear the cheering as the Piikani lined the opposite riverbank to watch the final stretch. Thinking he must be close to the ford where they would cross the river, he looked up just in time to slow the black and turn down the bank. Three Eagles and the Runner slid down the bank close behind.

Big Horse looked down and his image floated up from the mirrored surface of the river. He fell into the shining water.

Rides Fearlessly dove from the opposite bank and swam across to pull Big Horse from the water. By evening Big Horse had recovered but could not explain the dizziness that had caused him to fall. That evening he and Rides Fearlessly walked to The Fifteen Dead Warriors' camp to invite Three

Eagles to the Bow to collect the ten Runners. They spent most of the evening with the Warriors, talking about horses and hunting.

Blue Eye was sitting alone by the campfire when a familiar voice disturbed his thoughts.

"Otssko Moapsspiksi. Do you still fall from your horse?"

Blue Eye turned and saw his boyhood friend, Two Arrows, in the shadows. Blue Eye said and rose to his feet. "I learned to be more careful. Now I know enough to ride quieter horses than that splash-necked pinto."

"I learned too, now that I'm getting old!" Two Arrows said, stepping toward the fire. His face was still youthful and his dark eyes still intense and restless. He was dressed in clean leather leggings and a beaded jacket.

Two Arrows reached forward with his left hand. "*Oki,*" he said. After they shook hands, Blue Eye commented on Two Arrows' healthy appearance. "Life agrees with you. You look the same as you did when we went to the Sun Dance."

"I'm like your grandfather. The journey isn't tiring if you stay on your path."

"Yes," Blue Eye agreed.

Two Arrows took Blue Eye to his tipi and introduced him to his wife, a white woman with blonde hair he had met on the Milk River, and his two pretty daughters, Little Calf and the freckle-faced, Many Spots. Sitting outside the tipi, they talked into the darkness. Two Arrows had left the Bow after the smallpox. "I heard what happened to Sikssikapii on the Missouri," he explained. "I chose to keep to the path of my Piikani people, away from the white traders and whiskey, and from Sun On The Mountains.

"Look," he said, pointing to the tattered camps in the Great Circle. "In one generation, all we had is gone."

Then, almost instantly, he was the same boyish Two Arrows. "I almost joined the drive to Fort Union," he said with a grin, "but I didn't have a slow enough horse."

Despite the sadness on the prairie, Two Arrows had not changed. As he talked about his life, Blue Eye listened and then, as imperceptibly as the sun climbs a morning horizon, Blue Eye saw firsthand the gathering of Light in the Piikani horseman.

In Two Arrows next words, he heard the Light speak. "Many of my people know the value of what you showed them in the drive to Fort Union and what you have offered them tonight. They would thank you if they could."

Blue Eye answered with silence. The two men sat together for a long time.

"It is time to say goodbye again," Two Arrows said.

"The Sun has protected you well," Blue Eye said as they parted.

"And the Light has guided you well," the Piikani horseman responded. Blue Eye watched him leave, admiring the easy gracefulness with which he walked into the shadows.

The Piikani chiefs signed the agreement with Sun On The Mountains that winter. Three Eagles and The Fifteen Dead Warriors became regular visitors at the Bow. Nobody was surprised when Big Horse married Two Arrow's freckled daughter, Many Spots. In the spring, she announced she was pregnant and would not attend the races with Big Horse and Rides Fearlessly.

Crooked Smile visited Sun On The Mountains when Many Spot's baby, Mary, was born. Seeing that the baby had blue eyes and hair as white as Alexander's, she told Hannah, "The baby isn't like Big Horse or Many Spots. Sun On The Mountains will have a great trader."

Many Spots rejoined her husband and Rides Fearlessly the next summer at the races, leaving Mary in Hannah's care. Hannah thought for many months about Crooked Smile's prophesy, believing that, although Crooked Smile could not see the future, she did have an uncanny ability to sense a person's path. Hannah would never know the accuracy of Crooked Smile's prediction that Mary would become a trader.

THE ELBOW RIVER, SUMMER, 1871. Three Eagles and The Fifteen Dead Warriors Society took as their sacred mission in life a determination to drive the whiskey traders out of Blackfoot territory and across the Missouri. Pledging never to drink whiskey themselves, they rode their ten Sun On The Mountains Runners to all the Prairie people's they could to persuade more young men to join their society. None joined. Undeterred, The Fifteen Dead Warriors stopped the Piikani on the trails to the whiskey traders, urging them to barter for anything but whiskey. This effort, too, proved futile. The Piikani who survived the brawls at the forts returned disheartened, usually without their horses and frequently without their husbands and wives.

Many of the whiskey traders had taken up their profession following the American Civil War where brutality had become commonplace. The American Indian Wars, as well, encouraged the belief that extermination of the Indians was a necessity. The whiskey traders took these beliefs seriously and preferred to spill blood before they spilled any of their profitable whiskey. From the backs of wagons and from stout fortresses, the traders ignored the laws and poisoned the Blackfoot tribes. A smart trader could dilute a $5 gallon of whiskey enough to acquire buffalo robes worth $50.

The Fifteen Dead Warriors took their sacred mission closer to the whiskey forts, breaking up fights and regaining horses and belongings stolen by the white traders. Inevitably, the policing tactics of the Warriors led to killings. The shirts of the Warriors accumulated more and more black stars. The white traders barricaded their forts and stockpiled ammunition, refusing to trade with any Piikani if The Fifteen Dead Warriors were nearby. The whiskey traders continued to open profitable posts because many Piikani eagerly brought in the robes, furs and meat the white traders wanted.

Whiskey traders came closest to Sun On The Mountains trading house in 1871 when an arrogant American, Bob Kennedy, known for his outspoken view that Indians were vermin, opened a whiskey post on the Elbow River within a day's ride of the Sun On The Mountains trading house. From Montana to Fort Edmonton, the trader had shot any Indians and white traders — drunk, sober, armed, and unarmed — who challenged his dominance.

Kennedy, determined to squeeze every drop of profit from the whiskey he imported from Montana, built a solid log fort on the Elbow, with a windowless trading room inside. The outside walls had loopholes that the traders could fire their Spencer carbines and revolvers through whenever the Indians became, as Kennedy said, "surly."

Three Eagles told Kennedy to move on, saying the Piikani had given Sun On The Mountains the right to trade on the Bow. Kennedy and his three trading partners barricaded themselves in the fort and dared Three Eagles to do his worst. Thinking The Fifteen Dead Warrior's presence nearby would be enough to encourage Kennedy to move his fort closer to the protection of the American border, Three Eagles rode away to let the traders think about their choices.

Kennedy, assuming he had scared Three Eagles away, opened a keg of undiluted whiskey to celebrate and assured his partners that the Sun On The Mountains much talked about aversion to violence would hold The Fifteen Dead Warriors in check. Kennedy and his three trading partners were delirious by nightfall.

When the Fifteen Dead Warriors returned the next day, Kennedy and one of his partners were arguing over a Kootenay woman. Kennedy pulled out a revolver. Waving it, he shot and killed his partner. He then turned on the Warriors, threatening to shoot them as well. Three Eagles shot Kennedy in the shoulder, injuring him slightly. Kennedy, his other partners, and the Kootenay woman ran for their fort and barricaded the doors.

The Warriors sat out of range while the traders' delirium continued. The traders sporadically fired at the Warriors, declaring success as bullets hit trees that looked to them like Piikani. Late on the second day, Kennedy called out, asking if the Warriors were sufficiently beaten to accept a truce long enough for both sides to bury their dead. Three Eagles laughed at Kennedy's delusion. The only shot fired by the Warriors had been the one by Three Eagles and the only casualty had been the trader killed by Kennedy. Nevertheless, he agreed to the truce and pretended to haul bodies from the brush for burial. Kennedy insisted the Warriors bury his partner as well because they had killed him. On the third day, Kennedy requested another truce. The Warriors agreed and Kennedy sent for reinforcements from the traders on the Highwood River.

The Fifteen Dead Warriors left the Elbow when the men from the Highwood persuaded Kennedy and the woman it was safe to come out of the fort. Kennedy's third partner, still delirious, had burrowed a hole in the floor of the trading room and had to be dragged out.

Assured Kennedy would leave the Elbow, the Warriors and Three Eagles rode to Sun On the Mountains.

Kennedy later told a much different version of the skirmish to his friends, telling them Sun On The Mountains had ordered the attack. Kennedy did, however, retreat to the southwest to trade with the less troublesome Kootenay. But, before he left Blackfoot territory, Kennedy had made up his mind to have his revenge.

Kennedy, as cunning sober as he was ruthless when drunk, bided his time. Two years later, in the fall, he got his revenge. Secretly, he brought five Kootenay warriors along the slopes of the Rockies from the Crowsnest Pass to the Bow River. There, he gathered information from the missionaries on the activity at the trading house. Stands Early, he learned, controlled the trading house. Hannah supervised the horse herd but spent most of her time in the house with her three-year-old great-granddaughter, Mary. Shoots With A Smile and four boys kept watch on the horse herd. Blue Eye and Frances led pack trains to Fort Edmonton, refusing to travel south while the whiskey trade continued. Big Horse, Many Spots and Rides Fearlessly had ridden with The Fifteen Dead Warriors to the horse races by the Cypress Hills.

Kennedy's motivation for revenge received extra vigour when a band of Stoney Indians visiting a mission told him they had heard Sun On The Mountains kept a cache of silver and gold coins under the floor of the trading house. Kennedy planned his attack, waiting until Hannah and Stands Early were alone at Sun On The Mountains.

When he learned Blue Eye and Frances were on their way to Fort Edmonton and Shoots With A Smile was the only man watching the trading house, Kennedy sent two Kootenay to scatter the horse herd and keep Shoots With A Smile occupied. Kennedy and the other three Kootenay then rode to the trading house. As soon as he dismounted,

Kennedy turned his greeting into a threat, pulling out his revolver as he entered the trading house, and holding the barrel against Hannah's forehead. He asked her only once about the coins. When she refused to answer, he shot her through the forehead and grabbed Stands Early. He smashed his revolver down hard on her hand, crushing her fingers, and demanded the coins. When she refused, he turned the barrel of his revolver on the child, Mary, grabbing her long white hair.

Mary struggled, screaming at the pain as he yanked her head back. With her good hand, Stands Early clawed at Kennedy's face until the Kootenay pinned her arms. As Kennedy was about to return the barrel of the gun to Mary's head, the Kootenay guarding the doorway called out that he could see horses coming from the west.

Kennedy shot Stands Early in the side of the face, splashing blood on the trading house wall. He pulled Mary through the doorway and onto his horse. Moments later, he and the three Kootenay galloped through the Bow and into the brush.

Shoots With A Smile, his arm bleeding, pulled up his lathered horse at the doorway. He stepped over the crumpled bodies of his wife and Hannah.

"Mary!" he shouted. "Mary!" He searched the trading house and the outbuildings before slumping beside Stands Early's body. The three boys who had been with the herd found him there as they returned from gathering the horses. A fourth boy lay dead by the corrals, brought down by a Kootenay rifle. Shoots With A Smile had killed one Kootenay and wounded another. The boys had tied this Kootenay to the corral. Scared and bleeding, the Kootenay told Shoots With A Smile about Kennedy's plan to steal Sun On The Mountains' cache of coins. He knew nothing about Mary.

Shoots With A Smile and two of the boys searched the rest of the afternoon for Mary. By evening they had given up hope of finding her nearby. The third boy rode north to bring back Blue Eye and Frances. As he rode, he spread the news of the killings at Sun On The Mountains. By the next evening Big Horse, Many Spots and Rides Fearlessly were waiting at the trading house. By the third day, over fifty Piikani had gathered, including The Fifteen Dead Warriors. Three Eagles had left already, telling Big Horse he would track Kennedy and the Kootenay. He returned at dawn, his horse exhausted, but with the news that Mary was still alive and causing Kennedy and the three Kootenay so much trouble he was not sure how long Kennedy would bother keeping her.

As soon as Blue Eye returned to the trading house he knew Sun On The Mountains neutrality in the conflict between the Blackfoot tribes and the whiskey traders had ended. No matter what happened next, Sun On The Mountains was involved. The Family would recover Mary, even if it meant killing Kennedy. That afternoon he spoke to the Piikani gathered at the trading house. "Thank you for coming. But this involves only Sun On The Mountains. If we need you, we know we can count on your help." All the Piikani except the Warriors left.

Blue Eye turned to Shoots With A Smile and Big Horse. "Your minds are not clear. They are filled with revenge and anger. You cannot be the ones to find Mary and return her."

He turned to Three Eagles and Rides Fearlessly. "I am asking you to help me bring Mary back. You know the land between here and the Kootenay territory, and you know how to deal with men like Kennedy. But we are not asking you to kill for us. We cannot ask you to do for Sun On The Mountains what we would not do for ourselves. I will go with you."

"No," Frances interrupted. "I'll take care of this. You are needed here." She looked toward Many Spots. "Stay close to Blue Eye until we return. We will find your daughter."

"It will be a long ride and cold," Three Eagles pointed out to Frances. "We will be riding hard."

"I know where we are going," Frances replied without hesitation. "And I know what I will be doing. I am not afraid."

As the three riders left the Bow, Blue Eye turned to the rest of The Family and said, "We will build the scaffolds for Hannah and Stands Early. Then we will resume work with the horses and prepare another load to deliver to Fort Edmonton. If we do not work, we will not survive." He reached over to Many Spots, took her hand, and led her to the river bank.

"You and I will sit by the river for a while. I remember my grandfather liked to watch the sun shining on the river. He said there were two suns. Maybe they will both be shining today."

THE OLDMAN RIVER, SUMMER, 1871. The three riders followed Kennedy's trail south to the Oldman River and, on the flats where the river turned east from the foothills, they found a campfire and estimated he was no more than two days ahead, and not hurrying. They believed Mary was alive. The Kootenay had left Kennedy at the point where the entrance to the Crowsnest Pass became visible. Rides Fearlessly said she would follow their trail until she could see if Mary was with them. If they didn't have her, she would return and follow Frances and Three Eagles east past the Porcupine Hills.

Three Eagles went ahead of Frances, skirting the eastern slopes of the Porcupines and pushing his Runner hard, hoping to circle ahead of Kennedy. If Kennedy had Mary, he would be feeling secure with a hostage tied to his saddle. Frances stayed on Kennedy's trail.

The next morning Frances found Kennedy's campsite, the fire ring still warm. She cantered the Runner, hoping Kennedy would spot her before the end of the day and stop. Just after noon, Kennedy halted, turned his horse, and saw Frances riding against the western horizon. She rode forward. He dismounted, and untied Mary from the back of the saddle and stood her on the ground in front of himself.

She rode to within a hundred yards before he ordered her to stop. He waved his revolver. "Who are you?" he called out.

"Frances James. I am the girl's grandmother."

Kennedy snickered, thinking he had the Sun On the Mountains people figured. They had sent a grandmother to rescue the girl.

"Let Mary go," Frances called. "You can ride away. You have my word."

Frances dismounted and walked forward, to within twenty yards. Mary recognized her grandmother and struggled against Kennedy who held her white hair with one hand. He pushed his revolver against Mary's forehead, grinding it hard into her flesh until blood trickled over her eyes.

"I could kill her now. And you, too."

As Kennedy spoke, Frances saw Three Eagles ride over the ridge.

"Look behind you," Frances called to Kennedy. "That is Three Eagles of The Fifteen Dead Warriors. You know who he is. If anything happens to Mary, I will tell him to kill you."

Three Eagles dismounted, lifting his Spencer rifle from its leather case.

Kennedy glanced over his shoulder and recognized Three Eagles.

"If I let the girl go, you will kill me anyway."

"No. There will be no more killing. Let the girl go and you may ride away." Frances spoke as if she were discussing a trade for an old buffalo hide. Three Eagles had his hand on the stock of the rifle. He lifted it toward his shoulder. Kennedy kept the revolver pressed against Mary's forehead.

"Do you speak Piikani?" Frances asked him.

"No."

"I'm going to tell Three Eagles that I will count aloud the fingers on one hand. If Mary is not released on the fifth count, I will tell him to shoot you in the head."

Kennedy turned to Three Eagles and listened as Frances spoke in Piikani.

"I have told Kennedy I'm going to count to five. You are to shoot him in the head if Mary is not released." She lifted her hand and pointed to the side of her head.

"Three Eagles will shoot you right there, behind your eye," she called to Kennedy.

Kennedy swallowed. Frances lifted her closed hand high. "One," she said, extending her thumb. "Two," and she extended her forefinger so both Kennedy and Three Eagles could follow the count.

"Three."

Kennedy pushed Mary towards Frances. "All right. You win."

"Put your rifle down," Frances ordered.

Kennedy shook his head.

"Four," Frances called out. Kennedy dropped the rifle.

"Now get on your horse and don't look back. Three Eagles will shoot if you look back."

Kennedy mounted, turned his horse and jabbed his spurs into its sides. The tired horse galloped straight south and Kennedy never turned in his saddle.

Frances lifted Mary into her arms where the child clung to her shoulders. Using a small lump of vermilion she carried in her jacket, Frances drew small, Sun On The Mountains symbols on the back of Mary's hands and on her own. "You are safe," she repeated as she drew the symbols.

After they returned to Sun On The Mountains, Mary insisted Frances cut her hair. She would keep it short all her life, never forgetting Kennedy's grip, and she would always have a tiny scar in the centre of her forehead where Kennedy had twisted his revolver.

19 The Treaty

THE BOW, FALL, 1873. The reports of the killings and the kidnapping of Mary at Sun On The Mountains, as well as the spectacular rumours about Sun On The Mountains' hoard of coins, had spread throughout the Piikani territory, reaching Fort Edmonton and the Missouri where traders heard conflicting reports from the Piikani and from Kennedy's friends.

It was the Kootenay who killed the women, Kennedy later claimed. He said he met the Kootenay near the Crowsnest Pass where he bought the girl from them. He planned to take her to Fort Benton where she would be safe. It was Frances and Three Eagles that had caused the trouble, he told everybody, when they accused him of the killings and kidnapping. He had just been doing what any well-meaning man would have done, saving the life of a little girl.

Believing Kennedy's account, and because of the ever-closer friendship between Big Horse and The Fifteen Dead Warriors, the white traders on both rivers became convinced that Sun On The Mountains had joined the Piikani. The traders at Fort Edmonton began to treat Blue Eye and Frances with suspicion when they arrived with robes to sell.

Within a year, The Fifteen Dead Warriors travelled with Big Horse and Rides Fearlessly. Blue Eye wondered if his son's interests still lay in horse racing, having overheard two Piikani bragging about how The Fifteen Dead Warriors had burned a whiskey fort in Montana and escaped unscathed on fast horses.

Big Horse and Rides Fearlessly assured The Family that, despite the temptation to seek revenge following the death of Hannah and Stands Early, they had not taken part in the burning. The Family accepted their word.

An incident two years after the kidnapping pushed The Family directly into the conflict between the Piikani and the whiskey traders. Two whites and a dozen Métis drove three wagonloads of goods and whiskey north from the American border and set up a small camp on the Bow River flats, inviting the Piikani to visit. The white and Métis traders were deserters from the Dominion surveyor camps set up to erect markers along the 49th parallel, the boundary between The Dominion of Canada and The United States of America. They planned to trade the whiskey and continue north from the Bow to Fort Edmonton to obtain fresh supplies. The whiskey forts in the Territories had, by then, brought much of the Blackfoot Confederacy close to destitution. They had sold their best horses, and their clothing and tipis were rags after two years of neglect.

The Piikani had been invited to the traders' camp and the drinking had been going on for two days without a fight, although the peace was fragile. The Piikani outnumbered them two to one. The Fifteen Dead Warriors watched from a hillside as Big Horse and Rides Fearlessly rode to the camp with fifteen horses. Big Horse, bold and charming, generated enthusiasm for a race against the Piikani. Rides Fearlessly stepped in before the wagers could be made, saying she would bet ten good riding horses against all the remaining whiskey. When this wager was accepted, the Piikani bet their robes, horses and tipis against the supplies.

Big Horse won by four lengths and he and Rides Fearlessly rode to the wagons to collect the whiskey. The traders refused to give the kegs up, saying they wanted to bet again. "*Sa*," Big Horse answered. The whiskey would be poured on the ground. Now! The Piikani, many of whom had been anticipating a few extra drinks from the kegs, protested as well, offering to buy the whiskey from Big Horse and Rides Fearlessly.

The arguments grew heated. Only Big Horse and Rides Fearlessly wanted the whiskey poured out. Everybody else thought it should not be wasted, regardless of the outcome of the race.

Three Eagles and The Fifteen Dead Warriors clicked fresh rounds of ammunition into the breeches of their rifles and formed a semi-circle around Big Horse and Rides Fearlessly.

"This whiskey will be poured out," Big Horse announced. "We won it and it is ours to do with as we wish." He rolled the first keg from the back of a wagon and knocked the bung out with his heel. The whiskey trickled out. As he reached for the next keg, a trader rushed forward and pulled him aside. A drunken Piikani fired first, killing the trader. The Métis and the other trader backed away from the wagons, fearing the drunken Piikani would fire again.

Big Horse continued to kick the rest of the barrels from the wagons, breaking several and knocking out the bungs on the others.

"Harness your horses," he ordered the traders, "and take your wagons north along the Bow. We will follow you." He told the Piikani he would hold the supplies for them at Sun On The Mountains.

The Piikani stayed behind to scavenge the remains of the whiskey in the kegs. The Fifteen Dead Warriors kept watch. When the wagons and horse arrived at the Sun On The Mountains trading house, Big Horse described the fight to Blue Eye, adding he hoped the matter would end as soon as the wagons reached Fort Edmonton.

Before the wagons could leave in the morning over a hundred ragged Piikani arrived at Sun On The Mountains, wanting to kill the Métis and the trader. They demanded all the supplies in the wagons. Blue Eye agreed the Piikani had won the food, ammunition and clothing and ordered the Métis to unload the wagons, leaving themselves only enough supplies to travel to Fort Edmonton.

The Piikani spat insults at the trading house as they loaded their horses, saying Sun On The Mountains and The Fifteen Dead Warriors were friends to the Métis and the whites, and were traitors to the Piikani.

"If you were Piikani allies, you would not protect our enemies." The Métis and the white trader also cursed Sun On The Mountains, blaming Big Horse and Rides Fearlessly for the loss of their supplies and the whiskey.

Trading dropped off after the dispute. With the widespread availability of breech loading rifles capable of bringing down a buffalo from a greater distance and more quickly than a racing horseman could with a bow, the demand for Runners decreased. The hunters and traders only wanted steady, reliable pack horses. On the other hand, the ranchers south of the Missouri who had taken over the prairie needed good horses. The crossbreeding of the thoroughbreds and the Runners had been producing a larger horse, suited to the heavier work of the range cowboys. The problem was not selling the horses; it was getting the horses to Montana, being paid, and returning with the money. In Montana, the Indian Wars continued. "It will be a long time before we can sell a herd of horses in Montana and return with the money," Blue Eye told Frances.

Nevertheless, he asked Shoots With A Smile to begin planning a drive to deliver a herd of horses to Montana. Blue Eye, Frances, Crooked Smile, Many Spots and Mary stayed close to the trading house for the winter. With the entire Blackfoot Confederacy approaching poverty, the horse herd had many eyes watching it. The whiskey traders speculated about Sun On The Mountains' rumoured cache of coins.

THE TRADING HOUSE, SUMMER, 1874. Reverend George McDougall, a Methodist minister, arrived at Sun On The Mountains with important news in the summer of 1874. Hoping to make a big impression on Blue Eye, the missionary announced that The Great Mother was sending a troop of Police to bring law and order to the region and close down the whiskey traders.

"The Great Mother!" Blue Eye replied with amusement. "I am surprised that Victoria is meddling in the affairs of The Dominion of Canada. I would have thought the South African Boers would be a bigger concern to her." Taken aback by Blue Eye's knowledge, McDougall spoke in less dramatic style as he described the Northwest Mounted Police force that he expected to arrive before the leaves turned in the fall.

Blue Eye listened to McDougall, then surprised the missionary by saying, "The Government isn't sending Police. It is sending soldiers."

McDougall insisted they were Police, and their only role was to close down the whiskey trade.

"And then what will they do?" Blue Eye asked.

The arrival of the Police brought only disparaging scorn from Big Horse as he watched the men, lost in the wide prairie, trudging beside their wagons loaded with supplies and four enormous guns. Their horses, galled and hungry, could barely climb even the smallest hills. Big Horse ridiculed the recruits' misfortune, but did not think it worth bothering to help them. Why bother with men who could not ride all day, and did not have enough sense to look after their horses?

"If the Piikani wanted to capture their horses, they would have them in one night," he laughed.

THE POLICE FORTS, SUMMER, 1874. When Big Horse reported what he had seen, Blue Eye and Frances admonished him for not guiding the Police to the whiskey forts and for not supplying them with replacement horses. They sent Big Horse and Rides Fearlessly back with fresh horses. By the time they found the Police again, the Police had been forced to travel south to the Missouri to buy supplies from the Americans at Fort Benton. Big Horse and Rides Fearlessly stayed well back and watched them march to Fort Whoop-Up, the most notorious whiskey trading post in the territory. There, the Police aimed their field guns and mortars at the log walls. With no response from the fort to this threat, the leader of the Police, James Macleod, rode to the gates and knocked. No answer. The whiskey traders had already moved on, leaving only an old civil war veteran and several Indian women in the fort.

The Police marched further west to the Oldman River where, in early winter sleet, they built their first fort. Big Horse and Rides Fearlessly decided they had seen enough and delivered the horses. The Police, bundled up in buffalo robe coats, mitts and hats, gratefully took the horses and increased the patrols on the trails used by the whiskey traders. Big Horse and Rides Fearlessly returned to the Bow to tell The Family that, if nothing else, the Police deserved admiration for taking on wealthy whiskey traders while they, themselves, lived so poorly.

Nevertheless, the Police did their job. Within a year the whiskey trade was over. Reverend McDougall returned to the Sun On The Mountains trading house, praising the work of the Police and showing Blue Eye and Frances the cattle he had trailed from Montana. Blue Eye understood McDougall's good intentions, and his attitude softened toward the missionary and he inquired into the developments on the Missouri. McDougall, in turn, had given up trying to impress Blue Eye with his worldly knowledge of modern progress. He described the frequency of the steamboat arrivals and the installation of a telegraph service in Montana. The Missouri River area, he added, was not safe for Indians.

As the two men talked, they set aside their differences. Blue Eye always called him George McDougall, never Reverend McDougall. The missionary always called him David. Blue Eye showed McDougall the agreement Sun On The Mountains had made with the Piikani. McDougall, acknowledging The Family's foresight, could not say whether or not the agreement would be recognized by the Dominion Government that had already begun negotiating treaties with the eastern tribes.

"I could sign this as a witness and date it," McDougall offered. "At least my signature would substantiate that it was made before any other agreements for this land."

Blue Eye thanked him but declined the offer. "Sun On The Mountains cannot ask you to establish the legitimacy of this agreement. Only the Piikani can do that."

The Piikani's attitude toward Sun On The Mountains improved as the whiskey stopped flowing and the Piikani again had robes to trade for horses. The Cree, Assiniboin and the Métis were pressing hard on their hunting grounds to the east. The Piikani chiefs began to recognize that there would soon not be enough buffalo for everybody. Shoots With A Smile made an exploratory horse drive, taking only fifty head of good riding horses and pack horses as far the Police headquarters at Fort Macleod. Instead of paying in bulky coins, the Police paid in Dominion paper dollars. Several of the Police remembered the horses given them by Big Horse and Rides Fearlessly during their first winter on the prairie.

The next fall, Blue Eye and Big Horse rode to the new fort the Police had built where the Bow met the Elbow. Expecting to be treated there as respectfully as Shoots With A Smile had been treated at Fort Macleod, Blue Eye and Big Horse received a disturbing welcome. The commander of the new fort, Inspector Brisbois, refused to leave his quarters and told his sergeant to send Blue Eye away. When Blue Eye repeated his request, Brisbois pushed open the door of his quarters, his arm draped over the shoulders of a drunken, teenage Métis girl. A trooper attempted to speak to Brisbois but was shoved aside. "Back!" the Inspector ordered. "If this heathen insists upon meeting his Queen's representative, then I must do my duty."

Brisbois marched forward, dragging the girl, until he was face to face with Blue Eye. He peered at Blue Eye's right eye. "There must be some civilized blood in this one," he said in amusement to the trooper at his side. "Ask him if he knows his father's name."

Blue Eye turned back to the gate. Brisbois bolted forward, growled, and grabbed Blue Eye's shoulder, spinning him back. The Métis girl fell to the ground and lay there whimpering.

"I'm an officer of the Queen!" Brisbois bellowed in Blue Eye's face.

Big Horse's knife flickered. Blue Eye reached over and pushed the knife aside. "Wait," he said in Piikani.

Then, speaking in English, Blue Eye turned his attention to Brisbois. "You may be an officer," he said, "but you are not Victoria's representative." His clear voice echoed in the fort and several troopers standing behind Brisbois smiled. The trooper beside Brisbois never flinched as Blue Eye reached down and helped the drunken Métis girl to her feet. "Don't stay here long," he said.

Big Horse, Rides Fearlessly and Shoots With A Smile sold small herds of horses to the Police over the next year. James Macleod, the Police Commissioner in charge of the area, never met Blue Eye, although McDougall likely explained a little to him about the family of Quaker descendants living and trading on the Bow.

Macleod did arrange for one change that pleased Blue Eye; he had Fort Brisbois renamed Fort Calgary and convinced the unpopular inspector that any other career would be more suitable for him. In 1876 Macleod signed Treaty Number 6 with the Cree to the east at Fort Carleton. The Blackfoot tribes, hearing of this, requested a treaty of their own and in late summer, 1877, Macleod sent messengers to the Blackfoot tribes that a treaty would also be negotiated with them.

THE TRADING HOUSE, FALL, 1877. McDougall rode to Sun On The Mountains to persuade Blue Eye and Frances to have their claims for the land on the Bow recognized at the negotiations. The Family discussed the proposal, and decided not to attend.

"Sun On The Mountains signed a treaty with the Piikani eight years ago," Blue Eye repeated to McDougall. "The Piikani know this land is theirs to claim at the treaty. They have allowed Sun On The Mountains to trade here for eighty years and we only occupy it with their permission. We would not presume to tell them what to do with their land. The Piikani will make whatever treaty is right for their path. Sun On The Mountains has a path to follow. We are traders. If the Piikani want to share a path with us, they will claim this land by the Bow." The Family remained firm and did not travel to Blackfoot Crossing to attend the treaty signing.

During the negotiations, the Piikani argued more than the other tribes, with The Fifteen Dead Warriors threatening up to the last minute to attack the Police. On September 22, 1877, Crowfoot, of the Blackfoot tribe, signed, accepting for all the tribes that they would live on reservations. All that remained was agree upon where the reserves would be.

Two days later, Three Eagles and The Fifteen Dead Warriors rode to Sun On The Mountains with the news. They were all waiting there: Blue Eye, Frances, little Mary, Big Horse, Crooked Smile, Rides Fearlessly, Shoots With a Smile, Thinks Like A Woman, and Never Seen.

"The Piikani have chosen a reserve to the south, on the Oldman River," Three Eagles told them, the disappointment obvious in his voice. "It is their traditional land. They say that is where they have always hunted buffalo."

Blue Eye, his throat dry, could only say, "There are no buffalo."

He led his horse to the river and knelt by the bank, cupping his hands to drink. For a moment, all he could see was Grey Horse and his grandfather's sorrow. What Grey Horse knew, would never be known again.

All the good years and the sad years, the friends and the enemies, and the dying and the living drifted by, just memories now, twisting in the shallows of the Bow River. He wondered how Sun On The Mountains would continue.

And in his cupped hands he saw the reflected blue of his grandfather's eyes, flecked with black bolts, and heard, "*Oki.* Be a good Quaker. Be cheerful and answer to the Light in every one." His strength returned as the river's current ran through his hands.

The Canadian Pacific Railway's steel tracks and steam engines reached Sun On The Mountains in 1883. Surveyors measured the prairie, hammering in pegs to mark townships, sections and a town. Railway agents in offices sold squares of land marked neatly on a map.

Nobody needed a fast buffalo Runner, and only one sun crossed the prairie.

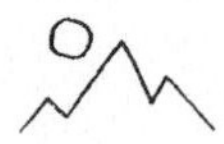

Author photo by Andrew Bakó

TYLER TRAFFORD has worked for many years as a reporter and editor, first with the *Calgary Herald*, and then in Australia with *The Australian*. Upon returning to Canada, he began a full time writing career, publishing a series of histories and biographies for others, before turning his attention to fiction. *The Story of Blue Eye* is the first of the *Sun on the Mountains* series that explores the history of Plains Indian horse culture, and the rise of western commerce, through high adventure. He shares time between Calgary and his studio on the Oldman River near Pincher Creek, Alberta.